A WIZA

Merlin is one of the most powerful names in the annals of fantasy, a name to conjure with, a name that is synonymous with Arthur, Morgan le Fay, the Lady of the Lake, Nimue, the Knights of the Round Table, Camelot, and Avalon. Was he the greatest of Druids, a true caster of spells, a weaver of tales and legends, a maker of kings, or a tragic hero in his own right? Whatever your own belief, here's your chance to see Merlin through the eyes of some of today's finest storytellers in such spellbinding tales as:

"One Morning at the Stone"—It was Arthur's destiny and Merlin's, too—the sword in the stone, the boy, and the wizard . . . or was it?

"The Magic Roundabout"—An old man and his dog, why should three teenage girls find them so fascinating? Maybe it was fate. . . .

"The End of Summer"—The King is dead and now his legend must begin, but will it be Merlin alone who spins heroic myth from an all-too-dark reality?

MERLIN

Merlin

EDITED BY

Martin H. Greenberg

DAW BOOKS, INC.
DONALD A. WOLLHEIM, FOUNDER
375 Hudson Street, New York, NY 10014

ELIZABETH R. WOLLHEIM
SHEILA E. GILBERT
PUBLISHERS

www.dawbooks.com

First Printing, September 1999
1 2 3 4 5 6 7 8 9

DAW TRADEMARK REGISTERED
U.S. PAT. OFF. AND FOREIGN COUNTRIES
—MARCA REGISRTEADA
HECHO EN U.S.A.

PRINTED IN THE U.S.A.

ACKNOWLEDGMENTS

CONTENTS

INTRODUCTION

by John Helfers

THERE are few figures in myth who stir the imagination like Merlin, the reputed wizard of Camelot and ally of King Arthur. Indeed, one cannot think of the legends of Excalibur and the Knights of the Round Table without Merlin's name coming to mind. Mystic, mage, adviser to kings, in the end he proved all too human, betrayed by Nimuë, the Lady of the Lake, and supposedly trapped in an oak tree (or cave, depending on which version of the story one reads) for one thousand years.

Interestingly, while there was a historical correspondent to Arthur, whom many scholars believe was an early sixth century Welsh warrior chieftain, Merlin is a complete creation of the Middle Ages author Geoffrey of Monmouth, whose book, *History of the Kings of Britain*, was written in 1136. While Monmouth claimed to have been translating from an older Welsh document, and that his writing was partially based on the character of Myrddin the Wild, a man who roamed the British countryside living like an animal, this is the first time that the sorcerer Merlin is mentioned in history or myth.

The French poet Robert de Boron shaped the magician into the mythic figure we know today. In his work *Merlin*, written in 1200, he created the sword in the stone myth as well as the Round Table. A thirteenth century anonymously written poem, *Suite de Merlin,* completes the cycle by telling of Merlin's final encounter with Nimuë, and his subsequent imprisonment.

Of course, retellings of the Arthurian myths have followed ever since, from the writings of Sir Thomas Malory and T.H. White to Disney's *Sword in the Stone* and the *Merlin* miniseries that aired recently on network television. Considering that it took more than a few centuries for Merlin's story to come together, it is only natural that there are some parts that have not been told. What of the rest of his time in Camelot? If Merlin is only trapped in that oak tree, what would happen when he awakens in the twentieth century? How would he react to the modern world?

These are the questions that were put to several of today's finest fantasy writers, with the result being the magical book you are reading right now. Authors such as Charles de Lint, Diana Paxson, Jane Yolen, Esther Friesner, and many others have been brought together in a new collection of stories about the mightiest of magicians, Merlin. So turn the page and immerse your imagination as mythology's most famous sorcerer comes to life in these tales of Merlin.

OLD MERLIN DANCING ON THE SANDS OF TIME

by Jane Yolen

World Fantasy Award winner Jane Yolen has written well over 200 books for children and adults, and well over 150 short stories, most of them fantasy. She is a past president of the Science Fiction and Fantasy Writers of America as well as a twenty-five-year veteran of the Board of Directors of the Society of Children's Book Writers & Illustrators. Recent novels include *The Wizard's Map* and *The One-Armed Queen*. She lives with her husband in Hatfield, Massachusetts and St. Andrews, Scotland.

> Here on the sands of time, slapping
> waters overlapping, his foot
> tapping to the waves' length,
> strengthening the bonds,
> boundaries, sounding boards,
> but bored with magic, that tragic
> moment of change, he alone remains
> unchanged.
>
> Chance was once his favorite game,
> gambling with life's odds;
> yet oddly counting no cards,

cardinal sins being his suit,
sweet temptations, like hearts,
a heartier hunger than a virgin
verging on her first inter-
course.

He remembers a girl in a tree;
tremendous power surging;
surgeonlike cutting through rock,
then rocketing hanging stones over sea;
seeing a sword slice stone—
astonishing—as if butter
were bettered by the slicing. He
curses

recall, that fall, that autumn,
that tumble of wintry verbs, nouns,
annunciation of endings. Never again
can he gain access to a first wish, a first
wisdom, a first sweetly opening girl,
girdle loosening to let him in,
let him enter that cave he will never
leave.

CAULDRON OF LIGHT

by Diana L. Paxson

Diana L. Paxson's novels include her *Chronicles of Westria* series, and her more recent *Wodan's Children* series. Her short fiction can be found in the anthologies *Zodiac Fantastic, Grails: Quests of the Dawn, Return to Avalon,* and *The Book of Kings.* Her Arthurian novel, *Hallowed Isle,* is appearing in four volumes over the next two years, with book one, *The Book of the Sword,* in stores now.

LIGHT glittered on the water, starry flashes reflecting a shifting glimmer across rock and tree and the face of the man who stood knee-deep in the pool. He blinked once, then stilled, allowing awareness to sink past that shimmering surface, seeking the silver flicker of the fish that drifted, suspended between earth and air, curving with the current of the stream.

He had been a fish once, a great salmon, returning home from the sea. He knew the myriad subtle messages of taste and touch and pressure, more meaningful to him now than the ways of courts and kings. His mind became that of the salmon once more, while his hands, forgotten, drifted against the current like water-weed.

The trout grew still, attention focused on the ceiling of

light. The mind of the man floated with it, perceived the ripple as a fly touched the surface. Silver sides flexed; hands flickered, scooping the trout out of its element. It wriggled furiously, protesting the impossible emptiness of the world.

Merlin straightened, his mind snapping free as the trout gasped out its life on the grass. He watched in unwilling sympathy—most of his life he had been out of his element, but Arthur, whom he had counseled and defended, was grown now, and a king. The mage was become a stranger to Camelot, his rightful home the wildwood, where he could be both more, and less, than a man.

He winced as back muscles began to complain against the unnatural angle he had forced them to maintain, and stretched, long arms, pelted with hair whose brown was grizzled now to gray, reaching for the sky. When he was a child, he thought ruefully, he could do this all afternoon. Where once he had been as flexible as a sapling, he was aging like an old tree. How old, he wondered? An oak could live until felled by disease or lightning or the hand of man, growing larger and stronger with each year. He had fortunately ceased to grow when he was a half a head taller than most men, and hair and beard had silvered. But he was still strong.

Merlin looked at the trout, whose colors were dulling already. One small fish was not much of a meal. The day before had been stormy, and he had huddled in his cave, fasting. He wondered if he could manage another fish, and bent once more to the stream.

Wind gusted suddenly, whispering in the trees, lifting the sheltering branches so that light flared blindingly from the surface of the pool. He swayed, all other awareness fleeing as his mind filled with light. The whisper of wind became a woman's voice that pierced the soul—

"Merlin! The Grail is gone! Merlin, help me!"

The wind passed; the branches, subsiding, veiled his sight. The vision released him then, and he collapsed gently into the pool.

The shock of the cold water brought Merlin upright, gasping. On her holy isle, the Lady of the Lake guarded the sacred Cauldron which was also called the Grail. He could not believe anyone had breached its wardings, but the Hallows sometimes moved of their own will. When they did so, kingdoms could fall.

He clambered out of the pool, shaking himself like a wet dog. First, he needed food, and then he would be on his way. Skewering the trout on a piece of green wood, he began to kindle a fire.

As Merlin moved south, he heard rumors. They spread across the land like a river in floodtime, murky with silt and choked with debris. Neither the Lady nor the Grail were at the Lake, cupped by its northern mountains. The only certainty was that the Hallow had appeared at Camelot, and now it was gone. Half of Arthur's war band, it was said, had ridden out to search for it.

What brave men might accomplish, they would do. It seemed to Merlin that he would accomplish little by running after them. Better to be still, and wait for wisdom like a fisherman at a weir. In time, he heard that the Cauldron had mysteriously returned to the Isle of Maidens. But men still sought the Grail. To Merlin, its true nature was now an even greater mystery.

As summer faded into fall, he settled finally in the woods near the ruined fortress of Mediolanum, where the road that angled across southern Britannia toward Londinium met the longer tracks that linked the north with the south and west. There he built himself a little hut of branches and heaped stones. Less visible, but stronger, was the net of power that he laid across the roads to catch the fragments of truth and the men who bore them.

On an autumn afternoon Merlin heard a horse approaching. The hoofbeats stopped outside his hut, and someone called for water. He emerged from the hut, head bowed

and body hidden by the voluminous white wool of a
Druid's robe, a wooden bowl brimming in his hands.

"Holy father, I thank you, in Christ's name—"

Merlin repressed a smile, understanding that the boy had
taken him for one of those hermits who sought the wilderness, finding even a monastery too worldly for their needs.
No doubt he had joined Arthur's band since the last time
Merlin visited the king.

"In the name of the god you serve, you are welcome,"
he answered gravely. "You look weary. Alight, and share
my simple meal, and tell me of your journey."

"I suppose it is no sin to accept the hospitality of a holy
man," the boy said, frowning. "My name is Amminius son
of Lucius, a warrior of Arthur's Companions, and indeed I
am in need of counsel."

"Then you are welcome," Merlin answered him.

"It is not a journey, but a quest that I am on," said Amminius when he had slaked his thirst and they were seated
by the hearth. "Perhaps you will have heard?"

Merlin nodded, and put another stick on the fire. "There
have been many rumors. What did you see?"

"It was the night of the great storm—" the young man
began. "All the folk in Camelot were gathered in the great
hall, listening to the timbers groan and the wind whistle
through the thatching, and praying to whatever gods they
knew. It was close to midnight when the doors were flung
open. A woman screamed—we all thought our last hour
had come. And then there was a great light, and a stillness,
as if we lay in the eye of the storm. The light moved
through the hall, and before each one, it paused . . ." He
lifted the beaker to his lips and drank.

"And what was it?" asked Merlin then.

"In truth, I do not know," Amminius replied. "I know
what I saw and heard, but I have spoken to others, whose
experience was quite different. To me," he continued, "it
was a chalice, such as the priest uses at the mass. But this
one was far richer, and it shone. And there was a Voice that
spoke to me," he added, but he did not tell what it had said.

Merlin did not expect it. His own visions had taught him how difficult it was to convey their real meaning in human words.

"I think it was the Cup of Christ's passion that I saw, but on the next day word came that the Cauldron they keep at the Isle of Maidens had been stolen. So I do not know now what it is I am searching for, or why—"

"Do you not? When you spoke, the memory of what you saw shone in your eyes. To deny that truth is to deny yourself!"

Amminius shook his head. "I was brought up in the faith, but I have never been devout. I always meant to be a warrior . . ."

"And now—"

"Now my only desire is to see that vision again! But I know that once I am back at court I will forget, and so I wander—"

"You are not searching for the Grail, you are fleeing the world." Merlin searched his memory for the teachings of the priests he had heard at the court of Vor-Tigernus when he was young. "If you follow this path you will remain in limbo, able to attain neither heaven nor hell."

"But what must I do?"

Merlin shook his head. He could preach Christian doctrine, but he refused to take responsibility for this boy's soul. "You must choose. . . ."

For a long moment Amminius sat with head bowed. When he looked up at last, the memory of glory shone in his eyes.

"Oh, good father, thank you!" His voice rang out joyously. "In the hills above my home there is a cave. I will go there, and live on berries and roots and the water from the stream. And perhaps, if I purify my heart and wait patiently, the Grail will come to me. . . ."

Merlin stared at him in amazement. "Do not thank me, but the god within you—" he said at last. *He has found his Grail,* he thought, *though he may not yet realize it. But if it is the Chalice of the Christians, what then is the Cauldron?*

* * *

On the heels of a winter storm another traveler found his way to Merlin's door. This one was older, a dour, heavyset man called Cunobelin, who had served with Arthur since the Saxon wars. In the old days, the mage had known him well. The mage came upon him as he led a limping horse down the road.

"What are you doing here?" he said as Merlin moved out from among the leafless trees. Cunobelin had never been one of those who made the sign of the Horns if they touched the mage's shadow, nor did he follow the Christians. Indeed, Merlin doubted the man had faith in anything at all.

"Waiting for you—" he answered. "Or someone like you. I have a shelter nearby. Come rest your horse and eat a bowl of soup by my fire."

For a moment Cunobelin considered him, then he nodded. "A friendly face and a little warmth will be welcome. This wind blows chill."

Merlin waited until the man had eaten before he questioned him about the Grail.

"What did I see?" Cunobelin laughed harshly. "A bright light that moved through the hall. So in truth I do not know what we are all seeking, but it is clear that I am not the one to find it. I am returning now to Camelot."

"You speak as one who has failed—"

"Is it not so?" Cunobelin asked bitterly.

"Perhaps you have been looking in the wrong place."

"What do you mean?" The warrior frowned.

"I think that you are one who must be able to see the object of his adoration. It is in this world, not the Other, that you will find what you are looking for."

"The sun and the moon are still in the heavens, as anyone can see, but no one has suggested we search for *them!*"

Merlin shook his head. "Surely the heavens hold wonders, but they do not make your spirit soar. Think back. Is there anything else that has made you feel as you did in the moment when the light passed through the hall? A person, an experience—in the Otherworld, things do not have to be alike to be the same."

"A person?" whispered Cunobelin. He closed his eyes. "Nothing that anyone else would think worth remembering. . . ." For a time he was silent. When he spoke again, it was as one in a dream.

"I was very young when I first came to Londinium to serve the king. The lads wormed out of me that I'd never lain with a woman, and they took me to a courtesan. I was ashamed of my ignorance, but she . . . was kind to me. And when she received me into her arms, it was like a great light breaking around me. . . ." He shook his head and looked up, an unaccustomed color in his cheeks. "But surely to remember that is blasphemy, when everyone is talking of a holy thing!"

"For you, her embrace *was* holy," said Merlin. "Why have you never married? You deny your nature."

"What could I offer a wife, when I was always going off to war? But I've dreamed of finding a woman who would come with me to one of those abandoned farms I've seen in my travels and make it bloom again." He stopped short, staring at Merlin. "Have you bespelled me? I have never told anyone these things!"

"I have cast no spells," the mage said softly. "I only point the way—"

Cunobelin was never seen at Arthur's court again. All that winter season, other men came to Merlin's hut in the forest, eager or disillusioned, proud in their strength or feverish with wounds. The weak he nursed and the strong he counseled, and from each one he learned something of the Hallow they were all seeking.

He had heard once an ancient tale of the blind men who were asked to describe an elephant, their reports all different, and all accurate descriptions of the part of the beast each man had found. On the Isle of Maidens, the priestesses guarded a Cauldron. He had seen it, and knew it for a thing of power. But was that the Grail, or only one appearance of something whose true nature could only be known by combining the myriad visions of those to whom it called?

Merlin's last visitor came riding by on a day when spring had drawn her first veil of greenery across the land and the skies were clamorous with returning waterfowl, borne north on the warm breath of the wind. Merlin had thrown off the heavy Druid's robe and donned his garment of skins. The hut where he had spent the winter seemed cramped and odorous, as tattered as the winter pelts the beasts were shedding to make way for the new growth of spring. His muscles twitched with the urge to action, yet still he tarried. When he met the young warrior's dazzled gaze, he understood what he had been waiting for.

"Eliuc—" Softly he called his name, waiting for the wide eyes to track slowly downward, for recognition to focus there.

"It is you . . ." the boy said at last. "I sought you . . . because you might understand. . . ."

"Why? Who do you think I am?"

"You are the Wild Man of the Woods, yourself half of faerie," the answer came.

Merlin grunted. This boy was too young to recognize him, but in a way, his words were true.

"Were you not one of those who rode out to seek the Grail? Your face seems to say that you have found it—" he said when the horse had been unsaddled and tethered to graze.

Eliuc sank down on an outcropping of stone. "I found . . . something. It haunts my dreams." His skin was luminous in the dappled shade of the young leaves.

"Tell me—"

Haltingly, the story came—the privations of a quest pursued through winter weather until despair was near. Eliuc had taken refuge at last with a shepherd, earning his keep by guarding the ewes as they dropped their lambs and keeping off the wolves. When the weather warmed, he set off again, letting the horse choose the way.

One night, he had made camp beside a small spring. He woke to the touch of moonlight that glimmered through the branches and reflected from the pool in a haze of light. He sat up, staring, for in that light a figure was forming, slender, luminous, beautiful beyond mortal ken.

"She smiled at me . . . she held out a vessel of pure silver, rimmed with river pearls, and I took it from her hand. It was brimming with what looked like water, but the taste of it overwhelmed my senses. I was lost, to myself, to the world, overcome by joy."

"And then?" asked Merlin, seeing him begin to drown once more in that rapture.

"Then it was morning, and I was alone." The desolation in Eliuc's tone made the mage's eyes prick in sympathy. "For a week I waited, but she did not come again. Since then I have wandered. Food has no savor, even my dreams are pale echoes of what I have seen. Was it in truth the Grail that I found?"

"For you it was," Merlin said gravely. "You have tasted the wine of the Otherworld. Be grateful for what you have seen, and do not seek to recapture it."

"That is cold comfort! How can I live in a world from which the magic is gone?"

"There are many kinds of magic—" Merlin began, but Eliuc shook his head.

"I will go back to the spring. Perhaps if I am patient, one day she will open the door to me once more!" He leaped to his feet, eyes once more afire with remembered glory, and before the mage could speak again, had run to his horse and was gone.

Arthur will not thank me for this day's work, Merlin thought sadly. The king's men had sought the Grail to bring healing to the kingdom, but too many, one way or another, had been lost to king and kin. To each of them, it brought the fulfillment most desired—for one, the Christos, for another, a woman's body, and the ecstasy of the Other-world for a third.

It was time for the hermit to leave the forest. The lure had become too strong—the Grail had appeared to him, if only through other men's eyes, and he had now no choice but to search for it.

What face, he wondered, *will the Grail wear for me?*

Merlin's way led toward the Lake and the Isle of Maidens. The Grail, it was clear, was not the same as the Cauldron, and yet by taking the Cauldron into the lands of mortal men, a way had been opened for the Grail to appear, establishing a connection between the Hallow and the men who sought it. For all his wizardry, he could take no path but the one the Hallow had already chosen.

He came in the evening, as the light of the setting sun, reflected from the heavens, was filling the Lake with gold.

Merlin had known the Lady since they both were young, and insofar as it was given to him to feel for a mortal woman, loved her. There had always been respect between them, but she faced him with hostility now.

"By blood you are priest of the Sword, and the god of the Saxons has given you his spear. By what right do you claim access to the Cauldron? It is a Woman's Mystery!"

"A woman bears the Grail, but it calls to men and women alike. Arthur is the Defender of Britannia, but I am his mage. When magic touches the land, it is my responsibility, and my right, to understand it. And it is your duty as Guardian of one of the Hallows to assist me."

For a long moment she looked at him, and then she sighed. "Perhaps it is so. Certainly I have not been so secure a custodian as I might wish, though the Goddess brought good from mischance in the end. But your reasoning does not entirely convince me—the lands of men have not seen you for years on end. Men thought you dead, or a legend. Why should the Grail draw you back?"

"Why, indeed? You are right to wonder. I have lived in the forest as a Wild Man, forgetting my humanity. I thought

I would die there, but I am still strong. Perhaps the Grail will show me, as it has shown to others, a way I may be released from the world."

And when he had said that, the priestess ceased to argue, and together they waited for night to fall.

"What is it that you expect to see?" asked the Lady of the Lake as she led him to the dell below the cave.

"A vessel, a container, a passage between the worlds. . . ."

"And does the greatest mage in Britannia need such devices for his journeying?" Her voice was cool, but in her words he heard echoes of the Otherworld, and the hair on his body stood out as if from cold.

"For this journey, I do."

"I will tell you once more. If it was the Cauldron that passed through Arthur's hall that night, it was borne by no mortal hand."

"Have you lost faith in your own Hallow, Lady?" He shook his head. "This is not the end of Desire, but this is where I must begin."

The opening to the cave was a dark slash in the rough rock that pushed through the turf of the hill. Torches set to either side hissed and flickered, sending ruddy light pooling across the worn stone. Merlin sank down upon the boulder that faced it, keeping his breathing long and slow. But he could not control the pounding of his heart.

The silence deepened until he could hear the whisper of fine linen as the wind stirred the Lady's veil. In the shadows of the cave mouth, something pale was moving. A female form, swathed in white, emerged from the darkness, torchlight flaring across the polished silver surface of the vessel she bore. She came to Merlin and set the Cauldron gently on the slab of stone before him.

It was half filled with water.

"It is only water from the spring," said the Lady. "What meaning you find there must come from within."

"I know it." Merlin lifted his hands in blessing and

invocation. "By fire and water I summon truth to me, by the radiance of the spirit and the darkness of the womb."

He felt, rather than heard, her leaving him. And then he was alone with the ripple of light on water and the surrounding shadows.

He saw, first, his own features, wild hair twining in distorted spirals like some ancient carving. Beneath the heavy brows, his eyes captured light from the torches' flames. Merlin continued to gaze, breath passing in a slow and regular rhythm that barely stirred the hair of his beard, waiting for the water to still, the fires to burn low, until he saw only the shimmer of backlit hair like a halo around a mask of darkness.

Gazing, he allowed his consciousness to sink into those depths, until he no longer saw the Cauldron or his own face within it. Presently new images formed within the shadow—stars in a night sky and the dim shapes of trees, a face framed by the rim of a cauldron.

But the cauldron he looked into was wrought of black iron, and the face reflected from the steaming brew it contained was that of a boy.

"Stir it, Viaun, you wretched chid! Have not I told you the liquid must always be kept moving?" A white hand reached past his head and cast pungent leaves of mugwort into the cauldron. The hand of Cerituend. . . .

His grip tightened convulsively on the ladle and he began to draw it sunwise through the liquid once more. Already the sharp scent of the herb was melding with others—mints and sages, leek, salt, and darker, heavier odors he did not want to name. It smelled like magic.

"It will not be long now. Do not fail me! I will be back soon!" Cerituend's voice was like honey, like the scent of her, fading as she moved away. A memory that was not his own made him shiver with mingled fear and desire.

Merlin who was Viaun reached out to the nearby woodpile and slid more sticks beneath the pregnant bulge of the cauldron. Soon the brew was bubbling gently. The roiling of the liquid intensified. He slowed his stirring, trying to calm it. Perhaps he should not have added more fuel to the fire. *She* had said the potion was almost complete—as he stared into the cauldron, its contents heaved as if that last addition had awakened it. The potion was meant to give her son wisdom in compensation for his ugly countenance. No wonder it seemed to have a life of its own.

He looked nervously over his shoulder, involved entirely in the vision now. Black branches netted the dim blue of the evening sky. And in that instant of inattention, he heard the bubbling of the potion intensify. In the next moment it was boiling over, splashing his hand. He squealed with pain and clapped it to his lips.

The concentrated liquid scalded, at once tart and sweet, bland and salty. Then the confusion of flavors became a maelstrom of meaning. He understood *everything,* the movements of the heavens and the growth of herbs, the ways of all beasts and the tongues of men. He comprehended, in that moment, the meaning of the Grail, and beyond that, overwhelming him with terror, knew that he had stolen the magic of the Goddess, and that She would destroy him.

He was Viaun and Merlin, he was every man who has transgressed Women's Mysteries. He dropped the ladle on the grass and began to run.

For a time he ran blindly, but soon enough his new knowledge told him that She was coming after him. He became a hare, coursing swiftly through the undergrowth. But the Goddess had turned herself to a lean hound bitch to run him down. When he leaped skyward as a sparrow, she became a plummeting hawk. He was the stag that fled the wolf-bitch, the salmon that twisted away from the otter's tooth, the vole that fled the owl. All these he had been, in that other lifetime when he was Merlin. As Viaun, he was pushed from transformation to transformation, fleeing the terrible Mother down the cycles of the years.

In the end he no longer possessed the strength or invention to continue his evasions. His last defense was to turn himself to something insignificant beyond her attention, one grain in a pile of corn. And there he waited, until the

huge black hen pecked her way across the farmyard and
swallowed him up into the dark.

For a time beyond time the soul that had been Merlin lay
cradled in the pregnant womb of the World. And in that
darkness came visions. He saw men of Camelot still searching for the Grail, some to give up the quest in despair, some
to die, and some, under a dozen different guises, to find
what they most desired. The veil of Time swirled, and he
saw Arthur facing Mordred upon a bloody field. He struggled then, sure he could stop it if only he were free, and
saw an oak tree in the heart of the forest whose trunk had
the shape of a man.

"Have I failed entirely?" his spirit cried then. *"Shall
Camelot fall, and all my wisdom pass with it from the
world?"*

"From whence did that wisdom come?" asked the
Darkness.

After a time, Merlin answered slowly, *"From the Cauldron, which holds the distilled essence of the earth."*

*"Then how can it be lost? It is men's knowledge of that
wisdom that will disappear. . . ."*

"I have lived long, but this body is not immortal—"

*"Then take a new one. I have taught you the way of trans-
formation."* The answer, slow and amused, came to him.
*"Let your power be rooted in the land, and your spirit pass
to the child of prophecy. Your wisdom will never be forgotten, so long as you remember that it came from Me. . . ."*

Merlin floated, thinking. The warm darkness that surrounded him was changing, becoming the slow surge of
the sea. At last a final question came to him. Other men
had asked whom the Grail served, but that was not what he
needed to know.

"Who are you?"

The attention of that Other intensified. Once more Merlin tried to get away, but how could he flee that which contained him?

"I am the Quest, and I am the Grail. Men seek Me, not knowing that they will gain their desire only when I find them. They flee, not knowing that flight forces the transformation that will bring them to My arms. I am the Divine Darkness and the Light that shines beyond the circles of the world. I am the Truth beyond all goddesses and gods. I am the Mystery. . . ."

The rhythmic motion grew more violent. Dizzied, Merlin struggled against the membrane that contained him.

"Who—" he cried. *"Who is the Child of Prophecy?"*

He was dying. He was being born. A last convulsion slammed him hard against an unyielding surface. The darkness that surrounded him was torn open and someone lifted him into the air.

"Look!" came a voice. "It is the Radiant Brow!"

When Merlin could think again, he found himself lying tangled in his cloak on the stones before the cave. The Lady of the Lake knelt beside him, but the Cauldron was gone. Had he dreamed its presence? It did not matter, for the vision it had given him still shimmered in memory.

"Are you all right?" she asked, helping him to sit up again. "Did you learn what you needed to know? You began to struggle, and then you cried out and collapsed."

"I think so . . ." he nodded. "Help me to rise and I will tell you what I saw, lest it disappear like a dream."

He finished his story sitting with the Lady on the stone bench on the lakeshore, watching the sky grow bright above the eastern hills.

"I must go back to Arthur's court," Merlin said finally. "I cannot change what is to come, but I can bear witness, and pass to the Child of Prophecy the story. . . ."

"But who is he?" asked the Lady.

"He is Taliesin, the babe with the Radiant Brow. In forty years, he will be born—for the first time. And I will be waiting to teach him, for in body and spirit I will be one with this land. That body will die, but his spirit, my spirit, will come again and again, renewing the ancient magic, re-birthing the old stories into the world. . . ."

A fish leaped from the Lake before them, the twisting body flaring gold. In the next moment it fell back again, but the impact sent ripples circling outward across the still water long after the fish itself had disappeared.

"And did you find what you were looking for?"

The mage nodded, gazing out across the shining expanse of water cupped within its sheltering hills. *This is the Grail,* he thought. *The Cauldron and all the other vessels, are but analogues for this precious and lovely world, which is itself a sacrament, given meaning by the life it holds.*

And in that moment the sun lifted above the rim of the hill, and sky and water and Merlin's spirit were filled with light.

FOREST OF STONE

by Charles de Lint

Charles de Lint is a full-time writer and musician who presently makes his home in Ottawa, Ontario, Canada, with his wife MaryAnn Harris, an artist and musician. His most recent books are *Somewhere to Be Flying* and the single author collection entitled *Moonlight and Vines*. For more information on his work, visit his Web site at www.cyberus.ca/~cdl.

"I lived in a tree," he said. "Not in some little house, nestled up in its branches, but deep inside the trunk itself where the sap flows and old secrets cluster. It was a time, let me tell you, but long gone now. Then I was a king in a forest of green; now I live like a beggar in a forest of stone."

I let him talk. He always had some story or other to tell, and if he invariably came back to this one, I didn't mind. There was something in the telling of this particular story that woke a pleasant buzz in the back of my head, a sweet humming sound like a field full of insects on a summer's day. His quiet voice created a resonance that made me more aware of my own heartbeat and how it resounded against the drum of the world below my feet.

There was a melody playing against that rhythm, but I

could never quite grasp it fully. Maybe we never do and that's why there's always a Mystery underlying the world.

"How long did you live there?" I asked when he fell silent, rheumy eyes gazing off into distant memories.

I tried to imagine him as he'd described himself in the story: strong and tall, dressed all in green, chestnut hair flowing down his back, a great beard half-hiding his face. Adviser to kings, a wizard in a tree. But all I could see in my mind's eye was the person who sat here with me on the steps of St. Paul's, an old broken man plagued with a continual cold, hawk's nose dripping, a cough racking his chest. The only green was an echo of the forest, hidden in those watering eyes.

"How long?" he said. "Forever and a day. Until I befriended a little girl in need of a friend and she pulled me out of my tree with her love. I was free to go then, across the water to the Region of Summer Stars, and so I did. But it wasn't what I thought it would be. I found no peace there, no rest for my old soul." He coughed, gaze turning from the traffic passing on the street in front of us to meet my own. "Perhaps it was because I didn't die. Because I crossed over, upright and on my own two feet, taking my blood and bones with me."

Like the forest with its prison tree, this place of summer stars was always vague to me. He gave no details that I could hold on to. From his description, or rather lack of the same, it could be any place or every place.

I took it to mean a pagan heaven, like Tir na nOg, some afterworld of the Gael, but that didn't tally except as metaphor. People, even a homeless man such as this with a mystic bent, didn't return from the dead. That was the province of avatars and saviors and I greatly doubted he was either. But what he was, or once had been, I was unable to say.

"You should leave your bones behind when you go," he told me. "I learned that quickly enough. Safely buried, or better still, leave them as ashes, burned in a bone-fire. Otherwise this world calls to them and you can never be content. Your blood moves to the tides you left behind and there is ever a yearning for something other than twilight. You long for the sun, and the dark of a moonless night. You long for life."

"Why is it always twilight there?"

He shrugged. "Maybe it isn't. Maybe it was only twilight for me because the ribbons of my life there were still entwined with this world, this life."

"Do you still want to go back there?" I asked. "To return?"

"I don't know what I want or don't want. I only know I've been too long in this world, if only viewing it through the bark of a tree for most of my years. I miss something, but I don't know what. Perhaps my old life, before I let curiosity snare me with its woody embrace."

"What were you in your old life?"

He took so long to answer that I thought he hadn't heard me.

"Let me tell you a story of a king and his adviser," he said finally. He smiled, eyes clear for a moment. "It explains nothing, but it will pass the time."

"What if pigeons were really angels?" Jilly said.

Geordie looked down the wide sweep of steps that fronted St. Paul's Cathedral. The usual, unruly flock of pigeons were mooching for handouts from the tourists and passersby up and down their length. In the midst of the birds he could see the old homeless man that everybody called Woody, ragged coat sleeves flapping as he tossed handfuls of sunflower seeds he couldn't really afford to buy. For some reason the sight of the old man made Geordie think of Tanya. Maybe it was because of the stories Woody told, rambling accounts that mixed up well-known fables and fairy tales with pure make-believe. That was the world Tanya lived in, more months out of the year than Geordie cared to dwell on. Hollywood. A more contemporary Land of Make-Believe.

"Sometimes," Jilly went on, "when I hear the flutter of their feathers in the air, I forget that we don't have wings, too, and I just want to fly."

"I'm tired of long-distance romances," Geordie said.

Jilly sighed. "I know you are, Geordie, me lad. That's why I'm trying to cheer you up with pigeon angels." She waited a beat, then added, "You could always move to L.A. to be with her."

"And be what?"

"Yourself."

"And you could always get a job doing storyboards for an ad agency."

"It's an honorable position."

Geordie smiled. "Maybe. But it's not you."

"This is true."

"That's how it'd be for me out there. I'm all scruff and too poor to be considered eccentric. Could you imagine me going to a premiere or some awards show?"

"You clean up well," Jilly assured him.

He shook his head. "I'd only embarrass her. She wouldn't say anything, she might not even think it, but come on. Beauty and the Beast is an old story. It doesn't play anymore."

Jilly put an arm around his shoulders and gave him a hug. "You're very broody today, and it doesn't suit you at all. Leave the brooding to your brother. Writers are supposed to brood about things. Fiddlers don't. Remember jigs and reels? Happy things?"

Geordie sighed. "I know. I hate mopey people, and here I am, doing it all the same."

They sat quietly for a moment. Below them the pigeons kept rising in nervous clouds as some imagined danger startled them—a tourist coming too close, the sudden whoosh of a bus—before the flock settled once more.

Without looking at her, Geordie said, "Do you ever get the feeling that although you've never seen a thing, you still know it?"

"Like what?"

"You know, when some one's describing a place you've never been, and it's all familiar, not because you've ever been there, but because you know that one day you'll go there?"

Jilly gave him an odd look. "I suppose . . ."

"That's how I feel with Tanya sometimes—like I can already see the time when we won't be together anymore."

"That kind of thinking makes things happen," Jilly told him.

"Whatever you think makes something happen."

"I suppose. So wouldn't it behoove us to think positively?"

Geordie had to smile. "Behoove?"

"It's a word."

"I know it is. I've just never heard it used in ordinary conversation before. Wait," he added, forestalling her next comment. "I know. Conversations should never be ordinary."

"That's not true. I like ordinary conversations. But I also like twisting, windy ones where we work out all the great mysteries of the world in whatever time we have and then sit back and have another cup of tea, knowing it's a job well done."

"I'd miss you if I moved to L.A."

Jilly nodded. "I'd miss you, too." She hesitated, before adding, "But maybe it's something you have to do."

"Perhaps it was only that you left something undone," I said the next time the old man and I talked. "That's why you came back."

"I'm not a ghost."

"Well, no. Of course not."

"And we all—the living and the dead—leave things undone. It seems to be part and parcel of human nature to put off today what we hope to do tomorrow."

"Well, then maybe you simply missed someone."

He considered that. "No. I don't think that. My lover betrayed me, my king had a sword sheathed in his chest, my father abandoned me to the forest. There was no one else."

"You sound bitter."

And had every right to, I suppose, if anything he was saying was true. Even if it was only true in a metaphorical sense.

"Do I?" he said, genuinely surprised. "I suppose I do. But I don't have reason to. Once you have lived as part of a forest, you learn to forgo such things."

"What about the little girl? The one you befriended?"

"The girl?" He shook his head. "She is gone now as well. I think it was a long time ago that we were friends."

"People don't just stop being friends."

"Of course. I only meant I hadn't seen her for many years."

He was quiet for a moment, wiped his runny nose on a raggedy sleeve.

"But perhaps you're right," he finally said. "I remember telling a reluctant knight once that if certain things don't happen, the spirit never rests. Perhaps some piece of unfinished business waits for me here."

I waited to see if he had anything more to say, another story to tell, but he looked down at the pavement, silent.

"Do you want a pretzel?" I asked him. "I'm getting one."

He patted his pockets. "Yes, that would be nice, but I seem to be a little short of the required currency . . ."

"I can cover it."

He smiled, still not entirely back with me yet. "And perhaps something for our feathered friends . . ."

I went to get us coffee and pretzels from one of the food carts out by the curb. The vendor gave me a plastic bag with some stale hot dog buns in it when I asked if he had any day-old bread. I took it back with me.

"I think you should do the honors," he said when I started to hand him the bag.

I took a sip of my coffee, then set it aside and began to break up the buns, tossing the pieces to the pigeons.

"I think I'm supposed to die," he said as he watched the birds eat. "That's the business I've left unfinished."

I shot him a worried look.

"Oh, don't worry. I'm not feeling suicidal or anything."

"Well, that's a relief."

"But when I do die, would you make a fire of my bones, burn them down to ash and scatter them from here to there, dust to dust and all that?"

"You're saying you want to be cremated." I made a statement of it, tossed some more bits of bread to the pigeons. "I guess I could do that . . ." Though where I'd get the money to be able to afford a cremation for him was a whole other kind of mystery, secular, but no less puzzling.

He shook his head. "Not in some . . . factory. No, in an honest fire, wood and bones. With a friend like you to watch over the flames."

"They've got laws against the illegal disposing of bodies," I told him, smiling, making a joke of it.

"There won't be a body," he assured me. "Only bones."

"This isn't like one of your stories . . ."

"No, of course not." He put a hand on my arm. "You're throwing too hard. Do it like this."

He took a handful from me and tossed it with an oddly graceful motion, like it was a dance, but only his arm was moving. I watched the way the little pieces of bread seemed to sail out and among the birds in slow motion.

"Now you try it."

I did, but I couldn't capture his grace.

"That's better," he said.

I gave him a surprised look.

"It's because now you're paying attention," he said. "Doing it like you mean it. You'd be surprised how much satisfaction you can get from the simplest task if you impart it with meaning."

"She's lined up some work for me," Geordie said. "A recording gig for this guy who's making a film. Tanya played him a tape of some of my music and apparently it's just what he wants for a couple of scenes."

Jilly beamed proudly. "That's great."

"I guess."

"Can you bring your enthusiasm down a notch or two—you're blinding me with the glare of your happiness."

Geordie gave her a rueful smile. "I know. I should be happy."

"So what's the problem? That you didn't get the gig on your own?"

"Well, yes. I mean, no. It's just . . ."

"It was your music on the tape, right?"

"Sure."

"So . . . what?"

Geordie sighed. "I don't know. It's like everything's slipping out of control."

"You're in a relationship," Jilly told him. "That means there's give and take. Compromise. She can't make a living here, but maybe you can make one out there. It's not like you're being asked to be someone you're not. And since when did you start worrying about control?"

"I don't mean that I want to be in charge of everything. It's just . . . I'll be leaving everything and everyone behind."

"You're scared."

He nodded.

"That's okay," Jilly told him. "Big, life-changing things are always scary. But that doesn't mean they're bad."

"I know."

"So when did she tell you about this?"

"Last night."

Jilly poked him in the shoulder with a stiff finger. "And? So what did you say?"

"That I'd let her know."

"Oh, Geordie."

"No, it's okay. She understands. I'm calling her tomorrow morning."

"We won't stop being friends if you move," Jilly assured him. "We'll just have bigger phone bills."

I guess I never really expected him to die. Or at least not so soon.

Like most of the street people I ended up talking to, I never knew where he came from—really came from, that is. If I believed his stories . . . but I didn't. People called him Woody, but he answered to a half-dozen names. Robin Wood. Jack Green. Sammy King. Merle Hode. Some others that I've forgotten now. Woody was the one that stuck.

I was busking the lineups in the theater district that night, always a good place to make a little money, when Bridie Grey gave me the message that Woody wanted to see me. She always reminded me of a gangly, wingless bird with her large eyes and twig-limbs. A recovered junkie, she still looked like she had a jones. Dark circles around her eyes liked smeared kohl, spiky blonde hair with an inch of dark roots showing, hollow creeks. Heroin chic. Some people never lost that look.

"He's waiting for you in the Tombs," she said, "up Flood Street, past MacNeil."

I was doing okay—pulling the popular tunes from the four strings of my fiddle: "St. Anne's Reel," "Greensleeves," "Old Joe Clark"—though not as good as when *Riverdance* was in town. Then any even vaguely Irish tune was guaranteed to fill my fiddlecase with change.

"I won't be long," I told her.

"Whatever."

She took off before I could ask what Woody was doing in that no-man's-land of abandoned buildings and old factories. The Tombs is a rough part of town, full of bikers, junkies, runaways, just a lot of people with a chip on their shoulder. The older homeless guys didn't usually go too far in once the sun went down, not unless they traveled in a group, and Woody was a loner.

I tried to play another tune, but my concentration was off, so I packed up and left my spot to a waiting guitarist. I took the subway as far as Gracie Street, then walked over to Flood and up into the Tombs. I could feel a prickle between my shoulder blades as I left the lights of Gracie Street behind. I don't like the Tombs in the day; coming here at night feels like walking into an ambush. But I had this going for me: I've been on the street scene for a lot of years. Most people know me and leave me alone. Not because I'm so tough, but because I've come to fit into the scenery. Like background. I hoped that Woody was as lucky. Sometimes people get the idea that it's funny to douse a bum with gasoline and chase him with a match. Or beat him senseless, just because they can.

There's an empty lot at the corner of Flood and MacNeil— one of those places where the demolition started but never got farther than knocking a few blocks of tenements down. It's been years now since the wrecking crews left, long enough for the rubble to be half-covered with weeds and scrub, some of which has actually succeeded in the struggle to grow into scraggly trees. I knew Woody didn't like being inside, so I started checking out the lot first, ignoring the abandoned buildings that were still standing on the other three corners. What I found gave me the serious creeps.

In about the middle of the lot, someone had piled up a heap of wood, an unlit bonfire of twigs and branches, scrap wood, old fixtures and other woodwork from some of the surrounding buildings. On top of it all was a bundle of clothes that I recognized as belonging to Woody and what looked for all the world like a human skull, artfully displayed on a pyramid of bones. I knew it couldn't be real, the skull, the bones, but it made my pulse quicken all the same.

"Okay," I said. "Very funny, Woody."

Because I remembered what he'd said. There wouldn't be a corpse when he died. Just the bones. I wondered where he'd found them.

Only then I noted the birds.

I don't know why I didn't notice them walking in. The trees, were full of them, more pigeons than I'd ever seen together in one place, eight or nine times the huge flock that gathers daily on the steps in front of St. Paul's. They were all quiet, except for the odd restless rustle of their feathers as one or another shifted position. Once you've seen that Hitchcock movie, you can't help but get a little weirded out over big gatherings of birds like this.

The streetlights of Gracie Street seemed a hundred miles away. Like this was another world. It is another world.

I sat down on some brickwork that had been a part of a wall in some other life and laid my fiddlecase down by my feet. I was seriously creeped. My night vision was good, so it was hard to ignore the unlit funeral pyre, the birds, the damned skull that seemed to be staring right back at me. I tried not to look at it.

I don't know how long I sat there, staring off into the dark. After a while, I heard footsteps, someone scuffling their way across the rubble. In this place it could have been anybody. A junkie, a runaway, some psycho. I was hoping for Woody, to hear him laugh and tell me, "Gotcha." Instead it was Jilly who came wandering up to me, out of the dark. I had to shake my head.

"How'd you know I was here?"

Jilly shrugged. "I don't know. It's just . . ."

"This gift you have."

She gave me a smile. I don't know why I was surprised. Jilly and I seem to have this connection, always running into each other whenever one of us wants to see the other. We don't even have to think about it. It just happens. And she's fearless when it comes to walking around the city at night. It's not like she doesn't care what happens to her. More like she's made some pact with the darkness, the city, the danger. Or maybe the night itself looks out for her, an unexpected random act of kindness pulled out of its shadows like a magician's rabbit.

She sat down beside me on my memory of a wall, and we looked at the bones for a while.

"Woody set this up," I said finally.

She nodded. "Joe told me."

Joe was Joseph Crazy Dog, a friend of hers who always makes me feel a little uneasy. It isn't anything he says or does, but something in his eyes. Or mostly in his eyes, because he can come out with the damnedest things, weird pronouncements that he lets drop like most people do comments about the weather. On the street everybody knows him as Bones because of this fortune-telling thing he does with a handful of small animal bones.

I sighed. More bones. There used to be an old woman who wandered the streets collecting animal bones that she tied up with wire and made into skeletons. With my luck, she'd be showing up here tonight as well.

Jilly tapped my knee with hers, a companionable bump.

"I didn't know Woody well," she said, "but I always liked him. It's too bad he had to go."

I shook my head. "He's not gone anywhere. This is just something he set up to get me going."

Jilly gave me an odd look.

"Whose bones do you think those are?" she asked.

"No way," I told her, starting to wonder if she was in on the joke. "If that's Woody, then who put all this together? The pyre, the bones."

"Geordie, me lad," she said. "We're talking about an enchanter. A magician. Didn't you listen to his stories?"

"Yeah, but . . ."

"You didn't believe."

"Well, no. I mean, Red tells me he's a werewolf. Am I supposed to believe that as well?"

She shrugged. "Depends. What's he like when there's a full moon?"

"Jilly . . ."

"I'm joking."

But I wasn't so sure. The things she accepts as matter of course would have most people knocking on the front door of the Zeb and asking for a padded room if they started seeing them as well.

"But not about Woody," she added.

I don't know why, but I believed her. I guess it's that I've known her too long. If this was a joke, she wouldn't be in on it, because it wasn't her style. She'd never go out of her way to make anybody feel bad, and if this really was Woody, bad didn't begin to describe the way it made me feel.

That's hard to explain, too, because we weren't as close as maybe I've made it out. I'd only known him for a few months, but I liked the guy. He had a certain dignity that most of us don't, and genuinely cared about, well, pretty much everything. Still, I only saw him once or twice a week, listened to his stories, bought him a meal or a sandwich when he looked like he needed it, which was all the time.

"Did you ever notice how many storytellers there are living on the streets?" I found myself saying to Jilly. "I wonder why that is."

"Everybody's got a story they need to tell," she said. "Stockbrokers, bankers, plumbers, housewives. The thing about street people is that often their stories are *all* they have."

I nodded, my gaze pulled back to the funeral pyre. I'd come all the way around to believing now, though I was no closer to understanding why there wasn't a corpse, only those bones. I only had Jilly's explanation and that was no explanation at all. But if I didn't know how we'd come to this place—Jilly, me, Woody's bones—I knew why. Woody wanted to get off the streets. He wanted back into that story he stepped out of all those years ago. The trouble was . . .

"I don't think I can do it," I said. "This is just too weird."

"You have to do it," Jilly said. "You made him a promise."

Like I promised Tanya things would work out, that I'd stand by her, except there she was and here I was, and it didn't look like we'd ever be together except for when she had a break from work and could get away to come back to visit me. I mean well, I really do, but I'm not so good at following through. It comes from a lack of trust, from having put up walls a long time ago, tall and thick and a lot stronger than the little memory of a brick wall we were sitting on. People didn't get in behind those walls so much as I looked over the stones at them.

Jilly was the only one who got all the way through, but that's because she's got her own walls. Everybody thinks she's this lighthearted piece of sunshine, and that's a part of who she is, no question, but it hides the shadows. Some people deal with their problems, others like Jilly and I, we simply put them away. Jilly uses her good humor and her art; I use my music. We've known each other for so long, been through so much together, that I guess our walls are made of the same stones by now. We're kind of standing there together, on the inside, looking out at the rest of the world.

"You can't break a promise," Jilly said.

Well, you can. But then you have to live with yourself after.

I felt the weight of her gaze on me and finally had to turn to look at her. She didn't say anything else, but she didn't have to. I nodded. Opening my fiddlecase, I took out a pack of matches I keep to light the candles in my apartment. Some nights all I want is a flickering light, something that moves like music.

I was hoping the wood wouldn't take. That it'd be damp, or the pieces too big, or something. So that I would have tried, but not been able to follow through, because I still didn't want to do this thing. But when I stepped closer, I saw that there were old newspapers, twisted into the wood. I lit a match and put the flame to one, moving on when the newspaper caught. It took me four matches to walk all the way around the pyre, to start the flames so that they rose up evenly on all sides, rushing up, the smaller wood crackling and popping as the fire reached for the pyramid of bones, the clothes underneath it, the skull on top.

A promise kept, I thought.

Woody seemed very close at that moment. I felt the echo

of the heartbeat of the world drumming inside me, slowly, softly, like it did when he was telling me his stories. It was inside my walls. So was Woody. And so was somebody else, though maybe she didn't know it yet. It was long past time that I did more than simply tell her how much she meant to me.

As I watched the flames lick the bones, I knew I had other promises to keep.

Things burn in the Tombs and no one questions what or why. The streets are too choked with rubble and abandoned cars for the fire trucks to get in, and the truth is, nobody really cares. If you took a poll, you'd find most people would like to see the whole eyesore this place is burned to the ground, the buildings leveled, the night people driven out because there's no place for them to hide anymore.

So we wouldn't be disturbed.

We sat there while the fire burned, bones and wood, the smoke trailing up into the sky throughout the night, thin tendrils still visible against the sky as dawn pinked the distant horizon. I felt like I was in a kind of dream state, an effect that was heightened when all those pigeons that had come to see Woody off suddenly took to the air at the same time. Their wings were like thunder as they circled around the fire, once, twice, three times, then went spiraling straight up, following the last trails of smoke as they drifted apart, high in the dawn sky.

I remembered what Jilly had said about pigeons and angels and watched the cloud they made fade into the distance. When I turned around, Jilly was smiling.

"What are you thinking about?" I asked.

"Just how wonderful the world is."

"Of course."

"No, really. And you know what's the best thing about it? That it doesn't matter if we're here or not. It just goes on being this wonderful place. That's what people forget. It's not here for us. It's just here, and the gift we were given is that we're allowed to experience it."

"I wish I could see it the way you do, but I guess I'm too much of a cynic."

"Oh, don't say that. I can think of nothing sadder than cynicism."

"It's the way things are."

Jilly shook her head. "Only if you see them that way."

Woody would have agreed with her. Nobody invested everything she did with as much attention and meaning put into the smallest parts of it as Jilly did. Maybe she didn't open up her own secret self, but she was open to everybody and everything. She was there to hear them, to mark the movement and meaning of their lives and bear witness, no matter who or what or how strange things were.

That was her real gift, and her burden.

When the fire had died down completely, I gathered some ashes in a paper bag and we went to scatter them on the steps of St. Paul's.

My brother Christy drove me out to the airport in an old clunker he borrowed from a friend, his girlfriend Saskia and Jilly coming along for the ride. They wanted to wait inside with me, but I knew that'd be too hard for all of us, so we said our good-byes outside. I got my seat at the ticket counter and went through security. All I brought with me was in a knapsack carry-on and my fiddlecase. Everything else, what little I'd accumulated over the years, I'd put into storage in the basement of Christy and Saskia's apartment. I figured for a new life, I'd need new belongings, things that didn't carry too much old history in them.

Walls are hard to take down. I hoped that Tanya would have patience while I fumbled my way through the unfamiliar task.

I listened to Woody tell me stories all the way out on the

flight to L.A. I'd swear he was sitting right there in the seat beside me, whispering in my ear, instead of in my memory. I promised him that I'd try my best to impart everything I did with meaning.

I'd start with Tanya.

ONE MORNING AT THE STONE

by Tim Waggoner

Tim Waggoner wrote his first story at the age of five when he drew a version of "King Kong vs. Godzilla" on a stenographer's pad. Since then he's published over forty stories of fantasy and horror. His most recent work appears in the anthologies *Prom Night, Twice Upon A Time, A Dangerous Magic,* and *Between the Darkness and the Fire.* He lives in Columbus, Ohio, where he teaches college writing classes.

"THERE it is, boy."

The old man kept his voice even, his tone noncommittal. Before them, in the middle of the town square, rested a large hunk of dark gray stone. Rising toward the overcast sky as if it were a silvery stalk that had grown forth from the rock's surface, a martial plant destined to one day bear blood-red fruit, was a sword. No, *the* sword. The only one that would ever matter.

Too bad the sun's swaddled by clouds. A voice, that of a man barely past apprentice age. Amused, mocking. *A shaft of light descending from the heavens would be an appropriately poetic touch right now, don't you think?*

A sigh like moving wind rustling desiccated, parchment-thin leaves. *An unnecessary adornment and a waste of power besides.* This second voice was rough, dry, its sound that of two tree limbs rubbing together, bark crumbling, flaking away, falling to the forest floor.

The old man ignored the voices for now, confident the youth in his charge could not hear or see their owners. Even to him, they were barely more than half-glimpsed shadows, the younger to the right of the stone, the far older to the left. But he didn't need to see them clearly to know who and what they were: in many ways, he knew them as well as—if not better than—he did himself.

The boy, still little more than a child, really, eyed the sword embedded in the stone with undisguised doubt. "I don't know. It looks . . ."

"What?"

"Stuck," the youth said.

The old man fought to repress a smile. The shadowy figures left their positions on either side of the stone and walked toward them. The old man noticed, but paid no mind. He shrugged, trying to keep the gesture from looking as calculated as it was.

"You have need of a sword; there's one waiting. Take it or don't. It's all the same to me."

The younger shadow let out a barking laugh. The older shook his head stiffly, the movement accompanied by the pained sound of a tree branch creaking under a heavy weight. The two shadows grew more distinct as they drew closer to the old man, their features sharpening, becoming clearer. Still, the youth took no note of them. For him, they didn't exist, which was exactly as it should be. Had to be.

So that's him, eh? said the Younger. *The King to be.*

The King that was, corrected the Ancient. *That perhaps never should have been.*

The old man felt a cold tightening in his gut at the Ancient's words, though it wasn't as if he hadn't heard them before, as if he wouldn't likely speak them himself one day.

It's all a matter of perspective, I suppose, said the Younger. He examined the old man's charge closely. Medium height, somewhat on the scrawny side, though with a frame that hinted at a future of muscle and strength. Brown hair shaggy, in need of trimming, cheeks and chin covered by down so thin and fine it looked as if it might never grow into a full-fledged beard. Skin pale, dotted with a blemish here and there. The simple tunic, leggings, and boots the boy wore gave little indication of his noble birth and the destiny that lay before him.

The Younger sniffed derisively. *Doesn't look like much to me.*

The old man wished he could rap his knuckles on the Younger's insolent skull. The boy was more than a mere pawn in Fate's chess match. The old man had practically raised him from an infant, taught him as best he could, helped shape him into the adult he almost was. The boy was the closest the old man would ever have to a son of his own.

The Younger, sensing the old man's thoughts, turned to him. *Ah, but do you love him?*

The Ancient answered for the old man. *More than you can imagine.*

That gave the Younger pause for a moment, but then he gestured toward the stone. *As the warrior loves his weapon, then. The hunter, his hound.*

The fool, the sound of his own voice, the Ancient countered.

The old man couldn't help it; this time he did smile. He knew he should maintain a certain emotional and physical distance from the lad, now most of all, but he placed a hand on the boy's shoulder anyway. "Kay will just have to do without a sword, then. It won't be the end of the world." The old man chuckled. "Though your brother may well act as if it is."

So that's the excuse, the Younger said. *Seems rather contrived.*

I preferred having the boy draw the blade during a contest, the Ancient said. *It was most satisfying to watch him embarrass all those loutish knights by freeing the sword when they—with all their strength and training—could not.*

The old man remembered, had watched the entire scene when it had been his turn to stand in the Younger shadow's place. Once the boy held the sword aloft, tip pointed toward the sky (which had also been overcast then—some things even a wizard couldn't change), events turned ugly very quickly. The knights declared that the boy must have fairy blood—or worse—in his veins, and swore to stand against him should he claim the legacy the sword promised.

It took quite a few skirmishes and more than a little spilled blood before they were ready to accept him, the Ancient admitted. *Still, the moment he pulled the sword, all eyes upon him, no one daring to breathe, the first soft sound of metal whispering against rock as the blade began to withdraw . . . it was glorious.*

The old man closed his eyes briefly, trying not to think of all the lives that had eventually been sacrificed to make that glory possible. This way—here, alone in the square, with the rest of the citizenry gathered outside of town to watch the tourney—was better.

The old man opened his eyes. "Why don't you at least go take a closer look?" he urged the boy. "No harm in merely looking, is there?"

Nothing merely *about it,* said the Younger.

No harm, indeed, sniffed the Ancient.

It'll be different this time. The old man spoke to the no-longer-shadows in a Voice that only they could hear.

That's what I told myself, the Ancient said. He nodded toward the Younger. *What he'll no doubt tell himself one day. No matter how many times we say it, even if we manage to fool ourselves into believing it, nothing changes.*

It's the boy's first time, the old man insisted. *It's never happened before, for him.*

And you think that makes a difference? the Ancient argued. *Seasons don't change; they merely turn their faces away from us for a moment until they come 'round again.*

The Ancient's form was clearer now, nearly as substantial as the old man's. His skin was the craggy gray of oak bark; his eyes smooth light brown, the color of acorns.

Autumnal leaves of red, yellow, and orange adorned his skull, and a layer of forest loam served in place of robe and cloak.

The old man knew he was looking at his own tomorrow, or at least one possible tomorrow. But it didn't bother him; there were worse fates.

The boy stared at the stone and the blade sprouting unnaturally from its rough surface. He made no move toward them. "I still don't understand how I could have misplaced Kay's sword," the boy said. "It's not like me; I'm a good squire." This last was said as a statement of fact, without boasting, though there was an edge of defensiveness in the youth's tone, as if he challenged the old man to dispute him.

"Very good, indeed," the boy's teacher and mentor soothed. "But you know how competitive tourneys are. It wouldn't surprise me if a rival knight took Kay's sword in the hope of forcing him to withdraw."

The boy's pale skin grew angry red, and his eyes narrowed dangerously.

How many times have I seen that look? the Ancient said. *How long it has been since I saw it last?* A sigh, as of a faint winter wind moving slowly between ice-encrusted trees. *I never imagined I would miss even his fury.*

"Then we must return to the field of honor, find Kay's sword, and expose the thief!" the boy insisted. "With your magic—"

The Younger guffawed and turned to the old man. *Let's see you talk your way out of this one!*

The old man ignored his more youthful self. He found the other's aspects—his strong frame, black hair, short beard, brown tunic, dark green traveler's cloak—far more disturbing than his words. The old man still remembered how it felt to wear that body, to move with sureness and strength, to feel that there wasn't any goal he couldn't achieve once he bent his fearsome will to the task.

Still remembered what it was like to be young and foolish. And now? Now he was old, but perhaps no less the fool. Still, he must press on, say his lines, take the next step in the dance.

"The thief who took Kay's sword would likely have made certain to obtain charms designed to hide the weapon from me. I could counter such simple magery, of course, given a bit of time to find the proper spell. But Kay does not have the luxury of waiting. As soon as it is discovered that he has no sword, he will be asked to leave the field of honor. And he will lose much face."

The boy considered this.

Why go to such elaborate lengths to get the boy to draw the sword? the Younger asked, clearly exasperated with the youth. *Just plant your foot on his backside, give him a shove, and tell him to bloody well get on with it!*

The Ancient answered for the old man. *He's obviously designed this version of the event so the boy's rule as King shall begin with an unselfish act. A nice touch. Still, it won't change anything.*

The old man bristled. *You're wrong; you have to be.*

The boy took one step toward the stone, took another.

What does it matter? the Younger said. *The boy's as much a tool as the sword. He may wield the blade, but it is we who wield him. All for the greater good, of course.*

The old man turned toward the Younger, started to yell, but stopped himself. It was possible that if the exchange between the three of them became too animated, the boy might somehow sense it, and the moment could perchance be disrupted. And the old man couldn't risk that. Besides, he knew it would be futile to attempt to make his younger self understand. How could he hope to communicate what it had been like to raise the boy? To hold and feed him, to rock him to sleep at night. To talk, sing, and laugh along with him. To dry tears and salve hurts—both those of the flesh and those invisible to the eye. To watch him grow strong and true and to know that it was in no small measure because of the old man's efforts. Because of his love.

The Younger snorted. *You gave the boy over to the*

knight Ector, who brought him up as his own son. You can lay no claim to parenthood.

Can't I? The old man said. *I visited often enough as the boy's tutor, came to him even more frequently in his dreams. I've spent more time with him than his noble foster father ever has. I know him better than anyone else could ever hope to. In every way that matters, he is my son.*

Another step, and one more besides, and the boy stood next to the stone. And the sword.

The Ancient looked at the old man with an expression of deep weariness and sorrow. *And yet you would set the boy's feet upon the same bloody path that I steered my own son down.* He nodded toward the Younger. *And he will one day do the same. Is that a father's love?*

The boy's eyes widened in wonder. "There is something on the blade . . . letters, becoming more distinct, almost as if they are rising upward through silvery water!"

Appropriate enough comparison, the old man thought. "Really? What do they say?"

The boy read slowly as the letters made themselves clear. "Whosoever . . . draws this sword . . . is rightwise king . . . of all Britain." He looked up, puzzled. "What does it mean?"

The Younger slapped his forehead in disgust. *Gods and demons, the boy can't possibly be that thick!*

The old man made a dismissive gesture. "An old folk superstition, I expect. Nothing to concern yourself with."

The boy frowned. "But the letters appeared by magic—I saw them. They must mean something. Something important, else why would a mage go to the trouble of enchanting them upon the sword?"

The Ancient chuckled, the sound of walnuts rustling in a tree's hollow. *The boy's smarter than he looks. Always was.*

The old man shrugged. "This isle is old, lad, and while there isn't as much magic about as there once was, still a good bit remains, hidden here and there. I'd pay no attention to the blade's legend. It is likely nothing more than a trick, perhaps one of the pranks the fair folk so delight in playing on us mere mortals."

The Younger frowned. *That's laying it on a bit thick, isn't it?*

The boy considered for a moment, looking at the sword intently, as if trying to see past the letters and into the metal itself. Finally, he took a step backward, away from the stone. "If the blade is ensorcelled, then it is not fit for Kay's hand. Whatever magic the sword possesses could give him an unfair advantage on the field of honor, or worse, it could turn against him, injure or even slay him somehow." The boy shook his head. "No," he said decisively. "We must look elsewhere."

Nice to see you've thought this through so thoroughly, the Younger said, sarcasm dripping from his soundless Voice.

The old man would've gladly cuffed his younger self if only he were able to touch him. "I wouldn't be too concerned, lad. The sword's been here for decades. Any spell placed upon it has surely weakened by now. And, at the risk of boasting, I'm confident I can counter whatever magics may linger in the blade."

You ought to be, the Younger thought, *since you were the one who put it in into the stone in the first place.*

The boy gauged the old man's expression, which the latter fought to keep carefully neutral. The boy must choose of his own free will.

What farce! the Younger exclaimed. *You're leading him to the sword just as surely as if you'd dragged him to it and wrapped his fingers around the hilt yourself!*

The Ancient joined in. *Do you truly believe the boy has a choice? And even if he did, that it would somehow absolve you of responsibility, keep your hands clean of blood?*

One must be informed to make a choice, the Younger added. *How much have you told him of his great destiny? Or perhaps I should ask, how little?*

The boy spoke once more. "Even if you can remove the

enchantments on the sword—and I have no doubt you can—what guarantee do I have that I can even draw the blade? Kay has tried to pull it free on several occasions. And though he's never admitted it, I suspect my father has had a go at it as well. How can I, a simple squire, hope to do better than they?"

The old man was tempted then to tell the boy everything, to let him know of the glory—and the pain—that awaited him if he succeeded in drawing the blade. Which, of course, he would, for the weapon was his by divine right. And by the machinations of a certain wizard.

The old man opened his mouth, hesitated, then said softly, "You can but try, lad."

The boy considered this for a moment, then nodded. He stepped forward, reached for the sword's hilt, and closed his fingers around the silvery metal.

The Younger and the Ancient drew close to the old man, so close that they would have touched had the other two possessed the same sort of physical reality that he did. Instead, they overlapped, merged, blurred at the edges, the way tendrils of mist might come together for a time, their mingled substance swirling and roiling until it was impossible to determine the precise place where one wisp began and the other ended.

This was the moment they had been waiting for, the moment when they would See.

The boy frowned in concentration, jaw set, grip tight, and pulled. The sword didn't move.

An image flashed through the combined consciousness of the three mages: the youth sitting upon a throne as a priest approached, holding a satin pillow upon which rested a golden crown.

The boy shifted his feet, searching for a firmer stance, and tried again. A slight hiss of sliding steel; the sword had moved the merest fraction of an inch.

Another flash: the lad, older now, standing in an open field, gesturing grandly as he described what his castle—his Camelot—would one day look like.

Another soft hiss of steel, several inches' worth this time. The blade was almost halfway free, and the boy's face held an expression of equal parts amazement and fear.

The images came in a torrent now. Knights flocking to the new king's side, land barons swearing fealty; the castle, the grandest ever conceived, completed. A wife, a friend, a quest; absence, betrayal, denial. Half sister, bastard son. Blood and fire, death and darkness.

The old man felt his blood turn to dust, his heart become a cold, useless lump of meat.

The Ancient sighed. *Minor details may change, but the pattern is ever the same.*

What does it matter how the boy ends up? the Younger challenged. *All that matters is that Unity is achieved, that humankind comes to realize the value of joining together in the service of something higher than the mere satisfaction of their base appetites. The man may die, but the King—the symbol—shall live for all time!*

The old man looked at the boy straining to pull the sword the rest of the way free from the stone that had been its home, prison, and guardian for so many years. Is that all the youth was in the end? A symbol? A figure for bards to compose treacly lays about, for poets to use as inspiration for banal couplets?

And how many times had this same scene—or ones close enough to it to make no difference—taken place? For of all the magics the mage possessed, the greatest was the ability to look both forward and backward in time, and to use the knowledge thus gained to alter the course of today. How many Ancients had bemoaned their inability to change the pattern of the boy's life? How many Youngers had been determined to press ahead when it came their time, to do better than their older selves had, no matter the price?

Yes, the world gained its thrice-damned Tale, as it always did in the end, but at what cost to the boy named Arthur?

"It's almost free!" the lad shouted. "One more good tug ought to—"

The old man clenched his right hand into a fist, and the sword suddenly stuck fast.

NO! cried the Younger. *You cannot! You must not!*

The old man stepped forward, disengaging himself from the others' substance. He strode toward the stone, the boy, and the sword.

"I don't understand," the youth said through gritted teeth as he struggled with the stubborn blade, a line of sweat beading his brow. "It was coming loose. I felt it!"

"Step aside," the old man said.

The boy hesitated, as if he somehow sensed that something wasn't quite right in his teacher's request. But in the end he released the sword's hilt and stepped back.

The old man reached out, gripped the hilt with long, spiderish fingers, and uttered a word of Power. He twisted his hand, and the blade snapped like a twig.

The others began to fade.

You may think you've won some sort of victory! shouted the Younger. *But I won't be so sentimental when it comes my turn to lead the boy to the sword!*

And I'll be there as the Ancient then, to try to dissuade you, the old man replied. *But even if I don't, I'll at least have the satisfaction of knowing that one Arthur was able to lead his own life, his own way. Perhaps he'll still be King, perhaps not. But for this moment in the endless cycle, it truly shall be his choice, and his choice alone.*

Howling in frustration, the Younger vanished, dissipating like morning mist burned away by the heat of a rising sun. The old man knew they would meet again one day, at a different point in the cycle, a different spoke on the wheel. But that was tomorrow's concern, not today's.

The Ancient nodded to his younger self. *When all is said and done, your gesture is quite likely to prove naught but a bit of grand futility.* He winked an acorn eye and smiled with craggy lips of bark. *Still, I wish I'd thought of it.* Then the Ancient's body shuddered and collapsed into a pile of dry leaves which were soon taken away by the wind and scattered across the length and breadth of the sky.

The boy stared at the spot where the others had stood, frowning, as if he thought he had seen something but wasn't quite certain. Finally, he shook his head as if to clear it and pointed to the broken length of blade protruding from the stone. The letters and their promise were gone now, the steel surface unblemished. "Why did you do that? Now Kay won't have a sword for the tourney."

The old man shrugged. "I guess I used too much power to try to free the blade." He dropped the broken hilt to the ground; it landed with a soft thud. "But does it matter? There will be other tourneys, other swords. But this is the only time that you and I shall be here on this morning, together." He put his arm around the boy's shoulders. "Why don't we go for a walk and enjoy the day?"

The boy grinned. "You know something, Merlin? Sometimes you don't make a great deal of sense."

The wizard grinned back. "Making sense is highly overrated." He turned his back on a sword that had meant so much, but perhaps never more than now, when it was useless.

"Tell me, Arthur," the old man asked as they walked, "what would *you* like to do today?"

REPRO MAN

by Esther M. Friesner and Anne Elizabeth Stutzman

Esther M. Friesner's latest novel is *Child of the Eagle*. She has written over twenty novels and coedited four fantasy collections. Other fiction of hers appears in *Excalibur, The Book of Kings,* and quite often in *The Magazine of Fantasy and Science Fiction* and other prose magazines. She lives in Madison, Connecticut.

Anne Stutzman was raised (though not born) in Madison, Connecticut. She is fifteen years old and a huge Anglophile. Anything British is good! She is also believed to be the love child of Elvis and Marilyn Monroe and the heiress to the throne of hamsters where her mother, Esther M. Friesner, sits. This is her first professional sale.

"WHAT ever possessed me to have children?" Merlin sighed and stirred more sugar into his tea. He was up to five lumps, but stressful situations tended to give him temporary amnesia in matters culinary. He still flinched when he recalled the time he'd been cooking up a nice steak-and-kidney pie and Maisie had come in to announce that she was preggers. Of course she wasn't, it was just another of her "jokes" on dear, dumb old Daddy, but the amount of salt he'd dumped into the dish was enough to raise the blood pressure of the entire East End for a week.

The great wizard stared out the kitchen window and sighed. It was March, it was cold, and it was raining. Rain always made him nostalgic and sentimental, no matter when it fell. Unfortunately this was a fairly volatile combination of emotions for Merlin. The nostalgia took him back to the palmy, carefree days before he'd had a daughter whose only sorcerous talent seemed to be for turning him into a raving loony, while the sentimentality conjured up visions of darling little Maisie in her pram, waving her tiny pink feet in the air, or toddling in to give her daddy a milky night-night kiss. When his mind shuttled between the two concepts too long, he developed a raging headache.

And there was still the matter of The Boy to be dealt with. Bother.

The wizard took a sip of tea, made a face at the treacly sweetness of it, and dumped it down the drain before forcing himself to face the unpleasant task at hand. He would not—could not shirk his duty. As he had often taught young Arthur, adulthood brings with it adult responsibilities, being accountable for your actions, being willing to face up to the consequences. Also, it helps if you don't get drunk and bed anything female with no more discretion than a tomcat on Spanish fly.

Well, Arthur hadn't exactly been taking notes on that last bit of advice. His half-sister Morgan managed to catch the green-as-grass king with his blood alcohol level up and his trews down, with Mordred the accursed issue of that ill-starred, incestuous coupling. Merlin still remembered how sternly he'd berated Arthur for his impolitic slipup, prophesying dire things to come.

"Lord, what a self-righteous ass *I* was," he muttered, shuffling down the hall to the front parlor where he took his favorite seat by the big bow window. It gave him a lovely view of the fashionable Knightsbridge street where he and Maisie had lived ever since her mother died. No sooner had he settled himself into the antique Morris chair than the family cat came trotting up, eager to reassert her territorial rights to the wizard's lap.

"That's my girl," Merlin crooned, stroking the gray tabby's fur. "That's my precious Titania. Who's a good moggie, then? Not a lick of trouble from you. *You* never give me a moment's grief, or a headache like this one. Of course I did have you fixed, but that's not an option with Maisie. Damn." He gazed out into the rain, which had lost heart and reduced itself to a drizzle. "Should've done the same with Arthur, if the chance had presented itself. But who am I to talk, eh, Titania?"

The cat meowed as if in agreement. The wizard scratched her head just so, in the purr-kindling spot right between her ears. When he stopped, she meowed again, this time wishing to lodge a complaint with Management concerning substandard service.

But Merlin had no more time to spare for the cat. He could no longer defer his duty. He knew that there would be hell to pay for it when Maisie got home, but he consoled himself with the thought that he had faced his share of demons in the olden days.

Yes, only they were adult *demons,* he reflected as he picked up the telephone and began to dial. *Not bloody teenagers. You could talk sense to demons, throw a little salt in their faces, tell 'em they're banished back to the pits that spawned 'em, and poof! Off they'd go, nice as pie. Not another word, no arguments, no tears. Oh, for the love of heaven, please don't let her start crying at me over this! I can't bear it when she cries. I'm even willing to put up with all of her cheek and then some, just as long as she doesn't cry.*

There was a soft buzzing in his ear and a click as the party he was phoning answered. He cleared his throat. It was now or never: "How do you do, ma'am, Merlin Ambrosius here. Am I speaking with Mrs. Collins? . . . You're Ahmad's mother? . . . Yes, well, very good, hrmh!, indeed, ah . . . Not to put too fine a point on it, it seems that your son and my daughter have been . . . well . . . seeing rather too much of one another socially. . . . Yes, that's so, and in an unacceptably clandestine manner . . . No, no, not *that,* Mrs. Collins! I have absolutely no reason to believe they're doing *that.*" *They'd better* not *be,* Merlin thought fiercely. *I'll kill the filthy little sod if he's so much as laid one hand on*— "However, I would prefer that it did not *come* to that, which rather seems to bring me to the purpose of this call . . . No, I do not wish your son to stop seeing my daughter entirely; I merely wish his attentions to be circumscribed by, er, the proprieties. In short, I want you to tell your son that he is forbidden to see my daughter again until such time as he presents himself to me in the manner befitting a suitably reared young gentleman. At that time he may declare his intentions—honorable, of course—and request my approval of all further contact between himself and my Maisie. Naturally I cannot *promise* your son said approval until we have had our interview, but should I find him unacceptable, I assure you it will be a wise and irrefutable decision, based not on his personal appearance nor other superficialities, but solely on any irremediable flaws of character he may possess."

There was a long pause on both ends of the line when Merlin finished. It hovered in the air with the substantial presence of an old London "pea-souper," and like those noxious yellow fogs of yore, it gave Merlin the uncanny sensation of being trailed down a dark alleyway by person or persons unknown, on mischief bent, with knives.

"Er, Mrs. Collins?" he ventured. The sound of his own voice breaking the heavy silence unnerved him. "Are—are you there? Have we been cut off?"

"We have not yet been cut off," said the deep, oddly lilting voice at the other end of the line. "The blade still thirsts to fall. You speak, but you know not to whom you utter your jackal-yappings. Your unclean mind defiles my pearl among pearls, my beloved son, ascribing to him the swinish motivations of one such as yourself. The thief locks away his own treasures with a hundred locks and still sleeps uneasily of nights."

"Well, I *never!*" Merlin snorted, restored to his role as the justifiably indignant father. "Madam, it is *you* who are unaware of whom *you* address. I am Merlin Ambrosius; *the* Merlin Ambrosius. You may have heard of me. Geoffrey of Monmouth's chronicles? The works of Chretien de Troyes? Malory's *Le Morte d'Arthur?* Roundtable Security dot com? The only computer system safeguarded with the guarantee that all intrusive hackers will be turned into the vermin that they are at the first *hint* of illicit access? *Now* do you realize who I am?"

"I do," the voice purred. "You're a nutter."

Merlin scowled into the phone. "My good woman, would you have me prove my identity? I am the greatest wizard that the world has ever known."

"Of a certainty. And Bob is thine uncle."

"*Harumph!* I would have given you proof before this—proof to break your heart. However, my sense of fair play and my consideration for a mother's feelings prevented me from manifesting my wrath against your son without due warning. Also, I realize that my Maisie is at least somewhat to blame for this situation, or by now you would be parent to a gerbil."

The telephone wires jingled with the sound of musical laughter. "By the seven thousand white camels of King Solomon, I shall have to offer up unending prayers of thanksgiving for the ineffable mercy you have shown my unworthy offspring!" More mocking laughter followed.

The wizard grumbled. "Before you do yourself an injury from so much unbridled merriment, humor me: Pick up the nearest small household object and hold it next to your telephone. Please."

After some small hesitation, the lady said, "Very well. I have in hand one of Ahmad's bronzed baby shoes. And now?"

"And now you may give thanks that you will always have the other one to remember his infancy by," Merlin replied. His free hand flicked nimbly through a series of bizarre gestures, salted with a spate of Latin incantations.

A gasp from the far end of the phone line made him smile.

"Well?" he inquired. "*Now* do you believe?"

"A rat," said the voice. "You have transformed my beloved child's shoe into a rat. How very . . . crude. And yet, you have found the way to transmit your spells over these electrical wires. Fascinating. Sir, your power is to be honored. I will instruct my son as to his duties concerning Your Reverence. He will attend you in five days' time to request your consent to his unworthy courtship of your fair daughter. Until then I shall see to it that he undergoes the most thorough and rigorous purification rituals, as are only fitting preceding an interview with a mage of your obvious endowments. In the meanwhile, I would deem it a favor beyond my humblest dreams were you to call upon me here, in my lowly dwelling place, and permit me to offer you what poor hospitality is mine."

"Er?" said Merlin.

"Lovely. Tea tomorrow, then. At five." And this time the silence that followed truly did stem from the fact that the lady had rung off.

They had it out in the front parlor as soon as Maisie came home from school that very day. She did not cry when Merlin told her what he'd done. Instead she calmly picked up his Waterford decanter full of fine old Napoleon brandy and let it drop from her fingers to the floor where the smash equaled the splash. A purposely insincere "Oops!" and a maddening smirk followed.

Merlin gave his daughter a scowl that might have cowed half a company of the minions of darkness. "Was that *quite* necessary?" he asked coldly. "Such a childish display of temper merely undermines all your arguments that I treat you like an adult. Need I remind you that an adult is aware of rules and follows them? We *do* still have a rule around here that you are to bring all your young men home to meet me. The only way I discovered you were seeing this . . . Ahmad-person was through a fortuitous accident."

"Yeah, while you were 'accidentally' nosing into my diary," Maisie snarled. "You wonder why I never told you about Ahmad? Well, it's 'cause you're never blimmin' satisfied with anyone I *do* bring home!"

Merlin pursed his lips. "There's no need to shout. Perhaps there's something not quite *right* about the boy? That might account for your reluctance to introduce us."

Maisie ignored her father's injunction against shouting and raised the decibel level: "I've finally found a lad I truly fancy and I don't want you to scare him off! Anyone's got something not quite right about 'em, it's *you!*"

"Tsk-tsk." All Merlin did was shake his head and wave two fingers.

Maisie opened her mouth to continue her harangue, only to discover herself unable to speak above a whisper. Still, she was a determined girl, her emotions just as fierce at whatever volume: "I knew you'd hissy-fit when you met him, so I saved both of us the embarrassment!" she rasped. She then launched into a tirade of foul language which carried just as much impact whether delivered in a shout or a whisper.

Merlin knew that she was quite capable of going on like that for hours. He might have clamped a spell of total silence on her, but he knew his daughter: She'd just go out, buy a can of spray paint, and relieve her feelings on every wall in the neighborhood. Reluctantly, he restored her voice and said, "It's not as if I'm asking you to be a nun, child. My own mother was a nun, and she wound up bedding an incubus. I definitely don't want you going down *that* road. All I want is what's best for you. Why won't you understand that?"

"*You* don't understand!" Maisie countered. "I knew you wouldn't! How could a bajillion-year-old man understand true love? Ahmad and me, we don't have time for your stupid courtship games; *you've* got all the time in the world! You'll just continue to outlive everyone!"

Merlin clicked his tongue again. "If that's what's troubling you, there are several excellent spells for extending human life. You wouldn't be so hard up for time to have a proper courtship if you'd only apply yourself to your grammarye, the way I've been telling you."

Maisie met her father's mild suggestion with a display of temper nothing short of ballistic: "Bloody *hell,* this is just what I'm talking about! Either you're nagging me about not putting any interest into magic or bugging me about who I fancy, but you never just try to understand me!"

"And I suppose *you've* ever tried to understand *me?*" Merlin couldn't resist giving Maisie a wicked smirk whose power to aggravate rivaled her own.

His daughter was not open to logic. She stalked over to the parlor door and gave the jamb a mighty kick with her bovver boots, leaving a huge black stain on the white paint. "Why don't you stick to your troubles and let me stick to mine," she muttered.

"You *are* my troubles," Merlin replied. "Which is why I make no apologies for having called your boyfriend's mother nor for having used my powers to secure an interview. I regret that my display of sorcery proved to be so embarrassing for you, but you left me no choice. I might never be able to make you learn magic, but I *will* make you into a properly behaved young lady."

"Magic." Maisie snorted. "Try not to deal with everything with spells and magic for a change. Then maybe you'll understand, for once be *normal.*"

Merlin looked down his nose at his petulant offspring. "I do not use my enchantments indiscriminately. I've *made* my point with Mrs. Collins, and so I promise that tomorrow's interview will be as normal and as entirely free of magic as you might desire. There. Satisfied?"

For her answer, Maisie only uttered a short, sarcastic laugh. Then she stomped off upstairs to her room where she slammed the door and played her Sex Pistols CDs full throttle.

"This is all that boy's fault," Merlin grumbled through

gritted teeth, fingers jammed in his ears. "My darling Maisie never used to talk back to me like this. Tomorrow can't come fast enough for me. I'll soon sort out matters with the boy's mother, see if I don't." Fortified by thoughts of how he would prevail upon Mrs. Collins to leash her brat, he sank gratefully into the Morris chair, first casting a quick spell that turned all of Maisie's music into *The Greatest Hits of Perry Como.*

The interview did not go precisely as the wizard had envisioned it.

"Lamp?" Mrs. Collins looked at Merlin as if he had requested some mashed lizard to spread on his scones. "What need have I of a lamp? The ceiling fixtures serve our illumination needs quite well."

The wizard held his teacup gingerly and cast small, sharp, nervous glances all around the dining room. "Oo, er, ah," he said. This was the gist of most of his remarks ever since crossing the threshold of the Collins home and getting his first look at the mistress thereof. "That is, don't you know, I mean to say . . . to live in?"

Mrs. Collins laughed, throwing her head back and letting her mirth shake an answering chorus from the strands of gold coins adorning her very ample bosom. She laughed so hard that the Coalport tea service on the table tinkled. She laughed so mightily that the trail of smoke which formed the lower half of her body frayed to wisps in several places.

Wiping tears from her eyes with one heavily beringed hand, she managed to gasp, "Oh, my good sir, you *have* been watching too much old American telly! In any event, I never was the Slave of a lamp, nor of a bottle, nor even of a ring. In fact, I never was bound as a Slave to any earthly object. I am a free-range genie."

"No!" Merlin leaned closer and sniffed. There was a powerful scent of sandalwood clinging to his beautiful hostess, but apart from that— "I say, not even a hint of iron nor the merest whiff of Words of Binding. You smell of nothing but freedom. You *are* what you claim to be. Astonishing!"

"You find truth to be so rare a quality that you must secure the proof of my words for yourself?" There was something kittenish in the genie's tone.

"I mean you no offense, madam." Merlin pulled back his shoulders rather self-consciously. "My experiences with the fair sex have been rather limited. Unfortunately both of them were fraught with deceit."

"What a shame!" Mrs. Collins leaned across the table and patted the wizard's hand, but the gesture assumed an autonomous life, changing from an innocent offer of comfort to an unspoken offer of something more. The genie's tawny skin flushed to a deep rose, and she jerked her hand away.

"Yes, ahem." Merlin looked away, pretending to be fascinated by the old lamp hook in the center of the dining room ceiling. "A shame, as you say. First there was Nimuë, who pretended love for me in order to learn my secrets. Once she had them, she had no further need of me and so—Hey, presto!—into an oak she clapped me the way a housewife might slam the linen cupboard door on an old sheet that's not *quite* ready for the dustman."

"The unfeeling bitch." Mrs. Collins's eyes flashed and a platter of fish paste sandwiches on the table burst into flame. "Oh, my! When will I learn to control my temper?" The genie gave a small, self-effacing laugh over her *petit faux pas*.

"Think nothing of it, dear lady," Merlin said, the very mirror of chivalry. "I fancy my sandwiches toasted, and your compassion means more to me than any bit of bread-and-butter. If only Maisie's mother had owned a heart as feeling as yours, our life together might have remained the stuff of romance."

"My Ahmad tells me she died."

"Only just in time. Forgive me if I sound callous, but the woman had me at my wits' end with her—hobby."

Mrs. Collins' black brows dipped into a frown. "Was

that cause enough to wish her dead? Most women have hobbies."

"Hers was adultery. I'd call it her profession, but she did it for free. To this day I believe that when she saw that lorry bearing down on her, she recognized the driver and threw herself over backward from force of habit."

"How did a gentleman of your obvious breeding wind up with a—a hobbyist such as she?"

"Ah! Well, you see, she was the first person on the scene when lightning struck Nimuë's oak. The tree was well off the beaten path, in an isolated woodland. When I emerged from the shattered trunk and saw her standing there, I thought it must be a sign from God, a miracle that someone so young and pretty just happened to be there, waiting to welcome me back into the world. People do get the strangest ideas into their heads when they've just been released from prison." He made a face. "Later on, when she was too late and it was too pregnant to amend matters, I learned that the only reason she'd been in that woodland was because she was on the run from a nearby school for young women of debatable morals. Few of us fulfill the promise of our youth as thoroughly as she."

There was an uneasy silence, broken at last when Mrs. Collins brightly offered: "More tea?"

While she gracefully refilled his cup, the wizard did his best to steer their talk onto less awkward topics: "If you're a free creature of magic, how did you ever come to live in London?"

"Oh, the usual story: I met a dashing young British officer during the War, threw a spell of Eternal Carnal Devotion on him, and we lived happily ever after until he died of exhaustion. Pity. Ahmad was already of school age by the time my Reginald succumbed, so I determined to remain here, for his sake. It doesn't do to uproot the young from familiar surroundings. The experts all agree that it gives them untold academic problems for years afterward." She lowered her long-lashed golden eyes modestly and added, "I shudder to think how much worse a scholar my Ahmad would be if we *had* left England."

"Not exactly the brightest will-o'-the-wisp in the swamp, eh?" Merlin leaned forward, his eyes full of understanding and sympathy.

"Nor the sharpest dagger in the assassin's belt." Mrs. Collins raised her eyes to his and for a moment the powerful genie seemed almost human in her vulnerability. "Good sir, I will speak frankly with you: To me, the life of the mind is all-important. I am no man's Slave of the Lamp, but mine own Slave of the Library. What better way to fill the empty centuries than in the quest for knowledge?"

"Exactly!" Merlin was beaming. "My *dear* Mrs. Collins, I could not agree with you more! Scholarship, learning, wisdom, these are the only things worth pursuing in this weary world."

"How good it is to speak with a kindred spirit." Again the genie reached out to pat Merlin's hand, but this time neither one of them seemed to notice or mind when she extended the duration of the caress. "Then you must understand the wormwood which my son has given me to drink. The lack of talent he shows for all things magical I could bear. The dearth of wizardly skill I could tolerate. But what sears me to the very heart of my heart is the boy's boundless want of *application*. I have tried to teach him the secrets of the darkest arts, the spells and conjurations for which generations of sorcerers have given their lives, their souls, their virgin daughters! I have offered him the way to establishing his dominion over all the kings and peoples of the earth! I have shown him the golden path that leads to supreme and unassailable power! But all the bloody little bugger wants to do is hang out with his layabout mates at the fish 'n' chips shop."

Merlin shook his head. "No ambition. Ah me, I know that curse all too well."

"You mean that your daughter, too—?"

"—cares more about memorizing the Spice Girls' songs

than performing the litanies which summon up the Princes
of Hell. Not that they don't have a lot in common."

Both parents slumped back in their chairs and released
massive sighs.

"Kids," said Merlin.

"Were it not for the unspeakable joy and wild, physical
pleasure one derives from their begetting, I would say that
the miserable pups are hardly worth the sack to drown
them in," said the genie.

"Er, did you say 'wild physical pleasure'?" Merlin sat
up a bit straighter in his chair.

"Why, yes." Mrs. Collins toyed with her teaspoon. "Yes,
I did."

"If you wouldn't take it amiss, might I inquire—strictly
to satisfy that whole quest-for-knowledge thingie we spoke
of earlier—how a being such as yourself, whose lower half
is not so much female as fog, is able to, um, *experience* the
aforementioned physical pleasure? You know, the wild
sort."

"Ah." The genie had beauteous dimples. They were
positively glowing as she wafted up out of her chair and,
with a wave of her hand, levitated Merlin from his. "I have
found that some intellectual inquiries are best answered by
demonstration." She tugged at an invisible tether and the
wizard found himself drifting after her into a candlelit bed-
chamber that smelled of jasmine and bergamot.

"Well, so long as it *is* in the name of pure scholarship,"
he muttered as the door closed softly behind them.

Maisie sprinkled vinegar on her chips and shoved the
bottle across the table to Ahmad. The young man mumbled
"Ta" without looking up. It was the longest verbal exchange the pair of them had had in better than a week. The
note which Maisie had handed him at school, urgently re-
questing this meeting, didn't count.

Since she had been the one to call for the meeting, she
took it upon herself to break the silence. "Well, this is
awkward!" she exclaimed. She was not referring to their

present lack of communication. Unfortunately Ahmad knew exactly what she meant.

"I know," he replied. "This may sound daft, but I keep picturing them . . . you know . . ."

"Snogging?"

"Yes! And—ugh!—it's—"

"Ludicrous?"

"That's not even the word."

"You're telling me." Maisie shuddered. "It's disgusting! And after all my old man's lectures about what's 'proper,' he and your mum have to go and—" She shuddered again. "Ought not to be allowed."

"Yeah, but what can we do? Tell 'em to stop? The 'rents don't listen to us to begin with." He popped a chip in his mouth and chewed it, looking glum.

Maisie slouched low; Ahmad was right. All those years locked up in that oak tree had given her father a bad case of wood pulp in the ears. He just *couldn't* listen, or *wouldn't*. She bent over and morosely fed her fish to the prowling chip shop cat. All his talk about how he'd *make* her behave properly, and now he and Ahmad's mum had to go and—and—!

"I'd like to have a way to make *him* behave himself proper . . ." He voice trailed off in mid-mutter, her eyes lighting up suddenly. "Wa-hey!" she exclaimed, making the cat scarper. "Why don't we give them a taste of their own potion?" she demanded of Ahmad.

"I don't believe I'm following you."

"C'mon, it's obvious! What is it they're always on us about?" She waited for him to catch on. When he didn't, she made an impatient sound and answered her own question: "*Magic*. They're forever after us to *apply* ourselves, to take an interest in magic. Well, we *will*."

"So's we'll make 'em happy and then they'll listen to us and leave off . . . what they're doing?" Ahmad turned a little green at the mental image.

"No," said Maisie, grinning. "So we can get even."

"You mean use magic on *them?*"

"Of course!"

"You're off your head. Your old man's got magic he hasn't used yet, and my mum—well, she *is* magic, i'n't she? It'd be like trying to get the drop on Darth-bloody-Vader."

"Yeah, *if* we were Luke-bloody-Skywalker. Old Vader knows *Luke's* got the Force behind him, he expects *him* to attack, but what'd happen if somebody went and made a Jedi knight out of a baby Ewok, eh? *That'd* catch Darth with his knickers 'round his knees, all right!"

"Uh . . ." Ahmad still looked puzzled.

"Look, you *know* what they think of us," Maisie pressed on. "We're their *very disappointing* kids who don't give a rat's bum for magic and never have. So when we do pick up some sorcery to use on them, we'll catch them completely off guard. They'll never suspect a thing!"

Ahmad let out a yelp of triumph and high-fived Maisie. "Genius!"

"Thank you."

"This is perfect! We're so smart!"

"Eh-hem . . . 'We'?"

"Well, *you*. But you couldn't pull this off without me."

"True. Still, I just wanted to make it clear who's the brains of the bunch." She smiled at him.

"Of course." He sprang to his feet, quivering with anticipation. "C'mon, let's get started on our—*your*—brilliant plan."

In the end, the most brilliant thing about Maisie's plan was its simplicity, a matter of setting up the sorcerous equivalent of a deadfall trap in Merlin's bedroom. It took only three months for her and Ahmad to acquire the requisite spells. It might have taken longer, since they did need to study and work in secrecy, but their parents became their unwitting helpers. The unabated intensity of the liaison between Merlin and Mrs. Collins made the two enchanted beings oblivious to everything save each other.

This sweet heedlessness ended abruptly on a sweet, lazy, amorous July afternoon when the door to Merlin's bedroom flew open at a crucial moment and a muslin sack full of catnip came flying in, followed by Titania.

"What's that?" Mrs. Collins tried to sit up, her body crackling with defensive magic.

"Nothing, my darling," Merlin crooned. "Just the cat. Where were we?"

Mrs. Collins was all too willing to remind him of where they'd been. The lovers embraced. Suddenly, Merlin froze.

"The *cat*," he said. "But who opened the door and tossed in that thingie she was chas—?"

He never got to finish his sentence. At that moment a second catnip bag sailed through the doorway, landing on the bed itself. Titania leaped up, unable to resist. It was only then that Merlin saw the amulet attached to her tail. There was a cool flash of blue-and-yellow light, then a slamming sound and pitch darkness.

"Beloved, where are you?" Mrs. Collins called.

"In the dark." Merlin snapped out a spell and a ball of soft light materialized at his shoulder. By its glow, the wizard gazed around him, then said, "I still don't know about where *I* am, but *you're* stuck in a bloody bottle."

It was so. Merlin found himself seated on a plastic replica of an easy chair, a piece of cheap dollhouse furniture like the other objects decorating the doorless, windowless, wood-paneled chamber. The aforementioned bottle rested on the table beside him.

"A bottle?" the imprisoned genie echoed.

"Yes." Merlin picked it up and studied the label. "Formerly used to house an unremarkable white Beaujolais."

"Well, what are you waiting for? Let me out of here!"

"Certainly. Won't take but a—"

"I wouldn't do that so fast if I were you, Daddy." Maisie's voice resounded through the room, making the tatty plastic furnishings rattle. Merlin stared up, one hand on the bottle, one on the cork, as the entire ceiling of his cell lifted away and his daughter's gigantic face leered

down at him. His little scrap of light blew away on
Maisie's first breath.

"Yeah, what she said, " said Ahmad, coming into view
over the girl's shoulder. "Not unless you want to spend
more'n five years in chokey."

"In . . . chokey?" Merlin turned red as a boiled beet.
"Now see here—!"

"No, Daddy, *you* see here," Maisie cut in. "Me and Ahmad, we're calling the shots now. In case you want to
know where you are, you're clapped up in Mum's old jewelry box, the one you gave her for a wedding prezzie. You
remember what *that's* made of, don't you?"

Merlin did. "Wood from Nimuë's oak tree. It still has
the power to bind me." He shook his fist at his daughter.
"Young lady, I insist that you release me from this place of
confinement at once!"

"Dream on," Maisie relied. "We'll let you out okay, but
when we say. Five years should do it, 'long as you two
don't do anything improper while you're in there."

"Five years?" Merlin exclaimed.

"Improper?" Mrs. Collins piped up from inside her
glassy prison.

"Yeah, like letting me mum out of the bottle and the two
of you—uh-snogging and the like," Ahmad said.

"It's embarrassing," Maisie provided by way of
explanation.

"What, even with us locked away out of sight?" Merlin
protested.

"You didn't need to see what me and Ahmad was doing
before you went and called it *improper,* did you now?" his
daughter countered. "How's that sauce taste to *you,* you
old gander?"

"But—but you can't leave us in here for five years! How
will you two manage without us?" the wizard demanded.
"You're just children! And how will you explain our dis-
appearance to the authorities? Oh, you've bitten off far
more than you can chew now, my girl. There'll be hell to
pay, just you mark my words! 'Old gander' indeed!"

Maisie was unruffled. "Chapter six of the Pontefract Grimoire, Revised Standard Edition, shows how to make a stand-in for just about anyone using common household pets. I used Titania. She went to the Roundtable office in your place today and your business associates didn't suspect a thing." She giggled. "Can't wait to see what sort of a curfew a cat's going to set me."

"And what about replacing Ahmad's mother?" Merlin asked.

"Yes, we never *had* a pet," the genie put in.

"Remember how you went and turned his old baby shoe into a rat?"

At this news, the bottle began to shake so violently in Merlin's grasp that he almost let it fall. A stream of hot words in a foreign tongue spewed from the vessel despite its cork. No one present knew exactly what Mrs. Collins was saying, but the sentiment behind her words was very clear indeed.

"Er, maybe we'll have another little chat with you after Ahmad's mum's calmed down," said Maisie nervously. She replaced the lid on the jewelry box and darkness returned.

Merlin spoke a few quiet words and the light rekindled. He sent it to hover near the lid, illuminating the whole box, while he used other spells to convert the plastic dollhouse furniture piece by piece into something a bit more substantial.

"You're taking this well," the wine bottle said bitterly.

"No help for it," Merlin responded. "At least I've got some walking-about room this time, a place to stretch out if I like, and I'm in for five years, not ten bloody centuries." He rattled out a minor incantation and sat down comfortably in his good old Morris chair. "And some good's come of it all. I always knew my girl'd make a fine enchantress if she'd only take the time to *apply* herself," he said with a contented smile. "Now she's had a taste of what magic can do for her in this life, there'll be no stopping her. Why, she might even outstrip me in her sorcerous accomplishments! Make her old Dad proud."

"My Ahmad has likewise at last shown himself to be an apt pupil of magic," the bottle remarked, though the words seemed to bristle with invisible quills. "Although I, too, have long desired such an outcome, forgive me if I do not rejoice with you. Some of us do not have walking-about room."

"My dear, I'd release you gladly, but I have no wish to upset the children and extend our capitivity."

"Let them try it! You will not be taken by surprise a second time, I hope? Surely your powers are still superior to theirs? You can easily overcome any spells they seek to hurl against you."

Merlin shook his head. "My powers only work within the confines of our prison. The enchanted oak wood sees to that."

"Ah, but if you were to set me free, things would be different." Now there was a sly, calculating note to the genie's voice. "Our children are bright, but they are still children; children never manage to think things through. They forbid you to release me solely because they do not wish us to indulge in the pleasures of the senses, in unbridled lust, in the fulfillment of our every carnal—"

"No snogging," said Merlin.

"That, too. But what they do not realize is the greater danger to their scheme if you open my bottle. For you see, on my release I would become your Slave, bound to grant your every wish. The powers of the bespelled oak wood do not bridle *me*. All you would have to do is wish for liberation from this box and then—"

"—and then the kids would see that it doesn't matter how hard you work to try to change things, the bloody grown-ups always win out in the end, so why bother?" the wizard concluded. "I'll not do that to Maisie. Five years isn't too steep a price to buy my child a bit of hope for the future. Do you love your boy enough to give him that much?"

The bottle fell silent. Then in a little while it asked, "But what of *us?* May *we* not hope for a happier future as well, O my beloved?"

"Oh, we'll have *that* without a doubt." Merlin stroked the bottle fondly. "In five years' time, we'll not only be free again, but we'll be living in an earthly paradise, a world where we won't even be able to find 'trouble' in the dictionary, a utopia beyond our wildest dreams!"

"How can you be so sure?"

"In five years' time, they won't be teenagers any more."

And for five years thereafter, Maisie had the devil's own time explaining to her friends why the old jewelry box in her bedroom kept on laughing.

ROOT AND BRANCH
SHALL CHANGE

by Andre Norton

Andre Norton has written and collaborated on over one hundred novels in her sixty years as a writer, working with such authors as Robert Bloch, Marian Zimmer Bradley, Mercedes Lackey, and Julian May. Her best known creation is the Witch World, which has been the subject of several novels and anthologies. She has received the Nebula Grand Master Award, the Fritz Leiber Award, and the Daedalus Award, and lives in Murfreesboro, Tennessee, where she oversees a writers' library.

THE character of Merlin is a very complicated one, entwined in such a weaving of various legends that the searcher can find many Merlins, each alike in some manner of power, yet unlike in the use of it. In one of the sage's guises, he uttered dire prophecies of the wild wrath of both elements and stars, foretelling that, in the future, the earth would exact from humankind payment for its befouling.

With Arthur, Merlin failed, and we are given several reasons for that failure. In some accounts, it is hinted that he was too impatient in striving to bring about what was necessary to achieve ends foreseen along one future path, and thus his power turned against him.

*Was Nimuë, his disciple and comfort, in truth a trai-
toress and one who chose a dark path? We cannot be sure
of the wisdom of accepting such a direct answer as legend
has presented. Certainly, though, she was the woman with
whom Merlin could share his dreams and desires, and the
mage—in all accounts—stood alone until her coming.*

*Yes, they list—the seekers-of-legends—a number of Mer-
lins, sometimes sundered by centuries of time. Perhaps,
then, the prophecies uttered by one of these wizards of the
past may also lie ahead. We are told that Arthur was, and
is, the Once and Future King; surely, then, Merlin is the
Once and Future Master of Powers.*

*Thus there might come a time when such a tale as this
could shape itself into reality.*

* * *

How fares a survivor whose world has collapsed, leaving no firm refuge or retreat?

First came the dreams—wisps of action in which I was
caught, but which I could not understand. Yet, in a way,
such visions were better than waking; and with each
dreaming, reality also became stronger. I awoke to find
myself talking to the air about me, not only arguing with
one I could not see upon awaking, but repeating strange
words and phrases. Strange, yes, and yet—once they had
had a strong meaning.

After a space, when I awoke from one of the dreams, I
could not put a clear name even to myself. I was no longer
Ninan Tregarn, once teacher to the young in a dull gray
city where the debris which humans had made cluttered
the breast of the long-suffering earth. *You see,* I would tell
myself unhappily, *you now stand apart, having left the
company of your own kind.*

The visions had begun even before the breaking of the
peace of the world. True, men had troubled their own
peace for generations, but now earth and sky, sea and stars

left their appointed patterns and changed, sweeping away most of the humans who had failed.

The meteor showers, the tumult of the oceans, those dark shadows across the moon, the fatal plagues— HE had foretold them in his time.

His time! But Time folds upon itself when Nature strives to throw away a past. Could there begin anew anything—anything?

It was cold, and it had hailed, battering my half-starved body. The ragged blanket I drew around me now as a shawl was heavy with damp. Only a small spark of defiance had kept me moving the past few days.

But, for the first time, my need was clear. I was no longer Ninan—no, I was again that other who had once gathered to her all she could hungrily grasp. Then there had been a parting, and thereafter ill repute had been cast upon me. Through the centuries, I was remembered as a traitor, a woman who had brought about the death of the only one who had ever tutored and—yes—cherished her.

However, Time was not finished with either of us, nor was the earth ready to take us into itself, to part flesh from bone, from—soul? Spirit was a gift, a loan from Her who rode the heavens at this hour, and it was surely She who sent me stumbling on my way.

That new-old part of me, which was growing stronger with every breath I drew, was my guide now. My head was no longer bowed; instead, I listened, perceiving something not heard as sound but rather felt as an inner trembling of the body.

The forest my budding other self remembered—that was long gone, swallowed up by the lava-tide of relentless human expansion. Nonetheless, as I moved ahead, trees rose about me, tenuous shadows of themselves at first, then strong, sturdy growths, complete. And that trembling within grew ever stronger, urging me on.

Suddenly I no longer moved alone, for there came another, well-shrouded in a tattered robe. Memory stirred. In the days just behind me, some had arisen who had, in their anger and fear, sought stern gods, turning fiercely against all who did not believe as they had come to do. This man was one of their Speakers. His face was as gaunt as if the flesh had already departed from the sharp bones, and it seemed to me that his eyes were mere pits of fire in a skull.

He raised his hand high, pointing toward me, and I could see that his taloned fingers held a curved carving like unto the bowl of a bell; this object he also swung, yet there was no clapper within its throat. Nonetheless, I knew that the unheard sound which had drawn me hither issued from that tongueless bell.

"Well do you ring! Wait you upon an answer?" I asked, realizing as I did so that I spoke a language long dead to men, yet to me strongly alive.

"No answer," the ringer grated a harsh reply. "Get you hence, woman of ill fortune, betrayer, thief of power never meant to be given to any female!"

Suddenly it seemed that he spoke in jest, for the way of his imagined god had never held any truth for me. I found laughter I had not known for many days upon my lips as I moved determinedly toward him.

The Speaker wore a mask of sheer horror now, as though his features in their warpings and wrinkles pictured all the evils his beliefs held that womankind had brought upon the world. "Begone—into darkness, begone!" he spat.

Fearsome the man might be, but he was only a final adversary, worn out by centuries of waiting. Knowing what must be done, I put forth my hand and snatched the bell from his grasp.

It was as if I had plunged fingers and palm into a cold that ate. Then the ice became fire, as violent in its burning as the meteors which the death-days had spilled upon the earth. Still, I held to the bowl; and for the first time I dared to summon, from those memories that had only recently

regranted me the ancient tongue, a lilting song of Power.
Once I had been taught to guard so, and now I stood, battle-
engaged, once more.

The one who faced me gave a sharp cry, spittle bursting
from between the stretch of his thin lips. He strove hard,
and the pressure of his will was nearly enough to silence
my own call for strength. Tearing through the air with his
claw-fingers, striving to regain what he had lost, he tot-
tered forward as though about to throw himself full upon
me and snuff out my life with the weight of his body.

But what he had held was now mine. I raised the bell
high, and it moved smoothly and well. As before, no sound
for the ear issued from its empty half-round, yet that trembling which reached into the body grew and grew.

He whom I had so confronted—false priest of a human-
created god—began to darken, seeming to draw upon
shadows in an attempt to rebuild himself. Such, however,
was not to be his fate, for darkness instead swallowed him,
and he was gone.

A glow brightened within the walls of the enringing
trees, as though the orb that is Her own hung there now,
and the silent song of the bell drew me on until I came
to the foot of a jumble of rock such as could be found
in many places since the shaking of the earth some
seasons past.

Once, I well remembered, a proud rise of stone had stood
there—a haven-fortress which he whom I now sought had
made his place of peace and study. Within had been stored
and safeguarded ancient slabs of stone patterned over with
symbols of power; books so great and weighty as to need
both hands to shift them; flasks; coffers. And I had known
them, too, drawing knowledge and skills from that which
they held.

Now only a shapeless mass of rubble was to be seen;
however, I would not accept that I had been brought here
only to confront a sterile and futile ending. At first I
thought to lay aside the bell and strive to remove the pile
of rock piece by piece, using my hands. Then I noticed

that, when I fronted the heap directly, the tremors I felt inside my body seemed also to resound in some fashion within its substance. Shivering free from their resting places, the stones rolled down the mound by the force of no touch save the call of the tongueless bell.

By the moon's silvery light, near the crest of the hillock so swiftly dislodging itself, a dark spot could now be seen—an opening made larger by the fall of every rock. In a few moments I faced a door, and then the stones ceased to tremble and tumble.

It was small, that entryway, and I had to stoop to enter. Before me was only all-swallowing darkness, but, taking one cautious step after another, I went forward.

The radiance of the forest-filtered moon seemed to rest fingers of light upon my shoulders and to make clear what lay before me. I saw shelves deep-carven into the walls of what had once been a cave and, upon those, the heaped remains of weapons of *his* kind, long since come to dust. All that lived now was the knowledge which was a part of me and which had been summoned from the past.

Against the far wall lay what seemed part of a great log. I stood gazing at the vast trunk, and tears filled my eyes once more, even as they had nearly overcome me when I had last paused in that spot to take a silent farewell.

I had come so far to do what must now be done, yet somehow I could not make the final gesture. Here—even in this very place—I had stood, tricking my love for his own sake, in the hope of saving him by defeating Time itself.

Time . . . yes, that had passed, and I had been caught up in a chain of many lives. I was a seeress, a dreaded woman of strange knowledge, whose body had been given to the fire by those who had feared her. Then, as the Old Beliefs had failed, so I, too, had faded, losing those abilities. I had toiled in fields, and—equally a slave—in the machine-filled pens of later ages. And never had love warmed me, for I had betrayed it, seeking in my pride to master death. Despite all such strivings, I had died, more often than I had any wish to remember—and lived again, in each new form withdrawing farther from that which I had been.

Yet I had been brought here and my memory reawakened; and that She had some use for me I was certain. Had I not come across a starved and dying land, living on what roots I could find, and pushing forward always against great weariness to crouch now in this place of sorrow?

Now I put aside the bell, for this spell I would break was one of my own setting in the long ago. Leaning forward and placing my hands flat on that seeming length of log, I called up the binding as it had been laid. For even as the ensorcellment was wrought, so it must be rescinded word by word, gesture by gesture—a thing which I alone could do. I began with great care, lest my tongue twist and give some fatally-wrong accent to a word. Gradually, with increasing confidence, I ordered the phrases, remembering the swing of the chant, the proper movement of the hands. Thus, and thus, and thus—

I had stepped out of time as humankind knew it. My body swaying to the rhythm of the incantation, I became only a voice, fueled by what was left of my strength. As was required in such a casting, I now closed my eyes upon that which lay before me; rather, I built and held to a mind-picture of what it was needful to bring forth by my wreaking here.

The flow of words slowed. I reached once more for the bell, and its weight seemed to draw my hand toward that tree-not-tree which had been shaped and set here to guard a most precious spirit. In answer to the bell's call, like the stones that had sealed the mouth of the cave, the illusion of bark covering began to slough away; and with the fall of each flake, a portion of my remaining inner power was lost, as well.

My last bespelling, this enchantment had once been. Now it was finished yet again, and I felt nearly as spent as I had with its making. The vibration from the bell died as I crouched down to see what I had uncovered, not truly sure that my will could be undone as it had been done. There was not now any threat from Morgause raised against him, such as had lent me strength beyond the might of mortals to send my teacher beyond her grasp. That jealous queen had had her day and place, as well as her hatred, which had been so strong it had led her to a murderous act. No, here there was only myself, and—

Light arose from the interior of the loglike coffin. The radiance blazed, and I held out my hands to it as one coming in from bitter cold would seek a beckoning fire.

I looked, and gave a little cry; then I stared fully down at what lay there. It had been majestic age I had sealed so against death in that far-off time; but—

—here lay a child. The hair, to be sure, was still silver, but the locks were vibrant with young life. The features likewise were as yet untroubled by time's passing. I had left an oldster, one who had lived longer in the world than many of his kin-blood; but it was certain that I now looked upon a youth of middle years.

Around the body was still wrapped the Master's cloak. Over its surface played rippling lines of color, each of which expressed the inner secret of some mystery not revealed to humankind unless such knowledge were hard fought for and the proper rites enacted.

On the quiet breast, the folds of that enshrouding garment had shifted aside. Lying there against the ivory of the skin was a length of substance I had never before seen. It was not the steel of a blade, nor any safe-ward I could understand. Nonetheless, though the thing had no place in my past, I knew what had to be done. Clutching the bell-bowl tightly in my left hand, I reached out with my right and raised the object from its resting place.

I held a cylinder measurable by my forefinger yet thicker than that, a rod not smooth but rather deeply graven. I brought it closer to eye level. This was very ancient—so old that it reached far back beyond any memory I could summon. The carving showed a woman's lush figure, heavy-breasts and wide-hipped—a shape such as an artist might craft whose purpose was not to show the real but the ideal. Though I had seen its like only once, and that many lifetimes ago, I knew what lay in my hand.

This was the Great Goddess as the earliest of our race had known Her: the Earth Mother Herself in all her fertility and strength. Hardly conscious of what I did, I put the bell and this new-found clapper together. The sound which shouted forth was no longer mere vibration; now it smote the ears like the brazen clangor of a mighty gong.

The closed eyes of the child-man opened and stared up into mine, neither blue nor gray in color and fiery with life and barely-leashed power. It was true, then—he who lay here in such strange guise was, indeed, restored.

The just-wakened one raised himself slowly, drawing the overlarge cloak about his body.

"So . . ." His voice had not the piping lilt of the youth he seemed but rather a stronger tone. "Welcome, Nimuë. *'Root and branch shall change places, and newness will come to all things, as is the measure of the Power.'* Greatly must the earth have altered since last we met here—so much indeed, that, as I forespoke, the place of the trees and the very land is changed.

"As once you learned from me, so now must I relearn from you. How fares this world into which you have drawn me?"

I did not answer him in words; instead, pictures passed through my mind of vast sufferings—evildoings and bloodletting by men and the uprising of nature itself against humankind. And he also, I knew, read my recent memories, viewing what I myself had seen and, beyond that, perceiving through me knowledge far wider and deeper than any I could offer him.

He shook his head when I was done. "Dark are the roads trodden by mortals, for a host of ills are shaken from the garments of those who travel there! The Great Mother cannot be denied forever."

"Yet," I ventured to question, "what can any do, if the skies, seas, winds, and the earth itself rise in battle against us, as they have done?"

"We must make a beginning," he answered. "I shall

draw from you in full all that lore I once freely gave. Thereafter—together—"

My master, now my pupil, hesitated only a moment; then his fingers reached out and touched the wrist of the hand with which I held the bell. A charge tingled through my flesh as though I had grounded lightning, and in that instant I, too, might have uttered a prophecy. Great, in truth, had he been, but it was in him to be greater still, and under Her tutelage he would become the mightiest of Her servants.

Pulling the cloak tighter about him, he rose up, freeing himself from the shell of the tree trunk. Again he put out his hand to clasp mine, and I understood that in partnership we were to bring new life to a ruined world.

Thus—Merlin and Nimuë once more—we stepped forth into the open of that strange forest, and the ring of the bell was in rhythm with each purposeful step we took in company. Out of the shadows came a great gray wolf with whom my lord had once walked in harmony. From over our heads sounded the harsh cry of a raven, and ahead of us, waiting majestically, stood a horn-crowned stag, king of that woodland court to which Merlin had paid homage long ago.

And Time turned, even as the stars move in their appointed paths, and Hope was born anew to light the Dark.

TOUCHED BY MOONLIGHT AND SUNSHINE

by Kathleen M. Massie-Ferch

Kathleen Massie-Ferch was born and raised in Wisconsin. She's there still, with a wonderful husband, two Scottie dogs, several telescopes, numerous rocks, and more books than she cares to count. She worked her way through college, earning degrees in astronomy, physics, and geology-geophysics. For the past twenty years she has worked for the University of Wisconsin as a research geologist. Massie-Ferch has made short fiction sales to a variety of places, such as *MZB's Fantasy Magazine*, *Sword and Sorceress*, *Warrior Princesses*, and *New Altars*. She has coedited two historical fantasy anthologies for DAW Books, *Ancient Enchantresses* and *Warrior Enchantresses*.

EVEN in the fullness of the day's glory, darkness ruled under the great trees where mighty branches caressed the sky by day and kissed the stars at night. The forest floor, wet from fog and soft from years of windfall, muffled his footfalls. The heavy smell of old leaves and juniper cloaked his scent. It was here he came to walk and learn the splendors of her magics. I often wondered if he knew she dwelled here or if he was first drawn only to the power he felt. The strength residing in the forest was great, but the power in my Lady was superior. It is said she had a name before, when she walked among men, before, when she first came to this land from her distant home. She had escaped the ravages of war and death in a land warmed by sun to come to this country of clouds and forests, but an age and more had passed since then.

Now she was as old as the oldest tree.

He walked the forest boldly, as if he were its master! For the first two days I felt only his wake as he moved, a cold, distant presence in the heart of life. Often he would pass so close I might reach out and touch him, yet he did not notice me. He paused, plucked a sprig of wild mint and crushed it. The scent of mint and man traveled on the breeze. It was then my Lady chose to approach him. Her dark hair fell in thick cascades past her knees, her eyes were the color of the richest mud, and her dress was the color of water from the forest's river. She took the mint from his hand.

"Why have you entered my home?" she asked.

"To seek knowledge," he answered.

"Knowledge or power?"

"Is there a difference? One is the other. I did not mean to trespass, but the forest drew me into its heart. I would leave if you ask me, but I hope you do not ask."

He then took her hand in his and kissed the palm where the crushed mint lay. I could feel his short beard, as if it touched my hand.

"Emmeline."

My mistress called. I broke from my daze and stood. He dropped my Lady's hand and stepped back in dismay.

"What magic is this? Where did you come from?" he asked.

"No magic," she answered. "Emmeline has lived here long enough to be inseparable with her home."

"She has not lived so long," he denied.

"She has lived here even longer than I, haven't you, Emmeline?"

"Yes, dear Lady." I had forgotten how it felt to speak.

How it sounded. We seldom had need to speak, my Lady and I. "Yes, I lived before you came, but I was not aware, then. You gave me form and substance and awareness."

He looked on me, and I found his eyes to be as blue as the early-morning sky. His hair, dark in this light, would be as burnished copper in the sun. I took his large hands in mine.

"These have known work," I began. "They are not the hands of a scholar or learner of the healing arts. You know the sword and spear and perhaps the ax."

We both, my mistress and I, looked at him in silence as I reluctantly slipped my hands from his.

"I am all of these things—a scholar and healer, but so, too, have I used a sword and ax."

"Have you come to destroy these woods?" Her voice was no louder, but it carried much farther in the thicket. He turned and looked about. I saw and felt anger in each shape, oak or spruce, that surrounded us. Could he feel it, too?

"I would never harm this forest," he began as he took my Lady's hands in his. "It is more alive than any other in all of the country. To harm it would be as if harming the king."

"We have no king," I said.

"That will change soon," he said.

"You would be king maker?" my Lady asked. "What else would you be?"

And so began the time when the man, Myrddin, learned from my Lady.

The man stood in the center of a small clearing, his eyes closed. She sat on the ground near. She was always near Myrddin of late. Soft, green moss lay under her youthful form. Even when they did not touch as now, still they touched.

"Where is Emmeline?" she asked him. "No, keep your eyes closed."

The sun moved farther across the sky as he searched for me in his unmoving silence. Still, we waited for him.

"She's not alone," he finally said.

My Lady laughed softly. How seldom she laughed out loud! Our world was silent to those who only listened to our human voices, but always she smiled. "We, none of us, are alone in this place. Even you have spirits following in your wake. Why? I can't imagine, but they are drawn to your power as a moth to the fire."

"Power?"

"Yes, Myrddin, power. You have your share as all mortals have, though quite a bit more, I believe. Use it, now. Where is Emmeline?"

"She is here, right beside you though her body rests near a lake. Ah, and what a lake. It is as if the moon has set within its waters and a silver-blue light is trapped beneath the surface. It is a power, but it isn't as bright as your power or the power of the woods." He moved toward my Lady, and I tasted fear. My own? He held out his hand to her.

"Why do you wear this mantle, this disguise?" he asked. "Foolish if you meant to hide your power thusly. I can see your true self."

I detected her fear now, or was it quiet surprise? She pulled him to her side and they kissed. Her mantle of youth slipped away to reveal her true appearance. Her skin, dark and well creased, rivaled the bark of the mightiest oak. Yet this was not the face I saw most often. Her dark hair became the color of moonlight, and still he continued to kiss her. She tried to pull away, but he held her close.

"Can you make love to this body?" she asked him. "This husk of an old woman?"

He kissed her neck as if he couldn't drink his fill of her. "Shall I show you the image I see of you?"

"Image?" she asked.

My heart caught in my throat. I rushed through the forest and was at their side in moments. "Myrddin, do not!" I pleaded softly.

"But why not?" he asked. He waved his hand and before

us stood the translucent recreation of a woman on the sun-dappled ground. She wore silver hair, the color of moonlight, as a dress and where exposed, her skin was just as pale. Her eyes were the color of water. She even smelled of water, spring water.

"She is beautiful. And this is your portrait of me?" she asked him.

"Yes, this is what I see when I look at you, but it is Emmeline's vision. The power of her impression of you is so strong I can see no other. Even when I touch your rough skin and you would have me believe it is the bark of a tree, I feel skin as soft as the finest cloth. If it were an image of my design, I would undoubtedly have placed a gown of delicate linen about your shoulders, but Emmeline has the right of it. Only moonlight should caress this skin."

She took him in her arms again and I walked away, back to the lake, slowly, step by step. I placed all the trees between us so they might be alone. And so might I as I sat on the Lake's central island. It was much later when the moon was high overhead that my Lady came to me and sat down behind me.

"Are you angry at me?" I asked her.

"Why? Because you love me?" She placed her arms around me. I felt safe again.

Her voice was quiet, as soft as the dew. "For so many years I have been bound to this place, the Lake and the Forest. I thought it was because of my love of it, but that isn't true. I am bound here because your love holds me. Time does not march forward here in the same way as in the land of men beyond this forest. Still, I would like to think those who traveled with me to this country are safe and with their new families, but I know they are no more. Even their bones are long dust and blown away. But for your love I would have died many ages ago. Yet we, you and I, live on. No, I am not angry, but I wished you had not given him your vision of me. I never felt so naked as then."

"I did not give it to him. I do not know how he came to see it."

"No true harm done. His abilities are not so great."

"I wonder. Do not trust him too much, Lady. He is a man wanting power. How great are his desires and wants?"

And so they played, and taught each other their magics. Although I thought Myrddin learned rather more than he taught my Lady. Still he seemed pleased with the bargain for I had never heard her laugh so much. I stood beside the Lake and watched the sun sink toward the western edge of the world. Bloody light painted the deep greens of the forest, canopy and grassy banks, nearly black. And suddenly he was beside me.

"Myrddin, you have learned a few tricks," I said. "You pass through the woods as if it is mere air and the distances, from one end of the land to the other, are of no consequence."

He smiled. His face had lost some of its fullness since he came, but his smile was as warm and bright as ever. "It's a good trick. Many places I wish I could have bypassed rather than trudged through. The traveling is seldom as important as the destination."

I shrugged. "I have found the traveling is often the most important part of any journey. For it is in the journey one learns the composition of one's soul."

"Ah, there I have you, for I am demon-spawned and have no soul."

Even though he teased, I wondered if he might have felt there was truth in his words. What would it be like to live with such a portrait of oneself? What was the truth?

I circled around him until he was between the Lake and me. I moved toward him, and he retreated a step. Then suddenly I pushed him backward. The surprised look on his face quickly turned to anger as he sat in the cool, shallow water. The water slowly settled around him.

"Now why did you do that? I don't suppose this is another test?"

"Yes, and you have passed this as all others. Your father may be a demon, but your mother is a holy woman. You

are baptized in your faith's water and in this land's water.
If you were a demon, you would have done anything not
to touch this holy water, but you did not fear its potentially
scalding effect because it would not hurt you."

"I thought you didn't believe in Christ?" he asked.

"He was a holy man. Even though I never met him, I
have met others. Good is good and evil shall not suffer the
touch of holy waters. You are not demon, Myrddin." He
started to get up, but I motioned for him to stay. "What do
you feel?"

"Cold."

"Is that all? You have seen the Silver Lady within the
spirit of my Lady. That wasn't easy. Even she didn't know,
and they have been one being for many years. You have
coupled with her. Did you only savor the warm body of the
woman and her passion, or can you feel more?"

He closed his eyes and held sand in cupped hands.
Slowly the water and sand dripped from his grasp as the
twilight descended upon the forest and the Lake. It was
full dark before he stood and walked ashore. I did not need
to touch him to know he was warm and his clothes were
dry. I could feel his presence all around me. The power
flowed through the air and toward Myrddin. I moved several steps away and still I could feel power moving toward
him from all directions as if a whirlwind. It rushed through
the woods, across the Lake and its central island, and
poured into him and was swallowed whole by his essence.
I sat on the ground in a huddle, afraid to leave, and yet
afraid to stay. Soon I felt my mistress' arms around me. I
had never seen her so pale as she stared up at Myrddin.
How long had it been since she knew this deeply of fear?

"What is he doing?" she asked me though her lips barely
moved. "Why is he calling the power? Does he know what
to do with it?"

All of a sudden the wind stopped. A bright, near-full
moon shone down on us. Had days passed? I felt the so-
still world around me. The power of the Lake remained untouched. Relief flooded me.

And the forest?

The trees above us looked healthy, youthful even. Yet there was a difference beyond their appearance. My Lady squeezed my arms painfully. Her face was even more pale. I followed her gaze and there stood Myrddin. His lovely copper hair was cloud white and his beard, just as pale, reached mid-chest.

"What did you do?" she asked him.

"Emmeline would have me feel the goodness of the forest to prove I'm not a demon. All I felt was the power which beckoned to me. It called me by name, and I knew its name, too. I felt every part of it and therefore knew every tree in this forest. I reached out and embraced all of the land as I would have you embrace my god. Now its power is mine. How could I refuse this gift?"

I reached out to the Lake as she went to him. Still, the waters were as always. He had not touched their power. I had been correct, he wasn't a demon. But was he a friend?

He took my Lady in his arms. "Is this how you came by your powers?"

"As a thief?" She shook her head. "No, it simply grew in me over the years, for I truly am an old woman."

I did not say anything, yet it was how she had gained her powers even if she didn't see it. But hers was a slow theft. A healing of an ancient tree, returning to it a vigor and health, and its power became hers. With each touch of her hand, her power grew and the years weighed more heavily on her, yet she never knew, it was so slow.

I had not seen it either, until now.

I reached out and touched the nearest tree. It smelled of new rain and warm sunshine. Each and every tree I could see was truly young and healthy once again. Their magic had grown even as the trees grew their own limbs over the centuries. But the forest was no longer a single entity united in their costly power, it was no longer the mighty force which had anchored this country in the sea all these years. He had stolen their power and with it their cohesion.

And I had shown him the way, even as I had shown my Lady so many centuries before.

"I have learned much," Myrddin began. "I must return to my young king and teach him many things. The more I teach him now, the greater a king he will be."

"You're leaving me?" she asked softly.

"Come with me. There is much changed in the world."

I could feel my heart cracking, and I couldn't breathe.

"No, I will not leave Emmeline or my home. Why do you care what these mortals do? You are beyond them now."

"My king needs me. He is my hope for this land."

I wanted to see what kind of man could drag him away from my Lady's side. I picked up some damp soil and formed a crude image of a man and caused it to float on the waters. Quickly a vision formed on the water's surface made out of silver light. It was of a boy, perhaps twelve, perhaps older; he was raking out stables.

"This is the king you find so important? Kings, even young ones, do not rake barns."

Myrddin turned to stare at the display. "Who is this? King Arthur is just a baby, perhaps he is learning to walk by now, but this is not he."

"But it is," I said.

"Time here is not the same as beyond the woods," my Lady said. "You could spend several lifetimes here and not a blink has passed beyond these green halls. Or the reverse is true."

"If you leave, you will never know peace again. I see war will surround you and your king." Both Myrddin and my Lady stared at me.

"Do you speak the truth, Emmeline?" my Lady asked.

I nodded. I didn't want him to leave either. I like hearing the sound of laughter, his and hers.

"Will the wars be lessened if he stays?" she asked me.

"No," he answered. He gazed at a nearby tree, but his vision saw things much farther away. "No, they will be worse, much worse. I would stay, but I am needed." He wrapped his arms around her. "You will not come?"

"No," my Lady said again. "I will wait here, by the Lake and when you tire of your games you will return to us here. But do not take too long, for I am an old lady and cannot wait forever."

I knew she meant it as a jest, but he did not see it as one. He hugged her tightly to his chest. I thought he would crush her. The wind blew across the Lake and wrapped us in its embrace. He kissed her and when she turned back to me, I saw she was the Silver Lady, but not in image alone. He had taken the years from her, and the image she wore was now her true appearance.

She looked down at her hands and then felt her face. "You have stolen my power, too! You are a greedy man!" Her voice did not move through the forest as it once might have.

"Only the power of the forest. I hold all within me. It would not be wise to separate it, I think." He looked at me.

"I do not know the truth of your words," I said. He looked even older now and his beard was now down past his waist.

"You could have asked for the power!" she said.

"I didn't plan this. The forest will grow more, and you are not without power." His shoulders sagged a trifle. "I will return it, if you desire it."

He tried to take my Lady in his arms again. She pulled away. It took him a moment to find his voice.

"You will now have the time to wait for me for you're a young maiden again."

"Why should I wait?"

"So we may be together again."

"Not long ago I would have hurt you considerably for this," her voice softened as she spoke. "But I had forgotten youth has its own magic. I will miss the power, but the freedom I shall savor. Why did you not take the power of the Lake, too?"

"I'm not greedy, and it's not my element. Wherever I walk, I will be surrounded by trees and never truly leave this forest. Otherwise, I could not bear to leave it either.

But the Lake is here. To hold its power would be to trap me here. I've a king to train."

He looked back at my image of Arthur. It remained, but now the boy was a man and he was reaching for a sword embedded in a stone. As he pulled it out, Myrddin gasped.

"Again more years have passed." He turned back. "Lady, I must leave and go to him or the wars will be lost before they are begun. Tell me you will forgive my theft?"

"Perhaps in time," she answered, but he could feel the hidden warmth in her manner and laughed.

"Tell me what name I may call you so when I speak to you only you will hear me."

"Name?" She asked.

"Nimuë," I said. "It is the name men have given to this Lake, before, when they still remembered it lay here and they worshiped it. Now they praise a different god."

He kissed her again, long and deep and then he was gone. Only a breeze stirred in his leaving, but on the wind we heard her name spoken.

I went to her and took her hand. Silver tears slipped down her cheeks.

"Will he know many wars, Emmeline?"

"Yes, he has already known wars and will know more until the land finds its harmony again. Time moves swiftly outside."

"How will the wars change him?"

"He is the power. Does the power ever change?"

Wind stirred across the lake and through the trees. There was a whisper of power on the breeze and a name. *Nimuë. My love, Nimuë.*

A restlessness stirred among the oaks and whispers of discontent moved through the junipers and holly. We sang, my Lady and I, a song of contentment and spring rain, lulling the forest into quiet, for now. How long would they remain so?

Nimuë, my love. The longing in his call spoke to us and drew us to him.

We were there at his side. They, the king's knights, had taken Myrddin from the battlefield to lie in the shade of a mighty oak. His wounds were many, but he lived. King Arthur and another knight waited closest as a healer tended Myrddin. The knights would stop us, but when they looked at Lady Nimuë they saw the Silver Lady and let us pass. She knelt at Myrddin's side and touched his forehead.

"He had been unconscious for several hours, my Lady," the king said.

"Yes, I know," Nimuë answered. "I have come for him."

"There is no hope, then?" Arthur asked. "Can you not heal him? We have need of his wisdom."

She stared at the king for a few moments. He was a man of advancing years, and he did not turn from her gaze as others might have. "His time with you is done."

The king paled. "Heal him, I beg you. We need him!" His voice was soft with fear.

"There is a cost for the magic," my Lady answered. "You cannot afford the payment."

From the depths of his soul the king's anger began to surface. "I'll pay it! I swear! There is nothing I would not give for him."

"Without even asking? If you always make such rash decisions, I see why you need him so." She turned from the king and knelt very close to Myrddin. I knelt on the other side. Slowly the wind around us grew until all the forest was filled with its voice and form. More than one of the knights took shelter among the giant roots of older trees. When the wind had diminished, the king and his knights came forward. Arthur knelt and touched Myrddin's chest.

"He lives," the king said. "But what wondrous healing is this? He is a young man again. He has always been the oldest among us. None alive can remember him as a young man, not even the grandfathers. Now he is younger than my children." He laughed. "What would you have me pay, my Lady?"

"I should like to receive this healing," one knight joked from behind me. I did not look at him, nor did my Lady.

"It is a heavy price, King, a very heavy price. And now Myrddin is as mortal as you."

"Have you taken his mind with his age?" one knight asked. The fear thickened his voice.

"No, his mind is as before. You may use his wisdom and his insight, but his power is gone. He is wizard no more. You must win this war by your own resources, King." She stood and then took the king's hands in hers.

"Sire, beware least she spell you!" A knight cried. All around us I heard the hiss of swords leaving sheaths and the clank of armor.

"She will not harm me," the king said.

"How do you know?" my Lady asked him.

"Because you are the one Myrddin loves before all others, even me. You are the one he thinks of every spare moment of his day and your name is the one he whispers at night, yet he has never spoken of you to anyone. Not even me."

"Then how do you know of me?"

"I've watched him when he didn't know. On a few occasions I saw a vision of a silver lady. You are why no other woman exists for him. I know the price he paid in leaving you. I would gladly pay to thank him for his gifts to me."

She closed her eyes, and the forest was still. When she looked at him, it seemed all began to breathe again. "You are indeed the king. The land has accepted you completely. You belong to it. It is the source of your power and strength. Use that power, and you will win your war."

"Thank you for your prophecy."

"It is not prophecy, but you don't understand I cannot teach you if Myrddin has been unable to. You must learn on your own."

She let go of his hands, glanced at the sleeping Myrddin, and began to walk away.

"You would leave before Myrddin wakes?" the king asked. "He will be disappointed. Stay but for a while."

"He will know we were here."

"Stay. I have more I would ask you."

"You have nothing of value to pay for the answer. I am Nimuë, the Lady of the Lake. When you are ready, you will come to me. Then we will answer all your questions." She walked away.

I kissed Myrddin's brow, stood, and followed my Lady back to our home. It seemed as if only a moment had passed before we heard his laughter among the trees. He suddenly swooped down on us, swept my Lady up in his arms and twirled her around. Her laughter filled the air from every shoreline of the Lake.

"I did not expect to see you so soon, Myrddin. Does your king not need you?"

"I could not stay away any longer. Now that my power is gone, I cannot touch you as I did before. I needed to drink in your beauty for a time before I return to the land of men."

"The king?"

"The war is over. The peace is strong. I am not needed."

"Have you forgotten times does not flow here as there?" I asked.

He sobered, but did not release my Lady. "I have not forgotten."

"This is a test for them, then?" I asked.

"Yes. I am learning from you, little shadow. They will pass my test, of this I am sure."

I stood and turned to the wind. What was it I heard? I stooped and grabbed a handful of soil. I would have thrown it on the water to spy on the world of man, but it wasn't necessary. The land itself knew all and whispered what I needed to know.

"Myrddin," I called, but my voice was a whisper.

My Lady looked at me not comprehending for a moment, then she heard, too. We moved through the woods and to the island in her Lake's center. Myrddin followed. We heard the sound of lute and harp on the breeze. Even the ground wept.

"No!" Myrddin screamed to the sky as he sank to his knees. He now understood and would have gone to them, but I stopped him. My Lady went forward on her own. She waded through the water and approached them.

"Is he dead?" Myrddin asked.

"No, not yet," I answered.

"Why won't you let me go to him?"

"Because you have left the world of men for this realm. To go back will confuse them. They must learn to live without both you and Arthur. She will bring him here."

"How long have I been gone? Without the power I don't know."

"Years."

As the sun began to sink below the western limb of the world, the music faded. We saw a boat coming toward us with two figures standing beside the injured king on his pallet. The boat gently nudged the shore; Myrddin waded out and gathered up his king and brought him ashore. His queen and my Lady followed.

"Myrddin," the queen began. She was all golden, the sun to my Lady's moon. You healed others in the past. Can you not heal Arthur now?"

"Arthur has nothing in return for payment," I said.

"Must there always be payment?" she asked

"Yes."

"Then hasn't he given the land enough? Isn't his blood payment?"

I shrugged. "He has given almost everything to free his land. All his power has returned from whence it came. What would you give for his return to health?"

"I? I have nothing but my love for him, and that has hurt him enough."

"What are you thinking, Emmeline?" my Lady asked.

"This queen is air to this king's land. I would not have thought two such powers could be happy together, but here she is with him, as you are with Myrddin."

"I can heal him?" the queen asked.

"You have the power to, if you wish."

"Show me!" Her face was bright with eagerness.

I spread my hands and gathered the waning sunlight in my hands. I could touch the power, but it was not mine to wield. She followed my example, and in her hands the sunlight danced. There was much she already knew. She lacked faith in herself. Later I watched the king and queen from a distance as they sat close to each other near the Lake's shore and talked.

"They have much to discuss?" I asked Myrddin.

"Yes, a great deal. I should not like to see them grow old and die. I hoped to escape that by coming here."

"Why should they die?"

"Because they are mortal," my Lady answered.

"They were mortal when they came," I answered. "But both have touched the power and will touch more. Mortals have a way of not remaining mortal in this forest. They will have time to talk."

"They will want to go back someday," Myrddin said.

"It is already too late. The world has grown without them and no longer needs any of us." I then got up and walked away through the forest under the waxing moon. Soon they would all forget the world outside this forest even as my Lady had and I had before her. This was all the world any of us needed.

THE FINAL BATTLE

by John Helfers

John Helfers is a writer and editor currently living in Green Bay, Wisconsin. A graduate of the University of Wisconsin-Green Bay, his fiction appears in more than a dozen anthologies, including *Future Net, Once Upon a Crime, First to Fight,* and *Warrior Princesses,* among others. His first anthology project, *Black Cats and Broken Mirrors,* was published by DAW Books in 1998. Future projects include more anthologies as well as a novel in progress.

THUNDER rumbled across the sky as a jagged bolt of lightning split the heavens, throwing a cold white light on the countryside below and the lone figure that walked through it.

Although his silver-white hair and beard and the long staff he walked with marked him as an old man, his step was that of one half a century younger. His strides were sure and purposeful across the moors, deftly avoiding the treacherous bogs and other obstacles on his journey. Given his powers, he could have reached his destination in a trice, but after centuries of imprisonment, it felt good to stretch his legs again.

Climbing a small hillock, the man stopped, gazing at the valley before him. The air here was still and heavy, as if the land had been waiting for this moment for many years. He turned his eyes heavenward, then raised the intricately carved staff over his head.

The dark skies above blazed for one brilliant instant as a crackling canopy of lightning rained down around the valley. The thunder that accompanied this light show was so loud it seemed as if the very heavens had splintered into thousands of fragments. The bitter smell of ozone was redolent in the misty air until the man waved his hand, causing a breeze to spring out of nowhere and whisk away the offending odor. As quickly as it had come, the electrical storm was gone, and silence reigned once more.

In the shallow valley stood a massive keep that seemed carved from one single piece of polished green marble. Surrounded by a glimmering moat that reflected the dim silver moonlight, the tower rose from the ground like a solid stone needle. Lowering his staff, the old man stood quietly, not wanting to disturb the peace in the valley. Then he resumed his walk as if he saw this kind of thing every day, heading down the small hill toward the keep.

Upon reaching the moat, he muttered a single word. A section of the swirled stone wall grew translucent, then descended to span the gap with a bridge of glowing color. The old man allowed himself a small smile, stepped onto the drawbridge, and entered his keep.

After more than a thousand years, Merlin had come home.

The next morning dawned clear and bright, and Merlin arose to take breakfast on the parapet overlooking his valley. Much had changed since he had been away, and he had even more to ponder before tackling the immense tasks that lay before him. But since the world had a thousand years without him, a few more hours would not make any difference.

As he watched the blue skies, a small form darted down from the clouds to land on his shoulder. Some mages went in for flashier birds such as ravens or hawks, but Merlin preferred sparrows for his familiars. Not as likely to break off in the middle of a mission to try to hunt mice, and they never brought unwanted trinkets back to the keep. They didn't attract attention to themselves like the larger birds did. Also, they were curious, yet easily controlled.

Chirping, the sparrow informed him of a man who was approaching the keep. Merlin nodded, expecting this, yet a bit surprised that it was happening so soon. Although the appearance of the keep would be a surprise, it was still in a remote location, and would take several days' journey to reach. Still, a lot of people had come to him in the past for advice on one matter or another. No doubt this was another one seeking knowledge or wisdom, or perhaps a little of both.

Merlin raised his cup so the pot floating nearby could refill it with steaming tea. He dismissed his breakfast table back to the kitchen and relaxed, preparing himself for the magic casting.

Closing his eyes, Merlin merged his vision with that of the bird's and commanded him to fly over for a better look at the traveler. The sparrow did so, winging his way to the edge of the valley to alight on a clump of bushes the stranger was approaching. As the man came nearer, Merlin could see that he was plainly attired in hard-soled boots, strange light blue breeches, and a simple long-sleeved shirt with a line of buttons down the front. The man stopped under the elm tree and looked up, right at Merlin's familiar. The man's gray eyes locked onto the bird's black ones. Merlin's breath caught in his throat when he recognized the man's face.

Mordred! It couldn't be, yet it so obviously was. Merlin would recognize him anywhere. The same long black hair, the same narrow face, the same foxlike features. Now it all made sense. Mordred had been waiting for this day, just as Merlin had, and had come to finish the last part of his vengeance against Arthur and the Knights of the Round Table. Merlin didn't know why Mordred thought he could destroy Merlin by himself, but he would be happy to prove the bastard wrong.

Merlin returned his concentration to Mordred, still standing near the bushes, his eyes on the sparrow. Faster than the mage could react, his enemy reached out and plucked the bird from the tree branch. As soon as he touched the familiar, Merlin experienced a wrenching headache, as if someone had reached into his head and twisted his brain a quarter-turn to the right. He grimaced involuntarily and opened his eyes. He found himself looking at the stone wall of his keep, his normal sight returned. He tried establishing contact with his familiar again, but there was no answer to his questioning thoughts, nothing at all.

Merlin rose so suddenly he spilled tea all over his robes. Not even wasting time on a cleaning spell, he strode to the edge of the parapet and looked for his sparrow. After a few seconds, he cast out with his mind and found the bird flitting away from the keep as fast as its wings could carry it. No amount of mental cajoling could bring it back. It was as if it had never been his in the first place.

He broke my familiar bond, Merlin realized. He must have seen it come from the castle, and recognized it as a magebonded creature. In and of itself, this was a minor annoyance; after all, there were plenty of sparrows. However, the mental bond between a wizard and his familiar could not usually be severed without effort. Which meant that Mordred had obtained magical power from somewhere. As if Merlin had needed any more proof, this was certainly it. Mordred had come to destroy him.

Merlin smiled as he realized this. *Rather foolish of Mordred to announce his intent this way,* he thought. Most assassins used stealth to get close to their target before attacking. He had never seen someone as openly contemptuous of an enemy as Mordred was. *Either he has some trick up his sleeve I'm not aware of, or he's so overconfident he thinks I'm no threat whatsoever. He'll soon see the error of his ways.* Merlin reached for the opal pendant around

his neck as he pondered the best way to dispose of his foe.
After a moment's thought, the pendant glowed an incandescent green, then released a bolt of energy that shot
toward the heavens. All that remained of the pendant was a
gray powder, which Merlin carefully brushed into a small
leather pouch. After all, one never could tell what might
come in handy someday.

After he had finished his task, Merlin returned to watching the completion of his spell. The energy bolt would
come down wherever he wished in a shaft of magical lighting that would utterly consume whatever it hit. Merlin's
offensive spells often worked that way, no muss, no fuss.
The poor fool wouldn't even know what hit him.

A flare on the horizon told Merlin his spell was finished.
While he enjoyed exercising his power, he was a bit more
squeamish about actually seeing it work. Taking a monocle
from an inside pocket, he put it to his eye and muttered a
single word. Instantly the lens made his vision as sharp as
an eagle's, so that he could view clearly what he had
wrought.

What he saw made Merlin blink, rub his eyes, and check
his monocle for damage. Finding none, he put it to his eyes
again. He saw the man, completely unharmed, still walking
toward him. He had suffered not so much as a singed hair.

For one of the very few times in his life, Merlin was at a
loss to explain what had happened. The spell never missed,
yet this time it apparently had. Merlin frowned as he realized he had underestimated Mordred's power, a mistake he
wouldn't repeat. Holding the monocle up again, he muttered a string of words that caused the metal frame of the
eyepiece to glow red. Looking through it again, he examined the walking man for any type of magical wards or
protections.

After several minutes of intense scrutiny, during which
time Mordred had come considerably closer, Merlin was
forced to give up. No aura surrounded him which
would have signified innate magical power. Nor was he
covered in the mystic tattoos that would afford him rune-

protection. There was no talisman shielding him, no ring or pendant or brooch to absorb magical energy. Mordred was not an illusion. He was just what he appeared to be, an ordinary man.

Merlin snorted and put away his monocle, for now the man was perfectly visible without it. There had to be something protecting hm from the lightning spell. *But it won't save him from this.*

Holding his hands together in front of him so that the distant man appeared to be walking through the valley of his palms, Merlin slowly brought his hands together, interlacing his fingers until they were clasped tightly together. As the spell went off, he was gratified to see huge earthen hands with claws made of solid rock rise up out of the ground on either side of his target. They curled over to pierce through him and drag him down into the earth, leaving no trace of anything behind. The hands folded into each other and sank back into the ground.

Or rather, that's what should have happened. For as the hands clutched at the traveler, they seemed to pass right through him on their way back into the earth. The man continued walking as if they had never appeared.

Merlin staggered as he felt the drain of energy upon completing the spell. He was just as shocked by its lack of effect. He wondered if Mordred might be more than even he could handle. For a moment, he pondered escaping, but immediately dismissed the idea. First, his pride wouldn't allow it. No one would force Merlin from his keep alive. Second, where would he go? *If Mordred is as powerful as he appears, there is nowhere I can flee that he cannot follow. I'll be damned if I'll run now, after all this time,* Merlin thought.

Recovering quickly, he reached for a pouch that hung at his belt. Opening it, he scattered the iridescent dust it contained over the moat below. Wherever the dust landed, the water it touched grew placid and still. Merlin finished his work and waited for the man to come closer.

A few minutes later, Mordred walked up to the moat.

Without pausing, he started wading into the water. Instead
of swimming across, he seemed to be walking across the
bottom. There was a small splash and a few ripples, then
silence.

Merlin let out the breath he had been holding. The dust
would allow anyone into the water, then solidify into an
unbreakable film that could not be cut or broken. Mordred
would suffer a relatively painless death by drowning.

Merlin shook his head as he thought about the close encounter. Without a doubt Mordred had been more powerful
that he had any right to be. What could have possibly
given him such a resistance to magic without being an in-
herently magical defense? *I'll find out once I examine his
body. Power such as that will certainly have its uses.* He
turned and started to walk away from the balcony when a
noise attracted his attention.

A splash, to be precise.

Rushing back to the edge and looking over, Merlin saw
Mordred climbing out of the moat and up the side of the
castle to the closed drawbridge. He was soaking wet, but
looked none the worse for wear. *He'll never get past the
drawbridge,* Merlin thought. *Nothing that has ever tried
has survived.*

The drawbridge Merlin had walked across the night before was not constructed of wood or metal, but of pure
magical force. Back in the old days, Merlin had riddled a
demon for three weeks before besting him, and as payment
had made the creature construct the door. It could only be
lowered by Merlin's command, and anyone who touched it
without the wizard's consent would be instantly killed.

Merlin cast a spell and sank through the floor, expecting
to see the man's lifeless body. The sight that greeted him
when he passed through the stone, however, was shocking
enough to break his concentration and send him tumbling
helplessly to the floor of the main hall.

Mordred, whole and alive, walked right through the
drawbridge as if it were nothing more than air. Behind
him, the barrier shimmered, quivered, and disintegrated,

falling apart in a multicolored explosion of light. Merlin felt the sun on his face, and as he looked up, he saw the keep crumbling around him, the invincible walls, walls that had waited for his return for more than a thousand years, now collapsing to dust.

Again, Mordred started walking toward him. A few more steps brought him directly in front of the wizard. He reached out his hand and touched Merlin on the shoulder.

Merlin tried to rise, to throw Mordred's hand off, only to gasp in pain as his leg buckled under him. None of the magical safeguards that were supposed to protect him from harm were working. The myriad of spells he had memorized fled his mind like a flock of sparrows on the wing. Blinking, trying to focus, Merlin suddenly felt every one of those hundreds of years catch up to him. He looked at his hands as he tried to rise, saw them becoming gnarled and wrinkled before his eyes. With a shock, he realized he was feeling his age. His true age.

"Mordred? What trickery is this?" he demanded, his voice shaking.

The man he thought was Mordred was looking back at him, not with hatred, but with sadness. He sat down beside the wizard and tenderly took him in his arms. "No, but I am of his lineage. I haven't come for vengeance, however, but because it is my duty. Mordred is long gone, as you should be. You are the only one of your kind left from a time long past. Mankind has moved on, and there is no place for you in our world now. I have come to tell you it is over."

Well, that answers one of my questions, Merlin thought. He could hardly believe it, even though it was happening to him as he watched, powerless. His first thought was still anger. *After all this time, to be defeated so easily. What has happened to the world I knew? How could it have turned so rapidly?*

The man stood over him now. Even though he knew this was the end, Merlin had to know. He had to know what power the stranger held to have defeated him, the most powerful wizard who ever lived. As his body aged centuries in minutes, Merlin had just enough time to gasp out his question, the only one he had ever asked that he couldn't find the answer to.

"How?"

And, looking at him with a gaze that already mourned his loss, the man told him. The words he spoke caused Merlin's centuries-old heart to beat its last, for all of his power and all of his protections could not help him when he heard the man's answer.

"No one believes in magic anymore."

THE MAGIC ROUNDABOUT

by Pauline E. Dungate

Pauline E. Dungate lives in Birmingham, England, and is a teacher at the Birmingham Museum and Art Gallery. Her stories have appeared in such anthologies as *The Skin of the Soul* and *Narrow Houses*. She has also written numerous reviews and articles under the name of Pauline Morgan. Other interests include gardening, cooking, ferret keeping, and truck driving.

THE three of us would walk Jenny's dog in the park most evenings. Some people, like my mum, would say, "Don't you see enough of each other at school?" They don't understand the difference. During the day, there are always other influences, pulling us in other directions. In the park, with just the dog and the grass to listen in, we could tell each other things we didn't want anyone else to overhear.

There were other reasons, too. Jenny wanted time to herself before being absorbed back into the seething maelstrom of four siblings in a terraced house. As an only child, I wanted the levity of my peers before being the third responsible adult in our household. Nimmi escaped briefly from parents who both pushed her to do well, though for slightly different reasons. Our walks were the safety valve for the pressure they put on her.

Rex was perpetually inquisitive and would make friendly overtures to anything. The moment he was let off the lead, he would hare off to investigate any non-grass object in sight. Several times last summer he had disturbed courting couples by placing a damp nose where it wasn't wanted. Occasionally, his enthusiasm would get him into trouble— like this time.

Highbury is a large park with areas of formal bedding, clumps of bushes, a small playground, and lots of open space. Rex saw a couple of interesting people in the distance and raced toward them. Their dog met him halfway. To look at him, you wouldn't think that Rex was the offspring of a Supreme Champion. Instead, he looks rather like an off-white, badly shorn sheep. All Bedlingtons do. This other dog, a bandy-legged Jack Russell, either saw him as a rival or as a large rat. Either way, the Jack Russell didn't even pause for the ritual bottom sniffing but went straight for Rex's ears. Rex squealed.

Jenny broke into a run. Nimmi and I jogged after, neither of us expecting to get there before there was slaughter. The third dog streaked out of nowhere. The gray flash bowled over the Jack Russell, which howled. Rex fled, leaping into Jenny's arms and spraying her with blood from the torn ear. The lurcher got the terrier by the scruff and shook it. It went limp as a dead rabbit and whimpered.

"Call off your dog!" The owners of the Jack Russell lumbered across the field, gasping rather than shouting.

Jenny shrugged helplessly. There was nothing she could do.

I just heard the edge of a high-pitched whistle. The lurcher froze, ears pricked.

"Leave!" The dog obeyed the shout. The terrier remained lifeless where it fell for a moment before haring off into the distance, tail between its legs.

The lurcher responded to a call to heel as its owner approached. The elderly man limped toward the group, using a hiker's thumb-stick to speed his pace. His beard and the long winter coat that flapped at his calves gave him the air of a storybook wizard. The terrier's owners squared up to him.

"Your dog's fucking dangerous," the younger, less breathless one said.

"It ought to be put down," the other wheezed.

"At least my dog obeys commands," the old man said.

I stepped forward to stand by him. "Perhaps you better find your dog before he causes an accident—or attacks someone else."

They looked at us, then down at the lurcher which bared its teeth in a silent snarl.

"You just watch it, then," the older one said.

"And keep that rat on a lead," the other shouted at Jenny.

Both of them turned away, though they glanced back at us occasionally as they headed off in the direction the Jack Russell had taken.

The old man stepped toward Jenny and Rex. The dog whimpered and was visibly quivering in her arms. He stroked Rex's head and gently touched the savaged ear. Remarkably, Rex seemed to calm and licked the old man's hand.

"You should get him to a vet," he said. "That wound will need stitching."

"What if they're waiting for us?" Nimmi asked.

The old man smiled. I noticed how young and bright his eyes were in contrast to his wrinkled, weather-brown face. "I will walk with you to the main road," he said. "Dulac and I will guard you."

I was just thinking that Dulac was an odd name for a dog when he half turned toward me. "We found each other at Earlswood Lakes," he said. "Someone had thrown the puppies in the water and he had just managed to swim ashore."

"It's French," I said, wondering if I had imagined that he had just read my mind.

He nodded, acknowledging both the spoken and unspoken responses.

* * *

Jenny couldn't talk of anything but the old man for the next two days. "He saved Rex's life," she told anyone who would listen.

"His dog did," Nimmi said. "Dulac was the real champion."

"We should buy him something."

"Like what?" I asked. "We don't even know where he lives."

"A cake," Jenny said unimaginatively.

"Dog biscuits," Nimmi said.

Soap was my contribution. I suspected that if he wasn't actually a tramp, he spent a lot of his life outdoors and somehow I couldn't share their enthusiasm. I thought it had been a lucky coincidence that he happened to be in the park at that time, and that we should forget the incident.

"How will we find him to give him these presents?" I asked again. It wasn't that I didn't want to thank him for his help, more that I didn't want to get involved.

"He'll be there," Jenny said. I could hear uncertainty in her conviction.

"We'll find him," Nimmi said, "I know we will."

I believed her.

Not far from Highbury Park is one of those large roundabouts that mark the junctions of the Ring Road with the major trunk roads that radiate from Birmingham's city center. Traditionally, the traffic islands are bright with flowers, the council renewing them each season to welcome visitors. The larger ones are planted with mature trees and shrubs. Once Rex's ear had healed enough for us to resume our evening walks, we took, by common consensus, the longer route to the park. We kept a wary eye open for men with Jack Russells. We'd walked past the roundabout loads of times before, but, since it was invariably submerged in swirls of angry traffic, we'd ignored it.

This evening, over the traffic noise, we heard barking. Fortunately, Rex was still on his leash or we would have lost him under the wheels of a bus as he strained to reach

Dulac. The lurcher stood poised as if to rush toward us through the flow of vehicles.

"He'll get hurt," Jenny said, obviously afraid for his safety.

"He's got more sense," I said. Most dogs would have gleefully launched themselves into the traffic, regardless of the havoc they would precipitate. I suspected that the old man was around somewhere and his unseen presence was restraining the lurcher's innate foolishness.

The moment there was a lull in the traffic, Jenny, Nimmi, and Rex made a dash for the island. I followed with a little more caution.

Dulac and Rex made a fuss over each other, yapping (on Rex's part), sniffing (both of them), and licking (Dulac). I am glad human etiquette is simpler. The fret Jenny made over the lurcher went largely unregarded by the dog. Nimmi noticed the old man first. He was sitting on a park-type bench, watching us. Nimmi moved toward him. I tagged along.

"Welcome, ladies," he said.

"This a weird place to . . ." I couldn't think how to finish the sentence. Surely, only a nutter would choose to sit on a traffic island surrounded by noise and fumes, regardless of the fact that it was overly large for a roundabout.

"Why do you live here?" Nimmi asked. I noticed then that a shelter was slung between the bushes, perfectly camouflaged within the clump of evergreen shrubs.

"Here I have the freedom to do as I wish," he said.

"But doesn't the council object?" I asked.

He smiled. "They might if they noticed. How many times have you walked or driven by? Have you ever seen my home before?"

"What about the parks people?" Nimmi said. "When they cut the grass."

"I am the parks people. What better job for someone who can't stand being cooped up inside?"

I looked more carefully. The island was a perfect circle. Lamp posts warded the cardinal points. I suspected no one would see the place unless he wanted them to. So why were we there? Why had he let down the guards to allow three teenaged girls and a Bedlington terrier in? I also wondered why or what he was hiding.

"Can we take Dulac for a walk?" Jenny said.

"Of course."

Nimmi looked dubious. "Does he have a lead?" she asked.

"He doesn't need one." The old man called Dulac over. He knelt down and whispered to him. "Go with them," he said aloud to the dog. "Guard them well."

Jenny giggled, Nimmi frowned as if working something out, and I felt cold fingers walking up my spine. A warning, perhaps, that this old man would break up our trinity.

In the beginning it was innocent enough. We would stop by the roundabout and pick up the dog before we went into the park. Jenny, always the most athletic of the three of us, would race off with Dulac, chasing sticks. Rex, more timid since his encounter with the Jack Russell, tended to stay close to Nimmi and me. Often Jenny would bring a gift for the lurcher; dog biscuits, a chew, a tin of food. I asked the old man once if he minded.

"Dulac goes where he will," he replied. "He chooses his own fate."

We seldom talked to the old man; he never told us his name—we never asked.

Summer passed. Our GCSE results came, and we all found ourselves embarking on A-Level courses. Jenny and I both did English and History, but whereas I chose Sociology (I had ideas of becoming a social worker), Jenny did Biology with Nimmi. Nimmi's parents had visions of her becoming a doctor, so she had no choice but to go for all the sciences. It was that interest that led her to ask the old man if he ever suffered from colds. This was a time when all of us, including many of our classmates, were sniffling from the latest infection to sweep through the school after a particularly chilly Christmas.

"I use herbs," he said.

"Got anything for flu?" Jenny asked. She was shivering in the orange lamplight and probably should have stayed in bed.

"Feverfew is good for bringing down a temperature," he said.

"I don't suppose you've got any?" She sneezed into an already soggy Kleenex.

The old man dragged a tin trunk from his shelter. When he opened it, we saw that it was full of layers of dried plants in plastic bags, all neatly labeled. He passed one to Jenny. "The leaves are better fresh but make this like tea—infuse a spoonful in a pint of boiling water. Drink half a cup every three hours."

"It won't poison me, will it?" she asked.

"No, but it may taste a little bitter. You can add honey if you want."

Nimmi was delving into the trunk as if she had found a chest of jewels. "I've never heard of most of these plants," she said. "What are they all for? Are they all used as tisanes?"

"It varies from plant to plant. And what you want to use it for."

Nimmi's eyes were bright. "Will you teach me?" she asked.

The old man hesitated, then shrugged. "If you wish."

"Magic!"

I now had a problem. I could either go with Jenny and the dogs, or I could stay and chaperone Nimmi. I knew Nimmi's parents would not want her left alone with any man, however harmless he might be. They were enlightened Sikhs, but not that enlightened. I was not sure that they would approve of her learning herbalism either. That was quack medicine, and she was going to be a real doctor. Nimmi tried to include me, making me part of a conspiracy against our elders but I couldn't get involved in herb lore. I wasn't interested. I felt that overnight I had become the outsider. Dulac had replaced me in Jenny's affections, as the magic of dead plants had in Nimmi's. I suppose I was jealous—of a dog and an old man.

I began to make excuses—too much homework, other things to do. I don't suppose Jenny or Nimmi believed me for one moment, but they accepted it as friends do, or people who are so wrapped up in their new interests that they haven't even noticed you aren't around any-more. The trouble was, we had always been such an ex-clusive group that I didn't really have any other friends. A couple of boys asked me out and I went out of bore-dom. I wasn't really interested, which showed as the relationships didn't last.

The guy I fancied didn't seem interested in me. Morde-cai Reddy was a sort of cousin. He was about five years older than me and only interested in cricket. Even though he lived about a mile away, we only met occasionally, at family gatherings. Obviously, I wanted to impress him so when we found ourselves as about the youngest people at Uncle Gareth's twenty-fifth wedding anniversary party I told him all about the old man and the dogs. I thought he seemed really interested, but it could have just been that my story was marginally better than all the other things go-ing on in the room. I don't know what I expected to achieve, perhaps the downloading of some of the angst that had built up after my friends had deserted me. I hardly expected Mord to go and tell the tale to the members of the Warwickshire Cricket Club's Youth Team. Even if it had occurred to me, you can't blame me for forgetting that Nimmi's brother was a member of the squad.

First thing I knew about it was two days later when Nimmi started shouting at me in the loo at school, then burst into tears and locked herself into a cubicle.

"What did I do?" I asked Jenny.

"Piss off, bitch," Jenny swore at me. I was too stunned to react. This was supposed to be my best friend, yet she looked and sounded as if she hated me.

"Did I say something?" I asked.

"You've said plenty." She was almost snarling. I

thought for a moment she might actually hit me. "I never thought you would do such a nasty, spiteful thing."

"I don't know what you mean." I was ready to stamp my foot in frustration. I genuinely hadn't a clue what she was going on about.

"Just fuck off. And don't speak to us ever again."

In my next lesson, English, Jenny pointedly sat as far from me as she could get.

"What's up with her?" Blanche asked as Jenny snubbed her as well.

"I haven't the faintest idea," I said.

"Bet she's jealous," Kai said.

"Of what?"

"Nimmi. I heard she was getting married."

I felt something cold and hard settle in my stomach. "Who told you that?" I asked.

"My brother. It's all over his college."

"What did you hear?"

Kai shrugged. "That she's leaving at the end of term and will finish her studies in London."

I got a sudden feeling that if the rumor was true, for some reason Jenny and Nimmi were blaming me. I didn't know why, but even her family wouldn't arrange a marriage that fast unless they thought they had cause.

When Nimmi disappeared, her brother came looking for me. I told him I hadn't spoken to her for weeks. I sent him to talk to Jenny, and I went to see the old man.

The roundabout looked exactly as it always did from the other side of the traffic flow—green and deserted, yet once I crossed over and passed through the circle of lamplight it all changed. There was a hint of smoke, though I knew the only heating he allowed was a small calor-gas camping stove. The air prickled with static. The dog wasn't there, but the old man sat on the bench almost as if he was waiting for me.

"Is Nimmi here?" I asked.

He shook his head.

"Do you know where she is? Her family is looking for her."

"So they can trap her into a marriage she doesn't want," he said. "They won't find her. She has already chosen her freedom."

"You don't understand," I said.

He smiled sadly. "I will miss her magic," he said.

"Magic doesn't exist," I told him.

"You are wrong. Your magic is with words. You can destroy with them. I had hoped that this time round, you would use them wisely."

I didn't understand. I thought that either he was hiding Nimmi or he had helped her run away. I did know that everything had changed.

They found Nimmi's body the next day. Two fishermen hauled her out of the water at Earlswood. The newspaper headlines called her "The Lady in the Lake." The old man was convicted of killing her. The evidence was all circumstantial.

That was ten years ago. Everyone knows that a life sentence doesn't mean you rot in jail until you are dead. Not in this country. They parole you to make room for more dangerous criminals. As a probation officer, I had to help them back into society.

I showed my pass to the guard as I entered the prison. He scrutinized it carefully.

"Faye Morgan. You're the new probation officer," he said. Some people always state the obvious.

I had recognized the name the moment I was assigned the case. He didn't recognize me. Ten years behind bars had destroyed him. They were letting him out because they had no facilities for a man who had been diagnosed with Alzheimer's. All I could do was to arrange accommodation for him in a home. I knew, though, that it had been the loss of freedom that had caused his decline. Between us, Nimmi and I had buried him alive.

OTHER AGENDAS

by Lyn McConchie

Lyn McConchie runs a small farm in New Zealand. She became a professional writer in 1990 and since then has sold short fiction in five countries. She has also written historical novels, a nonfiction book about the amusing incidents that take place on her farm, and most recently her second Witch World collaboration with Andre Norton, *Ciara's Song*.

NIMUË bent over her crystal and sighed. "The power he has," she said to herself. Living alone did that to you, she thought. There wasn't anyone else to talk to. "The power is—so impressive. It doesn't hurt that he's young and will be good looking either."

She had to admit that she wasn't getting any younger. Although that was something she'd only admit to her crystal. The other thing she wouldn't even speak aloud was the knowledge that she'd never been good looking. Her magic had allowed her to improve that. Just enough that she'd pass as growing old gracefully.

But of late it was getting more difficult to hold that appearance. And things slipped. If she held her aging back, then her looks faded. If she kept her looks, then age began to creak joints. She cursed vigorously. She'd found the

long-lost substitution spell. All she had to do was assemble
its ingredients. Await the right time and place. Set the
spell-trap and behold! She'd be Merlin.

Of course the spell she'd found did emphasize that
everything had to be just right. But she'd see to that. Just
as soon as the moon was in phase she would be a young,
handsome man, hugely gifted, at the start of his life and
career. And what was better, she'd be court adviser to
an even younger Uther. Her smirk revealed teeth which
needed brushing. She would live in luxury.

Nimuë glared about her. Her own small gift allowed
her to live in minor comfort for this day and age. The
roof didn't leak although the mist from the lake played
hell with her rheumatism. She had enough to eat even if it
was too often the gifts peasants brought her. She was sick
to death of oat porridge. As for her clothing—she looked
down at the shabby, faded, rather grubby robes she wore
and sighed again.

Then she brightened. She had coriander, sage, wolf's
gall, feathers from a hawk, what else? She read through the
spell. Oh, yes. She needed a pinch of bat dust, three hairs
from her head, and the yolks of four thrush eggs. Thrush
eggs. It was summer. Nimuë threw back her head and uttered several regrettable words. The damned eggs wouldn't
be available until next spring.

Her gaze sharpened. It *was* a substitution spell. Maybe
she could substitute something. Hen eggs might be a possibility. Her hens had been laying quite well lately. Nothing ventured, nothing gained. Now, she needed one last
thing. Something belonging to Merlin. Hummmmm. She
sat down to think. The boy wasn't given to dropping bits of
his possessions about. She'd have to steal something and
to do that . . .

The spell took almost a week before she was satisfied.
It didn't provide perfect invisibility, just encouraged anyone who saw her to think she was vaguely familiar, in the
right place, and not to be bothered. It worked. Nimuë returned with several threads from Merlin's second-best

robe. As a backup she'd taken a scraping of leather from the scabbard of some old sword he'd taken to carrying about.

That had puzzled her. Advisers didn't fight. But she forgot it once she returned to her home. Humming, Nimuë busily creamed the egg yolks, wolf gall, and herbs. She added the bat dust, beat the mixture, sliced in hawk feathers, and warmed the results. Then with one hand she dropped in three hairs from her head, with the other the threads and uttered the prescribed words. There was a bubbling sound as the ingredients blended.

She surveyed the result with satisfaction. Right. Better make preparations. She could be gone a long time, but after all, this was her home. She'd rather think of it as unchanged, waiting for her even if she might never return. That took a while. She had to seal it away, place the hens in spell-sleep—and what *that* would do to their egg-laying she hated to think. Hens went off the lay so easily.

She took up the potion and departed with it. The final spell left her lying on her bed. She would still be there untouched by time in a thousand years. She'd always been good at spell-sleeps. Even if her abilities hadn't been good for most other major spells she reflected. Now. She released the bonds just enough to allow her to swallow. Then, before the substitution could occur, she completed the spell-sleep. It wouldn't end unless she returned to this body again.

She wondered, as she vanished into a whirl of colored lights, what the last couple of lines on the parchment had been. Probably nothing important. Damn mice. They got into everything. Then she felt herself dropping in a slow spiral. She opened spirit eyes and grinned. Look out, Merlin. Here I come!

Merlin was reading. His room in the castle was pleasantly warm and sunny. Beside him lay a trencher of fresh bread, buttered and loaded with berry jam. Breast of roast chicken and half a bottle of good wine completed the meal.

Life was peaceful. If only Uther would stop chasing women. This latest fancy for someone else's wife could be trouble. The more so as he seemed to expect Merlin to arrange things for him. That was the trouble with kings. They wanted what they wanted when they wanted it.

An odd feeling swept over him, as if his robe had suddenly tried to crawl off his shoulders. He shrugged it back into place, thinking he must have been falling asleep there. He sat up. An idea was coming to him. He could help the king if it worked. All the woman needed was an excuse. His foresight activated, and he could see that this could be something important. He should help Uther this one time. He considered possibilities.

In a woolly way his robe was also considering events. On minute she'd been on track. The next, she was a robe. It wasn't unpleasant but it was frustrating. The more she thought about it the more frustrating it became. She was trapped. Without hands she couldn't work another substitution spell. Until the vessel in which she now resided was destroyed, she couldn't return to her own body either. Nimuë settled down to use all the rude words she knew.

Merlin shifted. Damn this robe. It seemed to be unusually scratchy today. Nimuë finished her tirade and lapsed into thought again. She'd just have to make the best of it. One thing could be to her advantage. A witch had to have a good memory. Merlin would be wearing her while he cast many of his spells. She'd learn those. Once she returned to herself she'd have more knowledge, greater power.

She relaxed. Things could be worse. That was true, but over the next two years Nimuë discovered that robes did not lead an interesting or comfortable life. The cat slept on her too often. The laundrywomen were rough. Merlin *snored!* That last was the most irritating. She endured as a robe, however. She had no other option, and she was learning. Nothing too much as yet. Small spells, cantrips which she'd put to good use once she was free again.

* * *

A year passed, and another, before the robe was deemed too old to keep. It was unwoven carefully, the wool to be reused. But its unraveling was sufficient to release Nimuë. Her spirit fled gratefully back to its body. She released the sleep spells and sat up creakily. Well, she knew something for that now. Her hands wove as she chanted and she felt her joints move smoothly, her limbs become more supple. Yes, she hadn't wasted her time.

Although what that fool Merlin thought he was doing was beyond her. Aiding a wretched half-barbarian king to steal an ally's wife. Disgraceful. The stupid woman had even produced a brat. Nimuë suspected Merlin had plans for the baby. Not that it was of any interest to her. She set about tidying her home, waking the hens—it was as she'd feared. They'd all gone off the lay. And making sure the peasantry knew she was back. She allowed a rumor to circulate that she'd been on a magical quest.

Nimuë was quite pleased with herself once she'd fitted back into her old routine. The stolen spells allowed her to live in greater comfort. She looked and felt younger and watching Merlin in her crystal, she saw the extra years had improved him.

"Not such a gangly youngster, eh. You're making a very handsome man." She nodded at the tiny figure in the crystal. "But you should stop helping that idiot Uther." She snickered. Not that Merlin's way of getting the king into a bed desired hadn't been smart. It was the sort of idea Nimuë could have thought up if she'd needed to. It surprised her faintly that Merlin's male way of thinking had produced it. But one never knew with magicians.

She bustled about for a moon until all was tidy and she felt ready to try the substitution spell again. At least this time she had the thrush eggs. It must have been that which sent her awry last time. She made her preparations, gulped the results, set the sleep spells, and lay back. The downward whirl began and ended. Nimuë would have choked with rage had a scabbard the ability to choke. How the *hell* . . . !

But there was nothing she could do. She was part of the scabbard until it was damaged beyond repair. She settled down in disgust to learn. At least Merlin kept her and the sword close by. Sooner or later she'd be free and could use what she had memorized. She guessed what the problem must be. She'd become a robe when she used threads from it. A scabbard from leather scrapings.

Next time she had to use something from Merlin himself, not just his possessions. Hair would be the easiest. He had that cut now and again. He did burn every strand with care, but she'd manage somehow. Below the stone ledge where she lay, Merlin was reading again. Didn't the man ever do anything else? All that reading. It rotted your brain.

Merlin *was* reading, but only casually. With the other half of his mind he was worrying about Uther's son, and the nobles of the land. He needed a way to persuade the latter to accept the former. He stood, pacing about the room. Then he glanced up. The sword. Wearing that had been Uther's order. He believed that it would give other mages pause if they thought Merlin could use a weapon as well as his magics.

Drat the thing. It was almost falling from where he'd placed it. He reached up to thrust it back against the wall. His fingers touched the worn leather. Trust Uther. The king never liked wasting money. An idea slipped into his mind. A sword, hummm? Not this one. He'd require something more attractive. The sort of weapon which made people think of power and magic the moment they saw it.

But wait. An attractive sword, yes. Merlin knew where he could lay his hands on one of those. The owner had been dead a long time and wouldn't care. He stopped pacing to sit. Not just the weapon. He needed the surroundings, the trappings. A way to make the sword appear even more. He settled back reaching for wine. What if the sword was found thrust into an oak. Or the door of the castle? He paced, pushing the sword farther back on its ledge. This required thought. He had time. The boy was barely a year old.

Nimuë would have wished for a lot less time. Being a scabbard was incredibly boring. She kept memorizing Merlin's spells. More to keep herself from going mad than because she wished to learn. After more than twelve years she would have killed to relieve her boredom. She was horrified when she discovered she'd have the opportunity.

Uther leaned wearily against Merlin's doorway. "That fool of a Saxon dares me to come out and fight."

"You will do so, my Lord King." The reply was quiet and cool.

"I have no choice." Uther's face was sullen. "But we are short of weapons." Merlin rose and bowed. Nimuë had time to wonder what he planned before his hand closed about her.

"Take this one, then, my Lord King. I wield other weapons. One of which shall come to you in the midst of battle. Be waiting." A different hand shut on her. A larger, rougher, sword-callused palm.

"Good man. This I shall give to Brys who has only a dagger. For the other weapon promised, I shall wait."

Nimuë was borne away, screaming inwardly with fury but unable to act. Scabbards have no magic. She could only hope she'd be freed soon. She was. Her bearer missed his blow in the midst of the battle. A Saxon struck the borrowed sword from his hand. Brys twisted to avoid the next blow. It bit into the scabbard at his hip, slicing it in two. The next swing took out his throat, but by then Nimuë's spirit had fled.

With a gasp of relief she chanted the words which would lift the spells from her home. Her body had not aged greatly while it had been tenantless. Merlin had once been almost forty years younger than she. Now there was only twenty-five years between them. His powers remained far greater. His youth, while less now than it had been, was still her desire. She would try once more.

This time would not be easy. She must obtain his hair, that sleek black hair which he trimmed so carefully. She sat, idly spinning out spells as she improved her home. Encouraged the hens to lay again. She turned to her own body. Spells drove out rheumatism, brightened her hair, turning the silver strands to red-gold again. The skin tightened, she became more slender, age spots on her hands vanished. The years turned back until a handsome woman in her mid-twenties stood there. Finally Nimuë eyed herself in the small mirror which was her treasure.

"Fit for a king, my dear. Fit for a Merlin perhaps?" She pondered her chances. But no. He was a mage. He'd see what she'd done. Better if she went in humbler guise. Merlin liked cats. There was always one about him. Fine. She'd be another cat who chose to sleep warm. The army liked cats, too. She should be safe. She could always catch a few rats and lay them at the feet of those who offered her tidbits. Soldiers liked that sort of thing.

It took time. Uther's brat was half-grown. Running about with that fancy sword he'd found. Giving orders to others, bowing to Merlin as if the man was his Lord. A pity the boy had no magic. If he had, she might have considered him for the other half of the substitution spell. She found she liked Merlin's cat, too. A placid black queen who was happy to share her human's bed with Nimuë when Merlin was absent and the nights were chilly. The cat's only complaint was that Merlin kept her spelled. A war camp was no place for kits.

Time slipped by, and Nimuë was quite surprised one day when she realized she'd been there as a cat for almost a year. It was time she acted. She watched harder, more closely. Now it was spring. Merlin would have his hair trimmed any day. She was away trotting about the camp when it happened. She returned to find Merlin flicking a cloak from about him, the trimmings being swept up with care.

Nimuë bit back a hiss of anger. She stared about. There! Under the table she spied a few strands. She slipped forward and sat on them. Even if they guessed some of the trimmings were under her, the bits might stick to her fur when she was moved. She needed only two or three snippets. No one moved here, and once the room was empty again she stood gloating over her treasure. This time her spell would work. She gathered the hair into her mouth and ran from the camp.

Since the spell into cat was her own, she could cast off the shape easily. Back at her small dwelling Nimuë spent time putting all in order. Then she set the spells, drank the potion, and sank with glee into the spiral of light. She felt herself fitting into the body and smiled. At last. She would take this kingdom and teach it a few good lessons. Merlin had always been too soft. There were ways of dealing with problems which he as a male never considered.

A hand stroked down her spine. Involuntarily she arched her back, waved her . . . her *tail?* How, what? She tried to speak and found she was uttering distressed mews. But she'd been so careful. She'd *seen* the bits of hair float down from the cloak about Merlin's shoulders as he rose. It had been his own hair. It had to be. The hand moved up to scratch behind her ears. Nimuë purred, then forced herself to stop. She was *not* a cat.

"You are, my dear." She looked up. Cat eyes recognized the mage and inwardly she groaned. How much did he know?

"All of it, I'm afraid. I hoped the first two disappointments would discourage you. Since they didn't, you aren't the only one who can work a substitution spell. You are indeed a cat, and a cat you'll stay until you decide to be Nimuë only." She eyed him shrewdly. There'd been another reason, she was sure of it.

"Quite right, my dear." How cheerful the wretched man sounded. "You had your agenda. I had mine. A woman thinks in different ways than a man. They use different tactics. While you were a robe and a sword, you had no magic. But I did." Nimuë swallowed her dismay. What had he done?

"Nothing much. I merely listened to your thoughts. When you produced an idea I could use—I used it."

Nimuë fluffed in fury. Of course. She remembered now.

The method of changing Uther's appearance so he could have the woman he desired. The sword and the tricks connected with that. They'd been her ideas. She'd forgotten them until now.

"That was my doing as well, my furry one. Yes, you have learned from me. I thought it only fair. I've learned so much from you." He leaned forward. "You are a cat, and you shall be so for nine lives of your kind. After that, take your revenge if you can and still wish to." She snarled at him, then sat. If she was in the body of a cat, it had to be that of Merlin's own feline. But he'd loved that one. Surely he wouldn't have killed her spirit just so he could trap Nimuë.

The mage's voice was shocked. "Certainly not. I swapped you over. She had some small cat magic. But she will sleep until the last of your own lives. When you begin on that, she will wake in your body and do as she wishes. When you die for the ninth time and return to yourself, she will be free to take her life back as my cat again." He paused.

"One other thing, the spell. I cannot see how you overlooked the final requirement. To substitute, you must also concentrate on the one you most wish to be. And their will must be weaker than your own." He studied her, looking puzzled. "I cannot understand, my dear Nimuë-cat, why you would think that should be."

Nimuë slunk under the table. Those eternally damned mice. She would kill scores of them for every life she lived. She was doomed. But not entirely. She had nine lives to live. Nothing said that each must be long. She'd be back all right. She just had to find a few painless deaths. This she managed for four of her lives. Cats can eat strange things and Nimuë found some which were very strange. But it all took time.

Arthur gathered men to war, Merlin aged, and through it all a sleek black cat held to her purpose. That faltered after the fifth death. It had been prolonged and not painless at all. She did not wish to suffer that way again. For the sixth death she contrived to slink from the camp. A dog found her, and his teeth bit down. A flash of pain, and she embarked on her seventh life.

But now she was desperate. She could feel her own mind sliding away. If she did not live more swiftly, she could forget Nimuë. Wild with determination she ran under a galloping horse. A flying hoof crushed her head and she went free. Again, quickly. She stole openly from the cook and made no attempt to dodge the flung knife. One life to go. She checked around her and blinked.

She had been so intent on freedom she had noticed little about her in the fleeting years. Why, Arthur was old. His hair had white streaks. His face lines. Merlin was older, his hands shook a little and he used a stick. But the affection between them was still there. Trust, love, she'd had none of them. The young men who had shouted so bravely were mostly gone. And the Saxons, too. They had their own place by the shore and came less often inland. The very world was changing.

She had only to die once more and she was free. Merlin was weak now. She would be younger and stronger. She could attack—did she wish to, though? Her own home would be welcome after so long away. No noise of a war camp. No deaths, no hatred. Only her warm bed and her hens making soft clucks as they laid their eggs for her. Suddenly she yearned for that. She raced madly through the camp. She would go home.

She would find a way to die once she was back. The transition would be quicker. She found the path, overgrown and damp. She found the spelled door. How should it hold against the one who had spelled it shut? Once inside she nosed about among her herbs. There, that one would do. She eyed her body where it lay. It seemed far younger than she remembered. And plumper. Spell-sleep had done well by her.

She pushed the flask down, worried the stopper loose, gulped the herb potion. Then she lay down. Free, she would be free. The whirl took her and dropped her back in a body she recognized. In thankfulness she wept. She was Nimuë again. She would risk no more substitutions. Let Merlin die in peace. She only wished a little wistfully that the rest of her life would not be lonely.

In the midst of a camp which prepared for the last great battle a mage smiled. Beside him a renewed placid black queen purred. Cats have a little magic of their own. Merlin had added something to that. She'd used it in her new body to change it, to rise and find a lover. A proud yet affectionate tom. Nimuë would have her company. She didn't know it yet and when she did, well. The queen purred. A gift for a sister cat. Nimuë would no longer be lonely—she was having kittens in the spring.

THE WILD HUNT

by Lisanne Norman

Born in Glasgow, Scotland, Lisanne Norman began writing when she was eight because, "I couldn't find enough of the books I liked to read." She studied jewelry design at the Glasgow School of Art before becoming a teacher. A move to Norfolk, England, prompted her involvment with the Vikings, a historical reenactment group, where she ran her own specialist archery display team. Her writing takes center stage now, with her creation of the Sholan Alliance, a universe where magic, warriors, and science all coexist. Her latest novel is *Dark Nadir*.

Old Sarum, Salisbury Plain, Wiltshire, England. September 2051.

HE sensed her presence long before he heard her soft footsteps. Though it was hard to ignore her, he continued scribbling in his book. This was the second time today she'd disturbed him. Normally he'd have welcomed her intrusions, but not now. He knew why she was here.

Coming round to his side of the desk, she stopped behind him. "It's time, Old One," she said, the gentleness in her husky voice stripping the formal title of its sting. "Time for you to Choose."

The familiar sweet smell of sun-warmed grass enveloped him, making his hand falter. As he forced himself to carry on, his pen nib spluttered, sending small droplets of ink across the page. She leaned against him, reaching across his shoulder to touch her hand to his cheek in a familiar caress.

Distracted, again his pen spluttered, but this time, conscious of the feel of her soft body pressing against his back, he was unable to continue writing. There had been many such as her during his long life—child-women, their physical development arrested for several years while they learned the old arts of the mind—but none like her.

"I'm not done yet," he whispered, closing his tired eyes as her hand slid from his cheek to rest on his shoulder. "There's still much for me to do before . . ." His voice petered out to silence as, triggered by her presence, visions of the past once more flooded through him.

I'd still been sleeping when rough hands took hold of me, flinging me on my face and trussing me up like a chicken. There had been no chance to cry out even when they bundled me up in the folds of my cloak. I tried, the Gods know I tried, but the fabric only worked its way into my mouth, threatening to choke me.

I must have passed out because the next I knew, I was lying belly down across the back of a horse.

The blood was rushing to my head, and I felt sick as the motion of the beast jolted me up and down. Feeling myself sliding toward the ground, I started to scream. A hand gripped the neck of my tunic tightly, hauling me back up.

"You'll pay for this!" I yelled, trying to turn my head up and away from the horse's flank. "My father will come after you!"

"Silence, brat! We've your father's permission to take you!"

I knew then who they were. "But not my mother's!"

The warrior laughed raucously. "Queen or not, her wishes don't matter!"

Through the bobbing curtain of my hair, I could see another rider draw level with us.

"They wait in the clearing up ahead, Niall," he called, the wind whipping his words away almost as soon as they were uttered.

"Remind them it's abduction by consent! The fight isn't for real!" Niall yelled as he began to slow down.

His companion nodded, turning his mount, then froze in mid-maneuver, his hand reaching for the arrow sprouting from his throat. Above me, Niall leaned out, grasping the horse's bridle as the rider, a look of confusion on his face, coughed once then collapsed across his animal's neck.

"Trap!" Niall yelled, letting go of the bridle as if it burned his hand. "It's a trap!"

Earth spattered up into my face as he pulled his horse up sharply. Moments later, the rest of the College's small war band had formed a living shield around us. The scraping of metal rang in my ears as swords were drawn.

"Take the boy, Niall!" a voice yelled. "We'll hold them off! Those are the Queen's brothers, not the King's men! I recognize their livery."

He hesitated, the horse snorting and dancing, impatient to be off. "Too dangerous."

"I said my mother wouldn't let you take me."

"She breaks the law and puts your life at risk with ours," was the short reply.

Even as he spoke, the ululating cries of the Queen's war band filled the air. Fear filled me then. This was no mock-battle with my father's men; this was real, and my life was the prize they fought over.

"Conn, Owain, stay with me!" Niall said, leaning forward to loop the end of the rope binding my wrists round his waist. He jerked it tight, making the bonds dig deeply into my wrists. I bit my tongue in an effort to still my cry of pain.

"Hold still, boy," Niall warned. "Jeopardize my life and yours will be forfeit, too." Then his war cry, echoed lustily by the men around him, deafened me as our horse leaped forward to join battle.

My head buried against the horse's heaving flank, I could see little but the pounding hooves and the flying clods of earth, but I heard the screams and yells of the warriors and their mounts as swords clashed on shields and flesh. Suddenly my mind did its leaping trick, and I could see it all through the eyes of Niall, my captor.

Hair and beard tangled together by the wind and sweat, what was visible of my opponent's face was covered with the blue swirls of war. Contorted by rage, I scarce recognized him for Diarmid, my mother's oldest brother. His sword arced down at us, blocked by our shield as Niall counterattacked with a blow to his side. I gasped, then forced my mind to stillness. Niall was right. Should he fall now, I'd be pulled to the ground with him to be trampled to death beneath the hooves of the horses. I had to remain a passive observer, but it was not easy, Great Goddess, it was not easy!

Diarmid's horse swerved at the last moment, taking my uncle just out of range, but Niall urged us after him. Swords clashed in midair as Diarmid's horse turned its head, neck stretching toward us. Mouth gaping, nostrils flaring, it snapped at our mount's haunch, narrowly missing my small body. With a scream of pain, ours reared up, throwing us against its neck as Diarmid's blow struck home. Pain seared our forearm, and I only had a quick glimpse of the blood coursing down Niall's arm before my mind was flung back to my own body.

A scream of agony, quickly cut short, rent the air. I saw my uncle fall to the ground, trampled beneath the horses.

I screamed then, over and over till my throat was raw. A rough hand grasped me by the hair, pulled my head up and slapped my face hard. Shock made me stop and open my eyes.

"Be silent, Llew! You dishonor your family with this wailing! Untie him," ordered Ywain, letting my head drop.

Ywain! I was safe now.

"Our Prince will travel in a more dignified position," he commanded.

"Prince no longer," said Niall's tired voice from above me. "He's been Chosen by the College, you know that."

"I know," my father's war leader snapped. "But till he reaches there, he's our Prince. The King ordered us to escort you."

My heart sank again. No rescue this. I was to be handed over to the Druids like a levy of grain.

"What of the Queen?" demanded another. "She broke our agreement, set this trap for us. We've lost kin!"

"The King will be told of her treachery. She'll be dealt with, never fear," was the grim reply.

Cold iron touched my wrists briefly as the rope was cut and I was hauled up to sit in front of Niall. Head swimming, face still burning from the blow, I grasped hold of the long mane for support. On either side of me were Niall's arms, one bound tightly with a blood-soaked rag.

"The College will hear of this," said Niall.

"I will make our apologies," said Ywain coldly as he turned to remount his horse. "Understand this, I would as lief not have any dealings with you or the Druids, but we do our King's will."

"And those who attacked us?" asked Niall.

"Will be returned for the King's justice. Enough talk! Let's get moving."

"I have that memory, Old One. You gave it to me weeks ago," she said, her lips gently touching his wrinkled cheek. "It belongs to one of the first Chosen, not you."

"Not mine?" Even he heard the slightly querulous tone in his voice. He frowned, locking his thoughts away from her. "But I remember it so clearly . . ."

"I know. Your mind is wandering in the past because you're tired. Leave your writing for now, you have plenty of time to finish it. You must come up to the courtyard and Choose the one who will follow you. Everyone is waiting."

"Already?" He sighed, letting her reach forward to take the pen from his now slack grasp. She laid it down carefully on the desk beside the inkwell.

Once he left these rooms that had been his home for so long, he'd never return. Though his journal would remain unfinished, it contained enough to guide his successor until he learned to trust the memories.

"It's that time," she agreed, stepping back from him to give him space to stand.

There was no avoiding it—or her—any longer. His chair scraped against the floor as he pushed it back from his desk and slowly got to his feet, turning around to face her.

Reed slim, she barely reached his shoulders. Her white robe, as much her badge of office as his blue one, clung to her boyish figure, accentuating her slight curves. Brown wavy hair cascaded over her shoulders, its color echoed in the calm eyes that watched him solicitously. Sensing her sadness, he reached out to take her hand.

She accepted it, letting him draw it to his lips to kiss. Of all the child-women who'd been sent to him over the years to teach, this, the last, was the only one he'd ever loved, the only one to become his lover.

"I still don't understand why you must choose a successor so soon. You're well and fit, for . . ." She faltered, a faint rose color flooding her cheeks.

"For my age," he finished with a wry smile. Every day brought him new reminders of just how old he was. "It has nothing to do with my health, child. This day of Choosing was decided by the position of the stars at my moment of birth. I am the Goddess' servant, I must obey Her will."

"They still have to find him and bring him here," she whispered, stroking his cheek when he released her hand.

She linked her arm through his as they began to walk toward the door. Thoughts still guarded from her, he wondered if he should tell her that he had to leave this world. Though she held his memories in trust, the contents of many were hidden from her, meant only to be understood by his successor. She was too young to understand fully what must happen, but he knew. He knew only too well. It was impossible for him to forget it, just as it was impossible for him to forget the way he and all his predecessors had been Chosen and taken from their families. For him, because of his burden of memories, it was not the first time he'd taken this walk.

As they left his study, he barely saw the black-robed Druid on duty bowing to them. He shivered, not from cold, but from prescient fear. Something was different about this succession, something he couldn't yet put his finger on.

Their footsteps echoed down the narrow labyrinth of corridors as they made their way to the staircase leading to the surface. Part college and part research establishment, this place of learning was hidden from those outside their Order. Its history, like himself, went back to the beginnings of their people. But those who had need of their services had always known how to find them.

Holding onto the carved stone handrail, he climbed the stairs slowly. Age had made him stiff lately and it had been some time since he'd last ventured out into the world.

This is not the end, he kept telling himself. *It is another beginning, for her and the one who succeed me.*

"Briana tells me you'll remain here till you've chosen your successor," she said quietly as with each step, the courtyard gradually came into view. "Then I must receive your memories of the Choosing so that I may pass them on to him."

"You must give him all you've learned from me, child," he said tiredly as he stepped at last onto the stone courtyard. "My memories, everything, including my journal. You will be his teacher, helping him understand the purpose of the College and his mental gifts until he reaches maturity."

"I've told you, I don't want to do that!" she said, her voice deepening with intensity. "I want to be with you, not him!"

"That isn't the way it's done. His first teacher must be a woman, so he can understand that side of his nature," he said, his mind drawn back to a similar conversation so many years ago.

"Why must you leave?" I demanded, holding her tightly, ignoring in my pain how stiff and unyielding her body felt.

"Because our time together is done," she said. "You must go on alone now, and I must leave to be married. A husband has been chosen for me—a king, lately widowed. It is a good match, as befits the position I held here."

"What of us? Why can't you marry me?" I buried my face in her long hair lest she see the tears that filled my eyes.

"Because that's the way it is. You're a man now, you must follow your own path, and I'm not part of it."

"But I can make you part of it! I'm supposed to be in charge, their leader—I can *make* it happen!"

Her hands came up and took hold of my face, lifting it from her shoulder so she could see me. "It isn't the way things are, Merlin. The Goddess calls me elsewhere."

"Don't call me that!" I said angrily, pulling her hands away from my face. "My name's Llew!"

"No. Llew ceased to be the moment you were Chosen," she said. "I was your teacher, here to give you the memories of the ones who came before you, help you understand them. My task is done now."

"We shared the nights from the first," I said, part in anger, part in appeal. "When I was old enough, you were my lover! You're more than just a teacher to me!"

She let me go, turning away from me with a sigh. "No, I was only your teacher. It was what I was trained to do by your predecessor."

"Trained?" I felt suddenly betrayed. "You were with him before me? *I* meant nothing to you?"

She glanced at me as she made her way to our bed where the robes for my investiture lay. "I cared for you, but I never loved you, Merlin, nor led you to believe I did."

"What was I supposed to think?" I demanded, hot tears scalding my face, not caring now if she saw them. "That our nights together were meaningless, just a reward for learning my lessons well? That your heart was as hollow as a maggot-ridden apple?"

"That's not so. I cherished you like kin, just not as a lover."

"I don't want to hear it," I said, dashing my forearm across my eyes. "You could at least have left me an illusion!"

"Life is full of illusions, Merlin. I've told you many times, you must learn to see what is true and what is not."

"Llew! My name is Llew!" Behind me, I heard the door open. I swung around. "What do you want?" I demanded.

The Druid inclined his head to me. "The College waits for you, Merlin. It's time for your investiture as Archdruid."

Impotent anger rushed through me, and I clenched my hands at my sides. I was trapped, with no escape, just as surely as I'd been from the moment they'd taken me from my mother's house.

"You may leave us," she said to the Druid. "I'll bring him to the courtyard."

"I'm not going," I said with finality as the door closed.

"You must. This is why you were brought here," she said, coming over to me, the embroidered blue robe held open before her. "It is your destiny. You are the Merlin."

"Merlin!" Someone was shaking his arm. He blinked, suddenly back in the present. "You were drifting again," she said, tightening her grip on his arm.

He stopped dead, reaching out to cup his hand around her face. "Did you love me? Even for a brief moment?" he asked softly, searching her childlike features for the truth he hoped he'd find there.

She frowned, brow furrowing in concern. "You need to ask me that?"

"I need to ask," he said, understanding part of the reason why the memories of the long dead Llew were returning to haunt him. "Tell me our time together wasn't a dream, just an illusion!"

"It's no dream," she whispered, leaning forward to kiss him. "Our love is no mist over the heath, Merlin."

Her kiss was as sweet and tender as always, giving him the reassurance he needed so much right now. He sighed as they parted.

"Everything has been made ready as you asked, Merlin," said a male voice from behind him. "The time of Choosing is here."

Merlin looked round at Euan. "I'm coming," he said testily. "You rush me too much. Let me enjoy these few minutes with her."

The Druid turned to look a the girl. "You distract him from his purpose. It might be better if you left us till you're needed again."

"I need her now," Merlin said, his voice becoming cold as he reached for her hand. "You forget yourself, Euan. Until I've Chosen, I'm still Lord here."

Euan bowed low. "Your pardon, Merlin. I was only thinking of your own good," he murmured.

Merlin ignored him, well aware his apparent obedience was nothing more than a sham. Drawing her with him, he began walking toward the chair that had been set by the fire pit in the center of the courtyard. Around them, flares burned in the College wall sconces, casting flickering shadows.

"Damned newcomers," he muttered. "Got no sense of the moment! Only thing they believe in is their man-made schedules. Not like in the old days when their protocols and rules waited on the Goddess' will."

"What did you mean you're still Lord till you've Chosen?" she asked. "What haven't you told me about this ritual?" There was concern tinged with fear in her voice as she glanced back over her shoulder at the dark figure of Euan following them.

"Later, child. It can wait till later," Merlin said, patting her hand.

* * *

The chair was old and comfortable. It had graced many incumbents before him, but as he took hold of the narrow padded arms and lowered himself into it, he noticed that the covering of blue velvet was wearing thin now. At his feet, the fire burned in its pit, sending occasional glowing sparks up into the cool night air as the resins in the wood sputtered. Beyond it, set low on the horizon, the full Moon hung swollen and ripe, its baleful orange glow matching that of the fire.

"Herne's Moon," he murmured, shivering again despite the warmth. "The Wild Hunt rides tonight." His uneasiness was growing now, taking form.

"The Riders of Chaos?" She paled, moving closer to him for comfort. "Surely it's dangerous to be out beside such a fire tonight?"

"No one here has anything to fear," he said, frowning slightly. Something was missing, but what? "My staff, I left it in my room. Would you fetch it for me, please?"

When she'd gone, he gestured Euan over.

As he watched the younger man approaching, the gulf of time separating him and Llew blurred once more, making him aware of just how different it all was these days. Where once everyone had gone robed, now robes were only worn on ritual occasions like today, or when greeting petitioners to the College. He was more used to seeing his chief administrator in a suit, and Euan looked out of place clad in a flowing black robe. It only added to the strange feeling of unreality that had possessed him since morning.

"What can I do for you, Old One?" Euan asked, coming to a stop beside him.

"Time for straight talking between us, Euan." Merlin settled back in his chair, refusing to crane his neck by looking up at him. "I know you've little time for all this," he said, gesturing around the courtyard. "You think it has no place in this age of technology, but it does. It's because we've retained our humanity that people come to us rather than consult some electronic oracle of wisdom. It's why they send their children to be educated here, just remember that."

Euan feigned surprise. "I don't understand what you're inferring, Merlin. Every college and university has its strange traditions. Ours are just a little stranger than most. Surely after all my years of service to the College, I've shown where my loyalties lie?"

Merlin grunted. "Soon there will be a new leader—a child—in my place, guided by another not much older. You will make no changes while they are too young to object, Euan. For once, follow your God of protocol, make sure it's done the way it has been for this past millennium. Let the other Druids guide you in this."

"Of course I'll see the traditions are kept, Merlin. I'm shocked you felt you needed to say that," Euan murmured.

"Oh, I know all about your little ways, shaving a penny here and there, cutting back on this and that, but it will stop during the Regency, you hear me? None of your tricks, because I have a feeling that this time, you'll have more on your plate than you can handle."

He frowned. "I don't understand you."

"You will, soon enough. Change is coming, Euan, I can feel it. Have you seen the moon tonight?"

Euan glanced behind him at the night sky. "It's autumn. You often get a moon like that at this time of year," he said. "It's a natural phenomenon."

"There was a time when all the College staff knew what that meant, especially the administrator."

"You're living in the past, Merlin. I don't mean to be unkind, but the College is a place of law and logic. It isn't necessary for us to believe in superstitions and folktales for it to carry out its main function."

"You think not?" He smiled. "We'll see, Euan. We'll see. Perhaps my legacy couldn't be left in the hands of a better man than you! Just remember, guard him—and her—well. Our world is changing fast these days, and much depends on his tenure as Archdruid."

"Is that all, Merlin? Because if it is, then we should get

on with this ritual. The sooner it's done, the better. The nights are getting colder now and I don't want complaints from the staff at having to spend hours standing in this chill air, especially now the wind's getting up."

Merlin hadn't missed Euan's faint sigh, nor failed to pick up the other's feelings of boredom and relief that the Old One's tenure would soon be over. So Euan had discounted her already and was planning how he'd shape the new Merlin to his ways, was he? He realized it was no mistake on the Gods' part that the night of his Choosing was the night of the Wild Hunt.

Sensing the girl returning, he smiled gently to himself and waved Euan away. He knew for certain that tonight's ritual would shake the College to its very foundations.

"Your staff, Merlin," she said, holding it out to him.

Nodding his thanks, he took it from her, glad to see she was now wearing a cloak. "Come and sit beside me, child," he said.

He reached into the pocket of his robe, pulling out the small packet of herbs and resins he'd prepared earlier. While she settled at his feet, close to the fire pit, he opened the packet then leaned forward to sprinkle some of the contents onto the fire.

Hissing and spitting, flames of purple and blue roared up into the night, lighting the courtyard around them, illuminating the still figures of the Druids he'd asked to stand this last vigil with him. Breathing in the scented smoke, he looked around. Mentally, he touched the mind of each one of them, giving them his protection, knowing that they all understood the importance of what was happening tonight. Those like Euan were rare, but for now they were the ones that held the balance of power and influence both in the College and with the world outside these walls. Tonight would change that, too.

As he turned toward the small building that was the College audience chamber, he saw Briana approaching, firelight glinting off the goblet she carried. He'd tried to forget this part of the ritual, the setting free of the child-woman who was his lover. This would allow her to reach the maturity that had been artificially denied her these last six years.

Kneeling down beside the girl, Briana presented her with the goblet. "Take this cup, Lady, that you may have the strength to welcome the Chosen One when he arrives."

Startled, she reached out to take it from Briana and looked up at him. He saw the light of understanding come into her eyes, felt it with his mind. She knew that once she'd taken it, her life would never be the same. Before he could stop her, she'd plucked from his mind the knowledge that the drink would also cause her to forget they'd ever loved.

The fumes from the fire had already begun to loosen his bonds to this world. Her face blurred slightly, the features changing, resolving into that of another before changing again, and again, each time letting him see the last love of those who'd gone before him. He shook his head, forcing the memories to stop.

Never taking her eyes from his, she raised the goblet to her lips, then stopped. "Do you wish me to drink it?"

No! his heart cried out. "You must," he whispered, unable to look at her, his heart breaking at the betrayal their roles were forcing on them. "But I swear you will be the last one this happens to!" The knowledge that he spoke the truth didn't help him, didn't stop him from beginning to die inside. "Tonight it changes forever."

"I do this only because you ask me." She drank the bitter contents slowly, then returned the goblet to Briana.

They sat in silence for several minutes. "You must feed the fire," she said finally, passing a piece of wood up to him.

He took it from her, saying nothing, still unable to trust his voice. As the eighth piece was added, he took the packet of herbs from his lap and sprinkled what remained into the flames, letting the scented fumes surround them.

She began to stir, knowing she should leave him to his visions as she usually did, but his hand closed on her shoulder, holding her still.

"Stay. Tonight you need to be with me."

"Is it traditional for me to remain during the Choosing? You've told me very little about it."

"After tonight there will be new traditions. Can't you feel it in the air?" he asked softly, his eyes gleaming in the firelight, feeling the air around them thicken and swirl with potentials and possibilities. "It's the wind of Chaos." In the distance, he could hear the faint baying of hounds. Exhilaration filled him at the thought of riding with the Hunt again.

"I feel only a gentle breeze."

"It will strengthen, then it will come howling through this courtyard, sweeping tradition with it as it's done so many times in the past. Nothing stands still, not man, not time, not the earth Herself, child." He could feel her fear begin to rise as the breeze changed direction, blowing from the east.

"Don't be afraid, no matter what you see," he whispered, taking tight hold of her hand and turning his face back to the fire.

He looked deep into the heart of it, where the flames burned the strongest, concentrating on the glow as he let his mind loose from the bonds of his body. It took but a moment's thought to link his mind to hers, then they were swirling upward with the current of hot air into the blackness of the night sky.

The baying of the hounds was getting louder with each moment. Then, heart leaping in anticipation, he saw them, the rider in front not quite human, his head crowned with the huge branching antlers of a stag. Behind him came his four kin, each with the look of Human men, each set high on a horse of a different color. Raucous laughter filled the night, voices calling to each other as first one then the other of the four pointed to the ground below them. He felt her fear and tightened his grip on her hand, remembering that this was new to her. Closer and closer the Hunt came until he could see those who followed in its wake. All manner of four-legged beasts were their mounts—

horse and deer and wolf—carrying on their backs those
not of this world—some horned, some with tails, some
furred, some scaled—all laughing and crying out to each
other, pointing and searching for their quarry. Hounds
bayed, darting this way and that beneath the hooves and
paws of the mounts, yet never passing the Horned One that
led them.

Lower the Hunt swooped until it drew level with them,
its leader nodding briefly in recognition to Merlin as he
passed by, his followers reaching out hands toward them
in welcome, sweeping them up behind them on their beasts.

Greenwich, London, same night.

Sleep refused to come to Khyan. His bed was too warm
and had become no more than a pile of tangled sheets and
covers. Now his pelt felt itchy and uncomfortable. Getting
up, he padded softly to his window, clambering up on the
covered seat in front of the bay window where the cool
night air could reach him. Squatting there, he leaned his elbows on the window ledge, looking out over the city.

From here he could see over the rooftops of the houses
lower down the crescent, right out to the heath and woodland beyond. They'd been here, in the Sholan legation, for
a month now, and his promised trip to the heath hadn't yet
materialized. The adults might be content to remain
penned within the walls, but not him. He felt trapped and
homesick for the wide open spaces of his own world.

Sighing, he looked up at the moon. It fascinated him
tonight, hanging there just above the distant tree line. Back
home they had two, but he'd never seen either of them sit
so large and orange in the sky. Reaching up, he put his
hand against the pane of glass, imagining he was actually
touching it. Tonight, despite the psychic dampers they had
fitted throughout the building, the air felt alive and electric
with promise, as if the woodland and the alien moon above
it represented some great adventure about to happen. As he

watched, it seemed to grow larger, filling the window till
he could see nothing but its hypnotic orange glow.

The wood sputtered and crackled, the leaping flames
that fed on it flickering first red, then blue before turning
almost white. The night air was chill on his pelt, making
the longer guard hairs on his arms and legs lift slightly as
the breeze grew stronger, bringing with it strange new
smells. Fear lapped at the edges of his mind, but curiosity
was stronger among his kind, and he suppressed it. He
couldn't understand what was happening, but he knew this
was no dream world he was in. It was too real for that.

Lifting his head, he sniffed the air as he looked around,
trying to separate out the scents. Ahead of him, dark
against the glow from the fire, he saw a chair with a seated
figure in it. It was from there the strongest scents came—
one male, one female. He reached out with his mind, trying to sense them, but met only an emptiness where he
should have found people. That puzzled him.

He felt himself pulled toward the seated figure. Although he tried to stop, he found it impossible. Now fear
began to take hold of him, gripping him with claws of ice.
Inexorably he was drawn onward till by the light of the
fire, he could see them both—the old male in the chair and,
at his feet, the young female.

A sudden burst of sound from above startled him. Looking up, he saw figures on strange riding beasts silhouetted
against the moon. Transfixed, he watched as they rode
toward him, growing larger and larger till suddenly he was
surrounded by a confusion of noise and scents and sights.

Around him the beasts pranced, hooves and paws clat-
tering on the stone-paved courtyard as they enclosed him
within a circle. Horses whinnied, their breath so close it
was hot on his pelt, while from their backs, the riders
called out, drawing each others' attention to him. Faces,
more alien than any he'd ever seen, leered and laughed, their
mouths wide-open and full of teeth. He spun around,
crouching low, pelt bushed out, claws extended, ready to

defend himself as he looked frantically for an escape.
There was none.

A voice louder and more raucous than the rest rang out,
then a bearded male, long hair blowing wildly behind him,
urged his horse forward and leaned down, holding his hand
out to him.

"Come up and ride with us, youngling!" he said. "It's
time your kind joined our Hunt!"

"No!" another voice thundered, this time from behind
him. "He's not for you!"

Again he spun to face this new threat, his senses reeling,
terrified to the core of his being. Where had these alien beings come from? How could their beasts fly through the
sky? What did they want with him?

A Human figure slid down from one of the beasts, stepping into the circle to join him. Blue-robed, his long gray-
ing hair blown back from his face, Khyan recognized the
old male from the chair.

Striding forward, the elderly male stood between him
and the rider, holding his staff before him in both hands.
"He's mine, Herne, not the Hunt's. I called him here. He's
the Chosen One, he has my protection."

But it was the female with him who commanded Khyan's
attention. In all this terrifying nightmare, she was the one
being whose mind had touched his. In the brief instant before the Horned One answered, he had time to form but a
few thoughts and receive a single answer. Her name.

*"We have other bael fires to visit, other prey to chase.
See they're taught the old ways, Merlin."*

The Horned One's voice seemed to echo inside Khyan's
head as the beasts began to move, circling around them
faster and faster till all became a meaningless blur and he
collapsed senseless to the ground.

Swept up behind the Hunt, their ride had been terrifying
yet exhilarating. This was the Old Magic, from the time
when the world of Llew was still young. For Merlin it held
faint echoes of his wild ride with Niall's war band. The Hunt

had taken them far across the land before returning them to the courtyard, with the boy who would succeed him.

Merlin had almost been prepared for the sight that met his eyes when he finally opened them, but no one else was.

She gasped, scrambling backward till she was at his other side, far from the brown-furred feline who lay on the paving stones beside them.

"What is he? Is he one of the hunters?" she demanded of him as Euan strode over to them.

Merlin laughed gently. "Hush, child. There's no need to fear him. No, he's not from the Hunt."

"How the hell did he get in here?" demanded Euan.

"He came because he's the Chosen One," said Merlin.

"You can't Choose him!" Euan's tone was an equal mixture of shock and outrage. "Have you any idea who that is?"

She looked up at Merlin, confused. "Didn't he see the Hunt?"

"Of course I know who he is!" Merlin said. "I watch the news, and read the newspapers. He's the son of the Sholan Ambassador—and my successor. As for me choosing him, I don't Choose! The Gods Choose through me. I told you change was coming, but not even I anticipated quite this great a change."

Merlin regarded the unconscious young male critically for a moment. "He's older than usual, quite a lot older, but then they mature later, so I've heard." He looked up again at Euan, standing impotent with anger.

"Nothing to say this time, Euan?" he asked. "That's a first. Don't just stand there, man! You've got work to do! Have him taken downstairs, then contact his family." He narrowed his eyes, looking beyond Euan to the woman approaching them. "Briana, dismiss the others and ask Sean to see our new incumbent is taken downstairs. Euan has a call to make to the Sholan legation. We'll wait for you here."

"You can't leave me to deal with this, Merlin," said Euan as Briana nodded and left.

He smiled up at him, eyes glinting with obvious humor. "Oh, yes, I can. My schedule doesn't permit me to have anything further to do with you or the College, Euan. I told you that the new Merlin would be more than capable of handling you!" He pointed to the unconscious youth. "He's no child like I was when I was first brought here. Now go and call his family, explain to them the inexplicable—if you can!"

As Euan stormed off muttering and swearing, Merlin relaxed back into his chair. He was tired. Dealing with the Entitites drained him, and Herne was always unpredictable. A hand touched his knee, reminding him she was still there.

"So your minds met, did they?" he asked.

"I didn't say that."

"Yet you know his name," he said gently. "You can't turn your back on him, child. You saw how scared he was. He will need your gentle hand. He'll be your pupil, yours to guide for the future."

"He was brave, too," she said. "But I don't know that I can do what you ask." Cautiously, she leaned past him to take another look at the Sholan.

He felt a wave of sadness wash through him as he sensed how she was already being drawn toward the alien youth. "You must. It's up to you now."

Lifting her head, she looked up at him. "Me? What about you?"

"My work is done. All that remains for me to do is give you the last of my memories." He stopped, sensing Sean approaching.

"I mean no disrespect, Merlin, but are you sure he's the one?" Sean asked as he bent down to examine the Sholan.

"I'm sure. Only Chaos could bring about the changes we need to make in order to survive, Sean. And tonight, we rode with Chaos to find him. He is the Merlin, trust me."

"I do, Old One. We'll guard him well, you needn't fear."

Merlin reached out to grasp Sean's shoulder. "I know you will, and in him you'll find a champion against the likes of Euan. They'll be hard pushed to downgrade the magic of the College when the eyes of two worlds are watching them!"

"That's true. Far hail, Old One," Sean said softly before lifting his burden and heading for the apartments below.

Alone again, he gripped her hand tightly for a moment before releasing her. "Now, child, take those last memories from me, and then I can rest," he said resolutely, locking his feelings for her and the knowledge of his final journey behind a wall she could not penetrate.

When Briana returned, it was over and Merlin sat alone by the fire.

"I'm sorry it took so long," she said, "but I thought it best that I reassure the others first."

He nodded, and leaning on his staff, began to push himself out of his chair. Briana reached out a hand to help him, but he brushed it away.

"I'm fine," he said. "Just stiff from sitting out here, that's all."

They walked in silence to the far side of the courtyard. He stopped there, turning back for one last look at the College. The smell of woodsmoke drifted toward him from the fire pit. Turning abruptly, he pushed the door open and entered the building.

"She'll be fine, Merlin," Briana said, breaking the silence as they made their way down the stairs to the ground floor. "I mixed the drug exactly as you said. She'll remember you only as a dream."

He said nothing, just gripped his staff more tightly. All they'd shared, all she'd felt for him was ebbing away from her mind now, but it was that or have her grieve for him, unable to give the new Merlin the help he'd need. At the vault door, he stopped, waiting for Briana to push her authorization card through the sensor. The door swung open slowly, allowing them into the bare anteroom. He waited at the second door while she sealed them in.

"You have to put your hand in the DNA scanner," she

said, indicating a recessed unit at waist height beside the door. "It will only open for you."

He stuck his hand in the opening, jumping slightly when he felt the sting of the sampler.

"Identity confirmed," intoned the computer. "You are authorized to enter."

The locking mechanism clicked loudly. He pushed the door open and stepped inside, momentarily blinded by the intensity of the lighting. The first thing he noticed was the gentle humming that filled the air. As his eyes adjusted, he looked around. The room was circular, its single wall lined with a dozen tall, narrow doors. Set into the wall beside each was a control panel. All were dark save one. On it, the lights showed green. To one side of the entrance stood a console.

As Briana went to the console, Merlin walked over to the active panel, placing his free hand over the door beside it. This was where his predecessor slept.

"Can you dream in cryo?" he whispered to the one within. "Are we allowed the luxury of reliving precious moments? Or are we consigned to a night without end, a living death against a time when they might need us once more?"

He started as the door adjacent to him slid back, exposing a transparent cylinder some six feet tall. Mesmerized, he watched as the empty cylinder was propelled smoothly out of its niche into the room.

Llew had died in his bed. Maybe that was preferable: it was at least an ending. This electronically controlled limbo was not. But then, they'd cut Llew's head from his body and hung it above the fire in the College to dry in the belief that in time of trouble, he would speak to them. Automatically he put his hand to his neck. No, he didn't fancy that either.

A section of the cylinder wall slid back as Briana left the console to join him. He could feel her sadness engulfing him. Blocking it out, he walked unsteadily toward the cryo unit, waiting for her. Impulsively, she flung her arms around him.

"I shall miss you," she said, her voice rough with emotion. "I wish you didn't have to do this."

He patted her back awkwardly. "There can never be two Merlins, Briana. I can best serve the College and our country by doing this. Khyan will have my memories, including these final ones that you take, but if I should be needed again, then I can be wakened." He pushed her away firmly. "Now, let's get this over with," he said.

She sat on a stool by the bed, waiting for Khyan to waken. While he'd been unconscious, she'd studied him carefully. There was less of the feline about this purple-clad young male than she'd first thought, despite his strange form. His hands were definitely hands, though different from hers. He had hair, long and light brown in color. She'd spread it out carefully on the pillow so that when he woke, he'd not be lying on it. His face was almost human. His nose felt cool on its unfurred tip, and his mouth was bifurcated, but it was a nice face. And his pelt was soft, pleasant to touch. She reached out to stroke his hand once more only to feel it close around hers.

Crying out in shock, she tried to pull back, but he held her firmly. As their eyes met, so did their minds, once more bridging the barrier of species.

"Nimuë," he said. Her hand relaxed in his as the memories began to flow between them—his to her and hers to him—their minds merging, becoming one, linking them together for life.

MOUSE AND THE MAGIC GUY

by Brian M. Thomsen

Brian Thomsen has been nominated for the Hugo
and the Tucker awards, and has had stories appear in
Alternate Generals and *Sherlock Holmes in Orbit*, as well
as in many other anthologies. Recently he coedited
the anthology *Mob Magic*. Currently he is a freelance
writer and editor living in Brooklyn, New York.

I'VE seen a lot of dungeons in the past few years, some
with dragons, some with torture chambers, some with
both, but never had I seen one that was home to as ugly a
brute as the one who now stood before me and was about
to cleave my neck in twain and permanently sever my head
from my shoulders, not to mention my life from existence.

My name is Mouse Chandler and it really looked like I
was headed for the great jousting match in the sky, but first
let me tell you a little about myself and how I wound up
that night deep down in the underbelly of a town that
would one day be called Camelot.

I was born Malcolm, the illegitimate son of a fallen
damsel and an unidentified chandler (you know, a dealer
in candles, oils, soap, and other newfangled stuff). I was a
bit on the runty side and growing up on the wrong side of

the kingdom and quickly found myself redubbed by my peers as "Mouse the wick dipper's bastard" which I quickly reworked into my current moniker.

My diminutive build, even for a medieval guy, mind you, kept me out of the knight training program, as Uther Pendragon had a thing against the vertically challenged and usually relegated runty recruits to vassalage under a blacksmith or a farrier. Being both decidedly un-stable oriented and having an exceptional sense of smell and an aversion to manure, I quickly left the realms of court-sponsored education and apprenticed myself to a fellow who specialized in the retrieval of lost things.

Fenwick the Finder had a great reputation and was paid good gelt to track down and return objects that were missing from various members of the nobility (the only ones who could actually afford possessions let alone Fenny's fees).

Fenny always played his skills rather close to the chest-plate and was not very forthcoming about sharing his secrets with a newly acquired apprentice. As a result, I soon found myself relegated to the clean-up squad. Then one day Fenny was recovering from a bender and a rather desperate client was willing to accept my immediate attention rather than waiting the two to four days it might take "ye olde finder" to recover sufficiently to take the case.

I took down the facts, put away my mop and scoop, and accepted my quest.

Well you'll never guess what I found out (unless Morgana the Big Mouth told you already, of course). It was a small wonder that Fenwick was so good at finding things, particularly since he was usually the one who caused them to go missing in the first place. Old Fenny the Finder should have been called more accurately Fenny the Filcher. Any two-bit gumshoe could have solved these cases and pointed the finger at my former master, but since he was offered all of the major jobs and could pick and choose at will, no one ever thought to challenge him.

But I didn't know any better and, as a result, Fenny was

soon doing fourscore and ten in Dungeon Pendragon, and I, a Year Two apprentice (now without a master), decided to put out a shingle and go into business for myself.

Despite the requisite bruises and beatings that occasionally go with the turf (and not to mention the overdue IOUs from wayward knights whose urgency to action never translated into urgency to pay), I've never looked back.

Mouse Chandler was now Avalon's A#1 finder of lost things (and professional peeper for a price).

I like to think that over the past few seasons I had acquired a nice reputation around the court as one of the "go to" guys of Avalon, a man with a plan, a knight of my day, you might say.

Not that this translated into any high class business. After all, if you could afford to hire a bunch of guys in metal suits who knew how to handle a mace and a lance, or perhaps an experienced wizard or witch to solve your problem, why bother hiring a guy who was a gumshoe of the people, if you know what I mean.

So needless to say, I was quite surprised when Merlin, the Magic Guy himself, decided to pay me a visit.

I recognized him immediately. Tall conical cap with matching star-and-moon-patterned floor-length robe, receding hairline and a midriff reaching white beard that also provided a home to a wide variety of indeterminate minuscule livestock, and a bushy pair of snow white eyebrows that wreathed his brow with quotelike accents on the left and the right.

He didn't materialize out of a swirling cloud of spangles, glitter, or smoke, or transform himself out of some unusual animal's form.

He didn't even cast a spell to transport himself to my presence or vice versa.

He knocked on the door, paused a second, and walked right into my one-room place of business like any other courtly clod.

Needless to say I wasn't impressed and already began to

think that his rep was more the work of Percival the press courtier than of actual deeds, merits, and accomplishments.

The fact that he was coming to see me could mean several things: his actual influence and powers were overrated, he needed some help in a matter of utmost discretion that he himself could not afford to be tied to (recently Sir Milhous was deknighted after a scandal that tied him to certain break-in at Templar headquarters and everyone had become exceptionally careful about traces of their own culpability, but that was all just water through the mill-gate, if you know what I mean), or he was really in over his head and was on the verge of desperation.

None of these possibilities boded well for my beloved Avalon as he was considered to be the kingdom's A#1 defender.

(I apologize at this point to my storytelling for my constant reuse of the A#1 rating system; prophecy has foretold that some guy named Arthur will be the Once and Future King, and A#1 has been the popular sound byte of the moment for points of favor in the public opinion in anticipation of this guy's coming. Me, I just wait until something happens—that way if it doesn't, I'm not really disappointed. The A#1 moniker, however, suits my needs, and thus have I appropriated it.)

"Am I addressing Malcolm, also known as Mouse Chandler, the seeker of lost objects?" the magic guy asked, sounding more like the senile old coot he resembled rather than the figure of awe I had been led to believe in.

"Indeed you are," I replied, and feeling a bit daring added, "and you are?"

The wizard harumphed, answering taciturnly, "Exactly who you think I am, and watch the wisecracks, or I'll turn you into some lower life-form like a newt."

"A newt? Like some kind of lizard?"

"No," he replied, "like a twentieth-century right wing loud-mouth Republican windbag . . . but that is of no consequence. I have the future pretty much down pat, it's the past that is giving me trouble."

"The past?" I inquired, exhibiting a great deal of patience as the magic coot took his sweet time about getting to the point.

"Of course, the past," he replied indignantly.

"Not the future?"

"Been there already, no surprises, except perhaps big ears running in the royal family. Who'd a thought that that would have been one of the drawbacks of inbreeding?"

I didn't hazard a smart aleck reply. He had lost me, and within a few seconds he realized it.

"Sorry, let me get to the point."

"Please do, your royal wyrdness, I mean, wizardness."

"I need you to track down something for me. Something that I will hide prior to its already having been discovered by the once and future king."

"Which hasn't happened yet," I added.

"Only for everyone else but not me," he explained. "That's the rub. You see, I have this problem—no, not really a problem, more of a situation, whereby I experience my life in reverse. You'll read all about in a book by T. H. White in a few centuries."

"Of course," I humored.

He was unamused.

"That's why I know that the sword will be discovered and . . . a certain person will discover it and lead England on to the future, provided, of course, I can discover where I hid it in my future, your past."

"So you want me to track down a lost sword that you haven't really lost because you know where it is going to be."

"Then, not now, and one must always preserve 'the now' in order to assure 'the then to be' of being 'the then to be.' "

"Or 'the then not to be.' "

"That is the question," he replied, quite animated as he realized that I possibly understood that which he was trying to convey. "I have no idea what would happen *then*."

"So tell me about this sword. Where did you, I mean will you, have it last?"

"In a churchyard, not too far from the place of the jousting tourneys."

"Was, I mean, will there be anything distinguishing about this sword?"

"It will be big, hard to lift, and its name will be Excalibur."

"Ed Scalibur?" I repeated, making a note of the unusual name.

"And it will be embedded in a rather large stone."

"Embedded?"

"Blade down," he elaborated, "so that the true born king of England can pulleth it out and prove himself."

"Of course. How did it wind up that way?"

"That's not important."

"Of course not. It's in 'the future past,' not 'the past future.' "

"Exactly," he replied, overjoyed in his illusion that I actually understood what he was talking about. "I knew you were the right mouse for the job. Now find the sword and bring it to me."

"I . . ."

My whole chamber was filled with a cloud of smoky gold dust before I had finished my question.

Merlin was gone, and my place was a mess.

I decided that the gold dust was probably my retainer, and immediately set about cleaning it up.

(Dirt Damosels, the cleaning service that came in twice a week, wasn't due for another two days, and, besides, I didn't want to risk them cleaning out my soon-to-be-hard-earned payment.)

The place once again a model of Dark Ages spic'n'span, the dust safely nestled in a hollowed-out illuminated manuscript, my favorite hiding place, I set out to find the legendary Ed Scalibur.

The Avalon Yellow Pages were of little help as too few in the kingdom earned enough to be listed let alone to be able to read and write, so I set off for the next best source of information—the popular pub Bedivere's Brewery.

Now I had known Beddy for a while and there was no love lost between the two of us since the day I reported him for serving liquor to miners (the law was quite specific—working in mines was extremely dangerous work and, given the amount of training involved, it was deemed wasteful to allow them to drink on duty and cause some mistake that might jeopardize their lives, their work, or the whole mine for that matter). Luckily, I also knew that Beddy was in the company of the king and had therefore left the pub in the custody of his firm and better looking right-hand Maiden Hughessay.

Huey, as I called her, was a real down-home girl, homespun yet savvy, a real dame's damsel who had managed to turn around Beddy's business faster than she had managed to turn his head which, as I recall, took less than a split-second.

She was also a good listener and made it a point to keep on top of news about time and beyond.

She also knew to keep certain bits of gossip to herself (and a few close friends), and, much to Beddy's displeasure, I was indeed a close friend.

"Well, if it isn't Pendragon's favorite peeper," she bubbled affectionately. "Come here, and give me a little of that chivalric sugar."

I quickly moseyed to her end of the bar, and gave her a kiss that I hope was quick enough to be chaste yet long enough to hint at the possibility of sin so as not to insult her. (Dames are funny that way—Huey would never cheat on her man, but that's not to say that she didn't enjoy turning down the occasional invitation or two; my expertise at such romantic jousts is only one of the reasons that I have managed to rise to prominence.)

"What can I do for you?" she asked going back to cleaning the top of the bar so as not to seem too interested. "No, let me guess. Your first stop was the Avalon Yellow Pages, which were, of course, no help."

"Of course."

"So now you have come to the number one dame-in-demand, the gal with the know how, the wench with the will, the . . ."

Time was a wasting.

"Ed Scalibur," I interrupted. "Ever hear of him?"

Huey placed a finger to a dimple (her normal thinking affectation), scrunched her brow, and thought for a moment.

"Scalibur, sounds familiar," she offered, having finished her cogitating and resuming her wiping, "not Ed, though. You've got the wrong first name."

"So, if not Ed, what does his squire call him?"

Huey laughed.

"He doesn't have one. A squire, I mean. He's a blacksmith who does a little custom sword work on the side. He used to be quite the boss of blades, really rolling in the gelt, but he was too quick to diversify—'Scalibur's Scabbards,' remember?"

"No."

"That was the problem. Unfortunately, he had leveraged everything on his designer scabbard line and the business went under, forcing him to go to work for his father at the old smithy shop."

"Where can I find him?"

"At his father's place over on the corner of Manure and Detritus—not the best part of town."

"I know my way around the hind of horse or two," I replied, reassuring her that she needn't worry about me venturing into the wrong side of town.

"Not surprised. I would imagine that horses' arses are one of your specialties."

Not really knowing how to take her last comment, I smacked a coin onto the bar, said thanks, and made my way to the door.

Huey called after me.

"And remember, his name is not Ed. It's . . ."

. . . but I was already on my way.

* * *

I had not even left the block of Bedivere's Brewery when I found myself coughing and wheezing for breath, having just become engulfed in a cloud of gold dust.

"So have you found my sword yet?" I heard over my own racking noises.

I opened my eyes and there was the magic guy, tapping his tasseled slipper in front of me.

"I'm glad I've run into you," I improvised, clearing my throat with yet another cough of enchanted dust, adding, "Damn cloud of dust . . . cough . . . Excuse me."

"You're excused," Merlin replied, not offering any apology for the distress his traveling spell was causing my upper respiratory system. "So have you found the sword yet?"

"I have an address for you . . ."

"I don't need a dress. I wear a robe . . . but that's not what I asked for."

"I mean the place where you can get your sword."

"You mean the place where you will get the sword. That is what I required from you, or perhaps I shall turn . . ."

"No need for that," I assured.

"Good."

Another cloud of dust (I thought to hold my breath this time to save my lungs) and he was gone. I started to shuffle off to Scalibur's.

I arrived in the more aromatic section of Avalon and quickly found myself at the corner of Manure and Detritus and the blacksmith shop of the mysterious Mr. Scalibur. I was about to go inside when I found my way blocked by an ogre of a fellow who seemed less than pleased about my presence.

"What do you want, you no good chivalric shamus?" the mountain of a man demanded.

"I'm looking for a Mr. Scalibur," I replied. "My name is Mouse—"

"I know who you are," he boomed, "and I don't deal in

stolen steeds. I run a strictly legit smithy here, so you go looking for your missing horses elsewhere."

"Horses?" I queried, just slightly recalling a recent rash of horse jackings. "I'm here about a sword."

A blanket of ignorance passed over the thug's face, smoothing the lines of rage with a patina of dumbfoundedness.

"Oh," he replied haltingly. "That's different. Forget what I said. Come inside, Mr. Detective. A guy in your line of work is always in the market for a good blade. You never know when you might come up against an ugly brute such as meself."

"Indeed," I replied, following him inside, then hastily adding, "which is not to say that I think you're ugly . . . I mean, I've met uglier."

"Indeed," he agreed, taking a torch from beside the door and proceeding to illuminate the smith shop by lighting various other torches along the way.

The place was surprisingly clean with nary a horse or its leavings in sight. Along one wall was a set of empty stalls decorated with the occasional bit of bridle work and horseshoes, while along the other side were various models of swords and armory.

"This is my showroom," the ogreish fellow explained. "My forge and ironworks are downstairs," he added.

Replacing the torch in its holder, he leaned over and put his arm around my shoulder, whispering, "You're probably looking for one of my 'specials.' "

"Specials?"

"You know, an untraceable."

Now this was indeed an interesting turn of events. This oaf was worried about being connected to horse thievery, but thought nothing of enticing me with illegal weaponry. A recent Avalon decree, brought about in response to the numerous cases of hack and slash that raged through our city streets, required that all swords, daggers, and other miscellaneous bladed weapons had to be registered with the seneschal. No less than my own client Merlin the magic guy had instigated a spell that would immediately engrave any blade with a serial number that could then be traced to its bearer.

There was, of course, no law specifically enacted to outlaw untraceable weaponry (since Merlin's magic took care of the engraving of the serial numbers automatically), but similar implied/inferred crimes were truly frowned upon, and usually greeted with some dangerous spell from the magic man himself.

I didn't say a word, just tried to look eager.

"I knew that's what you be wanting," he replied with a smile, "and, of course, I'm not breaking any laws . . .", he reached behind his back and presented me with a sword, ". . . one might say that I am just proud of my handiwork."

Before me was a beautiful blade, and in the place where the serial numbers would normally be was a boldly engraved design.

"The serial numbers are still there," he explained. "You just can't make them out. Let's just say I signed my handiwork."

The inscription read "EXSCALIBUR."

"It's Latin," he explained. "Means 'from Scalibur.' Soon everyone will have one, and not a single slicer traceable. I will be famous, and restored to my former glory in no time."

"Aren't you scared of Uther or maybe Merlin?"

"The former is a pudding and the latter is a fake, and, besides, this entire smith shop is enchanted and out of the old guy's reach. I pay a certain amount of juice to old Morgana Le Fey and she in turn keeps all of this in the shadow-realm and out of that old fakir's reach."

A candlewick went off in my head. This must have been the real reason for my assignment. Merlin needed someone to investigate this who wouldn't give himself away (thus alerting any wards cast by Morgana), and I was the dick he decided to use.

Lucky me.

"So how many do you want?"

"Well, I, uh . . ."

Just then a raven arrived from one of the barn's dark corners, a message held tightly in its beak.

"Excuse me," the oaf offered and explained, "but it will only be a minute. Mail order is an important part of my business."

Scalibur hurried over to stand by a torch to read his message.

Imagine that, I thought, *he can read.* I wandered over toward his sword display to wait for him to finish when all of a sudden the floor beneath my feet disappeared, and I found myself in the dungeon that housed two spans of apparently hot stallions (or maybe they were the stolen knights' mares—I never was much on horse plumbing, so I really couldn't tell), Scalibur's forge, his ironworks, and a one-eyed brute of a fellow who seemed ready to cleave me in twain.

"Sorry about that, Chandler," a voice from above hailed, "but Ms. Morgana informs me that you are working for the authorities, and as a result are undeserving of my talents, and of your own life for that matter."

For some reason Scalibur didn't seem to be so dumb anymore. Imagine that, give a guy the upper hand and his IQ goes up a few points. As he pontificated in typical bad guy style, I quickly scanned my whereabouts, never failing to keep one eye on the brute who made the guy upstairs look like the Queen of the May.

"I see that you have met Wrathbone, my associate. He does all of the heavy work around here. The poor boy was born impervious to pain, a condition that has led to the many mishaps which have scarred his body."

"Poor guy," I replied, still not seeing a way out.

"He likes to cut things in half for fun" (I noticed an anvil that had been cut in twain and was being heated up in the forge, as well as half a dozen half-carcasses of unknown origin scattered on the floor). "I will have to remember to have him clean up after he is done with you. I wouldn't want the smell of rotting flesh to disturb my equine equity. Cheers."

I looked up just in time. Wrathbone was about to bear down on me with the white-hot blade of a recently forged Scalibur special. I quickly ducked, covered, and rolled to the left under a cooling trough, and back by the forge hoping to find something to use to defend myself.

Nothing . . . and the big thug was lumbering across the room, drool of anticipation dropping from his well-scarred lips.

"Can't we talk this over?" I offered, noticing that the two half-anvils were suspended over the hearth by chains that were connected to a counterweight that ran right next to the trough. The anvils were then balanced in place on a single beam above the hot coals. "Maybe I can offer you a better job?" I pattered. "How would you like to be an apprentice PI?"

My inanities fell on deaf ears (probably a product of his scarring) as he closed in on me. I was about to meet my maker when a candle went off in my noggin.

The still white-hot sword came down again, and I rolled once more to the side.

Wrathbone was now between me and hearth and about to raise the freshly forged Scalibur special above his head again.

Acting in a flash, I grabbed the chains that held the counterweight and undid them with a twist while simultaneously swinging myself to the side, causing a ripple down the chain that disengaged both anvil halves from the beam and sent them careening toward the scarred oaf.

Wrathbone saw what was coming but couldn't react fast enough as one of the anvil sides kissed the white hot blade and immediately affixed itself in molten unity. His immediate reaction was to try to yank the blade away, but this only succeeded in bringing blade and anvil half in contact with the other anvil half.

In another flash I sprang back into action and threw a flying kick against Wrathbone that sent him backward into the cooling trough with the sword in the anvil on top of him, pinning him underwater.

Air bubbles came to the surface for barely a few seconds as the man who felt no pain breathed a last lungful of water and embraced death.

A rush of footsteps above indicated that Scalibur was no longer alone, so I carefully negotiated my way back up the trapdoor using a makeshift ladder from the equipment around me. I was just about to lift it back when it was opened on the other side by my old rival from the King's guards, Sir Flannery.

"What are you doing here, Mouse?" he demanded with a harumph. "Surely tracking horse-nappers is out of your line of business."

"It is," I replied, "but illegal sidearms aren't."

"Sez who?"

"Sez Merlin," I replied.

Flannery scratched his chin for a moment giving me the once over.

"Illegal arms, you say," he considered, then noticing the pair of legs that were sticking up from the trough below, gestured and asked, "Who he?"

"He dead," I replied.

Flannery was not amused.

"Everything here is impounded by order of Uther Pendragon," he ordered his sub-seneschals as Scalibur was led away in irons.

Flannery turned back to me, and said, "Get outta here. If you are working for Merlin, I'm not gonna get in your way . . . but don't leave town. You'll probably have to sign some paperwork about your dead friend in there."

I looked back at the corpse of Wrathbone and noticed that the sword and anvils were no longer weighing him down in the trough, and thought better than to mention it.

"No problem," I replied, stepping clear of the trapdoor, and moseying my way out of the shop and back to the office.

* * *

I wasn't surprised to find Merlin back in my office when I finally got there. If there is one thing you learn about magic guys it's that they get around fast.

" 'Bout time you got here," he said brusquely. "I've got better things to do around Camelot, I mean Avalon, than to spend my precious time waiting for a private eye."

"But if I read what you said before right, the backwards thing and all, you just got here, and the waiting is still ahead of you, right?"

The old guy chuckled, and said, "Touché! Job well done."

"Busting the illegal weapons racket?"

"Oh, that, too," Merlin replied with a chuckle, gesturing to the corner of the room. "And your finding Excalibur."

There was the sword with the engraving EX CALIBUR (the S must have rubbed off in the fight), standing up straight, the tip half of its blade embedded in the now whole anvil.

"I thought you said it was embedded in a rock?" I reminded him.

The magic guy laughed and shook his head, saying, "I am an old man with occasional memory lapses. Besides who can keep all these myths straight? I must have made a mistake."

I turned back to take a closer look at the sword in the anvil only to discover it had disappeared.

"Well, I will be off," the wizard said with a flourish.

"Wait a minute," I said, holding my hand up, "what about paying me for the job? I don't run a charity operation here, and I did risk my life."

Merlin turned back to me and said, "It was the second half of a two-for-one sale that you are going to run."

"What? The gold dust was just the retainer."

Merlin replied, "Your finding the Holy Grail was the first part, and this is the second part. You were giving a two-for-one sale, so this one is free."

"The Holy Grail," I replied, in confusion, "but I haven't

found any Holy Grail yet. You haven't even asked me to find it yet."

"Exactly," he replied with a smile before he disappeared into another cloud of glitter, "which is why I haven't paid you the rest . . . but I will, because from my point of view, I already have."

I thought about lodging a complaint with the castle, but thought better of it.

Sure, he might be cheating me, but I didn't want to be turned into a newt, whatever that was.

Besides, it's good to know that there is some work waiting in the future. Finding a Holy Grail can't be too hard, can it?

MERLIN AND VIVIANE

by Alan Rodgers

Alan Rodgers' stories are guaranteed to please even
the most discriminating reader. Whether he's writing
subtle fiction where the shocks creep up on you or an
out-and-out screaming terror tale, his command of
the genre and language are a force to be reckoned
with. His short fiction has appeared in such anthologies as *Miskatonic University, Tales from the Great Turtle,
Masques #3,* and *The Conspiracy Files.*

THIS happened after Merlin was no longer old, when he
was once more in his youth—in those years before he became the ancient timeless thing we all revere. It happened
long before that first king caught Merlin for a sacrifice, or
used him as a seer; it happened when the wizard was a boy
in years but after he had hardened down inside much older
than a man.

Time moves strangely for some people, and Merlin is
the strangest of them all.

Is it any wonder? Men like Merlin aren't made or educated; they're born to be the way they are, and because
they are unlike us, their loves are nothing like our own.

Still: Their loves are things that haunt them just the

same, out of phase with everything we know about the world and time.

It was that way with Merlin and Viviane, and everybody knows it. Most people know Viviane from when she was the Lady of the Lake, and remember her as the enchantress who gifted Arthur with Excalibur. But she had her place in Merlin's life long years before that day, and ages after; and the thing that so few know is that she was a Queen before she met the mage, and always was and would be.

When the mage first set eyes on his Lady of the Lake, she was Queen of the Fairy tribe at Dunmeller. This was before anyone knew to call that place Black Mountain; it was before the land had taken the shape we know to travel.

So long ago! And Merlin was so young then. But Merlin would have loved her sooner if he could. Not that he could—he never could, before that day. It was the day after the catastrophe at Dunmeller, the day after, when the world had broken Merlin like a bird cast from the sky. Because of what he'd suffered, Merlin was a different sort of person than he'd been till then.

Maybe that's why, when the Queen of the Dunmeller Fairies found him, it was love between them, almost from the first.

He met her in the wilderness at the south edge of the Caledon wood, which is the space between two spells as much as it is any place. The green things all around them parted there in the twilight, and they blinked at one another, half-surprised, the Fairy Queen and the then-youthful mage.

"I never knew," young Merlin said, his voice a mystery bent toward surprise.

The Queen of Night in Caledon smiled at him, hungry but uncertain.

"I knew that you were there," she said. "But I never could have found you if I'd meant to."

Merlin stepped away, almost as if to cloak himself among the branches.

It's a known fact that no man ever meets a fairy by accident, nor even by any purpose of his own. When a body
meets a fairy in the woods, it happens because the fairy
meant it should—but all of that is true of half-mannish
men like Merlin, too. The fact that those two met under
any circumstance at all meant that the fates had twisted
them around one another aforethought, maliciously or worse.

The fact that they tied them together on that day, with
Merlin broken deep inside and before he'd had the time to
heal—that meant they had a special destiny for him, a destiny that no man could renounce or deny.

"My Queen," Merlin said, kneeling. "I live to serve you."

The Queen of Night in Caledon scowled at him.

"Your fealty is a lie, Merlin Emrys. I would not have
you lie to me transparently."

"I would never lie to you," said Merlin, and though he
meant that with all his heart, it was untrue. Men like Merlin are complex creatures, after all; the truth as they see it
metamorphoses as they look upon it. "I would die for you,
my Queen."

That was probably untrue, too, for Merlin had a destiny
to live, and the lives of men with destinies are not their
own to give away. But he meant it when he said it, as much
as he meant any words he ever spoke.

The Fairy Queen shook her head and smiled patiently.
After a moment she took Merlin's hand and led him into
the dusk.

They walked together for an hour, not speaking. There
was no need for words between them—not so much because there was nothing they could say as because there
was no need for either of them to give voice to any of those
things.

Then she led him to her moon pool, and showed him
what he was.

"You are a destiny, my love," she said. "Greatness waits
for you to touch the world."

The wizard had already taken his name, then, but in that
moment he nearly stepped away from it.

"Stars and darkness," he said. "I can't be Merlin."

The Fairy Queen regarded him impatiently.

"I have no spells," he lied.

"You need no spells. Listen, Merlin—you could kill him with a glance," she said. "If you look into the nerves and veins that bind a man's head to his shoulders, you could behead him with a whisper. The bodies sing to you; the lines inside us are the lines that bind us all together, that mind everything together. A spell is not a ritual, but a word that whispers in our bones."

"Perhaps," the wizard said, for he had a sense about these things—it was in his blood, even then, when he was still untutored.

"I have murdered with my smile."

"I never would," the mage responded. "It isn't in me, not at all."

The Fairy Queen gave a little laugh.

"The day will come," she said. "It will be."

"Never," said the mage. "I never will."

The Fairy Queen scowled.

"Too soon," she said. "Too soon, your innocence will vanish on the wind."

Merlin laughed, because he knew he was transparent. "If I could have lied well, I would have made my fortune long ago."

"You need make no fortune," the Queen replied, "for you are fortune itself. You will be the treasure of a king." She smiled at him hungrily. "And you are my treasure now."

"I know," the wizard said, relaxing his reluctance, his pretense. "My gifts frighten me. I would turn away from them."

"You've thrown your life away for them, and now you contemplate renouncing them? You are an odd man, Merlin."

"Perhaps," the wizard said. "Perhaps that is my blessing and my curse."

The Queen gave a little laugh. "Kiss me," she said. It

wasn't a request, or a demand—it was the nature of the moment, overwhelming both of them as if it were a whirlwind.

Merlin wasn't one to fight the wind—no fool he—but he resisted that one, all the same. "It isn't right," he said. Which was no truer than any other honest thing he said that night. "There will be consequences."

The Fairy Queen looked up from the pool to meet the wizard's eye. "The Woodland King abandoned me an age ago, or more," she said. "But, yes, that much is true: if he should find us here and look into our hearts, he will have both our hides to hang as tapestries."

Merlin frowned. "Are you afraid?" he asked. "Should I be afraid?"

The Queen of Night in Caledon laughed. "Of course there will be consequences," she said. "But we never could avoid them. The fates do not bring those like you and I together without intent."

"Malicious intent," the wizard said.

And then, finally, he kissed her.

When he looked back on that night, the mage was never certain how he ended up in the Lady's chambers; he had little more recollection of how they came to make love. What he could remember clearly was dinner; it was a terse dinner, not scant, not scant at all—but it wasn't a feast, just a fine thin meal that left him fed but wanting more, much more. That was her nature, wasn't it? To leave him always in a state of want. Dinner, then hours by the fire—idle conversation, mostly. But after that, his memories were fragmented, as of a drunken stupor, no matter how they drank no wine.

In the morning he had clear memories of sitting on a broad chest at the foot of her bed, talking to her as she nestled in the pillows with her knees drawn toward her breasts. And he remembered moments maybe three quarters of an hour later—in the throes of passion, and how she stared into his eyes, a thing like shock and part oblivion as she stared at him, gaped, almost, and he knew that he'd been seen in the deep heart where he lived.

He never could recall a zenith of the act, but there was a sense in him of that moment, a powerful and abiding sense, as if it were a thing that had leached away the evening and left him only fragments of the man he'd meant to be.

Or made him into a thing he'd never meant to be.

There were repercussions in the morning.

Of course.

It isn't natural, the thing that happened between those two, and even if it was fated and ordained and scribbled in quicksilver light among the stars, it was still an offense against the natural order of all things upon the world.

"Tell me everything you know," said his Lady of the Morning, burrowing close to him beneath the bedclothes. "I want to hear it all, every moment of it, all of it."

Merlin snorted as he nestled into her arms. "I bet you'd like to know," he said. "I'll never tell. Ha!" And then he laughed and laughed and laughed.

The Queen put a finger under his chin and turned his head up till he looked her in the eye. She gaped at him with the strangest mix of hurt and indignation. "How can you deny me?" she asked. "I keep no secrets from you— nothing."

Merlin frowned. "You love what I am as much as you love me," he said. "And a Wizard is a thing made out of secrets. How could I tell you all the mysteries and still be true to you?"

And then the Queen laughed, because there were and are mysteries about her, and there always would be.

Mystery was in her nature, after all; far more than in the wizard's.

They took a breath, and then another, settling into the

mild warmth of morning love—till something rattled at the door, and the Woodland King's harbinger burst into the chamber.

"All rise for the coming of the King," he announced—no, he almost said those words. He would have said them if he'd had another moment. But he didn't have it, not so much as a breath—he burst in announcing and unannounced, and the wizard Merlin . . . *looked* at him. Looked into him, the way his lover had described the night before. Looked at the bones and sinews and vessels knit like delicate living laces in his neck—and in his startlement, in his pique, enraged at the intrusion, the wizard unbound the laces of the herald's throat.

And as the fairy herald began to speak, he died.

An instant later his head rolled gracelessly from his shoulders, across the carpet; when it came to rest at the foot of the Fairy Queen's bed, the eyes blinked three times, gaping, and then they closed.

His lips moved, mouthing words, for a pair of moments longer; but neither Merlin nor the Queen cared enough about him to wonder what he might be on about.

"Bother," said the Queen.

Give young Merlin this much, anyway: the harbinger died quickly. That much was a mercy.

"Fairy blood, damn it," Merlin said, covering his nose with the palm of his hand. "Oh, God, the stink."

It's a known fact that fairy blood reeks all to hell, and stains worse than henna; the very worst of the Wicked Fairies of Erin dye their hair with the blood of their own slaughtered children.

"Hide yourself, my love," the Queen said.

Merlin raised an eyebrow at her. He bridled in his heart, but he did not say a word.

"The King will be here in a moment. He will try to kill you if he sees you. I do not want your death—or his."

Merlin did not want to heed her. But she was his love, and these were her chambers; if nothing else, she had a right to keep her boudoir free of further reeking bloodshed.

So he hid himself among the linens in the closet, and listened as the Woodland King thundered uninvited into his estranged wife's chambers.

"Where is he?" the King demanded, bellowing. "I smell him, the hellspawned man. He's been here with you, demimondaine."

The Queen laughed an angry and resentful laugh. "I am hardly your demimondaine," she said. "We have not been lovers in an age, and if either of us lives kept above his station, it is not me."

The Woodland King blinked, and blinked again. Perhaps he missed the gibe; perhaps he had the sense to ignore it.

"My herald lies dead in your chambers," he said. "You will pay his wergild, or I will take the price of it from you."

Merlin shifted angrily in the closet, but he kept his peace.

"He burst upon me unexpected and unwelcome," she said. "I killed him before I knew what he was about."

The King scowled. "He was my creature. He went where I directed him—and your chamber's mine by right. You do recall that, don't you?"

The Queen grew angry. For a long moment, the room seemed about to burst from angry silence.

"He was not welcome, Rhys. You are not welcome either."

The King shrugged.

"Mine by right," he said. "I walk where I please."

And then, finally the Queen *did* rage. She rose from her bed in all her naked glory, furious and trembling. Walked toward the Woodland King, glowering.

"Be gone, Rhys," she said, "or I will make you leave."

The King trembled and he fumed, but in the end he knew who the Queen was, and he did not dare to challenge her.

And left without another word, skulking toward the woodland shadows like a cur that turns tail as it makes to leave.

The Queen stood naked and threatening in her doorway all the while that he went. Watching because she knew that he was going to make his threat, and she knew that she should hear it.

And she was right.

Because the King did stop at the edge of the wood, and turn to her, and shout.

"I know the hell-spawned man is yours," he said. "And I know he killed my crier. I will kill him for it, I swear to you I will."

The Queen listened to his threat. And looked him in the eye, and nodded.

And whispered under her breath. "No," she said, so faintly Merlin hardly heard her from where he stood just inches sinister, emerging from the closet. "If you try to touch him, it is you who will die."

And then the Woodland King vanished into the woods, still skulking like a cur that had its tail between its legs.

"You honor me when you say you'd kill to save me," Merlin said later, as they wandered the fairy groves, picking and nibbling at the star-crossed yield. "But you dare not, my love. Everything you own is forfeit if you become a regicide."

The Fairy Queen shrugged. "None of this is dear to me," she said. "You are precious beyond all measure."

Merlin (who was wise then, well before his years) shook his head. "You say that now," he said. "And I do not doubt your love, for I can see into your heart. But these are the first moments of our lives, and the day will come when you will prize your heritage again. Do not relinquish it for me. I can see after myself."

The Queen smiled indulgently, but she never paid him any mind till later, when it was too late.

* * *

On the third day Merlin woke with sad conviction, and knew that it was time to tell the Queen he had to go.

"Obligations call me," he said. "I will return to you."

The Queen gaped at him, stunned for the longest moment. And then she pursed her lips. And spoke.

"Do not abandon me, Emrys," she said. "Never ever leave."

Merlin winced. "The world makes demands of me in ways I can't ignore," he said. "You know it does."

The Queen frowned; her lower lip trembled. For a moment, just that long, she was neither a Queen nor a fairy of great dominion, but an ordinary woman, a little girl, almost, on the verge of heartbreak.

"Kiss me, love," she said. "And hurry back to me."

The wizard took his leave that very hour, without a meal or more than a lingering good-bye.

He didn't get far. Near the edge of the Caledon wood a robin whispered to him, and the wizard turned to listen just in time to thwart a silver arrow that would have pierced his skull.

"Damn you," the Woodland King bellowed. "Damn your hellborn hide, Merlin Emrys."

Merlin smiled at the robin, and wished a Grace upon it. Then he turned to face the blood-mad king thundering toward him through the forest.

"The trees entwine you," Merlin said, and indeed they did—the trees themselves turned upon the King of the Glen, their branches stretching to grasp and enfold him.

But they made no menace upon him. For he was King of the Glen, after all, and the spells that Merlin cast upon those trees hardly could contain him for a moment.

"The air contains you," Merlin said. And he whispered to the air, and it grew dense as stone around the King, hard as soil in the deep heart of the cliff.

The Woodland King only laughed.

"I am the master of this breeze," he said, and puffed breath great as a gale, till now the trees shook with it, and Merlin nearly lost his balance. The King rode toward him on the crest of the breeze, carried by the same air that Merlin had commanded only a moment before.

"The stones confound you," Merlin said, unruffled. "The earth itself devours you."

And that was the mightiest spell Merlin knew when he was that young, the spell that brings our graves up from the dirt to consume us.

But it did no good.

It didn't matter what Merlin did because the air had hold of the King, and it carried him across the glen, till now he overwhelmed the mage with the force of his weight and his anger. The big fairy (and he was an enormous fairy, a mannish creature hulking as a mountaineer) slammed into the mage, shoulder to his breastbone, and the two went tumbling across the forest floor.

"I'll grind your bones for bread, I swear I will," the Woodland King said as he wrapped his hands around the wizard's neck. "I will slaughter you and feed you to my dogs."

And then he smiled, wide as the crescent moon.

Leaned close to Merlin, to look him in the eye and gloat, silent and sardonic.

Forced the wizard's skull back and back and farther back, into the dirt—baring Merlin's neck.

"Your last breath is mine," said the Woodland King.

And then he bent touching close, and began to tear the wizard's throat open with his teeth.

Merlin struggled desperately to free himself, but it did no good; the Woodland King had hold of him, and pinned him like a crude and feckless lover; as he held the wizard, he bound him like an ardent paramour.

And the wizard closed his eyes, shuddering and degraded, welcoming his end.

Opened his heart to death as the Woodland King's teeth opened the flesh of his throat.

* * *

But only for a moment, as now the Woodland King's fetid kiss drew to an end—and now the big fairy's head rolled away from him, and there was light again—

"Murder me, damn you," Merlin whispered. "Be done with it."

There was no struggle left in him.

"You never looked into his heart, my love," a voice said, and when he heard that voice the wizard trembled with shame. "You could have torn him bit from bit if you had whispered to his bones."

Viviane!

As the Woodland King's head rolled farther and now farther away from him, and Merlin blinked three times to see it was set loose from his shoulders, severed cleanly and almost bloodlessly.

As she pushed the King's carcass off the wizard, Merlin saw Viviane was—*smiling.*

"And now I am a regicide," she said. "Everything I know is forfeit."

The wizard put a hand to his throat and charmed his thin wound closed.

Merlin ached for her, for even then he knew her heart, and knew that the life she'd loved was dear to her.

"Then come with me, and be my love," he said. "And we will walk the world together."

The Fairy Queen smiled at him, touched. And then she shook her head. "I never could," she said. "My path takes its own course, as does your own."

"Stay with me," the wizard insisted. "I love you with my soul."

And then the Fairy Queen smiled, and was gone.

But we all know that they saw one another many times again. The things that bound them bound them always, across the years and miles; they bind them still, some say, for Merlin and his Lady of the Lake both are long of years. When the wizard served the great King Arthur, she aided him from afar; when he left the great king's service, to sleep within the mountain, she tended to him there.

And when Merlin came up from his mountain deeps to rule the land as the Wizard King of England, she ruled beside him.

And who knows? There are those who say they rule us still, within our hearts. And perhaps they always will.

WAITING FOR TOMORROW

by Marc Bilgrey

Marc Bilgrey has writen for television, magazines and comedians. His short stories have appeared in numerous anthologies including *Phantoms of the Night, First Contact,* and *Cat Crimes Through Time.*

AFTER Nimuë, I swore I would never love again. But the centuries have been harsh and lonely and what is an oath made to one's self if not to be broken?

It was the spring of 1160, Henry II of the House of Plantagenet was now king. I was a traveling bard telling tales in the marketplace of a small northern city when I saw her. She was standing in the crowd watching my performance. After I concluded my stories and collected my hat, I approached her. She was fair of skin with flaxen hair, sparkling blue eyes, and a smile that reminded me of Nimuë.

Her name was Sarah, and she was a baker's daughter. She said she was so awed by my vivid tales of brave knights and long ago chivalry, it seemed almost as though I had lived through it myself. I told her if I had, it would mean that I was over five hundred years old. She smiled, then we conversed for a few moments about life in her city.

Thus it began for us. I stayed at a publick house and we met afternoons in the hills beyond the city walls. She

brought me fresh bread, and we talked. Of course, I told
her little of myself. As far as she was concerned, I was a
roving storyteller. I listened as she spoke of her family and
friends. All the while, I thought I should leave, not just for
her sake but for mine. I had no wish to inflict pain on anyone, but my mortal side lost each battle and I could not
bring myself to depart.

Weeks became months. I met her parents and siblings
and then, eventually, I asked Sarah to become my wife. She
consented, we were wed, and I accepted a position at the
local apothecary mixing and dispensing herbs and potions.

After so many centuries of wandering I found joy in the
simple pleasures of daily life. Quiet evenings alone with
Sarah, meetings with neighbors, and dinners with Sarah's
family. To watch Sarah at her wheel, spinning, an expression of complete contentment on her face, brought me a
peace I had not known before.

But despite my bliss, the years rushed by. Along the
way, I had somehow been able to convince myself that all
would remain as it was, simply because I would have
wished it so. Since I grew no older, I began to color my
hair and beard with a white pigment and affected a slower
walk. Nevertheless, I was always concerned that I would
be discovered. In fact, I was so absorbed in maintaining
my disguise that I paid scant attention to the actual aging
that went on around me.

But one day, the truth became impossible to ignore.
Sarah was at the hearth preparing the afternoon meal. It
was a stew made of venison she had purchased at the
marketplace and vegetables from our garden. She had just
added some beets to the pot and was stirring the contents
when she cried out.

"What is wrong, Sarah?" I inquired.

She grasped her right hand and said, "My fingers are not
as nimble as they once were."

"But what facilitated this pain?"

She smiled ruefully and said, "Old age, Husband. Surely

you have felt its effects yourself. The occasional twinge in the back or feet or hands."

"Of course," I said, though I had felt nothing of the sort.

She looked at me and smiled again, then said, "Well, now, talk will not cook this stew, will it?" She returned to the pot and continued stirring as I was left to ponder what she'd said.

Some years later, after a long and healthy life, Sarah took to her bed and I, standing by her side, held her hand. In the waning moments we pledged our love to each other and I thanked her for all the gentleness and devotion she had given to me. When the end came, I closed her eyes and quietly wept.

I had not cried since my Nimuë had been taken from me. At Sarah's funeral, in addition to the sadness, I also felt a great loneliness come over me.

Shortly after Sarah's passing, I left the city. I could not bear to be surrounded by reminders of our life together. I also knew that, as the children of friends and neighbors grew older, there would inevitably come the question I could not answer. How is it that others die but you live on?

On the old Roman road that led out of the city, I wondered, as I had many times before, why I had been given eternal life. And I even thought fleetingly whether I had the power to snuff that life out. But then, I reminded myself, there were greater issues at stake than my own personal well-being. I had a mission, a fact that emotion could easily obscure. My day-to-day comfort was unimportant. All that mattered was that I prevailed, so that when the time came, I would be there and ready.

The decades flew by like leaves in a cold autumn wind. Another century came and went. I tried many occupations and many names. My travels led me throughout Britain, and I took care not to linger in one place too long.

Memories of Nimuë and now Sarah sustained me. I also thought of the happier times in Arthur's court and the long afternoons when the sun would bathe Camelot in a pure golden light.

More years trickled past. The black plague claimed almost half of Europe. Forbidden to interfere in the fate of humanity in any way that would significantly alter its destiny, I stood by helplessly and watched the bodies being heaped upon ox carts and taken to be burned.

Kings and queens ascended the throne. The New World was discovered and explored. One day I found myself in the city of Bristol. I was now an itinerant peddler of cutlery, my wares contained in a rucksack on my back. A friendly shopkeeper suggested a possible sales prospect, directing me to a nearby house. There I was greeted by an auburn-haired woman named Catherine, who allowed me to enter her domicile. As she examined the various knives and spoons in my possession, she spoke of being a childless widow and the difficulties of taking in tenants. Catherine had been thrust into the position by her husband's death. Previous to that, he had seen to the repairs and collected the rents.

As she continued speaking, I looked into her eyes and once again saw my sweet Nimuë. It had now been ten centuries since she had been taken from me and over three had passed since losing Sarah. Once again, I felt the pull of my mortal feelings. The beauty of this woman's countenance, as well as her obvious intellect and strength of character seemed to light the chamber as a dozen candles could not.

After Catherine had purchased a number of my articles of cutlery, I asked her if she had a vacancy in her rooms. She smiled and said that one would become available in a fortnight. We agreed on terms, and on the appointed day I took possession.

In the months that followed, Catherine and I became acquainted. Long talks led to outings by the water as we watched the cod fishing boats. And then to plays at the Guild Hall.

As I had done with Sarah before her, I made no mention of my actual past, choosing instead to fabricate one. Catherine accepted my invented background without question. As far as she was concerned, I was John Cornwall, son of a sailor, family deceased.

She came from a line of weavers, some of whom were still active. One year after our meeting, Catherine and I announced our engagement. The following year we wed.

I was pleased to have companionship again and to know the affections of a woman. Soon, my caring for her grew into a very deep love. Though I knew my time with her would be limited, I was determined to savor every moment.

All our waking hours were spent together. Though I had taken over the administration of the house, she was always by my side. Whether at the marketplace or church, or on festival days, we were inseparable.

Queen Elizabeth was on the throne with no signs of relinquishing her power, despite unsuccessful attempts to usurp her. With a strong monarch I was freed from daily concern and my mission's objective relegated to the future.

During the many years since Sarah's death, I had begun to think that as much as we'd loved each other, there was one element which had been missing and that was honesty. I had never told her who I was, a decision I had grown to regret. How much happier might we have been had I not constantly needed to be on my guard for fear of exposure? I now saw the opportunity to have an even more tranquil existence with Catherine, free from the constant worry of discovery.

I resolved to tell Catherine the truth about myself. The day came. We had just eaten dinner together when I said, "Catherine, I have something important to discuss with you."

"What wilt thou tell me, my dear husband?"

"It concerns what I have told you regarding my family."

"Your family is dead, you have said."

"We love each other, do we not?"

"Very much, Husband."

"I can no longer deceive you, then. I am not what I

appear to be. All I have told you concerning my lineage is false."

"You are not the son of a sailor from the port city of—"

"All lies."

"Then who are you and where *are* you from? And why the deception?"

"As a form of self-protection and to shield you."

"From what do you feel the need to shield me, John?"

"Perhaps that would be the place to start. My name is not John, it is Merlin."

"Merlin, as in King Arthur's Merlin?" she said, smiling.

"Yes, exactly. You see, I *am* Merlin, not merely his namesake."

"Merlin, if indeed he did exist, lived centuries ago."

"Ten, to be exact. Yes, I have already outlived Methuselah."

Catherine smiled once more. "This is a jest of yours, a joke, perhaps recited from a play?"

"No, I am quite serious. King Arthur is my liege, I bow to no other. I lived in Camelot, I served in the same court as the Knights of the Round Table. I am Merlin, born of no human father. I am counselor and wizard, living in secret amongst humans till I am needed once more."

"You are ill, my husband. You have taken leave of your senses. In the morning we must bring you to a healer."

I stood up and looked at her. "I did not realize that I would be so easily dismissed by you, my dear Catherine. I must therefore resort to a vulgar display of theatrics to prove my claims."

Catherine stared at me, transfixed, as I held out my hands. Her eyes widened when glowing spheres of light appeared in my palms. I directed the spheres under a nearby chair. The spheres picked up the chair, floated it to the ceiling then gently brought it back to the floor as the lights vanished.

"What say you now, Catherine?"

With that, she grasped her bosom and fainted.

Upon my reviving her, Catherine regained her faculties and said, "How did you create this wondrous magic?"

"I harness the energy of the cosmos with my mind, and it is this power which flows through my fingers. The spheres you saw were merely the manifestation of that energy." I feared that many of my attempts to elucidate only served to confuse, but, having placed myself in the position of confessor, I was determined to see it through.

"Are you, then, all powerful?" asked Catherine.

"I am not," I replied, "though, through the centuries my abilities have often been exaggerated by folktales. I am not omnipotent, as some have portrayed me, a deity who walks among men. Unfortunately, while I am capable of many extraordinary feats, there is also much I cannot do. It is true that there are some injuries I can heal: broken bones and wounds, but I cannot cure disease, raise the dead, or bring rain to parched land."

Over the days that followed, after a thousand more questions and despite her initial shock, doubt, and misgivings, she came to accept all I told her, proving what I had surmised, which was that she was a most extraordinary woman.

Admonishing her to never repeat any of our conversation to anyone, we went about the business of daily life, attempting to live as we had before. Indeed, little appeared to change. There were still the usual problems with our tenants, church activities, community meetings, and all that comes with mortal living.

Some months after I had taken Catherine into my confidence, our first wedding anniversary approached. It was my wish to honor my wife with a gift befitting my love for her. I had heard of a jeweler in London who had recently come into the possession of a small shipment of exquisite silver necklaces. Concocting a story about a business trip to see about purchasing new building materials to make improvements on our house, I left immediately for London.

Though my steed was swift, the journey took a number

of days longer than I had anticipated owing to inclement weather. Once in London, I procured a necklace and set about making the return trip. Taking care to avoid highwaymen, I found night lodgings at a succession of roadside inns, one less hospitable than the next.

Upon my return to Bristol, I rode through the streets, greeting a number of neighbors, but all avoided my gaze. Puzzled, I reached my home, dismounted, and ran inside. Catherine was nowhere to be found. Perhaps she had gone to visit one of her relatives, I thought. As the sun had already started its descent, I was at a loss to explain her absence. I left the building, deciding to stable my mount, when William, one of our tenants, approached me in an obviously agitated state.

"John," he said, speaking in a low voice, "you have always treated me fairly, therefore, I shall give you warning."

"Warning?"

"Yes, your secret is known. Your wife spoke it to a friend during your absence. The friend told others."

"What secret?" I said, though I now knew what would follow.

"That you are a warlock. They intend to do to you what they did to her."

I grabbed William by his neck and demanded, "What has been done to my Catherine?"

She was knifed and stoned by townsmen. I wanted no part of it myself. I said, 'If she is a witch there should be a trial—' "

"They—they killed her?"

"A week ago yesterday, but take heed, they have been awaiting your return. They come for you now."

"Who are these men that murdered her?" I said through clenched teeth.

"There were many, they—"

But before he could finish speaking, I heard agitated voices. I turned to see a group of men approaching, carrying torches.

"There he is," said one. "There's the witch."

For an instant I considered unleashing my fury upon them, but I was outnumbered and had no way of knowing which ones had actually participated in Catherine's murder. Self-preservation seemed in order. Certainly, reasoning with such a mob was without point.

I turned and ran down the narrow street and into an alleyway. Standing in the shadows, I cast a simple spell of illusion, creating a dense fog. Then I went east and briskly walked out of town.

In the ensuing years, after a discreet but thorough investigation, I made certain each man who had taken part in Catherine's death met his own untimely reward. But this did nothing to assuage my own pain or guilt. Had I not felt compelled to bare my soul to her, Catherine would not have died. I was as responsible for her murder as if I had driven in the fatal blade or cast the lethal stone myself.

The years that followed were dark and solemn. I brooded no end upon Catherine's memory, reliving the short but happy times we'd had together. Then reliving, too, the sorrow of her loss and my part in the tragedy.

The decades passed as if on a turtle's back. The Stuarts ascended the throne. Colonies sprang up in the New World, wars, inventions. I paid it all no mind, so preoccupied with guilt was I. Then, as the pages fell from the calendar, I gradually came to realize that the pain would always be with me, but to dwell upon it to the exclusion of all else accomplished nothing.

Another century brought weariness in mind and spirit, but my wandering did not cease. As I had done previously, I took care not to tarry in any one place longer than ten or twenty years. I established no friends and kept to myself as much as I could.

The next century brought Wellington's defeat of Napoleon, the steam engine, and George III to the throne. By mid-century, I was in London and employed as a clerk in a bookseller's shop. It was during this time, in the flower of Her Majesty Queen Victoria's reign, that I had, I felt, come

to terms with my existence. Some are meant to be surrounded by friends and family, I reasoned, while others
must forgo these in favor of a solitary life of service. Re-
signed to this outlook, I was, needless to say, quite taken
aback when, one day, while arranging some volumes of
poetry in the shop, the door was opened by a woman who
resembled Sarah. Noticing my dumbfounded expression,
the woman approached and inquired as to my health.

After I assured her that I was quite sound, she said she
was looking for a history book. Knowing something about
the subject, I had no trouble locating a suitable book for
her. I told her that most such books are not very accurate.
This led to a discussion of a few of the events of the last
century. Afterward, I asked her how she came to be interested in such things. She then told me that she was the
private tutor for the child of a wealthy businessman.

She purchased the volume I had suggested (her em-
ployer had an account at the shop and encouraged her to
see to books for the child.) Before she exited, I inquired as
to her name.

"Beatrice," she replied, and then she was gone.

Though at that moment I assumed I would not see her
again, I found my thoughts drifting back to her over the
ensuing days. Not that I had any intention of acting upon
them, even if I, by chance, did happen upon her again.
Though much time and distance separated Catherine and
me, the tragedy still lingered in my mind like ashes on a
street urchin's rags. I could not, I felt, in good conscience
risk a similar circumstance with another mortal. But then I
felt the weight of the years upon me and the endless loneliness of the hours.

Walking through the gaslit streets one evening, on the
way to my flat, I attempted to place my emotions aside and
consider the facts. Other than Nimuë, there had been only
two mortal women, each separated by great intervals. One
had lived, by human standards, a long life and had died
naturally. The other had lived but a brief time, and had

died due to my carelessness. I had found some measure of happiness before. Perhaps, if I did not repeat my previous indiscretion, should the opportunity present itself once more, I could find happiness again.

This was a radical idea, I decided, but no more so than carrying the pain and anguish of two hundred years. It was another age. Is one obligated to wear the black armband through all eternity?

A few weeks later, I was still pondering these questions when Beatrice once again entered the shop. She was now seeking a science book for her young charge. As I searched the shelves for a suitable text, we conversed anew. Again I felt that indefinable attraction that poets have been trying to describe since the dawn of civilization.

Before she left the shop, I asked if I could call upon her. She answered in the affirmative and we agreed on an afternoon the following week.

The appointed day arrived. We dined at a fashionable restaurant and she told me of her life. She was an orphan, and had, previous to her present position, been retained at a millinery establishment. Through a friend, she had received a letter of introduction which had led to her current situation. Beatrice was unmarried and had no suitor. As she relayed more details of her life, I gazed upon her beautiful features and her shiny brunette hair which was piled upon her head and fastened by a bright ribbon.

That first outing was followed by others. Usually we would dine at a restaurant and then, depending on the weather, take walks in the park. Often we would go to the theater. As we saw more of each other, my affection for her grew. Gradually, we spoke of the future. Then one morning we took a train to the country and eloped. Beatrice moved into my flat where, for six years, all went well. As far as she was concerned, I was, as she, an orphan. I never spoke of my past unless asked, and then, I would give imaginary details. Once again, I knew contentment and the love of another.

One night, as we were returning from a play at the Haymarket Theater, Beatrice noticed an infant crawling out of a fourth-story window.

"That baby will be killed!" she cried.

And indeed she was correct. No sooner had she spoken those very words when the child tumbled from the ledge and hurtled through the air.

Without thought to the consequences, except to save the baby's life, I raised my arms and sent four glowing spheres to stop the child's descent. The spheres slowly brought the infant back up to the window out of which he had crawled, sent him inside, and quickly shut the window.

After I had done this, I turned to Beatrice, but it was too late. She had witnessed all of it. Without a word she ran from me. I followed her back to our flat, lit the evening candles, and attempted to remedy the situation. But none of my words elicited any response from her other than a shortness of breath and tears. This continued far into the night. I told her I was an amateur magician, then a mesmerist capable of inducing the mind to believe suggestions I had placed there. No explanation would quell her hysterical behavior. By morning, she had slept only briefly and each time had been awakened, apparently by nightmares.

Now staring straight ahead and muttering incoherently, she refused to leave her bed and stayed there for three days and nights. I recited ancient incantations over Beatrice till my throat was raw. I mixed healing brews, teas of rare herbs, and made impassioned pleas to the gods, but all my efforts met with failure. On the morning of the fourth day, I found myself much weakened from the effort and no closer to affecting a cure.

Reluctantly, I realized that I had no choice but to summon a physician. Despite my trepidation concerning their methods, I nevertheless hoped that this man could help her. His diagnosis confirmed my worst fears. "This woman is suffering from a madness unknown to me," he said.

He committed her to Bedlam Hospital where I hoped she would be helped, but my Beatrice did not recover. My visits only seemed to aggravate her condition, sending her scurrying to a corner where she cowered in fear. Eventually, the doctors asked me not to return. Words could not express the depth of my sorrow. Some years later, Beatrice died, institutionalized till the end.

What can be done when the sadnesses mount like storm clouds in a night sky? Having no reason to remain, I left London and took to the roads once more. If only the scenery could have alleviated the pain in my heart, but it did not. I moved from one location to another as if in waking slumber, the changing decades and the new century arriving almost unnoticed.

One day, in the waning years of the twentieth century, I found myself by the sea in Brighton. I sat on a bench watching the waves. So lost in thought was I, that I barely perceived someone sitting down next to me.

"Beautiful day, isn't it," said a female voice.

"Yes," I said, "quite beautiful." Then I turned and saw whom I was addressing. This woman who sat directly to my right was the *exact* double of my long-lost Nimuë. She did not merely resemble her, she could pass as her twin. My mouth went dry. Nimuë. For almost fourteen hundred years I had held her memory in my soul. She still haunted my dreams as we ran together in Avalon. How many times had I offered to make bargains with the gods for the chance to once again hear her speak a few words or touch her hand?

"Are you here on holiday?" asked the woman.

"No," I said. And I thought about my mission, to await and assist the return of the once and future king. Then I stood up and said, "There will be no more holidays for me." As I began walking, I thought I heard a coronet blare, but it was only a ship sounding its horn as it sailed into the distance.

CENTRAL PARK

by Bradley H. Sinor

Bradley H. Sinor has seen his work appear in the *Merovingen Nights* anthologies, *Time of the Vampires, Lord of the Fantastic,* and other places. He lives in Oklahoma with his wife Sue and three strange cats.

THE desk clerk at his hotel had given Anthony Zane a worried look after hearing that Zane was going for a walk in Central Park. It was two A.M., and that was definitely not the sort of behavior that visitors to New York were encouraged to practice.

"This might not be a particularly safe thing for you to do. Perhaps you might want to wait until morning," said the desk clerk.

"No. But thank you for your concern," Zane said. "I can take care of myself."

"Whatever you say, sir."

As he walked away from the check-in desk, Zane couldn't help but smile when he overheard a single, muttered word from the clerk.

"Tourist."

Personal safety hadn't been a worry for Anthony Zane in a very long time. Not that he felt any need for weapons, but fourteen hundred years as a soldier made him prefer to err on the side of caution. Tonight, a 9 mm Browning rode in a specially made shoulder holster under his jacket and a tempered steel knife lay hidden in a wrist sheath on his left arm. It didn't hurt to take precautions.

He had barely crossed the boundaries of the park when he noticed a group of shadowy figures in the distance. For perhaps five minutes they followed him, but then moved back into the darkness in search of easier prey.

Zane drew out his pipe, filled with a new blend he had purchased from the tobacconist this afternoon, and fired it up using an old-fashioned wooden match. Once he was happy with the way the mixture was burning, he carefully stubbed out the blackened end of the match and dropped it into his pocket.

Standing in the center of a small stone bridge in the southwestern part of the park he could look out over a small stream, at a grassy knoll at the far end of the bridge, and up at the moon, letting the sounds of the city fade, if only for a moment, into a distant murmur.

"It certainly isn't Camelot, but it does sort of remind me of that little stream about ten miles or so into the woods, near the waterfall."

"Oh, Lance, this place is just so lovely. It makes me want to stay here forever and listen to the sound of the stream and the birds."

Lancelot looked down at the face resting against his shoulder. He gingerly reached up and touched her cheek. The resulting smile sent a feeling of calm through him.

"Ginnie, I'm afraid if we tried to do that, there would be a squad of knights out scouring the forest in a matter of hours," he said.

"But how would they know where to look? We could lose ourselves here, forget politics, forget wars, just make a life for ourselves."

"Ginnie, oh, my Ginnie, if only we could. But you and I

*both know that is impossible. Neither of us was raised that
way. I know my best friend. If we are gone too long, he will
have a squad of lancers out searching for us, probably
convinced that we have been murdered by bandits or taken
for ransom by some rival."*

*"I suppose so. Arthur does tend to look on the gloomy
side of things at times. But, for a few hours, before we have
to go back, and I admit we do have to go back, let's just
live for ourselves," she said.*

*Very slowly Ginnie began to loosen the cords that held
her blouse in place.*

Zane knew that voice.

That he hadn't heard the speaker's approach didn't surprise him in the least. He just looked to his left, and the
man was standing there. The stranger was short, barely
coming to Zane's shoulder; his iron-gray hair was neatly
coiffed, a silver-headed walking stick was in his hand, and
his clothing, though simple, had an elegant cut and an expensive air.

"Good evening, Merlin," said Zane. "As I recall, Old
Crow, you were either ensconced in your tower or the cata-
combs or en route to a meeting with Arthur during your
tenure at Camelot.

"You never seemed to stop or even have time for a little
bit of fun. So it rather surprises me that you even noticed
the forest, let alone a stream."

"That's what Nimuë was always telling me. She said I
needed to just relax a bit," said Merlin. Memories drifted
across his face, giving birth to a smile that was gone in a
moment. "As if I had the time. I had a kingdom to help
maintain. Not only were there dark forces of magic and
evil abroad, there were political necessities, balancing acts
to be walked between petty rulers, deals to be struck that
would buy us a year or a month or even just a few days
more of peace.

"Even so, I did manage to steal a few hours when I tried not to let my mind linger on the next thing on the kingdom's agenda, but on Nimuë instead."

"Indeed?" said Zane.

"Oh, my dear Lancelot. There is a lot more to me than you've ever suspected."

It had been almost a century since anyone had addressed him by the name he had been born with, Lancelot du Lac.

"How, otherwise, fourteen hundred years after the fall of Camelot, would I be standing here talking with you? In those days, had anyone suggested it, I would probably have accused them of being quite far gone in their cups," said Zane.

"Of course, Lancelot du Lac was known to bend his elbow with the best of them," said Merlin. "As have many other men, whose shoes you have walked in, down through the years. Or perhaps I should be addressing you by the name that you go by now. What is it?"

"As if you didn't know."

"Indulge me, Lancelot."

"Zane. Anthony Zane."

"How many names have you worn over the years? How many lives have you led?"

Zane sighed; it was his time to remember as dozens of names, some his, some belonging to people he had known, now long dead, ran through his mind.

"Too many, I think, perhaps as many as you," he said. "After a while, one loses track. All of the names, the lives, the people become blurry, distant memories. Much the way Camelot is now, a faint and distant memory of a time when things were better, for me and perhaps for the world. Maybe that's what helps me keep my sanity, if I have any left, that is."

Zane noticed a group of three teenaged boys approaching the bridge. They were dressed in identical jean jackets, with matching bandannas around their heads, no doubt a local gang "uniform." The three paused for a moment, at the end of the bridge, half in and half out of the shadows.

Zane knew predators, or would-be predators, when he saw them. Zane shifted just slightly so he could reach his gun with no problem.

One of the teenagers came toward Merlin and Zane.

"Evening, don't mean to intrude on the time of two fine-looking gentlemen like yourselves" he said.

"Good evening," answered Merlin.

"Gents, let's get right to the point." At that moment the sounds of two switchblades opening came from the others. Zane was fairly sure he could see the handle of a gun shoved into one's belt. "We're collecting for our favorite charity this evening, ourselves. So why don't you two hand over your wallets, any jewelry, cell phones, stock certificates, loose change, you know the drill. Then we'll just leave you two alone and you can get back to making whatever arrangements you were going to, before I so rudely interrupted you."

"I think not," said Merlin.

"I guess we get to have a little fun, cut you up, and still get all the goodies," said one of the other boys.

"I'll handle this," said Zane.

"Unnecessary."

With that word, Merlin came 'round, his walking stick raised, and hit the first teenager hard in the stomach. The young man doubled over in pain. Before the other two could do anything, Merlin sketched two quick gestures in the air. All three of the would-be muggers were frozen in place.

"So what are you going to do now?" asked Zane. "Something creative, I hope, that will leave a lasting impression."

Merlin walked over to each one. First he touched their temples, then placed both his thumbs on their foreheads just above the eyes. Once he had finished with the last, they dropped their weapons and walked slowly off into the darkness.

"So are they going to turn themselves in to the police?"

"Please, Lance, give me credit for more originality than

that. Our young friends will have a strange and eerie tale to tell, about how they barely escaped with their lives from a horrendous monster.

"If the rumor mill, not to mention the local tabloid press, works the way I expect it to, two days from now people will say that there are half a dozen such beasts prowling the park.

"After that our young friends will find themselves drawn to a profession that is more honest and worthwhile, perhaps professional wrestling," he said.

"My compliments, Merlin," said Zane.

"Thank you. Now, getting back to the question of your sanity. You are quite sane, I have no doubt about that. If you weren't, then you wouldn't have any worries about your sanity," said Merlin.

"You're as reassuring as some of the talk shows," replied Zane.

The old magician laughed, pointing in a southwesterly direction. "I think the last time I saw you was not quite a hundred years ago. Just outside of Teddy Roosevelt's office at the Port Authority."

"You still haven't lost your ability to change the subject at the drop of a hat. Besides, Theodore's office was at City Hall, not the Port Authority," said Zane.

"Oh, yes. I suppose it was, wasn't it?"

"So how did you know I was here?" asked Zane.

"I have my ways."

"Come now, Merlin, I've known you far too long to let you get away with a comment like that."

Merlin reached over and touched the heavy ring on Zane's right hand. In its center were two stones, one gray and one amber, wrapped in wire. The amber one began to glow, illuminating three tiny dots of red at the center.

"Let's just say I always know when my work is near," he said.

Zane stared at the ring. He needed no light to see the glow; he rarely needed light to see anything. Three tiny

bits of blood: Arthur's, his own, and Ginnie's; he knew
they were there, where they had been for fourteen hundred
years.

    "Lancelot!"
    *Merlin grabbed Lancelot's sword arm. The French
knight had not even realized a weapon was in his hand.*
    *A dozen steps away stood Arthur Pendragon. In the long
months since Guinevere had fled Camelot, his hair had
grown grayer and the lines in his face deeper. The king's
iron grip held his queen by her arms, even as she struggled
to escape his hands.*
    *Only this was not the beautiful woman who had dazzled
all of Camelot. This woman, her skin white and bloodless,
was snarling like a beast. In the flickering torchlight
Lancelot could see the long canine fangs and the blood
that ran from them, staining her lips and face. . . .*
    *"Lance! Lance! Help me! You've got to help me. Arthur
and Merlin are mad. They want to murder me!"*
    Guinevere.
    The Queen.
    The woman that both Lancelot and Arthur loved.
    *That voice, whispery and sensual, was the same one that
had enchanted him and haunted his memory since the first
day he had arrived at Camelot. He had seen her standing
near a flower-covered lattice, supervising one of the many
gardeners who worked around Camelot, and from that moment Lancelot du Lac had been in love.*
    *"No," said Merlin. "She can never be yours or Arthur's
again. If you truly want to free her, it must be done my way."*
    *Merlin held a sharpened stake of hawthorn wood, three
feet long, in his left hand. Lancelot looked at it, at Ginnie,
and then at his best friend.*
    Arthur nodded.
    Merlin moved toward Guinevere.

★   ★   ★

"You know I wanted to die that night, the night we killed her. And I should have as well. One vampire died that night; killing a second one would have been no problem," he said

"Even after she had ripped your very soul to shreds and made you a creature of the night, you still loved her," said Merlin.

"Of course. One's heart knows little of the real world, of political realities, of dabbling among the shadows and the light. Yes, she made me into a vampire, nosferatu, a blood drinker, a creature of the night. But that doesn't change the way I felt about her, even to the end," said Zane.

"I know, and she would have approved of what I did for her and for you. Thanks to my arts I gave you back the day, and helped to add to the strength within yourself to fight the Beast that consumed her," Merlin said.

"Yes, but why did it have to be with *her* blood?"

"And your own. It was that blood and the love that you had for her, she for you, and Arthur for both of you that gave you back some measure of your humanity."

"Humanity? Was that what it gave me? Or an eternity of punishment, full of recriminations and pain?"

"We had no choice in the matter, Lance, no choice at all. I needed you, Arthur needed you, the kingdom needed you to help hold it together. They needed a hero and that is what you were and are, my friend, a hero, nothing more, nothing less," said Merlin.

"So what did me being this hero get us? The table broken, Camelot fallen, Arthur dead, and every bit of good we had done lost to the winds of history. What did it accomplish? To most people now, Camelot is two hours in a dark room with pretty pictures flashing on the screen, a book of tall tales, or a bunch of people prancing about on the stage singing.

"As for me being a hero? Now, that's a laugh. I fought to

stay alive, to hold the Hunger at bay. I wasn't always that successful. When the Hunger comes over me, it's more beast than soldier that my foes face," said Zane.

"Lancelot, Lancelot, after all these centuries, you still tend to feel sorry for yourself at the drop of a hat," Merlin said. "I suspect that if I could change one thing about you it would be that."

"Lancelot."

The chill that went through Zane was as cold as the grave. It was not the low, familiar voice of Merlin.

He turned toward the figure standing next to him. Merlin was nowhere to be seen. He had been replaced by a tall lean figure dressed in chain mail, a rough woolen cape around his shoulders, a familiar long sword hanging at his side.

Arturius Rex. Arthur Pendragon.

"Remember, as long as you live, no matter where you go, everything that we have believed in, fought for, died for, will continue. As long as you live, Camelot lives."

"My liege, I am not worthy of the trust that you placed in me."

"You are worthy, my brother. You have proved it many times over the years, and will continue to do so."

Then Merlin stood at Zane's side once again. "He knew this road would not be easy for you. That's what made him such a good commander and king for so long."

"But not for long enough," said Zane.

"Lance, we've had this conversation before. Why are you bringing it up again?"

"Maybe because you're the only one around who can understand me, even a little bit, Merlin. After all, how many other people are there walking the streets of New York who have stood on the same piece of land as Richard the Lionheart and The Beatles?

"I've been struggling with the idea that all I've done has been for nothing, that no matter how much trust Arthur had in me, it was for naught. I struggle, and it seems to do no good.

"Plus there is the date. I think the reason I'm so despondent is the date. Fourteen hundred years ago, this very night, I watched you drive a stake through the heart of the woman that I loved."

"You think you're the only one who loved her, Lance? Arthur loved her. It may have been an arranged marriage but he still cared for her. All of the kingdom loved her. I loved her, in my own way, like a daughter," said Merlin.

Before he could say anything else, Merlin looked down at the ground.

"Well, it seems we are not alone," he chuckled.

Standing next to the magician's leg was a gray tiger-striped cat. The animal didn't appear to be afraid. It just stood looking at Zane and Merlin as if expecting to be the center of their universe. Carefully, Merlin reached down and picked up the cat. The animal studied the two men, then began to wiggle itself around until it could shove its head under Merlin's chin and begin to rub.

"I think you've made a new friend," said Zane. "I'm sure you could use one."

Merlin ignored the comment, but did begin to run his hand along the cat's back.

"Lancelot! You have a problem."

"I know that, so be serious, please."

"I'm very serious, young man. You are a young man compared to me, and don't go asking how much older than you I am. You won't get an answer. Look, given everything that has happened to you since you left Joyous Guard, I can understand that you are feeling depressed. Hell, you would be insane if you weren't, and I think we have established your sanity.

"There have been times when I felt the same way. Like you, I have buried friend after friend, watched those I love die, the work of decades crumble away to nothing, wondered why I even bothered.

"I think what you need to bestir you from this blue mood, friend Lancelot, is a quest," said Merlin.

"A quest?"

"Yes! A quest!"

"For what? The Holy Grail? Been there, done that."

"I know, I was the one that suggested to Arthur that you and the rest of the Table be sent to search for it. Besides, you wouldn't need to look far for the Grail. It's in my New Orleans condo, next to one of the bird statue props from *The Maltese Falcon*."

"Then what?"

Merlin didn't say a word. Instead he shoved the cat into Zane's arms. The animal was as startled as Zane. After a moment, it attempted to scramble out of his hands, first by leaping down to the ground, then by sinking its claws into his jacket and scrambling over his shoulder. However, Zane's hands went tight around the cat's body and held it firmly in place.

"There is your quest, Sir Lancelot du Lac!"

"Have you lost all grip on reality, man? What in the hell are you talking about?"

"Your quest is to find this cat's owner and return it to him."

"Yeah, right, some 'quest.' "

"Whoever told you that all quests had to be grand things with lives and the fates of nations balanced on the edge of your blade? Did you not swear an oath to do whatever you could to help not just the greatest but the least of people who were in distress?"

"You know I did," said Zane.

"Well, this cat is too friendly to be a feral animal, so it obviously belongs to some family who are no doubt in distress at its being missing. So there you have your quest. Find that family and help them," he said.

"Why don't you just turn yourself into a cat and escort the animal home? I think that would be much simpler," said Zane.

"Lance, you've read too much T. H. White and seen too many Disney movies. You know that shapechanging was never in my repertoire. So get on with it," he said.

Zane realized that he had begun to gently rub the cat behind its ears. He was about to say something to Merlin when he realized that he and the cat were alone.

"So why don't you tell me where you live?" Zane said to the cat.

A little after ten o'clock the next morning, Zane had a cab drop him on West 35th Street. He knew the area. A few blocks farther on was the office-home of a private detective he had occasionally had dealings with.

From his pocket he produced a small piece of paper with an address written on it. The cat, who rode quietly in the crook of his left arm, watched the whole thing with an air of indifference.

It had not been all that difficult a task to find the cat's owner. Covered by the animal's hair was a rather expensive collar, complete with the name of the pet shop where it had been custom made. Two phone calls and a ride across town had brought Zane and his companion here.

A minute or two after ringing the doorbell, the light on the intercom came on.

"Yes, can I help you?"

"I believe that you folks are missing a cat."

"Lancelot?"

Zane froze at the sound of the name. The door came flying open, a small form barely four feet tall appeared, and the cat leaped toward it.

"You're back! Mommy, Lancelot is back!"

Zane found himself looking at a young girl, about ten years old, with long blonde hair hanging down to her waist. She clutched the cat to her chest like the long-lost member of the family that it was.

"I'd say you are home," he said to the cat.

"She's been worried sick about that fool cat for three days," said a woman standing just behind the girl. She was the image of the child twenty years later, lithe figure, long blonde hair, a knowing smile. "Hi, I'm Elaine Appleton."

"Anthony Zane. I'm just glad I was able to bring what was his name?—Lancelot—back," he said.

"Camelot just hasn't been the same without you." The girl ignored the two adults and spoke directly to the cat, who acted as if it were his due. Which, in the cat's opinion, it was.

"Camelot?" asked Zane.

"That's what she calls her playroom, where the cat sleeps. She is totally enamored of this Knights of the Round Table thing. She has a very vivid imagination," said the girl's mother. "But then, considering her name, I suspect it would be a little hard not to."

"Her name?"

"Guinevere, Ginnie for short."

Zane felt a hard lump in his throat. Yet it was a good feeling. The quest had come to a very pleasant conclusion.

"Mommy, may I show this nice man Camelot?"

"Ginnie, I think he probably doesn't have time."

"On the contrary, I have plenty of time," Zane said. "Lady Guinevere, if your Lady mother will give permission, and would join us, I would love to see Camelot."

"Good! Then it's on to Camelot!"

A crow with gray streaks cutting across its black feathers sat on a tree branch just outside of the brownstone door. Teaching lessons to hard-headed warriors was not a new experience for him.

The bird lingered for a few minutes after Zane had gone inside, then leaped off into the air. Maybe it was time to take that vacation Nimuë was always nagging him about.

LAST FLIGHT OVER THE GIANT'S DANCE

by Jean Rabe

When not writing, Jean Rabe feeds her goldfish, visits museums, and attends gaming conventions. A former newspaper reporter, she is the author of seven fantasy novels for TSR, Inc., including the *Dragonlance* Fifth Age trilogy. She has written numerous fantasy and science fiction short stories, and she edits a BattleTech magazine for the FASA Corporation.

"ALTIMETER." I spit the word out as if it were a piece of spoiled meat. "Altimeter. Altimeter. Altimeter."

"Pardon, Lieutenant?"

"Nothing. Altimeter." *Ah, there it is! This is the altimeter. This the airspeed indicator. Flap controls. Clock. Turn and . . . turn and . . . hmmmm . . . turn and bank indicator. Engine controls. Ambrosius Aurelianus and the stones be damned. Twin Lewis guns on a Scarff ring. Rudder pedals. Compass.*

I pulled back on the control column. It was heavy, normally something that would be too unwieldy for a man my age who'd for decades wrapped himself in scrolls and scholarly pursuits. However the body my mind was occupying was young and strong, and I put all those muscles into my task and felt the aircraft's nose steadily rise. The

wheels bumped a few times against the grass runway of
the Liegescourt airfield, unkindly jarring my borrowed
bones. Then we were free of the ground.

I felt my stomach sinking into my toes, and I must
have muttered something disparaging, as Roland, my
newly-assigned front-gunner, offered up another "Pardon, Lieutenant?"

I ignored him and pulled back harder on the column, ex-
perimented a moment with the rudder pedals. Shoes be
damned. I longed for my comfortable slippers, not these
regulation fur-lined boots with laces more easily tangled
than tied.

Out of the corner of my eye I watched drops of sweat
form on Roland's forehead as we narrowly climbed above
the tree line, imagined that the rear-gunner nestled in the
tail of the plane was sweating, too. What was his name?
Nigel? Yes, that was it. Nigel Pennysworth. A "good chap,"
the airmen in the squadron called him. Seemed likable and
not nearly so talkative as Roland. He made a fine cup of
tea, and I trusted him with the dozen bombs we carried in
the plane's belly.

I eased the tail back and selected a heading, opened the
throttles a bit, and brought the airspeed up to eighty.

Higher and we passed through a low-hanging cloud that
was a lacy bit of gossamer as thin as a newborn faerie's
wing. Had I the inclination, I could have cast a spell to
hold the moment so that I could appreciate the view. But I
was too busy this night. Perhaps on the next flight. This
body and this plane had an assignment. I pulled back
again.

We went higher still, passing through another low, thin
bank. Then suddenly the stars winked brightly into view
all around us, suspended just beyond the glass of the windshield. No one could sweat here. So many feet above the
ground we were chilled—despite the summer and our
heavy flight jackets and woolen socks. How many feet?
"Altimeter. Altimeter. Altimeter." Ah, a little more than
three thousand. Unbelievable to be so high above the

ground. Unthinkable that we'd have to climb almost twice that soon.

"Compass. Compass. Compass. There we go." I banked a few degrees to the east and felt the plane shudder. For more than a dozen heartbeats we bobbed like driftwood on an agitated sea as we passed through a sheet of wind. Then we were free of the turbulence, and I opened up the twin engines farther. Rolls-Royce Eagle Eights, water cooled and capable of three hundred and twenty-two horsepower at eighteen hundred revolutions per minute. Ha! Wait until I tell Arthur about this. Would he believe me? The incessant roaring of the Rolls-Royces was unpleasant and more than a little unnerving to me.

Roland was unnerved, too, though I suspected it was my flying, rather than the noise, that was bothering him. The fingers of his right hand were anxiously drumming against the instrument panel, the fingers of his left were busy rubbing the black cat patch on his pocket—our squadron's symbol. I'd learned this latter gesture was meant for good luck and was practiced by most of the pilots and their crews. The black cats I had employed as familiars through the years were the most disagreeable and unlucky of creatures. Better a plump, happy toad to heed one's proverbial beck and call. I never touched my squadron patch.

Roland's thin lips were feverishly working themselves into another question. "Ah, sir? Lieutenant Myrddin, sir? They said this was your fifteenth solo flight. I was just wondering. . . ."

"Are you questioning my ability to fly this . . ." I searched for the proper term of the time. "Uh . . . this crate?"

"No, sir, it's just, sir! Down there . . . the lighthouse."

I see it." One more tug on the column and I leveled off the plane. "Barely see it." *Now that you pointed it out to me, my good Corporal.* Staring down through the gossamer, I was able to make out the faint lighthouse beacon. The glow of a sprite's tail. It was a landmark, one of several we were to follow, and I adjusted my course accordingly. The planes which had left the airfield minutes before us would have steered by it, too—as well as those that would come behind us. An entire flight of heavy bombers headed deeper into France directed by compasses and sprite glow.

"Sir?" He repeated the word, drawing it out and adding more volume to it.

I nodded and mumbled something about indeed flying fifteen solo missions. I suspected the Lieutenant, whose form I occupied, had indeed flown that many. This was actually only my third flight—in a plane. And as we hit another sheet of wind, I considered it three too many. At least I was a fast learner and was somehow managing to keep this canvas monstrosity in one piece. I wanted to fly this thing with my hands, not with my magic.

Roland's fingernail caught on a fraying piece of thread on the patch, and with an unthinking tug the cat's tail was freed and flapped forward.

I had decided early this morning that I would only fly this "bird" a few more times—just long enough so I could absorb more about the people of this time, about their cars and planes and politics, their clothes and weapons, about this war that began four years ago when the Germans entered Liege and that would end who knew when.

Satiate my curiosity.

Then I would devote my efforts to getting home and back to King Arthur, allowing the real Lieutenant Myrddin control of his body once more. The real lieutenant was with me now, tucked away in a secret spot in his mind, observing everything and unable to act. I didn't dare risk calling on his expertise, lest his mind come to the fore and shove me into that secret spot where I'd be trapped. Better that he think this all a nightmare—Merlin the great wizard absconding with his body and flying a Handley Page.

"Sir? Lieutenant Myrddin? Did you get your training over Stonehenge? Most of the Handley pilots in the two-oh-seventh did. I want to train there."

"Yes, yes, I trained over Stonehenge." *Damnable rocks. Why did I ever convince Ambrosius, Arthur's grandfather,*

*to have them moved from Ireland? Chorea Gigantum. The
Giant's Ring. The Giant's Dance. Stonehenge.*

I wanted the rocks in England. I wanted a monument to
the men who had died during the battles with the Saxons.
Of course, I also wanted the formation close to my home
because of its great healing powers and ability to channel
magic. But if the stones had never been reassembled in England, I wouldn't be here. I wouldn't have used the magic
of the formation in that spot . . . where the bomber pilots
were training . . . to look into the future at Arthur's behest.

He wanted me to discover a weapon to defeat the Saxons.
Not that I blamed him. Vortigern had not managed it. Nor
had Ambrosius or Uther. So it had fallen to Arthur to push
the Saxons back. But by my beard! I hadn't intended to look
so far into the future for him. Whatever had I been thinking?
I just kept looking forward and forward and suddenly felt
the presence of a man moving like lightning so far above the
stones. In a heartbeat, I cast an enchantment to place my
mind in that body. For Arthur, I told myself. Though I knew
it was for me, to settle my own ever-thirsting curiosity. I had
to know what magic allowed a man to move so quickly
through the air above Stonehenge. And now I knew.

"Magic had nothing to do with it."

"Sir?"

"Well, Corporal Roland, my very first flight was over
Stonehenge. In fact, Corporal, I . . ."

There were tiny flashes below us, looking like angry
fireflies. Gunfire, I had learned. More of this time's tech-
nological magic. I imagined the soldiers dying—British
and German and whatever other nationalities had been re-
cruited by both sides. With the magic of The Giant's
Dance I had quietly observed other wars. The Pelopon-
nesian War, the First Punic War, The Wars of the Second
Triumvirate—now that was an interesting one in which
Caesar Octavianus defeated Marcus Lepidus and Mark
Anthony, and Augustus became emporor—the Hundred
Years War, the War of the Roses, the War of 1812. And
now this Great War, which I was more than observing.

"What is so great about it?" I mumbled too softly for
Roland to hear. "The great destruction this technology can
hand out? The greatness of these Handley Pages?" Until I
had visited this war, I believed only my magic was capable
of such devastation. But these bombs, the ones carried in
the belly of this plane—such destruction they would be in-
flicting if things went according to plan.

This plane. This amazing creation. Again I directed my
concentration to keeping it aloft. It was a big craft, the
largest the Allies had, a Handley Page 0/400. So dark
green that even in the light of day it looked as black to me
as a starless sky. A "Bloody Paralyzer," some of the pilots
named it, a heavy bomber built in retaliation for the German air raids over England's fair cities. Wings that stretched
a hundred feet across. It weighed a little more than four
tons empty, seven with us and the guns and the bombs. All
that weight, hard to imagine it staying aloft. It could travel
more than ninety miles an hour, climb to eight thousand
feet, and remain airborne for eight hours at a time with the
help of this horrid-smelling fuel. These men without
magic, in the year 1918, had created something magnificent. What Arthur wouldn't give for something like this.
The Saxons would not stand a chance.

"Sir! Another lighthouse!"

I banked to the northeast and climbed to five thousand
feet. Through the darkness ahead, I saw specks of red, tiny
demon eyes. It was the exhaust of the other bombers, and it
signaled we were not far behind them and not far from our
destination.

"Corporal?"

Roland was still rubbing the patch. "A half hour to the
railway, sir. Then we'll give those Huns what-for. Foul up
their supply lines, and we'll bring the war to an end
faster."

The time passed quickly, and though the air grew colder
inside our Handley, we no longer seemed to notice. The urgency of the mission, perhaps with a dash of fear and ex-

citement thrown in, was keeping our minds occupied.
Three more lighthouses swept by far beneath our wings.

Six thousand feet.

Ahead, beams of more intense light were cutting
through the dissipating gossamer, moving in steady lines
and circles. The enemy's searchlights. I swallowed hard. I
knew if even one of those lights caught us, it would be like
pinning a butterfly to a board—and that might mean I
would never get home. My consciousness trapped in a
dead body. I shuddered and rolled our Handley to the
right—and just in time. Off my left wing a searchlight
sliced through the sky. So close! I leveled her. Her. They
call the planes her. Odd that this hunk of canvas and wood
would be assigned a sexual persuasion. Then I rolled
again and climbed a few dozen feet as another searchlight
reached out.

A Handley more that a hundred yards in front of us was
not so fortunate. The light caught her belly and held there.
Before I could breathe, a burst of red and white sparks
arced up through the beam. Tracers and Archie! Ack-ack,
anti-aircraft fire! The shells ripped through the canvas of
the Handley. Suddenly smoke was churning out of the un-
fortunate plane, hauntingly illuminated by the searchlight
that continued to stay with her. More ack-ack pounded her.
There were flames, too, venting from the cockpit, and I felt
myself sweating despite the cold, my fingers growing slick
against the control column. I could smell the stench of the
ack-ack and burning fuel, and I fought to keep down what
had passed for dinner.

Roland's hands were on the Lewis gun controls, swivel-
ing them right and left looking for enemy planes to target.
He was sweating again, too.

I banked to the left and dove just as the searchlight left
the dying Handley and swung toward us. Then I wrestled
with the column to level off and banked right as another
searchlight panned by.

There were great explosions erupting from the ground,

flashes of crimson and orange to signal the other Handleys in our squadron had released their bombs.

Our turn.

But there was so much fire and smoke that it was difficult to make out the railway so far beneath us. The enemy's searchlights helped a bit, and as a pair of beams swept toward us again I spotted the curving of the rail line and a dark building that stretched over a section of rail. Roland saw it, too, and he released his gun controls to skitter back through our plane to inform Nigel.

Heartbeats passed, and I managed to hold her steady. Fighting nausea, clamping my sweaty fingers tighter about the controls, I heard a soft, mechanical groan from somewhere behind me. Then I felt the plane drift upward, lightened by the release of our bombs. One set away. I would have to make another pass so that the rest could be released before I could turn us toward Liegescourt.

"Should have settled for two flights," I muttered. "Or the one. Should have known better than to take this third trip. Ambrosius Aurelianus and the stones be damned. My own curiosity be damned."

"Pardon, Lieutenant?" Roland had returned and was squeezing into his seat. I waved away his comment and began a wide circle.

"One more pass."

I had told myself I would not use magic to fly this plane or to carry out this mission. And though I reminded myself of that pledge now, I mumbled a string of what Roland would consider unintelligible gibberish. My face flushed and my eyelids tingled, and in the span of a few heartbeats I had cast a spell to let me see what was going on far below.

Hell probably looks like this, I decided, as the magic revealed the battered landscape. Fires burned everywhere—ravaging buildings, cars, and people. Sections of railway twisted upward like curled ribbons, and the ground was chewed terribly. The living were running madly about, waving arms and weapons, pointing to the sky, and trying to find cover.

I blinked as a flash of yellow-white light practically blinded me. Another bomb had struck. Bodies were propelled through the air, and a greater chunk of the rail line was destroyed. Fortunately, I had not enhanced the enchantment to permit me to hear what was going on. Fortunately. . . .

Roland was tugging on my sleeve. I shook my head and dismissed the spell. The sky around us was lightening— from the searchlights and the trails of enemy fire, from the fires that blazed below where more of the Handleys had dropped their bombs.

There were strings of green lights shooting into the sky off our right wing. Flaming onions! Worse than ack-ack, Nigel had explained that these German guns spewed chains of green balls, deadly phosphorous that were keenly synchronized to double the Huns' chance of setting our planes on fire. The green globes hideously lit up the night sky, brightening the billowing clouds of smoke that were pouring from more British planes that had been hit.

We were coming around to our mark again, the rail beneath us, shattered in places. The building. I wanted to hit that, figuring something important was inside. This might not be my time or my war, but I might as well accomplish something while I'm visiting—give the real Lieutenant Myrddin a medal for his chest. Accomplish this mission and then go home. I dove and inhaled sharply as a searchlight beam caught us squarely.

I felt the Handley lift again as Nigel dropped the remaining bombs. Then I felt her lift higher still, propelled by the ack-ack that was riddling her taut canvas belly. The stench of the shells, coupled with the stench of our fuel and smoldering canvas, was unbearable, and the fear that constricted my heart was greater than anything I had experienced before.

"The stinkin' Huns got one of our fuel lines, Lieutenant!"

I pushed forward to increase our dive, swung the plane to the left, then to the right, all the while fighting the urge to use my magic again. My feet jabbed at the rudder controls, and I narrowly avoided putting us in a spin. In the end, we managed to escape the clutches of the searchlight, but I feared we could still be seen. Fires continued to rage below us, and one of our bombs had managed to snare an enemy fuel dump. The veritable blaze was setting the countryside aglow.

My fingers flew over the controls even as my mind forced me to precisely recall what each dial and lever did. I pulled back on the control column, opened the engines as wide as they would go, and breathed a small sigh of relief that apparently our engines—and at least one of our fuel lines—had been missed by the enemy fire.

"Let's go home, Roland," I said.

"Yessir!" He was skittering backward again, to assess our damage. I was grateful for the few moments alone. I would return Roland and Nigel to Liegescourt, take the plane on to Stonehenge and . . .

"By my beard!"

I saw a form shoot up in front of the window, black like a bat but with wings so angular I knew it was a construct of man. Double wings, an enemy biplane. Too small to be a Handley bomber, I stared with a mix of horror and fascination as another form joined it, this one a triplane, as they banked around and flew straight at me, their guns spitting shells. I must have lost my voice, for I did not call out a warning to Roland and Nigel, not that either could have heard me over the roar of the Rolls-Royces.

I dipped the right wing, hoping that would serve as a signal for trouble and at the same time present a more difficult target to the German fighters, and again I fought the urge to use magic.

Tat-tat-tat-tat-tat! Their small guns spat streams of red that thudded sharply against my plane. Tat-tat-tat-tat-tat! The noise was coming from behind me, too, signaling the presence of more enemy fighters. I envisioned that pinned butterfly, then shook the image from my mind. There was Arthur to consider, the Saxons to drive back. I couldn't get caught in this horrid time and place.

Roland squeezed by me, panting and reaching for the controls of the twin Lewis guns. In an instant we were returning fire, our shells spitting into the night sky this time and arcing toward the German planes.

"Nigel!" Roland huffed as he swept the guns up and fired again. Smoke billowed from one of the enemy fighters, and I watched with some measure of satisfaction as the enemy plane spiraled down and out of sight. "Nigel's dead. He was a good chap." Roland was firing again, gulping down air and scanning the sky for what he was mumbling were "damnable Fokkers." The air was filled with the tat-tat-tat-tat-tat of the enemy, with our return fire, with the roar of the engines, and the pounding of my borrowed heart. "And we'll be dead, too," he was shouting. "if we can't shake these Huns!"

I pulled on the control column and felt the plane tremble. One of the engines caught and coughed like an old man trying futilely to clear his lungs. We drifted to the right and I changed tactics. Pushing the control column forward as fast and as hard as these arms could manage, the Handley dropped into a dizzying dive. The shadows of the German planes rushed by the windshield, left behind. But not far enough.

I still could hear their tat-tat-tat-tat as I searched my mind for a spell to protect this plane, something to give it armor like Arthur's knights. I began reciting the arcane words.

Roland swept his guns to the right as a lingering shadow tried to keep up with us. He fired again and again, filling the air with noise and death even as that shadow returned the same.

There was an odd pack-pack sound as enemy shells cut though our windshield, causing spiderweb-fine cracks to race through it and causing me to pause in my enchant-

ment. The wind whistled coldly and keenly through the
holes, and I rolled the plane to the left to evade that enemy
fighter.

The ground was looming up by the time I abandoned the
thought of magic and struggled with the control column to
level us off. I glanced to my right, wanting to ask Roland
to search for lighthouses. He was slumped forward in the
seat, head resting on his gun controls. My breath caught in
my throat as I pulled up harder and urged the plane to respond. Urged my gunner to respond. "Roland? Roland!"

His chest was rising and falling, his flight jacket just
above the black cat patch growing dark from blood. Dying.
Such a Great War the Britains and Germans had created,
greater than anything Arthur and the Saxons could wage.

I felt the Handley's engine cough again, the nose growing heavier and failing to respond to my efforts. The other
engine seized, and I knew we were billowing smoke and
venting flames. Dying.

"No alternative," I muttered, as I pulled back one
more time on the column, reached deep into my mind for
the greatest of the magic that I held there. So hard to
concentrate with the noise and the smell of smoke and
fire and blood, the sound of enemy's guns. So hard. Too
hard. "Find the magic!" I cursed. "Find it!" And in an instant, I had.

I felt the arcane energy suffuse these borrowed fingers,
travel into the control column and into the mass of
wounded canvas and wood. The nose lifted, a little at first,
then higher as I directed more energy into the Handley.
The ground whizzed by beneath the wings, then I brought
her higher, above the trees that had appeared from out of
nowhere. Higher and I directed the magic outward into the
wings where the sputtering Rolls-Royces rested. My mind,
my magic, cooled them, smothering the fire in an arcane
blanket.

I could see the wings in my mind's eye, so riddled with
shells that the canvas flapped like castle banners. Fuel

tanks and lines had been cut by the Fokker's fire. I concentrated and coerced the magic to seal the holes. Then I moved my senses backward and around the fuselage, noting the riddled top and belly, the empty bomb racks, the prone form of Nigel. "Good chap," I whispered.

I felt a deep sadness overtake me, for Nigel Pennysworth and the dozens of other men in the two-oh-seventh who had been lost this night, for the men in my time who had fallen to the Saxons. I would do my best to save Roland.

Tat-tat-tat-tat!

"The stones be damned!" I hissed.

The Fokkers were on my tail and closing, and I knew that I could not lose them. My magic was formidable. Indeed, I believed myself to be the most powerful sorcerer who ever lived. Better than Morgana and Mordred!

Still, as I had learned this night, my magic could not equal all aspects of this Great War's technology. I could not make this plane travel as fast as it could if it were under its own power. And therefore I could not escape the Fokkers.

But perhaps I could. . . .

My senses flowed over the Handley, racing toward the tail where more Lewis guns waited. They flowed over the rounds—tracers and explosive, found the triggers, pulled the guns back and mentally aimed.

Shells raced through the night again, raced toward the Fokkers that with my magic I could clearly see behind us. Five enemy planes, single-seat bi-wing fighters. The arcane-guided shells cut through the canvas, shredding it.

One plane belched a gout of black smoke and began a spiral to the ground. The four others remained in dogged pursuit. They were spreading out, one slipping to the side of my Handley, making themselves more difficult targets. Perhaps more difficult to a gunner, but not more difficult to an old wizard.

I trained my eyes on the horizon, my senses to the rear of the craft. I concentrated on the enchantment and contin-

ued to play a mental finger over the trigger of the Lewis
guns. Another plane was stuck, careening to the west and
out of sight. And my Handley was struck, too. A barrage of
enemy lead cut through the tail section, cleaving the air
where a gunner would have been positioned—where Nigel
should have been positioned. The tattered canvas flapped,
the added sound distracting me just a bit. More bullets tore
into my plane.

"By my beard!" Phenomenal wizard I was, but even I
was taxed at the moment—using my magic to keep the
Handley in flight and using it to shoot at the planes behind
us. "One in front!" I hollered.

The Fokker that had slipped to the side had banked
around in front and was coming in for a head-on shot.

The arcane energy tingled wildly in my fingers, warm-
ing my borrowed body and angling toward the front Lewis
guns. I mentally thumbed the trigger even as I registered
more bullets ripping into my plane from behind.

The magically-guided shells leaped out at the daring
Fokker, riddling its fuselage while at the same time the
Handley's was riddled from the enemy planes creeping up
behind me.

I directed all my energy into the Handley's guns, thumb-
ing the triggers, guiding the bullets forward and aft. The
shells cut through Hun canvas and windshields, pelted the
German pilots' bodies, lodged into the engines. Even as
they died, they returned my fire, their tat-tat-tat-tat-tats
ripping away part of the tail section and right wing.

In my mind's eye I watched the two planes behind me
plummet into the woods below. My borrowed eyes
recorded the Fokker's descent in the front. The Handley
should be joining them. This plane should not be flying—
not without part of a wing, a broken tail, and no fuel.

Only my magic was keeping it in the air. And on course.

I turned to Roland. His breathing was ragged and shallow. I squirmed out of my flight jacket so I could get at my
clothes beneath. Ripping off a piece of my shirt, I pressed

it against his wound and tried to staunch the blood flow. "My magic is formidable," I whispered, "But my magic can't heal you." I tugged free another strip, and then another, until I was barechested and struggling into my flight jacket for warmth.

"But the magic of the stones can."

Somehow Roland survived the trip to England, and survived my rather rough landing on the outskirts of the training field—the one he had hoped to someday train at. Blessedly, he was unconscious. And equally fortunately no one had seen us, though my magic had a bit to do with that.

I cradled him to my chest as I made my way toward Stonehenge and laid him in the center of the ring. The stones looked so weathered in the early-morning light, the intervening years between Arthur's time and now harsh on them. I concentrated on the angular stone to the northeast, the one I had discovered was richest with healing power. Its energy was palpable, thrumming against the ground as the Rolls-Royces had thrummed in the Handley. I pulled the energy toward Roland, then rested back on my haunches.

So pale. He'd lost a lot of blood. And so young. I waited and found myself praying. I watched the sun climb, and I faintly heard the sound of machines and men—from the nearby training field. I waited a bit longer, until I saw Roland's face reddening a little and his chest rising and falling with more strength and regularity.

"Time to go home." I rose and paced the circle, touched each stone and began the incantation that brought me here. I felt the coolness of the rocks beneath my borrowed fingers, and I felt the years rushing away. My senses receded from the Lieutenant's body, and I registered his consciousness coming to the fore.

As my own time came racing at me, I urged the Lieutenant's hand into his flight jacket pocket and forced his fingers to close about a hunk of metal. "My souvenir," I whispered, as my mind left his body.

Then 1918 was a memory, and I stood an old man again, white beard waggling in the early-morning wind. The stone formation circled me.

"Altimeter," I muttered. In my hand I clutched the hunk of metal I'd salvaged from the Handley.

THE WELL-MADE KNIGHT

by Brooks Peck

In addition to being an author, Brooks Peck is the associate publisher of *Science Fiction Weekly,* a review magazine on the World Wide Web. He has just completed his first novel.

THE first thing he ever saw was sunlight falling between the leaves of trees to form a dappled pattern on the ground. A breeze shook the tree limbs, making the pattern shimmer and sway. He heard rushing water, looked down, and saw a creek. Near his feet the bank had been scraped free of ferns and moss, exposing reddish clay. A pit had been dug out of the clay, over four feet deep. Downstream, the waterway widened and emptied into a small lake, which was bright with flashing sunlight. It was the most beautiful thing he'd seen yet. He thought, *I am alive.*

Then he noticed an old man in a threadbare tunic standing a short distance off, squinting at him. The tunic may have once been dyed brown, but years had turned it a dull rusty color. Over it hung a coarse wool robe the same color as the man's long gray beard. A belt of skin and fur around his waist held various oddments: a pouch, some claws, polished sticks inscribed with runes, a round stone. The old man wore no shoes.

"Not bad," the old man said. "Chaim said this might be useful someday, not that I believed him. Can you speak?"

He started to speak but felt a rough object under his tongue. He reached to remove it.

"Don't touch that!" the old man snapped. "That parchment is the talisman that gives you life, and mustn't be removed. Just leave it alone, you'll get used to it."

He cleared his throat. "Who are you?"

The old man bowed. "I am Merlin, adviser to the new king, Arthur."

"And who am I?"

"Ah, you're ahead of me there, quite precocious. Let's consider." He tugged his beard. "The name must fit the man and his task. Though calling you Cuckold-Maker wouldn't really do. We need something subtle, something that embodies your talents. Peter? Rod? Too common. I know! *Lancelot*."

He chuckled to himself, then stood still, staring away for long seconds. "We must hurry," he said. "They're almost ready. But first—" He kicked a sack that lay near his feet. "Take those, they're to be yours." In the sack Lancelot found a round wooden shield strapped with iron bands and a sword wrapped in greased rags. "They're rude but sturdy; belonged to a Saxon who'll never fight again. If anyone asks why your weapons are so poor, tell them you gave all your money to the Church. That will teach them to be less prying. Come, come."

Merlin set off through the trees, and after a brief hesitation Lancelot followed. He imitated the way Merlin moved his legs and feet, one after another, and after a few wobbling steps found the process was quite marvelous. New things kept coming into view before him—new kinds of plants, outcroppings of rock, small animals that didn't seem to notice Merlin, but who scampered away before Lancelot's own thrashing steps. He looked back to see the lake, but it was hidden by the trees now and he stopped, feeling a pang of sadness.

Suddenly Merlin was at his side. "Come," he said. "And listen." They walked on. "The king has married a whore. She charmed him with her fine looks and an alleged Roman lineage, but she's nothing but a whore. She likes power and men, this Guinevere, and that's the problem. She'll tire of Arthur's boyish charm soon, and her attention will fall upon the knights. They are mostly good men, but they won't be able to resist those wiles. Even now they love her—everyone loves her."

"You love her?"

Merlin gaped at him. "Don't be an idiot. I see her for the danger that she is to this land. Arthur may call himself king, but his domain is small and the Saxons grow bolder by the month. He needs the support of his knights and their families, or we lose all. *But she will destroy that.* Jealousy will divide them, they'll squabble and kill one another, and the kingdom will crumble. Then she'll move on to whatever bearfat-smeared Saxon is the strongest. Arthur is the best chance this land has had for unity since the Romans left, and I've worked very hard to bring him to this point. That trollop isn't going to destroy all that."

"What will you do?"

"Ah!" Merlin smiled. "Such a bright lad. I created you to help me destroy her. I shall introduce you to Arthur as a knight from a distant land, and you will take up residence at Camelot. You don't know it, having seen no other men but me, but you are an Adonis that I'm certain she won't be able to resist. And when she cleaves to you, I shall expose her—now, before Arthur is too fond of her. And then we'll be rid of her, hopefully because he's taken off her head."

Lancelot mulled this over. "So you want to make her do what she would do anyway."

"Yes, yes, but at the time of my choosing, while her position is still weak." Merlin turned to look Lancelot right in the eyes. "You will obey my instructions, and do everything you can to achieve this goal. At the same time, you will not reveal your true nature to anyone, but will be humble and good, do you understand?" A wave of dizziness passed through Lancelot, and colored spots clouded his vision. "Yes, of course," he said.

They joined a small track which soon led out of the forest to a broad slope of land that slanted down from a scarp to the south. Some of the land had been given over to fields of rye, which women harvested with scythes. There were long, one-story buildings here and there, with huts and shacks scattered among them. A few dozen head of cattle wandered inside a wooden corral, and sheep grazed along the slope. Smoke from numerous fires hung everywhere in a gray haze, and Lancelot breathed deeply, enjoying the smell. There was *so much* to see—horses, running children, a smith hammering hot iron, a bubbling pot of stew. He tripped over his feet as he twisted his head this way and that.

North stood a wide, flat-topped hill with a timber-framed rampart circling its crest. Merlin tramped toward this hill, ignoring everyone and everything along the way. As they reached the rampart's gate, a party rode out. First came a bored-looking man with black hair and a somewhat muddy cloak. Several boys followed on foot carrying bundles and tall spears. Then came a large man wearing a white tunic with a purple border, much finer than any other clothing Lancelot had seen. The man had thick brown hair and his hands were extraordinarily wide. His eyes lit up when he saw them.

"There you are, Merlin! Coming to hunt after all?"

"I'm afraid not, Sire. You know how the horses feel about me."

"Oh, indeed. And who's your companion?"

Lancelot suddenly became terrified, realizing he would have to speak to this giant man whose gaze was friendly, but clearly missed nothing. An aura of vibrant life surrounded him, was apparent in his every gesture, and in comparison Lancelot felt empty and dull.

"An itinerant knight by the name of Lancelot," Merlin

said. "Son of an old friend, come to help us fight the Saxons."

"Indeed?" The king dismounted and shook Lancelot's hand. "Where are you from?"

"The lake," Lancelot replied.

"Du Lac," Merlin said hastily. "He's from France. His full name is Lancelot du Lac. Lancelot, this is Arthur, King of Britain."

Lancelot bowed, which seemed to suit Arthur. "Sire, I hope you will allow me to lend you my services, however meager."

"Certainly. We'd be glad for you to join us—"

"If you pass the test," the black-haired knight said.

"Ah, yes." Arthur looked apologetic. "With our success we can be somewhat selective. Not like the old days when *you* joined me, eh, Parsifal?"

The other knight dismounted. "Indeed. Now almost half the army can grow a beard."

Arthur laughed. "Perhaps after our hunt we can arrange a suitable match."

"Why not now while we await the Queen?" Parsifal turned to a boy. "Fetch my second shield and two practice swords, quick."

The boy returned at a run, though struggling under the weight of his burdens. He presented Lancelot with a thick wooden sword, quite dented and gouged. "Let me help you," Merlin said, removing Lancelot's own sword and shield. "Do you know what to do?" he whispered.

"Not really."

"It's a contest. You want to hit Parsifal with your sword and avoid getting hit by his. Only hit him lightly—you're vastly stronger and could cripple him."

Merlin, Arthur, and the others stood away. Arthur said, "Begin!"

Parsifal's whole demeanor instantly changed. He crouched, yet seemed to grow larger. He moved with smooth strength, circling Lancelot, then lashed out with his sword in a

wide, sweeping blow. Startled, Lancelot stepped backward, and found that in his fear he moved very quickly.
Parsifal's sword hummed through the air where Lancelot
had been less than a second ago. Looking confused, Parsifal moved closer. He feinted another swing, but Lancelot
didn't move. Time had slowed for him, and Parsifal's intent
was clear from his footing and the shift of his hips and
shoulders. Then Parsifal swung again, cutting up and
across, and once more Lancelot hopped well out of the way.

He glanced at Merlin who gestured, pantomiming holding sword and shield, and remembered that he was supposed to strike back. That was what the shield was for, he
realized, to provide protection so you could stay close
enough to your opponent to strike back. Interesting. He
raised his shield and stepped forward, studying Parsifal's
attacks, blocking them all handily. At last he tried a blow
of his own, down and toward the center. Parsifal caught it
on his shield and immediately struck Lancelot's arm a
jarring blow. Lancelot retreated, stunned, but with a new
understanding of the contest. Attacking made you vulnera-
ble. Timing was everything.

He rejoined the combat, trading light blows with Parsifal,
then lashing out to thump him on the arm just as Parsifal had
done to him. Parsifal growled, breathing heavily. Lancelot
blocked his counterstroke, then slipped around and hit him
on the thigh. His next two blows caught Parsifal on the hip
and shoulder. He wondered if he was winning.

Now a gleam appeared in Parsifal's eyes, and he came
at Lancelot with renewed strength and speed. He'd been
holding back, Lancelot realized, but no longer. Before,
he'd been a fighter; now he was a warrior, and his look
was murderous. He battered Lancelot back with furious
blows, the two of them skidding on the damp ground. Lancelot tried to attack, but Parsifal blocked his every stroke and
nearly hit him in return. Finally Lancelot rushed Parsifal,
shoving him backward with his shield, then whirling
around to hit him on the back of the knee, making him cry

out. Before he could turn, Lancelot struck him in the back, sending him tumbling right over the crest of the hill.

Frightened at the strength of his blow, Lancelot started to go see if Parsifal was all right, but noticed that someone new was watching him. He turned and saw a woman holding the bridle of a horse. She wore a fine embroidered tunic and a fur-trimmed cloak. Her hair was deep auburn, and although carefully braided, pieces had pulled free here and there. There was something about her face, her expression, that arrested him completely. And as he stared at her, so she stared at him. After long seconds her eyes suddenly widened and she looked about to cry out.

Someone crashed into him from behind, driving them both to the ground in a clatter of wood and iron. Parsifal. He grinned down at Lancelot, bits of grass in his beard and hair, then stood with a groan and gave Lancelot a hand up. "He'll do," he said.

"Well fought, both of you," Arthur cried. Then noticing the woman he said, "Ah, my dear, there you are. Look, look—" he took her arm and tugged her over, "—this is Lancelot, who's come all the way from France just to help us keep out those barbarians."

Lancelot bowed. She was smaller than he'd thought, with a delicate, almost tiny, nose and chin. "You're a fighting man," she said, looking into his face with the same unwavering gaze as before.

"Only when I must."

"Well you've come to the right place. Arthur is, above all, a warrior." At last she looked away, to her husband, smiling with affection.

After the hunting party left, Merlin led Lancelot down the passage through the fifteen-foot-thick wall. "Excellent, excellent. You've already caught her attention. I knew I made you well. Now all you need do is be kind, attentive, and let nature take its course."

A number of timber-framed buildings had been constructed inside the ramparts: barracks, stables, storehouses. One building stood out from the others for its size—almost sixty feet long and thirty wide—and its high-pitched roof. It was the Hall, with the royal apartment in back. Next to that was a church, rather small but well built, with a wooden cross at the roof's apex.

"What if she won't love me?" Lancelot asked.

"Don't fear. She'd love a parsnip if there were no men about."

Lancelot thought about how Guinevere looked at Arthur, how she touched his arm. "Isn't it wrong?"

Merlin looked furious. "There's not question in that regard! It's right for Arthur and for this land. Don't doubt, don't even *think* about what I tell you to do. Just do. You are under my geas and must obey me."

At the edge of a new field, Lancelot unloaded stones from a sledge hitched to a packhorse. Many of the knights wouldn't help with the common labor, but Lancelot saw how the peasants especially hated digging out, loading, and unloading the great rocks, which for him was so easy, and their gratitude made him feel very good.

He rolled a hog-sized stone onto the pile growing at the base of an oak, and as he straightened up an acorn hit him soundly on the head. Two more struck him a second later, and he heard a giggle. "Who's that?" he asked. The oak's leaves had only just begun to fall, so he couldn't see very far up the tree.

"I am the spirit of the oak, O knight. Come up that I might bewitch thee."

Curious, Lancelot leaped up to the lowest branch, then climbed steadily, the whole tree trembling under his weight. Halfway to the top, he thrust his head through a cluster of leaves and found not a spirit, but Guinevere.

She sat a good distance out from the tree's trunk, holding a limb above her for balance. Her tunic was hiked up near her waist and her leggings were quite dirty, with twigs and pieces of bark stuck to the wool.

"My lady," Lancelot said, startled.

Guinevere smiled. "Fancy meeting you here. Especially when you go to so much trouble to avoid me."

He could hardly think of what to say. "I do not avoid you."

"Yes, you *do*." She put her feet on a lower limb and edged out even farther.

"Do be careful."

"I've climbed trees since before I could talk. But look at you and your white knuckles. Have you never climbed a tree?"

"Well, no."

She nodded, a shaft of sunlight playing on her face. "You walk about with a wide-eyed look, like the whole world's new."

"Britain is quite different from France."

Guinevere laughed. "But back to the subject at hand." Now she looked him full in the face, and he couldn't look away though her gaze made him feel as if he would crumble into pieces. He wondered if she were truly as beautiful as she appeared, or if Merlin had made him in such a way that he would think so. "Do I offend you?" she asked.

"No."

"Are you afraid I'll sap your strength?"

"No, no, it's not that."

"Then it *is* something?"

"No!"

"You keep saying that."

Lancelot was now thoroughly befuddled. He wondered if anyone could see them.

"I'm sorry," Guinevere said, her face softening. Then she turned away, and Lancelot found her silence more unnerving than when she addressed him.

"What troubles you?"

"It's just that, well, I really don't know how to be a queen. I've never been one before and I'm not sure how it all goes and there's no one to tell me. So when you keep such a distance, you who've been to foreign courts and all, I think I must be doing something really quite terrible."

Lancelot climbed up to sit on the same branch as Guinevere, but next to the tree's trunk. "I know little of foreign courts, but you seem to me to be everything a good queen should be. Arthur smiles like the sun when you are near. You give him great happiness and strength."

Guinevere looked down. "He's very busy."

"It's a busy time, but just knowing you are here is good for him. And besides Arthur, all the people love you."

"All of them?"

"Yes, all of them."

Guinevere turned away, dabbing her eyes with her sleeve. "You must think I'm silly. It's not as though I have to go fight barbarians." She faced him suddenly. "Do you suppose any other queens climb trees?"

"Some must." At that she smiled, and Lancelot felt a wash of relief and delight. "Can I help you down, Queen of the Tree?"

"I'm quite capable."

"Of course, but if you did happen to fall while I was at hand, I would . . . it would be a catastrophe. Please."

She looked at him again with that deep, open gaze. "All right." Lancelot took her hand, which was very warm.

Parsifal groaned as Lancelot helped him across the yard toward the barracks. Every Thursday he insisted on a rematch, and it always ended this way. As they reached the door, Merlin stepped out of the evening shadows and said, "Lancelot, a word." Parsifal waved Lancelot off. "You won't get off so easy next time, you stinking inbred foreign dog, I promise you." So saying, he clutched his bruised ribs ad limped inside.

The two walked away, and once out of earshot Merlin said, "By the heavens, what's taking so long? You've wooed her, I've seen that. She follows you around, praises your name to everyone. But there it has stopped. Why haven't you taken the next step as I ordered? She's willing."

"I'm not."

"Why?" Merlin peered up at him. "I didn't make you funny, did I? You like women?"

"I like women."

"And you like Guinevere?" Lancelot didn't answer, and Merlin grinned. "So why don't you take her?"

"It's a sin."

"A *sin?* Have you become a Christian now? I'm sorry, my boy, but even if Christianity weren't only a cultish fad, you were not created by God and you have no immortal soul to endanger."

"But she does."

"Bah. She damned herself long ago. One more tumble won't make any difference."

"Don't speak of her that way."

"Ah, you do care for her. Good. She cares for you, too, I can tell."

Despite himself, Lancelot felt a flutter of excited happiness to hear Merlin say it. "Even so, our relationship must remain the way it is."

"What's made you such an expert in the ways of the world? You're barely six weeks old. Don't you think that perhaps I know just a little more about men and women than you? Oh, I understand how you feel. You smolder for her. You want to touch her neck, you want to see her bare shoulders, her hips."

"Stop it."

"It's *natural.* Completely normal. And if she looks at you the way you look at her, you know she's thinking the same things."

"No." They walked for a moment in silence. "Truly?"

"Of course. Now why fight that urge? It's a good thing, believe me, a wonderful thing for two people to share. You won't know what it is to be a true man until you've had a woman." Lancelot wondered what the difference was, what it felt like to be a true man.

Then Merlin gripped his arm, turning him so they were face-to-face. "But it must be *soon.* My patience is running out."

* * *

Arthur, Merlin, and thirty other men huddled in a ravine
about five miles from Camelot, taking what meager shelter
they could from a sudden snowstorm. Clumps of wet snow
streamed through the air, clinging to clothes, beards, and
skin; dripping down collars and boots, making the ground
treacherous. It was impossible to see more than eight or
ten feet, and night was falling.

Word had come that a party of Saxon raiders had landed,
but either they'd fled by the time Arthur and the others
reached the sea, or they had been nothing but a rumor.
Then, as the group traveled home, the storm had come up
abruptly, the clouds appearing to coalesce out of clear sky.
The knights huddled under pines whose branches sagged
with snow, cloaks pulled over their heads, listening to the
wind's wail and the snow's *swish* as it struck the ground. A
fire was impossible.

From outside the tree where Lancelot crouched with
Parsifal and Gawain, Merlin's voice called, "Lancelot!
Come help me." The others growled as Lancelot's depar-
ture shook more snow on their heads. Beyond the tree, a
soaked and disheveled Merlin took Lancelot's arm, leading him to where the horses were tied at the most sheltered
end of the ravine.

"The time has come for you to perform the mission for
which you were created. You will ride on to Camelot
where Guinevere waits, alone and worried."

"I won't reach it."

"Don't fear, this storm is my doing. It barely extends a
half mile. Ride west and you'll soon be clear. Then you
can join the one who loves you."

Lancelot stopped walking. "No, I've decided that I cannot. Perhaps she loves me, but she is Arthur's wife. She's
pure and good—you'd see that if you didn't enjoy hating
her so much. She's no danger to the kingdom. You tell
yourself she is because you're jealous. She has Arthur's attention now—and you don't."

Merlin struck him in the face, his knuckles cold and sharp. "There's no time for you to spout your ridiculous theories. This is an order, do you understand? *You will go.*"

As Merlin spoke those words, Lancelot felt an enormous compulsion to leave the ravine. He *had* to. The urge was a twisting pain in his body that cried out for relief, and he knew where that relief lay—Camelot. Only there would he feel right again. He dragged his horse away through the drifts, ignoring Merlin completely.

Quite soon the snow thinned, then died away. Looking back, Lancelot saw a mountain of cloud rising in the moonlight, roiling with black and gray billows, shot through with lightning and snow. The edge of the ice on the ground was like the border of a frozen kingdom.

He brushed off the horse as he walked west, forgetting the others back in the storm. His mind felt dulled, as if shrouded in a blanket, and he thought little except to notice that with each stop toward Camelot he felt a tiny bit less anxious, a tiny bit more at peace.

Toward the very middle of the night he arrived at the silent encampment, which sat cloaked in a smoky haze. As he rode up the hill, stars faded into view—tens, then hundreds, then thousands. He told the sentries at the gate that the others would arrive in the morning.

Inside the rampart it was completely dark except for a line of light gleaming under a shuttered window at the back of the royal hall. Guinevere was awake. He should tell her the others were safe, he decided. That would be a kindness.

The Hall's great wooden door thumped loudly shut behind him, echoing in the dark chamber. He groped his way across, aiming for the glimmer of light at the far end. Just as he reached it, the door to the apartment opened. Light blinded him. Squinting, he saw Guinevere, her hand at her mouth, her eyes wide.

"Lancelot! Oh—no." She looked shattered.

"All is well," he said hastily. "The Saxons were just phantoms. The others will return tomorrow. I rode ahead."

Her whole expression changed, filling with relief. In the
low light of the hearthfire she was more beautiful than
ever. "Thank Christ. And thank *you* for bringing the news.
But you must be cold. Come in and warm up."

Lancelot never felt cold. He went into the apartment.

The sitting room was as lavishly appointed as Arthur
could manage. Tapestries hung on the walls to keep out
the cold, and a colorful carpet from somewhere in the
east covered the floor. It was too big for the room and was
discreetly folded under at one end.

Guinevere went to a carved wooden table by the hearth
and poured liquor from a glass bottle into a cup. Their
hands touched when she handed it to him. She wore a
long-sleeved undershift and a wool robe over it, open
at the waist. The outline of her body was clear to see.
Lancelot suddenly realized how he must appear—dirty
from days of riding and sleeping on the ground, wet, stinking of smoke and horse. A monstrosity next to her delicate
beauty.

Yet she did not seem repulsed. She stood unnaturally close,
and when he didn't drink, she took the cup and sipped
from it. Lancelot was confused. It was clear she loved
Arthur, yet here he stood in her chamber. Now she looked
at the floor, not meeting his gaze. "Do you think it's possible to love two people equally well?" she whispered.

A part of Lancelot's mind wobbled dizzily. He suddenly
yearned to hold her to him, feel her warmth down the
length of his body. He wanted to kiss her, touch her, feel
her touch. In all his short life he'd hardly ever been
touched, and never tenderly.

He carefully rested his hands on Guinevere's shoulders.
She did not stir. *Just a little,* he thought. Just a little
wouldn't do any harm, and he wanted it *so much.*

Guinevere moved closer. She leaned up, lips parted.
Lancelot tilted his head down.

But stopped. Even a kiss might open a door he could not
close. He couldn't do that to her. Couldn't betray Arthur

and Camelot for a brief pleasure, no matter how sweet. He knew he must only love her from afar, and so he started to pull away.

Don't get cold feet now, boy, spoke a voice inside his head.

Lancelot felt his grip on Guinevere tighten without his willing it. Merlin's voice sounded in his ear as if he stood close by, whispering. *I knew that when the crucial moment came, you would fail. Seems I didn't make you quite man enough. Well, no matter. Just relax and enjoy it.*

Lancelot's body moved against his will, pulling Guinevere to him. He roughly kissed her lips, then her neck, and she stood stiffly for a few seconds before relaxing and kissing him back with equal ardor. He tried to stop, but his body with all its strength had been stolen from him. He couldn't even speak.

His hands pushed Guinevere's robe off, sliding along her breasts and stomach while she pulled off his cape and unclasped his belt. He knelt, still kissing her, took the bottom of her undershift and drew it up. She raised her arms so he could pull it over her head, then stood naked before him, her hair spilling over her shoulders. He picked her up, kissing her face and neck as he carried her into the next room. It was dark. He was vaguely aware of the bed as he placed her on it and climbed above her to kiss her shoulders and breasts, then lower still so she squirmed and gasped, twining her fingers in his hair. After many long moments he raised his head, dizzy with overwhelming sensation, yet feeling distant from himself, an observer. Perhaps this is what dreams are like, he thought. Guinevere was helping him free of his clothes, and they drew together again, joining. His movements were quick, but Guinevere matched them, clasping her arms tightly around his neck, her forehead pressed against his shoulder. Lancelot tried to hold back but could not, and soon reached a shuddering, pounding release.

And when it had passed, he found his body was his own again. He looked at Guinevere, her body intertwined with his, strands of her hair stuck to her forehead with sweat.

Such beauty, and an innocence that he had now taken. He found he was silently crying. Guinevere touched his face where it was wet and hugged him.

Voices in the hall made them both start. The sitting room door burst open and new light shone in. *"Where are you?"* Arthur's voice boomed. He strode into the bedroom carrying a torch that lit the whole room, and gazed down at the bed in speechless fury. Behind him stood Parsifal, looking disgusted, and Merlin, whose face glowed with pleasure.

Lancelot rode through the woods, guiding his horse between the trees toward a place to which he'd never returned, yet knew unerringly how to find. Winter had stripped the trees of leaves, and ice crusted the creek's edges. When he found the place where the creek emptied into the lake, he dismounted and let the horse wander.

He waded into the creek up to his calves, thinking how the water's coldness would be painful to men. He searched for the pit in the clay bank, but there was no trace. Looking up, he saw Merlin standing on the bank. Lancelot stared at the old man for a long moment. All the rage had drained out of him that afternoon as Arthur declared his banishment. Now whenever he thought about what had happened, he felt only dazed and horrified.

Merlin attempted a smile. "I know you're angry right now, but in time you'll see this was for the best."

"How could it possibly be for the best?"

"It's best for the kingdom. We individuals must put aside our personal desires for the greater good."

Abruptly Lancelot laughed. "What a noble sentiment, when actually the opposite is what's true. All you really wanted was to lie with her."

"Posh. I only stepped in because you were weak and, I must add, a fool for refusing such a delight. It was a necessary step in plans that reach farther than you can imagine."

"No. You state grand goals, but in truth you only play with people like chess pieces. You're like a child delighting in a puppet show." He waded along the bank a few steps. Yes, this was the place. "Well, did it work? Has he killed her?"

"He sent her away. That's good enough."

He felt profoundly relieved. At least there was that. "And what of Arthur? Now he'll be lonely and bitter—what kind of king will he make then, without Guinevere to make him appreciate the good things in this world? You're going to destroy what you claim you would save."

"I've told you before to spare me your groping attempts at profound thought. You've had your cry, now it's time you got over this. We have other work to do."

"No!" Lancelot cried. The rage had not left, it had only been sleeping. "I won't get over it. Camelot is all I've ever known. It is my home, and I love those people. I love my king. And they loved me, but you—you took it all away! They all *hate* me now, and it's your doing. You made me into a monster."

Merlin folded his arms. "Well, you're not a man."

"I'm more of a man than you. I'm strong, and I'm good . . . or I was."

With that, he reached under his tongue and pried out the parchment there. Even as he did, he reverted to a statue of lifeless clay. Its raised arm split off at the elbow and splashed into the water. After a few minutes, the rushing creek eroded its legs, and it toppled over into a crumbled pile of distorted body parts. The water smoothed its features, erased and dissolved it while Merlin watched.

THE BALLAD OF THE SIDE STREET WIZARD

or
Those Low-Down, Dirty, Eternally Depressing, and Somewhat Shameful Post-Arthurian Dipshit Blues

by Gary A. Braunbeck

Gary A. Braunbeck is the acclaimed author of the collection *Things Left Behind* (CD Publications), released last year to unanimously excellent reviews and nominated for both the Bram Stoker Award and the International Horror Guild Award for Best Collection. He has written in the fields of horror, science fiction, mystery, suspense, fantasy, and western fiction, with over 120 sales to his credit. His work has most recently appeared in *Legends: Tales from the Eternal Archives, The Best of Cemetery Dance, The Year's Best Fantasy and Horror,* and *Dark Whispers.* He is coauthor (along with Steve Perry) of *Time Was: Isaac Asimov's I'Bots,* a science fiction adventure novel being praised for its depth of characterization. His fiction, to quote *Publishers Weekly,* ". . . stirs the mind as it chills the marrow."

"What is truly Divine escapes men's notice because of their incredulity."

—Heraclitus

"MYRDDIN," he says to his own image in the mirror over the bathroom sink (wondering if he should pronounce it as

Merlin, seeing as how that's the name he's remembered by . . . if, indeed, he is who he thinks he is): "She loves you not, oh, she doesn't, you poor fool."

He's put the makeup on, packed the bag of tricks— including the rabbit that he calls Mordred, and the bird, the attention getter, that he calls LeFay. He's to do a birthday party for some spoiled five year old on the other side of the river, in the Morgan Manor Estates. A crowd of babies, and the adults waiting around for him to screw up. This is going to be one of those tough ones. He has fortified himself with some generous helpings of Crown Royal, and he feels ready.

He isn't particularly worried about it.

But there's a little something else he has to do first.

Something in the order of the embarrassingly ridiculous: he has to make a delivery. This morning at the local bakery he picked up a big pink wedding cake, with its six tiers and scalloped edges and its miniature bride and groom on top, standing inside a sugar castle on a thick bed of caramel. He'd ordered it on his own; planning to offer it to Gwyneth, the young woman he worked with. He managed somehow to set the thing on the back seat of the car, and when he got home he found a note from her announcing, excited and happy, that she's engaged to her hunky Arturo the Wonder Mechanic. He's had a change of heart; he wants to get married after all. She's going off to Cincinnati to live. She loves her dear old Myrddin with a big kiss and a hug always, and she knows he'll have every happiness. She's so thankful for his friendship. Her magic man. Her sweet side street wizard. She actually drove over here and, finding him gone, left the note for him, folded under the door knocker; her notepaper with the tangle of flowers at the top. She wants him to call her, come by as soon as he can, to help celebrate. *Please,* she says, *I want to give you a big hug.*

He read this and then walked out to stand on the sidewalk and look at the cake in its place on the back seat of the car.

"Good God," he said.

Then thought: *I'm not supposed to be here, not like this, am I? Wasn't I the wizard above all wizards once, the magic man against whom all others must compare?*

Sometimes in sleep, other times during waking hours, he has flashes of memories, centuries-old, of a great, mythical kingdom, and of his place there; he remembers glory and enemies and a spell cast upon him, causing him to sleep, and now that he's awake he's living . . . backward somehow. That's right, isn't it?

He's old, and most times he forgets.

He stares at the ancient-looking staff he carries with him; the majority of its body a long, thick limb of knotted wood from a grand tree long dead, a sacred eagle's talon attached, upside down, to the top, holding a crystalline ball in place. Sometimes the ball fills with light and wondrous things happen, things he *commands* to happen.

He remembers the cake in the back of his car.

He'd thought he would deliver the cake in person, an elaborate proposal to a girl he's never even kissed. He's a little unbalanced, and he knows it. Over the months of their working together at the KMart department store, he's built up tremendous feelings of loyalty and yearning toward her. He thought she felt it, too. He interpreted gestures—her hand lingering on his shoulder when he made her laugh; her endearments tinged as they seemed to be with a kind of sadness, as if she were afraid of what the world might do to someone so romantic—as something more than, as it turns out, they actually were.

In the olden days—providing those weren't just a fantasy concocted by a failing mind—he'd simply have waved his hands and set the universe right and had her fall hopelessly in love with him.

She talked to him about her ongoing sorrows, the guy she'd been in love with who kept waffling about getting married. He wanted no commitments. Myrddin, a.k.a. Buster Francis, told her that he hated men who weren't willing to run the risks of love. Why, he personally was the type who'd always believed in marriage and children, lifelong commitments—*eternity-long* commitments. He had caused difficulties for himself, and life in this part of time was a disappointment so far, but he believed in falling in love and starting a family. She didn't hear him. It all went right through her, like white noise on the radio. For weeks he had come around to visit her, had invited her to watch him perform. She confided in him, and he thought of movies where the friend sticks around and is a good listener, and eventually gets the girl. They fall in love. He put his hope in that. He was optimistic; he'd ordered and bought the cake. Apparently the whole time, all through the listening and being noble with her, she thought of it as nothing more than friendship, accepting it from him because she was accustomed to being offered friendship.

Now he leans close to the mirror to look at his own eyes through the makeup. They look clear enough. "Loves you absolutely not. You must be crazy. A loon. A threat to society. A potential man-in-tower-with-rifle. Not-quite-right, even. You must be the Great Myrddin."

Yes.

With a great oversized cake in the back seat of his car. It's Sunday, a cool April day. He's a little inebriated. That's the word he prefers. It's polite; it suggests something faintly silly. Nothing could be sillier than to be dressed in a pointed wizard's cap and star-covered robe in broad daylight and to go driving across the bridge into the more upscale section of Cedar Hill to put on a magic show. Nothing could be sillier than to have spent all that money on a completely useless purchase—a cake six tiers high. Maybe fifteen pounds of sugar and a quart of caramel.

When he has made his last inspection of the face in the mirror, and checked the bag of tricks and props, he goes to his front door and looks through the screen at the shadow of the cake in the back seat. The inside of the car will smell like icing for days. He'll have to keep the windows open

even if it rains; he'll go to work smelling like confec-
tionery delights. The whole thing makes him laugh. A
wedding cake. He steps out of the house and makes his
way in the late afternoon sun down the sidewalk to the car.
As if they have been waiting for him, three boys come
skating down from the top of the hill. He has the feeling
that if he tried to sneak out like this at two in the morning,
someone would come by and see him anyway. "Hey,
Buster," one boy says. "I mean, Myrddin."

Myrddin recognizes him. A neighborhood boy, a tough.
Just the kind to make trouble, just the kind with no sensi-
tivity to the suffering of others. "Leave me alone, or I'll
turn you into spaghetti," he says.

"Hey, guys, it's Myrrdin the You-Could-Do-Worse."
The boy's hair is a bright blond color and you can see
through it to his scalp. "Did you remember to tape last
night's episode of *Sapphire the Sorceress?*"

"You know it's my favorite show. I enjoy looking at her
aqua eyes and long magenta hair. Many is the night I've
dreamt of that hair draped over my thighs."

"You're a perv."

Myrddin stares at the boy. "How can one not think
things when confronted with the magnificent enigmas of
Sapphire's ethereal mammalian protuberances?"

The boys look confused as they say in unison, "Huh?"

"Her Winnebegos. Floodlights. Rack. Bodacious Ta-Tas.
Bazooba-Wobblies."

He sees that he's still not getting through to them.

"Her *tits,* you post-Arthurian dipshits. Sapphire the Sorceress has got great tits."

"Jugs," says one of the boys.

"Boobs," says another.

"Knobs," adds the third boy.

"I feel as one with the aesthetic side of life," Myrddin
says. "Now scram. Sincerely."

"Aw, what's your hurry?"

"I've just set off a nuclear device," Myrddin says with

grave seriousness. "It's on a timer. The time for the Great Revolution is nigh. A few more minutes and—*Poof.*"

"Do a trick for us," the blond one says. "Where's that scurvy rabbit of yours?"

"I gave it the week off." Someone, last winter, poisoned the first Mordred (which somehow seemed like misdirected justice to him, for reasons he never quite managed to fathom). He keeps the cage indoors now. "I'm in a hurry. No rabbit to help with the driving. Elwood P. Dowd wouldn't let me borrow Harvey for the day."

"Huh?" says the boy.

"Your lack of culture depresses me."

But they're interested in the cake now. "Hey, what's that in your car? Jesus, is that real?"

"Just stay back." Myrddin gets his cases into the trunk and hurries to the driver's side door. The three boys are peering into the back seat.

"Hey, man, a cake. Can we have a piece of it?"

"Buzz off before I zap you all into newts," Myrddin says.

The blond-haired one says, "Come on, Myrddin."

"Hey, Myrddin, I saw some guys looking for you, man. They said you owed them money."

He gets in, ignoring them, and starts the car.

"Sucker," one of them says.

"Hey, man, who's the cake for?"

He can't stand it any longer. He pounds the bottom of his staff into the ground. The crystal ball fills with light, and with a wave of his hand the boys are turned into toads. He stares at them, all slimy and ridiculous-looking on the bikes, then returns them to their normal state. It amuses him to see them entangled in the pedals and chains of their bikes, each one wondering why his tongue is darting out for nearby flies.

He drives away, thinks of himself leaving them in a cloud of exhaust. He tells himself he's his own cliché—a magic man with a broken heart. Looming behind him is the cake, an irate passenger in the back seat. The people in the cake store had offered it to him in a box; he had made them give it to him like this, on a cardboard slab. It looks like it might melt.

He drives slowly, worried that it might sag, or even fall over. He has always believed viscerally that gestures mean everything. When he moves his hands and brings about the effects that amaze little children, he feels larger than life, unforgettable. He learned the magic while in high school, as a way of making friends, and though it didn't really make him any friends, he's been practicing it ever since. It's an extra source of income, and lately income has had a way of disappearing too quickly. He's been in some travail, betting the horses, betting the sports events. He's hung over all the time. There have been several polite warnings at work. He's managed so far to tease everyone out of the serious looks, the cool study of his face. The fact is, people like him in an abstract way, the way they like distant clownish figures: the comedian whose name they can't remember. He can see it in their eyes. Even the rough characters after his loose change have a certain sense of humor about it.

He's a phenomenon, a subject of conversation.

He stares at the staff, wondering if he truly turned the boys into toads, albeit momentarily.

This is not a world where the great, ancient magic has a place.

Perhaps it is better that he cannot remember.

There's traffic on the East Main Street Bridge, and he's stuck for a while. He stares out over the railing at the water of the ersatz-river below. For a moment he thinks he detects some sort of movement—something of flesh, something of silver—but all too soon it's gone, and the traffic crawls forward again. He looks at his Pinky and the Brain watch. It becomes clear that he'll have to go straight to the birthday party. Sitting behind the wheel of the car with his cake behind him, he becomes aware of people in other cars noticing him. In the car to his left, a girl stares, chewing gum. She waves, rolls her window down. Two others are with her, one in the back seat. "Hey," she says.

He nods, smiles inside what he knows is the glorious-wizard smile.

"You do magic, huh?" she says.

"Magic," he replies to her. "What the bloody hell do you know about magic? What the hell does anyone in this world *care* about real magic?"

"Take a chill pill," she says, cracking her gum.

If there were room, he knows he would pound his ancient staff and turn the gum to Perma-Glue in her mouth. "Do you know what lies at the core of all magic?" he asks her. "Everything is connected in Nature. Everything acts on everything else at a distance through a secret sympathy. The two basic assumptions in magical thinking—in *belief* and *need* for magic's purpose—are that like produces like or that an effect resembles its cause. That's the prime law of magical contact, the duct tape that holds all wizardry in place: Things which have once been in contact with each other contrive to act on each other at a distance even after the physical contact has been severed—hell, even if their connection is merely through a third, fourth, or fifth entity."

"You mean like that 'Six Degrees of Kevin Bacon' game?"

"You're very pretty. What a pity you lack a brain."

But the traffic moves again. He concentrates. The snarl is on the other side of the bridge, construction of some kind. He can see the cars in a line, waiting to go up the hill into Morgan Manor Estates and beyond. Time is beginning to be a consideration. In his glove box he has a flask of Crown Royal. More fortification. He reaches over and takes it out, looks around. No fuzz anywhere. Wouldn't do to get busted by the Man today. Just the idling cars and people tuning their radios or arguing or simply staring out as if at some distressing event. The smell of the caramel on top of the cake is making him woozy. He takes a swallow of the Scotch, then puts it away. The car with the girls in it goes by in the left lane; they are not even looking at him. He watches them go on ahead. He's in the wrong lane again; he can't remember a time when his lane was the only one moving. He told Gwyneth once that he considered himself of the race of people who gravitate to the nonmoving lanes of highways, and who cause green lights to turn yellow merely by approaching them. She took the idea and ran with it, saying she was of the race of people who emit enzymes which instill a sense of impending doom in marriageable young men.

"No," Myrddin/Buster said. "I'm living proof that isn't so. I have no such fear, and I'm with you."

"But you're of the race of people who make mine relax all the enzymes."

"You're not emitting the enzymes now, I see."

"No," she said. "It's only with marriageable young men."

"I emit enzymes that prevent people like you from seeing that I'm a marriageable young man."

"I'm too relaxed to tell," she said, and touched his shoulder. A plain affectionate moment that gave him tossing nights and fever and an embarrassingly protracted stiffy. A virtual political uprising in his pants.

Because of the traffic, he's late to the birthday party. He gets out of the car and two men come down to greet him. He keeps his face turned away, remembering too late the breath mints in his pocket.

"Hey," one of the men says, "look at this. Hey, who comes out of the cake? This is a kid's birthday party."

"The cake stays," Myrddin says.

"What does he mean, it stays? Is that a trick?"

They're both looking at him. The one spoken to must be the birthday boy's father—he's wearing a party cap that says **DAD**. How original—or perhaps he's like Myrddin, has a tendency to forget who he really is and the cap is simply the family's way to remind him when they're not around. Myrddin hopes there are plenty of mirrors in the house if that's the case, or **DAD** could be in deep sewage. The man has long, dirty-looking strands of brown hair jutting out from the cap, and there are streaks of sweaty grit on the sides of his face. "So you're the Somewhat Impressive Myrddin," he says, extending a meaty red hand. "Isn't it hot in that outfit?"

"No, sir."

"We've been playing volleyball."

"You've exerted yourselves. Perspiration can get in the way of an odor-free show. You all must shower at once, lest I turn you into roadkill."

They look at him. "What do you do with the cake?" the one in the **DAD** cap asks.

"Cake's not part of the show, actually."

"You just carry it around with you?"

The other man laughs. He's wearing a T-shirt with a smiley face on the chest. "This ought to be some show," he says.

They all make their way across the lawn, to the porch of the house. It's a big party, activities everywhere and children gathering quickly to see the wizard.

"Ladies and gentleman," says the man in the **DAD** cap. "I give you Myrddin the Not-So-Terrible."

Myrddin isn't ready yet. He's got his cases open but he needs a table to put everything on. The first trick is where he releases the bird; he'll finish with the best trick, in which the rabbit appears as if from a pan of flames. This always draws a gasp, even from the adults: the fire blooms in the pan, down goes the "lid"—it's the rabbit's tight container—the latch is tripped, and the skin of the lid lifts off. *Voila!* Rabbit. The fire is put out by the fireproof cage bottom. He's gotten pretty good at making the switch, and if the crown isn't too attentive—as children often are not—he can perform certain sleight-of-hand tricks with some style. But he needs a table, and he needs time to set up.

The whole crowd of children is seated in front of their parents, on either side of the doorway into the house. Myrddin is standing on the porch, his back to the stairs, and he's been introduced.

"Hello, boys and girls," he says, and bows. "Myrddin needs a table."

"A table," one of the women says, proving that all the family must share the same awesome genetic intelligence.

The adults simply regard him. He sees light sweaters, shapely hips, and wild tresses; he sees beer cans in tight fists, heavy jowls, bright ice-blue eyes. A little row of faces, and one elderly face. He feels more inebriated than he likes and tries to concentrate.

"Mommy, I want to touch him," one child says.

"Look at the cake," says another, who gets up and moves to the railing on Myrddin's right and trains a new pair of shiny binoculars on the car. "Do we get some cake?"

"There's cake," says the man in the **DAD** cap. "But not that cake. Get down, Ethan."

"I want that cake."

"Get down. This is Teddy's birthday."

"Mommy, I want to touch him."

"I need a table, folks. I told somebody that over the telephone."

"He did say he needed a table. I'm sorry," says a woman who is probably the birthday boy's mother. She's quite pretty, leaning in the door frame with a seater tied to her waist.

"A table," says still another woman. Is there no end to the brilliant think tank of people assembled here? Myrddin sees the birthmark on her mouth, which looks like a stain. He thinks of this woman as a child in school, with this difference from other children, and his heart goes out to her.

"I need a table," he says to her, his voice as gentle as he can make it. She doesn't notice the little wavelike gesture he makes with his hand. It probably won't be until much later, when she's washing her face before bed, that she'll notice the birthmark is gone and her face is clear-skinned and lovely.

"What's he going to do, perform an operation?" says **DAD**.

DAD is beginning to annoy. Sincerely.

It amazes Myrddin how easily people fall into talking about him as though he were an inanimate object or something on a television screen. "The Impressive Myrddin can do nothing until he gets a table," he says with as much mysteriousness and drama as he can muster under the circumstances. Then he belches and the children laugh. He tastes Crown Royal in his mouth and wonders once again if there isn't something he's missing, some sign to prove he's really a magic man, a true wizard, out of time and out of place.

"I want that cake out there," says Ethan, still at the porch railing and pointing at the magic man's car. The other children start talking about cake and ice cream, and the big cake Ethan has spotted; there's a lot of confusion and restlessness. One of the smaller children, a girl in a blue dress, approaches Myrddin. "What's your name?" she says, swaying slightly, her hands behind her back.

"Jeffrey Dahmer. And I've not had my lunch. Now go sit down. We have to sit down, or Myrddin can't do his magic."

In the doorway, two of the men are struggling with a folding card table. It's one of those rickety ones with the skinny legs, and it probably won't do.

"That's kind of shaky, isn't it?" says the woman who until recently had the birthmark.

"I said, Myrddin needs a *sturdy* table, boys and girls." Mensa could more than fill its membership roster here.

There's more confusion. The little girl has come forward and taken hold of his pant leg.

She's just standing there holding it, looking up at him. *"Jeffrey,"* she says, somewhat sadly, as if there is some secret, precious request she wishes to make but is afraid to give voice to.

"We have to go sit down," Myrddin says, bending to her, speaking sweetly. "We have to do what Myrddin wants."

Her small mouth opens wide, as if she's trying to yawn, and with pale eyes quite calm and staring she emits a screech, an ear-piercing, nonhuman shriek that brings everything to a stop. Myrddin/Buster steps back, with his amazement and his inebriate heart. Everyone gathers around the girl, who continues to scream, less piercing now, her hands fisted at her sides, those pale eyes closed tight.

"What happened?" the man in the **DAD** cap wants to know. "Where the hell's the magic tricks?"

"I told you, all I needed is a table."

"What'd you say to her to make her cry?" **DAD** indicates the little girl, who is giving forth a series of broken, grief-stricken howls.

"I want magic tricks," the birthday boy says, loud. "Where's the magic tricks?"

"Perhaps if we moved the whole thing inside," the woman without the birthmark says, fingering her left ear and making a face.

Use a Q-Tip, Myrddin thinks.

The card table has somehow made its way to him, through the confusion and grief. **DAD** sets it down and opens it.

"There," he says proudly, as if he has just split the atom.

In the next moment, Myrddin realizes that someone's removed the little girl. Everything's relatively quiet again, though her cries are coming through the walls of one of the rooms inside the house. There are perhaps fifteen children, mostly seated before him, and five or six men and women behind them, or kneeling with them.

"Okay, now," **DAD** says. "Myrddin the Somewhat Terrific."

"Hello, little boys and girls," Myrddin says, deciding that the table will have to suffice. "I'm happy to be here. Are you glad to see me?" A general uproar commences.

"Well, good," he says. "Because just look what I have in my magic bag." And with a flourish he brings out the hat that he will release LeFay from. The bird is encased in a fold of shiny cloth, pulsing there. He can feel it. He rambles on, talking fast, or trying to, and when the time comes to reveal the bird, he almost flubs it. But LeFay flaps her wings and makes enough of a commotion to distract even the adults, who applaud and urge the stunned children to applaud. "Isn't that wonderful," Myrddin hears. "Out of nowhere."

"He had it hidden away," says the birthday boy, who has managed to temper his astonishment. He's the type who heaps scorn on those things he can't understand, or own.

"Now," Myrddin says, "for my next spell, I need a helper from the audience." He looks right at the birthday boy—round face, short nose, freckles. Bright red hair. Little green eyes. The whole countenance speaks of glutted appetites and sloth. This kid could be on the Roman coins, an emperor. Caligula without the whimsical wit. He's not used to being compelled to do anything, but seems eager for a chance to get into the act. "How about you?" Myrddin says to him.

The others, led by their parents, cheer.

The birthday boy gets to his feet and makes his way over the bodies of the other children to stand with Myrddin. In order for the trick to work, Myrddin must get everyone watching the birthday boy, and there's another star-covered, pointed hat he keeps in the bag for this purpose.

"Now," he says to the boy, "since you're part of the show, you have to wear a costume." He produces the hat as if from behind the boy's ear. Another cheer goes up. He puts the hat on the boy's head and adjusts it, crouching down. The green eyes stare impassively at him; there's no hint of awe or fascination in them. "There we are," he says. "What a handsome, mysterious-looking fellow you are."

The birthday boy takes off the hat and looks at it as if a large, mythical bird has just dropped a large, mythical turd on his head.

Myrddin takes a deep breath. "We have to wear the hat to be on stage."

"Ain't a stage," the boy says.

Definitely an Einsteinian brain trust here.

"But," Myrddin says for the benefit of the adults. "Didn't you know that all the world's a stage?" He tries to put the hat on him again, but the boy moves from under his reach and slaps his hand away. "We have to wear the hat," Myrddin says, trying to control his anger. "We can't do the magic without our magic hats." He tries once more, and the boy waits until the hat is on, then simply removes it and holds it behind him, shying away when Myrddin tries to retrieve it. The noise of the others now sounds like the crowd at a prizefight; there's a contest going on, and they're enjoying it. "Give Myrddin the hat. We want magic, don't we?"

"Do the magic," the boy demands.

"Give me the hat."

"I won't."

Sometimes life for Myrddin is just too fun to endure.

He looks around. There's no support from the adults. Perhaps if he weren't a little tipsy; perhaps if he didn't feel ridiculous and sick at heart and forlorn, with his wedding cake and his odd mistaken romance, his loneliness, which he has always borne gracefully and with humor, and his general dismay; perhaps if he were to find it in himself to deny the sudden, overwhelming sense of the unearned affection given this lumpish, slovenly version of stupid, complacent, spoiled satiation standing before him—he might've simply gone on to the next trick.

Instead, at precisely that moment when everyone seems to pause, he leans down and says, "Give me the hat, you little prick."

The green eyes widen.

The quiet is heavy with disbelief. Even the small children can tell that something's happened to change everything.

"Myrddin has another trick," Buster says loudly, "where he makes the birthday boy expand like an ugly pimple and then pop like a balloon. It's especially fun if he's a *fat* birthday boy."

A stirring among the adults.

"Especially if he's an ugly, offensive, grotesque slab of superfluous flesh like this one here."

"Now just a minute," says **DAD**.

"Give it up," Myrddin says to the birthday boy, who

drops the hat and then, seeming to remember that defiance is expected, makes a face. Sticks out his tongue. Myrddin is quick with his hands by training, and he grabs the tongue.

"Awwwk," the boys says. *"Aw-aw-aw."* Myrddin keeps pulling and pulling on the boy's tongue, which keeps coming out, more and more, like toilet paper from a never-ending roll, gathering in great, slimy loops at his feet.

To hell with it, thinks the magic man, and with a free hand grabs his staff and thumps it on the ground, returning the birthday boy's tongue to it's normal size and erasing the memory of the sight from everyone present.

"Abracadabra." Myrddin lets go and the boy falls backward onto the lap of one of the other children. More cries. "Whoops, time to sit down," says Myrddin/Buster. "Sorry you had to leave so soon."

Very quickly, he's being forcibly removed. They're rougher than gangsters. They lift him, punch him, tear at his costume—even the women. Someone hits him with a spoon. The whole scene boils over onto the lawn, where someone has released Mordred from his case. He moves about wide-eyed, hopping between running children, evading them, as Myrddin the Befuddled and Put-Upon cannot evade the adults. He's being pummeled because he keeps trying to return for his rabbit. And the adults won't let him off the curb. "Okay," he says finally, collecting himself. He wants to let them know he's not like this all the time; wants to say it's circumstances, grief, personal pain hidden inside seeming like brightness and cleverness. He's a man in love, humiliated, wrong about everything. He wants to tell them, but he can't speak for a moment, can't even quite catch his breath. He stands in the middle of the street, his ancient robe torn, his face bleeding, all his magic strewn everywhere. "I would at least like to collect my rabbit," he says, and is appalled at the absurd sound of it—its huge difference from what he intended to say. He straightens, pushes the grime from his face, and looks at them. "I would say that even though I wasn't as patient as

I could've been, the adults have not comported themselves well here," he says.

"Drunk," one of the women says.

Almost everyone's chasing Mordred now. One of the older boys approaches, carrying LeFay's case. LeFay looks out the airhole, impervious, quiet as a bad idea. And now one of the men, someone Myrddin hasn't noticed before, an older man clearly wearing a hairpiece, brings Mordred to him. "Bless you," Myrddin says, staring into the man's sleepy, deploring eyes.

"I don't think we'll pay you," the man says. The others are filing back into the house, herding the children before them.

Myrddin/Buster speaks to the man. "The rabbit appears out of fire. By the way, have I mentioned that I don't really belong here? I'm out of place, out of time—you know, in the midst of a Billy Pilgrim: Unstuck. *Po-tweet.*"

The older man leaves, and **DAD** is back, carrying a baseball bat which hangs threateningly at his side. "You should leave now."

"You don't . . . you don't understand," says Myrddin/Buster, his voice cracking and tears forming in his eyes. "I shouldn't be here, I have no place. My *magic* has no place, not anymore. I'm not even sure that I'm who I think I am. Living backward in time can confuse a person." He's sobbing now, a pathetic sight, but he doesn't care. Before the day is over he must make *someone* understand.

"This world no longer believes in magic, and what magic there is, is quickly dismissed. Did you read the paper this morning? The Swiss have turned lead into gold! Okay, okay, okay—forget that they did it with a particle accelerator and that the process is so damned expensive that it renders the process pointless . . . the *act itself* was the truest, most miraculous kind of magic. I mean, I could have done it for them, but no one asked. Besides, what's the point?"

He thumps his staff into the ground. The crystal ball fills with light. "Now, *right now*, I could lay some magic on you that would make your head spin! I could gather the whole neighborhood and have all of you watch as I cause the sun to do figure eights in the sky . . . but how long would that wonder linger? How long until you started chalking it all up to stress, or weariness, or the heat, or mass hypnosis or delusions or some trick of digital technology?" He's really weeping now, and wishes he were back in the car so he might chug down more Scotch. "What need is there for my kind of magic? *Any* magic? Can you tell me that?"

The man nods. "Go home and sleep it off, asshole."

"Right. Thank you. Compliments are always appreciated." He makes another unseen wave with his hand and changes the large letters of **DAD** to smaller letters that say: **I AM A CONVICTED PEDOPHILE: THANK HEAVEN FOR LITTLE GIRLS. OR BOYS. I'M NOT PICKY.**

He puts Mordred in his compartment, stuffs everything in its place in the trunk. Then he gets in the car and drives away. Around the corner he stops, wipes off what he can of the makeup; it's as if he's trying to remove the stain of bad opinion and disapproval. Nothing feels any different.

Soon he finds himself on the East Main Street Bridge again. The traffic has cleared up. He pulls over to the side and gets out of the car, leaning against the railing.

It's not a great drop to the water below, but if he threw himself off at just the right angle, he might manage to land headfirst on that pile of cement blocks on the shore.

"Show me the magic," he whispers to no one in particular.

Then—there it is again: a glimpse beneath the surface of flesh and silver.

He takes in his breath and holds it.

The surface of the river ripples, and a long, bright, mighty silver sword rises from the water, held by the long-fingered, delicate, elegant hand of an unseen lady.

"Myth," he whispers. "A literary archetype of sorts, buried in the mass subconscious. Jung could explain you away in a heartbeat."

The unseen lady's other hand then breaks surface, her

lovely fingers flexing for a moment before folding into her palm.

All except one, that is.

With Excalibur held high in one hand, the Lady gives Myrddin the finger with her other hand.

"Okay, maybe Jung'd have a problem explaining away this."

You are who you think you are, Magic Man, says a voice from unseen lips.

It is a song his heart cannot contain.

He decides to forgo offing himself under the circumstances.

He gets back into the car and drives to the suburban street where Gwyneth lives with her parents, and by the time he gets there, it's almost dark.

The houses are set back in the trees. He sees lighted windows, hears music, the sound of children playing in the yards. He parks the car and gets out. A breezy April dusk. "I am Myrddin the Soft-Hearted," he says. "Hearken to me." Then he sobs. He can't believe it. "Jeez," he says, "I'm a bit pathetic today, aren't I?"

But at least you know who you are, he reminds himself.

Perhaps he can find hope in that.

He opens the back door of the car, leans in to get the cake. He'd forgotten how heavy it is. Staggering with it, making his way along the sidewalk, intending to leave it on her doorstep, he has an inspiration. Hesitating only for the moment it takes to make sure there are no cars coming, he goes out and sets it down in the middle of the street. Part of the top sags from having bumped his shoulder as he pulled it off the back seat. The bride and groom are almost supine, one on top of the other—a precursor of pleasures yet to come. He straightens them, steps back and looks at it. In the dusky light it looks blue. It sags just right, with just the right angle expressing disappointment and sorrow. Yes, he thinks. This is the place for it. The aptness of it, sitting out like this, where anyone who might come by and splatter it all over creation, makes him feel a faint sense of release, as if he were at the end of a story. Everything will be all right if he can think of it that way. He's wiping his eyes, thinking of moving to another town. Failures are beginning to catch up to him, and he's still achingly in love. He thinks how he has suffered the pangs of failure and misadventure, but in this painful instance there's symmetry, and he will make the one eloquent gesture—leaving a wedding cake in the middle of the road, like a pylon made of icing. Yes.

He walks back to the car, gets in, pulls around, and backs into the driveway of the house across the street from hers. Leaving the engine idling, he rolls the window down and rests his arm on the sill, gazing at the incongruous shape of the cake there in the falling dark. He feels almost glad—almost, in some strange inexpressible way, vindicated. He imagines what she might do if she saw him here, imagines that she comes running from her house, calling his name, looking at the cake and admiring it. He conjures a picture of her, attacking the tiers of pink sugar, and the muscles of his abdomen tighten. But then this all gives way to something else: images of destruction, of flying dollops of icing. He's surprised to find that he wants her to stay where she is, doing whatever she's doing. He realizes that what he wants—and for the moment all he really wants—is what he now has: a perfect vantage point from which to watch oncoming cars. Turning the engine off, he makes another imperceptible wave with his hand. The cake is now the size of a castle, taking up all of the center of the street and several feet of surrounding yards.

He decides that, when he gets home, he'll watch *Sapphire the Sorceress*. Maybe he'll even thump his staff and conjure her up for some Horizontal Medieval Humpty Dancing.

He's Merlin, after all. He can do that sort of thing.

Grinning, he stares at the cake, then makes it a bit bigger. "Indeed, I shall dub thee *Carmelot*."

Not a great joke, but it makes him laugh. And so he waits, concentrating on the giant castle-cake and the brouhaha that will undoubtedly ensue once someone notices it. He's a man imbued with interest, almost peaceful with it—almost, in fact, happy with it—sitting there in the quiet car and patiently awaiting the results of his labor and thinking that maybe, just maybe, magic still has a place, after all.

*For William Peter Blatty,
with respect, admiration, and thanks.*

THE END OF SUMMER

by R. Davis

R. Davis currently resides in Green Bay, Wisconsin, with his very patient wife Monica and his beautiful daughter Morgan Storm. He holds a B.A. in English from the University of Wisconsin, and writes both fiction and poetry. His current projects include a book-length manuscript of poems entitled *In the Absence of Language* and several novel projects that may never see the light of day.

CARRION birds circled on thermals above the battlefield. Hundreds of foot soldiers, the last tattered remnants of the war band, lay dead or dying. The birds were waiting only for the last twitches of movement to stop, and the groans to cease. In the distance, the great castle of Camelot stood silent vigil over the ground where Arthur had made his final stand. In the fading gray sunlight of late afternoon, the walls themselves appeared to be mourning his passing. I watched as Queen Guinevere slowly made her way toward the battlefield along the road leading to the castle. She was riding her favorite horse, a bad-tempered milk-white stallion. Her gaze was fixed on the silhouetted figure of a large man walking toward her. Lancelot. He was limping slightly on his left leg, and still carried his shield and

sword. They met at the halfway point between the castle
and the field. I remained where I was, hidden in the trees,
to watch.

Lancelot spoke first. "My lady, it is finished."

Her eyes flicked over the bodies littered between the
river and herself. "And Arthur?" she asked softly.

"No, my lady," Lancelot said. "He fought well, but died
at the climax of the battle. It was Mordred's spear that took
him." As her face momentarily sharpened, he added, "It
was very quick, my lady. And he killed Mordred at the
same exact moment, so justice was done."

She nodded, always the composed queen. I remember
Arthur teaching her that there was always time for grief—
in private. "Now what will we do, Lancelot?"

"My lady?"

"You heard me," she said.

"It is over. Mordred is dead and can trouble us no more.
But the war band is destroyed. And the king, my king, is
dead."

"Yes, that is so," she said, while I marveled at her calm.
"But what will happen to Camelot, to Britain? Will the
realm survive? Will I still be Queen?"

I chose that moment to answer her from the shadows of
the trees. "Of course not."

They both turned toward me in surprise. I was exhausted
and no doubt looking my age. Guinevere had a look of dis-
taste on her face as she did whenever an elderly person
was around. She was incredibly vain, and no doubt feared
that the wrinkles of old age might somehow be contagious.
Still, I could never fault her manners. "God be praised!"
she said, as I staggered my way toward her. "Merlin,
you're alive!"

"Oh, yes, Queen Guinevere," I said. "Still quite alive,
much to the chagrin of many." I looked at the battlefield
and in memory replayed my part in it. "It would take
worse than this pitiful battle to kill Merlin," I said.

"Still, it must be by the grace of God that you live," said

Lancelot. "I thought I saw you during the battle, though perhaps I was mistaken."

"You are not mistaken. I fought in the battle, not far from Arthur's side." Here I paused to let the words sink in, and Lancelot paled somewhat. "Still," I continued, "Arthur is dead. The Kingdom of Summer has come to its end, as do all things. There will be much strife, much chaos. And there will never be another like Arthur." I turned back to Guinevere. "You asked what will happen, my lady?"

She appeared almost eager. "Yes, Merlin. What will happen now?"

I looked at her then, to try and judge with my eyes what had become of the black-haired girl who had come here so long ago. She was not a girl now, but a woman grown both in body and in power. Her hair, once black as jet, carried a large streak of white from the crown of her head. Her eyes were a pale blue today, but I'd seen them range from that to almost lavender on various occasions. She had become comfortable with power, perhaps too comfortable. It would be best if I shattered her quickly-forming image of the future now. "Well," I said, "it seems a little late for the asking, but as you wish to know, I will tell you what I see."

The vision fell upon me then, and the voice that spoke next was my own and yet not my own. "I see Britain falling apart, a land torn asunder and entering into a darkness where once again barbarians plunder at will. I see the light of God dimming in the land, the trees having no leaves, and the fields bearing no harvest. Animals will starve and children will die. Camelot shall be lost, a home for ravens and jackals. And I see death. Death, plague and fire," I said, shuddering. It was a hideous vision, but when the sight comes and places the words of the future on the tongue of a true bard, he cannot fail to utter it. As my vision cleared, I said bitterly, "Is this the vision you hoped to hear, my Queen?"

Guinevere had paled under the onslaught, and Lancelot had stiffened and half-raised his shield to ward off an unseen blow. "Surely, Merlin, it is not as bad as all that," she said. "There must be some hope."

"Hope, my lady?" I asked. 'There is always hope."

Lancelot looked up with interest, and turned toward me. "What would that be?" he asked, with that slight sneer of his. Oh, he was an arrogant bastard for all of his greatness as a knight. Now, even that was ruined.

"Justice and bard's tales," I said. "In these lie Britain's only hope."

Guinevere stared at me. In the last glimmer of sunlight, her hair had taken on the color of blood in snow. "What do you mean, Merlin?" she asked.

"Yes, Merlin," Lancelot seconded. "Tell us what you mean. Don't give us your normal gibberish and riddles. Give us answers!"

"Oh bother!" I said. "You see, yet you are blind. You hear, yet fail to listen. Must I teach you everything, now that all is lost to you? Are you children who must be guided through the dark time of night by the hand?"

Guinevere laughed suddenly, perhaps caught up in the image of herself and Lancelot being led by me though the darkness. In that moment, I was almost able to forgive her. Her laughter was girlish and light, and dispelled the growing tension around us, at least momentarily. "Come now, Merlin," she said. "You are being unfair, my old friend. When have we done wrong?"

And that tore it for me, but I knew the game I played and laughed anyway. "Wrong?" I asked. "Bah! Lady you have wronged so many it is a wonder that the dead of Britain do not rise up to strike you down where you stand! All of heaven cries out for justice and you wish me to absolve you? Now of all times?"

Guinevere gasped. "What do you mean?"

"I know!" I said bitterly. "I know about you! About both of you! Arthur knew, and said nothing out of love for you. Worse still," I added, pointing at Lancelot, "I know the secret of his heart that not even you share at this moment."

Lancelot flushed, and his hand unconsciously dropped

toward his sword hilt. I turned to face him, and raised a hand in warning. "Beware, Knight. Though your prowess would surely test me, there is no doubt about who would be the victor should you try to harm me."

He moved his hand away calmly. "I am not surprised, Wizard. You were always the meddler, steeped in secrets. It is said you cannot be killed by any man now living. Is this true?"

"Who can say?" I replied. "It was not my vision, but Morgan le Fay's that began that rumor." I shrugged. "Perhaps it is true, perhaps not—though you'd be unwise to test it."

Lancelot nodded once, as though this answer somehow satisfied him, but I could not imagine how. "Why did you not call us out?" he asked. "It is treason, both of the hand and the heart, to commit adultery with the queen. Why did you not demand fit punishment?"

He sounded slightly desperate to me, and I felt this a good sign. He was feeling his guilt. "It was not my place to accuse you, but Arthur's. And he chose to forebear doing so for both your sakes, though it broke his heart."

Lancelot hung his head. "You cannot wound me further. You do not accuse me of anything that I myself have not felt in my heart."

I shook my head in bewilderment. *Fools in love,* I thought to myself. "I couldn't do it because of love," I said, turning to make my way down the hill. "Love is the foundation, the very cornerstone of the world."

Guinevere quickly dismounted, and she and Lancelot followed me on foot. I could hear them talking softly together for a moment, but I chose not to listen in. Declarations of love, no doubt, and perhaps of regret. Either way, I had not the strength remaining to listen to such things.

As I began winding my way among the bodies, the birds overhead circled lower while the field physicians removed the last of those who might live.

* * *

They caught up to me as I stood over the dragon standard. It was muddy and torn from being trampled underfoot. All around us, the bodies of those who were the last to fall were locked in their grim poses of death. Guinevere averted her eyes. "What do you do here, Merlin?" she asked, softly.

I reached down and picked up the standard. Then I slowly began to fold it. "I am saving something for the future," I said, "bleak as it now is."

She reached out and touched my shoulder. "Please, Merlin," she said.

I whipped around so hard that my long white hair swirled cloudlike above my head. Guinevere actually took a step back from me upon seeing the anger and revulsion in my eyes. At that moment the thought of her touching me filled me with dread. "Please?" I said. "Please? That is all you can say? You are the one at fault here. You are the one who was disloyal. And you ask me 'please'?" I said.

Lancelot stepped between us. "No Merlin, it was not her fault. I am to blame."

I sneered at him. "You are both to blame! If it were not for the distraction you caused with your callous disregard for propriety and honor, Arthur would have been able to withstand Mordred's schemes. Now he is dead and the realm with him."

Guinevere held up her hands. "No, Lancelot, he is right. There is fault in both of us. We are both to blame. I, perhaps, most of all." She lifted her head and turned to me. "But what I did, I did out of love. God help me, it is true. I loved—still love—them both."

I took the folded standard and placed it in a large sack I carried with me. Reaching out, I placed my hand under her chin and tilted her head up as though she were but a child. "Love. It is man's greatest joy and his most common downfall. Arthur loved you, and look what it brought him."

"I know," she said. "Still, you must tell us what to do now. Is it too late to fix things?"

I was stunned. "Fix things!" I repeated. "Now you want to fix things? Haven't you done enough? Isn't it enough that because of you, the Summerland is no more?"

"I know I wish to make it right, if I can." She bowed her head again.

Lancelot nodded in agreement. "Yes, Merlin. Tell us what you think we should do."

"You wish to fix things, too, great champion?" I asked.

"I do," Lancelot said.

"Then tell her—no, show her—your unspeakable crime."

Lancelot's eyes widened. "I cannot. It would be too much."

Guinevere looked at him. "What is it he speaks of?" she asked.

"My lady, it is nothing," he said hurriedly. "Come, let us go away from here. I will take you back to the castle. We can decide what to do from there."

I laughed. "Nothing, he says, it is nothing. Well, what a perspective love has given you, Lancelot. Come now, are you afraid? Is the mighty champion of the Round Table afraid of the truth?"

Lancelot's breath hissed between his teeth. He was always a man who lived on the outside of his skin, and his anger with me was growing. "No, meddler," he said. "I do not fear. There are some things a lady should not see."

Guinevere stiffened. "I am still queen, Lancelot, lest you forget. What is it that you do not wish me to see?"

"Please, my lady. It is nothing, as I said. Let us go." he said, gently taking her arm.

She shook him off. "Merlin, what is this you speak of? Do you now wish to sow dissension between the two of us?"

I smiled. "Not at all, Guinevere. When have I poorly served you? Ever have I been loyal to the crown." I looked at Lancelot. "Will you tell her?"

"Only if I must," he grated.

"You must," I said, "or I will. You speak of making things right. That is a hard road to walk, even when the light shines brightly. Truth will start you on that path."

Lancelot turned back to Guinevere. "Must you see this, lady? It is not a thing I would wish you to see or know."

She nodded, her eyes bright with curiosity. She had always been curious, I remembered, then realized it was probably that same "curiosity" that had led her into Lancelot's arms. "Come," she said. "Let us at least be forthright with each other. We've been lying to everyone else for so long, can we no longer even tell each other the truth?"

Lancelot shook his head. "Very well, I will show you. I could not have long kept it from you anyway. Already this thing eats at my heart. But first, I require two things, if I may be so bold."

"What is it?" she asked.

"One, that you hear me out before sitting in judgment on my crime."

"That is only fair," she said. "Besides, with the exception of loving me, you have always been a man of high honor. It is unthinkable that you would commit a crime."

His face burned with shame. "Perhaps once that was true, lady."

Guinevere raised an eyebrow at this, but did not comment. "And the other?" she asked.

He pointed at me. "I require that Merlin come with us. It is he who cast this stone, and I would have him there to see the end."

"Done," I said. "I wouldn't miss it."

Lancelot set down his shield and pointed toward a cluster of bodies. "That is where we must go," he said beginning to walk.

"Where do you take us?" Guinevere asked.

"To Arthur," he said, not looking back.

Guinevere went white. "But the messenger said his body had not yet been found!"

"I know where he lies," said Lancelot. "Follow me, if you insist on the truth of this matter."

We stepped carefully over the bodies around us, and made our slow way toward the crumpled figures that

Lancelot had pointed out. The carrion birds had landed, crows and buzzards, and were beginning to feast. The raucous cries echoed in the slowly gathering dark.

Lancelot reached the dead soldiers first, and quickly moved the bodes aside. Just as Guinevere and I came upon him, he reached the bottom of the pile. "There," he said, pointing. "There is Arthur, my King."

Guinevere knelt down. Arthur's face was dirty from blood and sweat. His blue eyes were—mercifully—closed. His armor, once burnished and bright, was dented and broken. Lancelot and I were silent. Guinevere took Arthur's hand and held it to her cheek. "Oh, my bright lord," she whispered. "Would that all had never happened, that I could take this cup from your lips and drink it down, I would." She clasped his hand tightly, and removed his amethyst ring. "For the future," she said. She was crying openly now, her tears washing his hand. I was a little taken aback. In all the years I had known her, I had never seen her display grief so openly. She sobbed, and said, "I am so sorry, my lord." Then she carefully placed his hand across his chest, and started to rise. Suddenly, she stopped. "Lancelot?"

"Yes, my lady?" he asked

"Where is the sword? Where is Excalibur?"

"I . . ." he said. "I have it." He pulled back his tattered cloak to reveal the hilt of Arthur's sword.

"You?" asked Guinevere. "Why?"

"I thought to return it," he said.

"Where?"

"To a lake or pond of still water. Often I have heard Arthur speak of how he came by the sword. It seemed right to return it from where it came."

Guinevere nodded as though this answer pleased her in some small way. Then, she handed the ring to me. "Here. Like the standard, keep this against the future. One day, the darkness may recede." She turned to Lancelot. "This is what you wished to show me?" she asked. "What crime in this? He is dead, as you said."

"Yes, my lady. This is what I wished to show you."

I laughed again. "Oh, come now, Lancelot. You have to tell her. She is no veteran of battle to see the truth in the shadow of how the bodies lay."

"Why, meddler?" Lancelot shouted at me. "She has seen enough I say. Let it be."

"Not enough!" I roared back. "Not by half! Or even half of that! Tell her, champion of honor."

Lancelot's shoulders sagged in defeat—something I had never expected to see. "I cannot," Lancelot said, subdued. "It is beyond me." He sat down and lowered his head. In a muffled voice, he said, "You tell her. You seem bent on destroying what light there is left for me, so you do it."

Guinevere went to him then. "Rest easy. I see no crime here. There is nothing he can say that will take me away from you." She sat down next to him, placing her clean white hand over his. "Speak, Merlin. I am curious as to where your riddle leads."

"Oh, it is no riddle, Guinevere. But perhaps a picture will do better than words."

"What do you mean?" she asked.

"I mean I shall conjure it for you. Arthur's last moments, exactly as they happened."

She looked dismayed at the prospect, but then shrugged. "If you feel it important, Merlin."

"I do," I replied, and set to work.

Taking up my staff once again, I inscribed a circle upon the soil. Then, I bade Lancelot to find enough wood for the fire. He mumbled something about ". . . not being a damned errand boy," before wandering away to do so. Guinevere watched me with interest, sitting composedly on the ground nearby. From my back sack I removed those herbs necessary for the conjuring. Lastly, I went to Arthur and removed a lock of his blond hair. By then Lancelot had returned, and was building the fire within the circle I had drawn upon the soil.

Once it was burning nicely, Lancelot stepped away and gestured to me. "Well, Wizard, make your magic."

I could tell he was frightened. Lancelot had always had a somewhat unreasonable fear of Druids and magic. I chuckled to myself. "Lancelot, I require yet one more thing."

"Oh?" he said. "My blood? You already have my soul, and the heart that moved it. What more could you want?"

"Nothing so exotic, I assure you," I said. "I merely wish a small sample of your hair."

"What for?" he asked, looking first at me, then at the fire suspiciously.

"It will aid me in conjuring the truth of what really happened here today," I said.

Lancelot shrugged. "What choice have I? You have forced the issue, and so I must go along." He removed his dagger from its sheath and lopped off a small clipping of his curly black hair. He handed it out to me with some small measure of grace before returning to his seat beside Guinevere.

"Excellent," I said, turning at once for the fire. I didn't really want to do this, having been through the battle myself. Nor had I any wish to hurt Guinevere. While she would never have been the choice I would have made for Arthur, he had loved her, and in time I had come to appreciate the quality of her mind—if not her heart. Love is often like a battlefield, I thought to myself, filled with small triumphs, joys, and even camaraderie—but there's a great deal of suffering, blood, and usually a few lies to go with it all.

I placed the herbs which I had wrapped around Arthur and Lancelot's hair on the top of the fire. They began to smoke and as they did so, I spoke softly in the language of the Druids.

This was the old tongue, rarely heard anymore. It was the language of the fields and the trees. Of green growing things and clouds, of rocks, and dirt, and mice. It was the language of the birds. The incantation rolled off my tongue, and in the cloud of smoke hovering over the fire, a picture began to form. It was the battlefield earlier that day. . . .

Arthur is strapping his shield on to his left arm with the help of a squire. He speaks (though it was impossible for us to hear him) *to several of his cavalry commanders. He gestures toward the far side of the field where Mordred is also organizing his forces. Those gathered nearest him laugh, and Arthur smiles. He glances around one last time as though seeking someone, and then finally he shrugs and mounts his horse. . . .*

A soldier is making his quick way around the encampment toward Mordred's side of the field. Crossing through their picket lines, he goes unnoticed. He is not wearing knightly armor, but rather armor that is old and dented. . . .

Mordred and Arthur face each other. Mordred makes a contemptuous gesture with his spear, and Arthur smiles as though expecting insult. They come at each other, hacking and slashing. It is quickly obvious that Arthur is the more skilled. . . .

The soldier is carving a path through the battle. All around there is death, but it does not touch him though he deals it out with quick efficiency. The soldier's blade flashes in the sunlight as he draws closer to where Arthur and Mordred continue their fight. . . .

Mordred's face is marred by cuts, and his helm is dented. There is a look of pain, and animal desperation on his face. He lunges toward Arthur, who turns his enemy gracefully away, forcing Mordred's spear out of his hand. It lands some distance away, and Mordred draws his sword. . . .

The soldier has, for the moment, run out of enemies. At his feet is Mordred's spear, and he reaches down to pick it up. He hefts it in his hand, testing the balance of the weapon. A few feet away, Arthur has disarmed Mordred again. He begins to close the gap, intent on finishing this combat. . . .

The soldier raises the spear to shoulder height and takes careful aim. Arthur's broad back is clearly visible and over it, the face of Mordred, seeing his own death. The soldier lets fly with the spear in the same moment that Arthur swings Excalibur at Mordred's head. The two weapons, sword and spear, strike their targets. . . .

Mordred's head rolls into the dust, his eyes wide and staring. Arthur falls to his knees, still clutching Excalibur. Slowly, he drops to his side, forcing his body to turn so that he can see his new attacker. . . .

The soldier walks quickly to where Arthur has fallen. Reaching down, he places a booted foot to either side of Arthur's back and pulls the spear out. Arthur screams as the serrated edge severs his spinal cord. His blood is pooling on the ground beneath him. . . .

The soldier tosses the spear away, and it lands in the dirt near Mordred's body. He kneels down beside Arthur and removes his helm. As the light fades from Arthur's eyes, an expression of betrayed recognition passes over his face. He dies, and the soldier—Lancelot—takes Excalibur, stands and walks quickly away. . . .

The smoke cleared away on a light breeze as the vision faded. In that span of a few seconds, the only sounds that could be heard were the carrion birds continuing their grisly feast.

Guinevere leaped to her feet, and turned to Lancelot. "You told me he died fighting Mordred. You said they died at the same time!"

Lancelot stared guiltily at her. "I am sorry, my lady."

"Where, then, lies Mordred?" she asked.

I pointed to another mound of nearby bodies. "There, Guinevere," I said. "There is where Mordred fell."

We sat for some time, silent in the near total darkness. Finally, Guinevere spoke, and her voice had aged. "Merlin, can you give us some light?"

I spoke a word, and the crystal at the end of my staff flared. "Better?" I asked.

She shook her head. "Nothing will ever be better again. My lover, who was once the most honorable man in the kingdom, has killed my husband who was the light of the world. There is no *better*."

I smiled at her, a little sad. Wisdom, when it comes, is always painful and usually late. "Do not fear, my Queen. We may yet salvage something from this mess."

She looked up at me, and I could see she'd been holding back tears. "How so?" she asked.

"In a moment," I replied, then turned to Lancelot who had remained silent and brooding for some time. "Will you tell her all now?" I asked.

"What choice have I?" he answered. "Now that you've shown this much, what else is there but to confess all?"

"None," I said. "But by telling all, at least she will know the truth. As for the rest, well, we shall see." I must admit it now. I wanted him to suffer then. I knew telling it would bring him pain, but I was angry. His crime, though committed for love, was heinous and evil.

Lancelot nodded and shrugged. "Is it your wish, also, to hear this tale, my lady? For I would not do it merely at his bidding."

"Like you, what choice do I have? Until a few moments ago, I believed at least my future with you be secure. Now, thanks to Merlin, even that is gone."

"Be patient, Guinevere," I said. "I only do which must be done. Do not hold anger in your heart for me."

She sighed. "Just tell it, Lancelot. Let us light this final darkness."

"So be it, my lady. Though the telling brings me no pleasure and I am no bard." Lancelot stood, and walked over to where she had reseated herself at some distance from him, on the ground. "This is the way of it, then," he said.

"Some time ago, you and I became lovers. That is the bald truth. We had always been friends, but I knew from the moment you came to Camelot that I loved you. Never have I loved or wanted a woman more. Yet you belonged to Arthur, my king. I knew that I could never have you—entirely—and I could not find it in my heart to take you from him. I could see the tear in your heart as well. You loved Arthur, too. Many times, as we lay together in regret, you said as much. We both knew it had to end.

"Yet I still sought some solution. Eventually I hit upon it. What if Arthur were to be killed in battle? Who, then, would be crowned king? Why, most assuredly, the Council would vote for me. As war leader and with Arthur having no heir, I was first in line for the throne. Not that I wanted it, but to have you, and with Arthur out of the way, I would find a way to make it happen.

"But we have lived at peace for so long. Arthur gave us that. Peace and prosperity throughout the realm—his vision of the Kingdom of Summer. But I had heard of a young mercenary of some renown in Ireland. Mordred. The travelers said he was gifted in battle, and had many knights among his war band. I sent him a message and asked him if he would be interested in making some amount of fortune for himself here in Britain. He responded with interest, and we arranged a time to meet and make our dark plans.

"I explained to him the situation here, and together we decided upon a solution. For long and long, the rumor had abounded that Arthur was possessed of a bastard son. Mordred looked the part almost perfectly with his blond hair and well-muscled body. In fact he didn't look Irish at all. The plan was simple and direct. Mordred would come to Camelot and present himself as Arthur's son, come to claim his due. Arthur, of course, would refuse, and Mordred would continue to badger him, eventually forcing a battle. When he came here, Mordred had his story in place. He was a gifted actor. He whispered, insinuated, he lied, distracted, and finally forced Arthur into defending his honor.

"But things went wrong. Even before the battle, I saw it clearly. Arthur would win unless a miracle should happen." Lancelot stopped and took up one of Guinevere's hands. "I could not face that, dear heart. I could not see all my fine work to possess you completely, wasted by a fool. It was obvious that Mordred had not only misled Arthur, but he had misled me about his battle skills. I was determined to end it for certain.

"I stole some armor and fought on Mordred's side of the battle, making my way to where Arthur fought. I killed— again and again—sword-brothers I knew. Then, I came to where he and Mordred fought. And I killed him. I, Lancelot Du Lac, his champion and his war leader, killed him. It shames me to say it, but it is all truth."

He shook his head and stared out across the ravaged field. "As I said, Arthur killed Mordred. Still, his forces were tough, and they fought like wild men. All well-paid mercenaries do. But when our troops saw Arthur fall, all the heart went out of them. Then the standard was lost, and the battle with it."

He looked at her. "I did it for you."

Guinevere said nothing, only stared at the man she once thought she knew. I felt a brief surge of pity for her, and yet triumph in that Lancelot's character had been truly revealed. Suddenly, she snatched her hand away from him and slapped him with all her strength. His head rocked back, and he raised a hand to his cheek, his eyes flashing. "Go ahead," he said. "It is far less than I deserve."

She sprang at him, hissing like a cat. "You bastard!" she cried. "This was for me?" she asked, pointing wildly around the field. "The war band destroyed? Arthur dead? We agreed to end it!" She slapped him again, and he did not defend himself.

"I love you, and could not bear the thought of life without you next to me. Could not stand the thought of you with Arthur, though I loved him well. I was incensed. I was not thinking of him, or honor, or anything else, but you," he said. "What else could I have done?"

I stepped between them. "Stop!" I shouted. "Stop it this instant! Do you want everyone in Britain to hear your confessions?"

Guinevere backed off slightly, as did Lancelot.

"There," I said. "That's better. Now, let's turn to your original question, Guinevere."

"What question?" she asked, her voice suddenly dull and tired. "I have no questions."

"Ah, but you did," I said. "You wished to know about hope."

"There is none," she replied.

"Yes, there is," I said. "There is justice and bard's tales."

"What have those to do with anything?" she asked. "There is no justice, for if there were, Arthur would still be alive. And the bards have not yet sung this grim tale."

"But they will, my Queen," I said. "Be assured of it. Still, it were better for all if the tale they told was, shall we say, a bit more palatable than the whole truth?"

"What are you saying, Merlin?" asked Lancelot.

"I am saying that justice has already been served. And we can see it to that the bards' tales are told in the best manner possible. Your story of Mordred and Arthur killing each other, a father and son dying on each other's blades has real possibilities."

"What about justice?" Guinevere cried. "What justice has been done?"

"Look you here, lady," I said. "Knowing the truth, will you now stay with Lancelot?" I turned quickly to him, and added, "And Lancelot, knowing the guilt that eats at you, will you stay with her and share this poison of your heart?"

"Never!" Guinevere answered. "He—he betrayed me, Arthur, Britain, and worse still, himself. I could not have him in this way. I will leave Camelot only to enter a convent. Perhaps in serving God, I may yet save my soul."

Lancelot also replied in the negative. "No, I am guilty, as you say. I will leave Britain, never to return. I know what I did was grievously wrong. And I could not be with her, for I am poison now."

"There you have it," I said. "Justice is done. The betrayer is repaid with exile, and the adulteress with solitude. It is enough."

Lancelot stood. "What happens now?" he asked.

I pointed to the forest. "We will take Arthur's body and bury him there, with all due *private* ceremony." I looked at Lancelot. "It is only fitting that you should help with this. Then, I will travel the land. The story will be told as Lancelot has started it. That Mordred was Arthur's son and they killed one another. Also, I will add a few refinements, so that all hope should not be extinguished in the land."

"Such as?" Lancelot asked curiously.

"That the king was not killed, but only horribly injured. That he will one day return when the land needs him most. That you, Lancelot, took Excalibur and threw it into the lake where the Lady who gave it to Arthur appeared and took it back. I will tell them that she is holding the sword against the day of Arthur's return. In short, we will make it honorable and fittingly tragic."

"That is good," said Lancelot. "It will give the people hope."

"Yes, Merlin," added Guinevere. "We will do as you have suggested."

Lancelot bent down and with a grunt of effort hoisted Arthur's body onto his shoulders. "Come," he said. "Let us get the worst of it over with before the gawkers come to loot the bodies. Light our way, Merlin," he said as he walked toward the woods.

The three of us walked together, my staff lighting the ground in front of us. It seemed we were in perfect accord, acting in the best interests of the realm. As we entered the forest, we stopped on occasion for Lancelot to rest his tired body. He had a small but painful wound on his hip from the battle, and this—added to the effort of stealing the armor—had taken its toll. Still, Lancelot was a warrior, and his body was strong. We continued on, and made good time.

In the battlefield, the birds had ceased their gluttony,

temporarily sated. They now roosted among the dead. At first light, they would start eating again. It would take them some time to pick the bones clean.

I led them deep into the forest, treading along paths known to few humans. Eventually, we came to a hidden glade that I knew of, and Lancelot lowered Arthur's body to the ground with a sigh of relief. I waited for a few minutes, allowing Lancelot to catch his breath. As he did so, I paced the glade and marked an area where we could lay Arthur to rest.

Once recovered, Lancelot said, "So we bury him here, then?"

Noting his cold turn of voice, I replied, "Yes, of course. Unless you'd like to carry him farther." I was in no mood to be taunted. We were here to bury the king, and that was in itself a serious matter. I had buried several kings in my long lifetime, but none had been Arthur. Lancelot's statement seemed callous, and I continued, "He was more than your king, *boy*. He was your friend and your better. Events have proved this true. I would suspect that even you could dredge up some amount of respect."

"Whatever you say, Merlin," Lancelot said, removing his cloak. He knelt down beside Arthur and wrapped his body in it. While he did so, Guinevere came forward, her eyes shining in the dim pool of moonlight that illuminated the glade.

Kneeling beside him, she cut a small piece of her hair and placed it like a flower in his hand. "For you, my King," she whispered. Even I must admit to being touched by that small gesture. In that space of time, she was singularly beautiful.

Lancelot and I set to work cutting away the sod in square pieces. Once those were removed, we began to dig. With the few implements to hand, the work was slow going, and it would have been impossible to dig extremely deep. While we worked, Guinevere hovered over Arthur's body. It appeared to me that she prayed. *Perhaps*, I thought, *she seeks forgiveness from his shade.*

We finished the work as the sun began a slow crawl over the horizon. In the forest, the birds began to stir from their sleep. I motioned to Lancelot, and together we lifted Arthur and placed him in the hole. I stood there, looking down on the form of the greatest king to ever sit the throne of Britain. *How inappropriate for him,* I thought, *to be so still. To lie not in state among other kings, but forgotten in the cold ground of the forest. Yet I will remember, and perhaps it is fitting for him. He was not like other kings.* I raised my hand in silent benediction, praying a swift journey for him.

I turned and saw that Lancelot was leaning against a tree, resting. Guinevere knelt near the grave, her hands clenched in the folds of her robe. "It is done," I said. "We have but to fill in the soil and return to tell the tale."

"Indeed," said Lancelot, "but there is something I would know."

"What is that?" I asked.

"What is there to keep you silent about this night's work?"

"What do you mean?" I said. "It is for the good of Britain that I do this."

"I've no doubt of that, mighty Merlin," he said. "But you could hold this over us until we die. What favors will you demand over the years to keep silent?"

"Favors?" I asked, incredulous. "When have I ever sought my own fortune? I will demand not favors. I need none."

He remained silent while I continued, "And why should I hold it over you? While it is not easily imagined, even Merlin has loved. I don't pretend to think you have done right, but what you did was done out of love."

Lancelot nodded. "That is true, and all well and good. Yet, I require your assurance of silence."

"I give none," I said, truly vexed. "If my word is not enough for you—when it has always been good enough for the most righteous of men, your king—then all is surely doomed from the start."

"That is where you are wrong, Merlin," he said.

"How so?" I asked.

"Because the only doom here is yours!" Lancelot said, and nodded almost imperceptibly.

I spun around, but was not fast enough to do more than see the dagger—Arthur's dagger!—coming toward me. It seemed as though time slowed to a crawl, yet I was unable to stop it. I watched as Guinevere plunged it into my chest with all her strength. I felt my mouth gape in surprise and my hand release my staff. Slowly I fell to my knees, plucking feebly at the dagger hilt now sticking out of my breastbone. I could feel myself dying and for one wild moment, it occurred to me that Morgan Le Fay had been right. I had not been killed by any man now living. I looked up at them. "Why?" asked. "I would've kept faith." My voice bubbled weakly.

"There is no faith," Guinevere said, "and you saw too much." She shoved me and I fell backward, into Arthur's grave.

Lancelot sneered down at me. "You were always the fool for love, Merlin. I can trust Guinevere; her guilt is as great as mine is. But you! You've always been so caught up in honor that there was no reason in the world to trust you." He laughed softly, as he saw the light of realization in my eyes. "That's right, Hawk of Britain. She's a superb actress, don't you think?"

"You . . . you planned all this?" I gasped.

"Most certainly. Though it was last second planning, I admit. I knew you had seen me at the battle. Fortunately enough, I was able to find a messenger and let Guinevere know that she needed to play along." He turned to her, "That was good work. You did well."

She smiled prettily. "Thank you, beloved." Then, looking down at me, she said. "I am sorry, Merlin. But it had to be this way. I've loved Lancelot for a long time, too long,

and Arthur would have been forced to expose of us eventually." She looked at Lancelot, who was still grinning
down at me, obviously pleased with his handiwork. "It
was fortunate that you could send the message on paper
and sealed," she said, "rather than by word of mouth. All
would have been undone otherwise."

"Indeed," he said. He picked up my staff and tossed it
into the grave atop my body. I clutched it feebly. I was already feeling light-headed from blood loss. Lancelot began filling in the grave, starting at my feet. I thrashed
uselessly, with no strength left in my limbs. He talked to
Guinevere while he worked.

"We should get back as quickly as possible. We'll want
to start spreading the story immediately. Most likely, there
are already people at the battlefield."

"What will we tell them?" she asked.

"The same story from before," he said, then paused
looking at me. "But I think I'll use Merlin's suggestions as
well."

"How long do you think it will be before we can be together?" she asked. "It seems we've waited forever."

"Soon, I would think," he said, eyeing her lithe form.
"Very soon."

Suddenly, she jerked upright. "I just thought of something!" she said.

"What?"

"People will ask about Merlin as well. What should we
tell them?"

Lancelot laughed. "I've already got that figured out. In
fact, it's just about perfect. We'll say that at the height of
the battle, he was attacked and captured by Mordred's
mother, Morgan le Fay, in revenge for her son's demise.
That she swore she was going to seal him in a crystal cave
where he will remain for all eternity, neither alive nor
dead." He laughed again and looked down at me. I was
barely conscious. "Does that sound 'enchanted' enough for
you, old man?"

I was unable to do more than grit my teeth in frustration.

Guinevere placed her hand on his shoulder. "It is perfect, my love. You should have been a bard."

Lancelot said, "You never knew, did you?"

"What?" she asked.

"No one ever knew where I was from, except 'across the sea.' I was a bard there, cast out from my people for attempting to seduce the king's daughter. So I fled, and beguiled an elderly knight into training me. Then, having heard of Arthur's court, I came here. To start a new life, and achieve my goals from other directions."

She said, "It makes perfect sense to me now."

It occurred to me then, in the last fading minutes of awareness, that Lancelot had even beguiled her. There was no way she would know it—bards have a magic all their own. I could not warn her. She belonged to him, heart and soul. He had planned this from the very moment he set foot on our shore.

"I think," he continued, "that everything is going to work out just fine. Once all the commotion has died down, you and I will marry and rule Britain. Perhaps we'll visit your father in Ireland after we've taken our vows." He began to finish the grave when I realized I still held my staff.

One last spell, I thought to myself. I began to mutter an old incantation under my breath. Lancelot heard me, recognizing perhaps the quality of the Druidic words. Quickly drawing Excalibur from under his cloak, he knelt down at the edge of the grave.

He saw the crystal at the top of my staff flicker. With one smooth motion, he brought Excalibur down forcefully onto the glowing orb. It shattered, the pieces slicing into the flesh of my face and neck. I barely felt the pain, was only dimly aware of my final failure.

Lancelot tossed Excalibur into the grave, resuming his task of putting the dirt back in. "There's no way we could keep it," he said to Guinevere. "It's better that it gets buried here, along with the rest of the past."

She nodded, and I knew she felt nothing for the dead, or for me.

The dirt quickly covered my head. I closed my eyes and dreamed of flight. As the last of the life force left my body, I saw one last vision . . . the long cold winter coming to Britain, and with it, carrion birds by the thousands, feeding on the betrayed dead.

RETURN OF THE KING

by Michelle West

Michelle West is the author of *The Sacred Hunt* du-
ology as well as *The Broken Crown, The Uncrowned King,*
and *The Shining Court,* all published by DAW Books.
She reviews books for the on-line column *First Con-
tacts,* and less frequently for *The Magazine of Fantasy
& Science Fiction.* Other short fiction by her appears in
Black Cats and Broken Mirrors, Elf Magic, and *Olympus.*

YESTERDAY, in the city:
   A man with half a mind and no place to live pushed a
young woman just past twenty into the path of an oncoming subway train because he thought she was laughing at him, because in the confusion of bodies and the
terror of his own dim sensibilities, she was all people
who, having the grace and the life that he did not, had
ever laughed at him.
   One strike for justice.
   Justice was not done.

   Yesterday, in the city:
   A thirty-two-year-old man with two children—both under the age of five, and both by dint of modern miracle,
healthy and unaware of the boon of health—attempted to

stop a mugging. He was brutally beaten and stabbed several times, and although he was successful in his goal, the victory was Pyrrhic.

He served Justice.

They fled before help came, and before help came, he died.

We stir, in our somnabulent state. We sir, and we are angry, and if we catch our anger quickly enough, we can settle its flames, bank its fire.

We want *justice*.

We look to the West.

I hear it, in the streets, the whispers of people who stop at newsstands and shake their heads, either at the loss of the man or the loss of innocence that breeds contempt for his bravery. I hear the anger in their voices at the death of the girl, as if that death could have been avoided by anger alone, by simple death.

Simplicity.

Let me stop here. This door would not have existed two hundred years ago, although with work and an eye for— yes, the simple—it might have been made. Glass as thick as an old man's wrist, thick as mine, framed by steel and crossed by it. We push—just so—and it swings.

Within: food and drink, the small space uncluttered by the hands that might once have worked to make them. There was no coffee, that I recall, not then; there was wine and sour ale and bitter bark tea that was somehow sweeter than the coffees sold here. But I like this place. I can't see my reflection in the glass that houses the food, but I can see the reflection of the man on my left and the woman on my right. He is tall and round, bearded and dimpled as his face breaks into a smile at something clever the woman behind the counter has said. She—the woman to my right, not the young girl behind the counter—is bent, not bowed, with age, her hair still dark by either artifice or grace. I see her here frequently; we are, on the surface, of an age. We do not speak, of course.

I tried to be a younger man, and even, for a time, a younger woman. I have been older. I have been ancient. I have not been a child since I was, in fact, a child, and I would not go back there, not even for Him.

"Excuse me, sir?" She—the girl behind the counter, plump in a way that youth hates, but that is so very attractive—is patient with me. She thinks me deaf, and she is less patient with those she doesn't know. Aren't we all? Day in, day out, we have set up our rhythm and she follows it; I have earned patience, if not affection. But it has been a long holiday season, and a relentless one. I offer her my apologies, she makes me my coffee.

This might have been a feast; it might have been a *waste*. When the days have been long and the visions longer still, I walk past the wastebaskets, these things that are receptacles for food not eaten or not cared for, and I shudder. The days are not often that long.

Not often, but today there is a chill in the air, and the New Year, old rites forgotten, is being ushered in. The new year is always the most dangerous.

Out in the streets.

Winter-veined and white in the early morning of snow-strewn city. Flurries have buried cars whole; the landscape, were it not for the steel-girded bridges, the vast skyscrapers, the flat, wide streets, could be any winter landscape. It is always when both warmth and food are farthest away that the new year is needed; it brings hope.

And it brings things just as old, and vastly less necessary to the day-to-day lives of the city's inhabitants: ghosts, clever creatures that have long since been forgotten by any fortunate enough to be able to ignore their existence.

From under the vast wraps of old newspaper, Brown Bear rises. "Hey, Merle," he says, because he assumes it will irritate me. It does. I say nothing, having chosen to wear a tattered dignity that his easy youth won't penetrate. "Time's a'coming. You can smell it in the air." He draws a deep, long breath; two birds plummet down in the wake of it and he swallows them whole. They'll find shelter there, somewhere in the hidden depths of his girth.

"Not yet," I tell him quietly.

"But soon. The King's a'coming." He coughs; feathers fly. "Funny how the old stories never die."

"Funny."

He slaps me on the back. On purpose, sly bastard; sends me half a block through the snow that, scant hours from now, salt, sand, and steel will have fought back.

I used to be better at hearing his bravado. I used to be better at a lot of things. I'm almost in her lap before I realize where he's sent me. To the King's sister.

Sister blood. If she's here, Brown Bear is right: He can't be far behind. After all, there's no King without a Queen. No day without a night. I cannot speak. I have not seen her in what feels like millennia, may indeed be that long.

Her skin is as white as winter, white as falling snow; her eyes are just as warm, steel gray, pale. Her hair is white; easy to miss her on a day like this, snow falling. Easy, and damn foolish.

The old habits never die. You can beat them, but like any addiction, they lurk in wait. And good thing, too, today. Good thing. "Lady."

Her eyes are all edge. She gathers the snow around her shoulders in folds and billows, standing as tall as old pine, as slender as young maple. "Where have you been?" she says at last.

I don't have an answer for her. She is of His blood, after all; the deaths that lie between them are other people's. They stand, like two pillars, across the battlefield, and win or lose, the field always looks the same.

Gods, how the mighty.

"I've been here," I say at last.

"The time is almost come," she says. She shakes her head and her hair falls about her shoulders like the promise of the perfect drug. I want to—and I would never—touch it. "The King will return."

I knew this. I've been telling people this truth—where they will hear it and when they will listen—for centuries. But I have not seen *her* in all that time, and I had forgotten what it was like to stand at the feet of the eldest. I, who am reckoned immortal and ageless, the keeper of the King, the watcher at the gate.

Her gaze is cold; winter is warm, and I remember now why the snow has never bothered me: it can't. Old roots are shaking free of dirt.

"You are here before Him," I hear myself telling her, "just as I. But if you seek to gain purchase in the world before His return, think again. You have never bested Him."

"Not on the open field," she replies, falling into the discussion that is not to her liking, but at least more to her nature. "But there are other ways to win a battle." Her smile is sun on snow; I have to look away. I *have to* look away. This is the one mistake He made, and it cost him dearly.

"Do you see how slender I am? I will not remain so," she says, running her hands along her smooth stomach, her smile sharp and cutting. "Something will be born to bind us."

I remember that it is always better to make her laugh than to let her slide into the ice of her own silence. I bend a little with the weight of her regard and the desire to live up to it, and I am bitterly glad that, on this winter day, no one mortal can actually see what I see.

"No," she says, the laughter leeching from her voice, "but they *will.*"

I have served my time.

I say this as penitent. I say this as an ex-convict. I say this as a man who has had faith and lost it, or rather, has had faith and found different, but whose roots, whose essence was born in the flame, and comes back to it, time and again. Once an addict, always an addict.

He was our shining moment. Arturos. Artur. Arthur. King. King in a time of war and inhumanity, in a time when magic was not what it is now—not the diminished

shadows that hide at the feet and behind the skirts of
women in garish costumes with heavy glass balls on
skirted tables and electric signs announcing their pre-
science. Then, magic walked the land. It rode upon the
shoulders of his enemies, great and small; it made of them
giants, and in the shadows of giants, men fell.

Here what do we serve? Commerce. Bureaucracy.

I see my reflection in glass. And in glass such as bishops
and archbishops, who ordered glass for their great cathedrals that the sunlight might touch and color the masses
who gathered in the nave beneath the clerestory lights,
would have wept for joy at the sight of: solid, clear,
smooth, and perfect; a thing to stand the test of time, like
the stone of the cathedrals themselves.

Glass is cheap. It is not made to enhance glory; merely
to give those who pass it a clearer glimpse at the wonders
their money might buy. I press my hand against the window; I leave no prints.

But while I stand like shadow I see clearly: the men and
the women who gather around small tables, their elbows
bumping dishes and each other, their children struggling
for either food or attention. This is a part of their lives.
Their lives are small.

That boy, russet-haired and young, his hands occupied
with something plastic and steel, his lips ringed by melted
chocolate, is three years off the age at which a boy became
a man, took sword, took oath, and dedicated his life to a
cause when the King lived.

He will feel that call, when he is of the age. They all feel
it, the great restlessness. Called puberty, explained away
by science until it is something embarrassing and dimin-
ishing, it will afford him no greatness, where once, once it
might have driven him to the King's side.

That boy is the King's boy, when the King returns.

But now he belongs in the half-world between state and
parent, the laws governing his behavior and theirs a tangled mess. They are beginning to argue.

Sometimes the argument is amusing, in a quaint way;

today it is merely irritating, and I wish they would take their child and their argument and go elsewhere with both. And I remember that it is *I* who am eavesdropping on their lives, and I upon whom it is incumbent to travel.

A month ago:

A young man, angered by the rejection of the countless women over whom he had spent his endless affections, took his life into his own hands. He walked into a store, glassed in like the restaurant, but with a different counter and a different clientele, and he purchased a gun.

This story, played out countless times, was larger: Not one woman, but many, not the women who scorned him, but *any* woman whose life might somehow exceed his own. He had to reload his gun, but no one—except for a woman, who chose to stand and speak, to try to turn him from his course—stopped him until he tired of the slaughter, or was satiated by it, and turned the gun upon himself.

A husband's last image of his wife in the national picture of the crime: lifeless body bent almost backward over a chair. A father, an officer of the law, come in haste to the scene to find his daughter among the dead.

There, in the streets, like an echo of the words of the dead: In a just society, this would *never* have happened.

And the footnote to the incident? The thing I most remember—and I am sorry for it, and I pray that the families of the dead will forgive—is this: a small article about the mother of the madman. About her grief and her loss and her confusion and the anger turned toward her by the mothers of the dead and the mothers of the living who fear that *this* is the what they're raising their daughters for. About the fact that there was a funeral, and it was empty of everyone but mother and reporters and the idle curiosity seeker who wished to see a fallen monster.

It did not ask us to define love. It did not ask us to condone it. But it asked for our pity.

* * *

"You're maudlin," Old Crow says.

"You're interfering."

He shrugs his sleek black wings, sends snowflakes flying. "So I'm interfering, that's what I do. You don't like it, you can jet your ass back across the pond."

I hate the provincials. But I came here to get away from the older magics, and this is how I pay for it. "I don't like it, and I'm not jetting my ass across the pond," I tell him. "And if I were you, I'd watch my tongue."

"Oooh, oooh, big words. You going to try something?" He hops from foot to foot like a taunting child. "Nothing you ain't already tried."

"No. Nothing I haven't tried already. But she's here."

"Who, she?"

He's trying to annoy me. "You know who."

He shrugs. "I never bought into all that glory and death stuff," he says, hopping about a bit more before settling into the snow, and glaring out at me with one wide round eye. "Thought we taught you better than that."

"You don't have much to teach me."

He laughs. A lot. It's irritating.

"You been around a long time," he says. "But I been around for longer, and I never got bit on the backside by no angels and no big organized religion."

"No, you settled for the petty, stupid ones."

He shrugs, completely unruffled. "I didn't settle," he says with a cackle. "They settled for *me.*"

I don't get a chance to ask him why he's come, and it's just as well. I'm waking, and the world is not the world I went to sleep in.

I hate to wake.

There is a story that is told of me, a myth that has become as much a part of my substance as the truth—whatever that might have been—that lies buried in past centuries, past realities. The story is an old one, of foolish age and unrequited love. It isn't very pretty, and it paints me as a fool—but we're all foolish in our own time.

In these tales of folly, I served the King, the One True King, with my wisdom and my magical wiles. I did not joust or fight with obvious weapon; even then I had not the build or the sheer physical presence such a task required. No, I served with wit, and the grace of wit, and I would send the morons to their deaths when they displeased me by an artful turn of phrase and an attribution to perhaps the wrong speaker.

That part, incidentally, is true.

We jostled like children for His regard, and in the end, I was the wiliest of our number; I sat by His right hand, and I guided Him—as I was able, and He was willing to be guided—to victory. Where He was unwilling to be guided, I eased His defeat. Even in the end, even then.

But I digress.

There is a story told of me. That I fell in love with a nymph, that I taught her, that I gave her power over me, and that she, in the end, imprisoned me. In some tales—for tales, like tree roots, branch in many different directions—she was in the employ of the King's sister, and through the artifice of love and lust entrapped me, that I might not come to the King's defense in time, thus bringing about his downfall. It is a flattering take, and one that is so entirely false I would never have conceived of it myself, and I have begun many, many myths in my time.

The truth is more complicated. There was love, yes, and lust, and there was power taken and power given—as, in these two things, such power resides—but in the end, when I went into the darkness and she closed the door behind me, it was no act of malice on her part, no act of foolishness on mine. The King had passed, and the keeping of the King's legend was not to be guaranteed by anyone who had not served Him quite so long and quite so hard as I. I felt His loss as I had felt nothing in life, not even His presence.

I understood eternity: that is the prison she made for me, fashioned at my direction and with my aid.

I loved Arthur.

I loved Him in His wild youth, and in His prime.

I loved Him in His rages.

Do you understand what I am saying? No, perhaps not. Perhaps I do not understand it myself. I am, as I said, waking, although I have been among you these many years.

It started simply enough. I accepted the burden, for I knew that Arthur was not human, and not bound by the laws of life and death that bind and hold those who followed Him and died in His shadow. I desired that He not be forgotten, and as I traversed the countryside, I felt His absence the way any lover, any child, any parent must feel the loss of their dead: the world was grim and ugly, the conflicts bloody and meaningless, the politics petty and foolish.

Everything tasted of emptiness.

Have I mentioned that I was called poet? Have I told you that words were my gift and my skill? You must know that misery loves company, and I was determined—so very, very determined—to be miserable. Arthur was Camelot to me; Arthur was everything. Those quests that He undertook, the justice that He sought—by sword and skill at war—to bring to an unjust, barbaric land, were the only true quests.

We mourned, who had survived His great sleep. And we spread His story.

I remember it clearly: the days after the battle, the carrion animals barely driven away. We could not bury our dead, but my magics—diminished and trivialized as they were without His presence to anchor and strengthen them—were enough to set fire and make ash of the fallen. We took swords and shields to set about the castle as emblems of the heroism of His knights; we kept signet rings to return to the wives and the children who had been left behind, that their sons might choose to follow the greater example of their parents.

And through the villages that we had traversed to reach our fields of battle, we returned. Without Arthur to steady

them, the army had disintegrated, and the crisis of food—
always a crisis at that time—meant that the villagers starved.
They hid what they could from the army, but the army
itself, in defeat, was ugly; there were more bodies to be
burned as we made our way to the castle, and all of them
our own.

Shall I draw this picture clearly? Children shortened by
food's lack, stunted in growth, sallow-eyed, sallow-faced,
constantly fearful under our watchful eyes. They spoke
when we spoke to them, if at all; we suffered impertinence
only from those too young to speak clearly.

And we, of course, were the judge of that.

I return to the restaurant. The boy and his family have
finished their argument, but not their meal. The boy is
playing with straws and sugar packages and the stand-up
menu that slides into plastics that would have been a miracle in an earlier age. There is no wilderness about him. But
how could there be? There is no great forest, no mountain
ranges, no wild streams or rivers; there are no horses, and
behind him no fields under the heavy winter snows. He is a
boy who is not anchored in our reality.

But he picks up a book—a book, a thing whole villages
were not worthy of owning—and he opens its pages, flips
them, immerses himself in the small, neat words he finds.
Words not scribed by men of God, not written by men of
Kings, but finally, stamped by soulless machines, over and
over again.

And he smiles.

There is no embodiment of Death; that's fable. Nothing
to come to you in the night and take your hand—or nothing that I've seen. Stories of angels abound, and take your
comfort from that if you can; me, I would rather die alone.
I've *seen* angels.

It's the flaming swords that remind me of His sword.

And why would I be thinking of flaming swords? Surprise. The crackle in the air has nothing to do with the snap of thin ice beneath boots.

"Raphael," I say, because the texture of crackling flame is somehow distinct for each archangel.

"Nice winter," he replies.

Small talk is small talk no matter how powerful you are; it passes the time. I've learned a lot over the years about just passing time.

For example, my afternoon: I've just ventured through a mall that looks, with its sweeping glass arches and its multilayered stories, like a cathedral—except that it lacks the transept across the nave, and it faces in the wrong direction. That, and it stretches out at such a glassed-in height for a full city block, devouring sunlight, casting shadows back. Tucked behind its west face, there's an old church nestled between mall and the single road that gives cars easy pickup or drop-off access. The church once owned the land the mall stands on, but belief in God has grown unfashionable, and it sold that land bit by bit to developers in the downtown core. That's what they call it; the core, as if the rest of the city were apple, and the seeds that germinate all rest here.

Now, the church stands surrounded on all sides by the mall, and the mall reaches heights that the church, once a respectable building in its own right, probably never dreamed of. A fitting statement, in and of itself.

But fitting, as well, that the church holds its ground, letting go what it can, and holding on to what it must. Embattled, of course, is what the archangels know best. If Raphael is waiting, he'd wait here. Michael would wait someplace else entirely, but Michael has a glimmer of something that might be humor in another creature.

"Merlin." Raphael crosses his arms, sword nowhere to be seen, although if one knows how to listen, it's never far away.

"I haven't seen you in a while."

"I've been busy," he says. "Attempts at cultural genocide always attract my attention. Bosnia," he adds, when

I don't respond immediately. His gaze is measured. Intent. Almost as beautiful as the King's gaze. "Kingdom's coming," he says at last. "Michael's waiting across the ocean."

"Why are you here?"

"I heard the White Queen was walking. We can't have that."

"You heard right. She's here."

His silence is a threatening thing. My silence is a shield. "I am not a boy, Raphael, who has been caught hand in cookie jar, or worse, magazine under pillow."

"You have to love the facility of modern metaphor. Do you even remember your old ones?"

It's meant to be an insult. I reply in kind. "You understand the metaphors, so you haven't risen above them yourself. Face, it, bright sword, we're all caught in the same web."

It works. He shuts up and gets back to business. "You had a weakness for the White Queen."

"I had a weakness for the Black Queen, if you recall, and look where that got us. I do not think I will make that mistake again."

"Mordred?"

"Still dead, as far as I know."

"Merlin."

"She's not pregnant. There'll be no child until the King returns."

"Good. You know what to do this time."

"Yes."

He meets my gaze and holds it; I let him. We play these games, but we're not really testing our power, and we each believe in a fight, we'd have the upper hand. "You should come to Bosnia," he says, leaning against the brick of the old church walls. "It'll remind you of the old days, but with bigger guns and more bodies."

"More bodies?"

"Well, population's denser."

"Yes," I tell him. "I should go to Bosnia. But there are other places in the world that will do."

"Pockets of the ideal," he says sweetly, his voice devoid of the saracasm that any other being—any human being—would put there, "where people are fighting for something they believe in. You amaze me; you can live among the prostitutes."

His word.

My word, once, for people who live like these people do: for comfort and money, not necessarily in that order.

"I amaze me, too," I tell him, because it's true and he'll know it. "But you know what? The White Queen didn't go to Bosnia. She came *here*."

He snorts, and the sword is in his hands. "Work to do," he says, and his eyes are all fire, blue fire. "But you know why she came to this place."

"Oh?"

"Fine. Play stupid; it's not that far off the truth. She came because this is where *you* are. And she knows that you'll bring Him the rest of the way here."

The King is coming.

The King will return.

That was His promise. That is the myth. And the truth, although He has been made a man and He was never that. He was larger, greater, uncompromised by morality; He vied with the Host for the hearts and minds of men, and He succeeded in winning, for in truth He made us feel that we were valued; not sheep to be watched, not children—not precisely—to be punished; but rather the denizens of the new world order, the world which He would create in an image of the heavens that only the living could share. He did not despise God; He did not abase himself before God either. That was not their relationship.

Complicated, the truth. And simple.

He came to the world and by dint of strength and will, by His ability to forge of flesh what lesser men made of steel, He became King, and the only man Kings called King.

He promised us Justice, and in His name, and for His goal, we fought, we killed, we died.

We were *so* certain.

I cannot remember when that certainty faltered. Certainly, I was frail. I am frail. I learned the mysteries at His side and with His guidance, but my magic was channeled by Him, and when He left, the fire behind it guttered. Slowly, so slowly that at first I did not recognize its passing. I built an empire, not in His name, but in as much of His image as I could master. I was a kingmaker, but the material of kings passed between my fingers as if it were water; I could not hold or shape it to my will. And I let it be known. I told His story, that was my strength.

These days, I tell no stories. I have no audience and I desire none. I tell myself that this is true.

I'm lying.

I desire Her and I desire Him, and I desire a kingdom in which the sword of Justice is absolute. I'm tired of living with the gray and dreary mortals; I want sharp perfection, I want glory, I want the hunt for honor.

I settle for a drink instead.

I've settled for a drink instead for so many centuries they're like an old married couple, the desire and the distinctly second best choice.

And as I sit in the bar, I think of other drinks and other times, and I know when it first started.

I had stopped at a village in East Anglia. A small village, relatively clean, but denuded of the men that had perished in the war between Harald and Harold. The battle itself was an echo of glory, but an echo was all I could find, and I came too close, in the end, to the fight itself. You might recall I am not a man of the sword, and by dint of sword I was laid low.

I did not fear for my life; that is not my fear, and never will be. But I dislike unnecessary pain. I repaired from the field when the fight was lost and won, won and lost, and, stumbling and bleeding—for my wounds, like my life, last an imeasurable length of time compared to mortal wounds and mortal span—into a village I will pretend I no longer remember the name of. A pretty enough place, all the women thin and the children thinner; the food had gone to feed the army.

Some of the girls had gone to feed the army as well, and were heavy with child; the mood was dark. But I looked like no soldier, and in the end, I adopted the role of priest and they adopted me, seeking either comfort or safety or the promise of an end to their pain. I should not have stayed. Their homes, clean, were simple, and their ignorance was a type of squalor in and of itself that is beyond distasteful. But they had the will to grace and kindness, and in truth, I was *tired,* and I accepted their hospitality.

"She's watching you, you know," Old Crow says.

I shrug. People pass us both in the street, averting their gaze; they're afraid we'll ask them to part with their money, and they'll be forced to confront the truth about the callousness of their comfort. Better to avoid being asked. Old Crow is a black-hearted bastard at times; he delights in making people feel worse about themselves than they already do. But he's busy, bothering me. They should be grateful. They don't notice.

"She's watching you. Merle?"

"Don't call me that."

"Sorry. What should I call you? High Muckety-muck?"

"That's a new one for you. You've been watching television again."

He shrugged. "It's winter. All the girls are sleeping. You promised you'd keep one awake this year."

I promised him that every year; it's my way of telling

him just how much I like his attention. "Well," I say, "this year, I kept my word."

"I don't see any of the girls, old man."

"There is the Queen."

His face freezes a moment and then falls into that grotesque twist of expression that denotes amusement. I hold up a hand to stop him, but it's too late. He starts to laugh. He slaps my back, his great pinions contained by a human shape, but contained poorly. I'm heartily sick of flying half a city block because of the joviality of the local forgotten deities. Old Crow is in a good mood; he catches me. "Why don't we go visit the kids," he says.

I roll my eyes. I don't want to visit the children. I don't even like them. He knows this. But he also knows that I won't struggle when he carries me above the city streets to the hospital row in the heart of the city's business district. Because he knows, the old bastard, why I came.

The English and the French had different rules; they were governed by different laws. Old battles changed that. It's often said that the people at the lowest end of the political ladder never really notice the changes at the upper end; that they can't look up from their plowshares to see the thrones and the towers of those born, in God's name, to lead them.

I believed it when I sat beside those thrones and within those towers. I believed it when I came, bleeding, in from the battle.

The King is coming. I feel it in the air. I have worked this past century toward no other end: the return of the King. Old Crow stops in front of the hospital windows, where children racked with fever can see him clowning about as if he were a toy and not a danger. It's the only time they'll see him so clearly, that and if they're dying. I recognize the look of dying children. They don't have it. They won't. There is a miracle in these tubes and plastics and steels, in the hands of these careworn nurses and busy doctors. Life. And it's taken for granted so often even I don't see it as the miracle it is.

"See the little cutie over there? Watch this."

He does something with the shape of his face; his eyes grow enormously large, like the eyes of some cartoon puppy. Beyond the window's glass, I see the child he speaks of, and I fall.

The bastard. Never trust Old Crow. He makes himself seen so harmless you forget that his beak has scratched out the eyes of a god, and his talons have torn out the tongues of tribal heroes.

Leofgifu.

It's not her, of course. She's dead. The only child I ever—the only child who wasn't completely revolting. Years ago. Centuries ago. Golden-haired, hollow-cheeked, serious, she defined the word precocious. I had never loved any mortal being the way I loved her. It was her mother who took me in when I came, injured and sickly, to the post-conquest village, and she did so not out of charity but out of need; her part of the common field needed tending, and she was recovering from the loss of a babe. I proved to her I could work, and after a time, in the depths of a depression that I recognize now but had only contempt for then, she would send the other child along with me. Leofgifu. Pretty name for a common child.

She was like a plague. She was constantly trying to kill herself, and after the first ten times, I stopped her because I was not a man who liked to admit defeat. She almost drowned six times; she could not—could *never*—be taught to stay away from the water. She couldn't be trained. It was like having a cat—one without the survival skills and instinct. The stupid child was nearly trampled by the four cows the village and managed to drive far enough away from the army that they weren't eaten, and once by the horse of a merchant in the nearby county. I hated her. I did. I couldn't wait until she was old enough to be put to better use. I couldn't wait until she was noticed by—or more likely, noticed—some other idiot villager.

And she did. I was grateful for her absence. I'd spent years in the village doing *nothing* but guiding their moral instincts—such as they were—and *baby-sitting*.

Baby-sitting and telling my stories with a terrible turn in conviction. She asked me—when she was still young enough that I felt obligated to answer her incessant questions— what the world would be like when the King returned. If He would need a wife (Yes). If He was a good man (Yes). If God liked Him (Yes). I had to explain the notion of beloved several times, and the concept of honor, which came surprisingly easily to her. In another life—as if humans are ever granted a different one—she would have been a warrior, and the concept had never occurred to me before then.

I did not desire warriors; I merely made them or turned them aside—but I had hopes, I invested them not in Arthur, as I had always done, but in a girl who persistently refused to be nameless, although that was what she was.

And I was to remember it. The first time I remembered it clearly was when she came home. Ah, no, when she came to me, her mother having succumbed to some passing disease three years previous. I can remember clearly the ruined line of what had once been her perfect face. Her husband, her first husband's, enraged gift. She was brutalized and she was afraid, but she was not a gibberer. She came to me, cursed child, and like a fool—like the man who pulled her from stream and brook and lake's edge, the man who turned aside the charging horse and angry cow, the apathetic parent, I went to where she lived and killed her husband. A moment of fire burned and sparked, and I said, as clearly as I had ever said the words, *Justice is done.*

Aye, for a moment, Justice, and peace.

We did not speak of his death. She stayed with me, and in time, when I thought her ready, and when I found a man who I felt was worthy of her, she married again. But between then, the death of the first and the vows to the last, years of sun and toil, years of burying babies and children who had not the constitution to survive either harsh winter or slim harvest or high taxes.

I should have left. I had not, since the casting of my imprisonment, stayed so long in any one place, for I understood what it meant to remain *objective*. People are frail. She was frail.

When the war came across the land again, and it came, it devoured her village, and in an attempt to protect *her* children—and it pained her deeply that I could never care for children as I had learned with time to care for her—she was devoured with it. And I, who had stood at the side of Kings, watched men who served them. I told myself, *these are diminished men and diminished times, when so much pleasure can be taken out of the destruction of so helpless a handful of villagers,* and I killed them; I killed them all. Slowly, which would have pained her, and with pleasure, which would have disgusted her.

Afterward, I left, but she had devoured me as the war had devoured her, that delicate scion of life.

I did not realize it at first. How could I? The concepts that had come to me through her were strange and foreign. But her passing was so bitter to me, so very bitter, that I *could not* let it mean nothing. And in the annals of history, how has she been remembered? She hasn't. The priest that eventually replaced my own ragged teaching did not survive the soldiers, poor fool; they did not clearly differentiate between his rank and the rank of the villagers; he was a layman and far too common. And besides which, he could not write.

So I did what was to be a pattern—if two such occurrences can be counted a pattern—and buried myself in making meaning of the loss and the void it left me. I could not make a myth of her; I tried. Her name did not have the resonance and the richness of Kings; it was a name, it belonged to a mortal who would die having achieved nothing more than twist the heart of an old, old man.

What would be a fitting legacy for a girl named Leofgifu who had died in pain and unspeakable sorrow? A world in which she could never die that way again. A just world.

There were the experiments. You know that I was an adviser to the one true King; how could I be less of an adviser to those who were his palest echo? I tried many things, retaining a fondness for Britain because it was the heart of His myth—and her brief life. I learned from trial and error that too quick a change led to more death and destruction, and I moved as slowly as I could. Here, a schism in the church. There, a denial of the church. A clash of the two. The cant of reason (forgive the pun), the great promise of communism, the great promise of commerce, the pragmatism that forged a compromise between these two. And for what?

The Winter Queen is the most beautiful woman the world has ever seen. She draws the eye and holds it tightly, coldly, all the while scorning the heart. She comes to me after I've managed to lose Old Crow. "Merlin," she whispers, and the hair that I have—little enough, and damp with winter—stands on end. *"When will He return?"*

"Soon," I tell her. Soon. It is the truth.

At her feet, the soggy remnants of yesterday's headline. Dead people. No heroes.

I have so little time, so little time to prepare, and in truth, I do not know what I am going to do *to* prepare. "Lady," I whisper, as her shadow passes my face, as my knees hit the the snow and the ice scrapes the skin from them.

The shadow that falls across her is not mine. Brown Bear rises from the snow, shaking himself clean, and not incidentally roaring loudly. "We don't need no stinking King!"

"A friend of yours?" she asks coldly. She looks him up and down. "Merlin has served me well, little forest creature; he bears me no love, but his great anger has anchored my myth. If you wish to argue about kingdoms, argue with Merlin. Or, indeed, if Merlin will not argue—and I see no reason why he should, given his current position and his known loyalty—you may argue with the angels."

"Indeed, argue with the angels," one of them says. Raphael. "For we have prepared the kingdom a long time now, and we are ready for its coming. Merlin, *when?*"

"Soon," I tell him. "Soon," I tell her. I gather my cloak around me, and there is enough power in it that I can leave them unseen.

The King is coming.

Old Crow settles on the roof above my head. "Don't try that invisible shit on me," he says affably. "It never works unless you take a bath first."

"I'll kill you," I tell him, without much fire, "after all this is over."

"And when will it be over?" he says, and the light in his eyes is a gleam I don't like because it reminds me of blade's edge. "Remember, I do the carrion thing part-time. And the battlefields always look the same no matter who wins or who loses. "When's He coming, old man?"

I laugh. "You took me to the hospital, you showed me what you wanted me to see. Don't play that game with me."

Brown Bear saunters over. Somewhere, in the alley, Red Fox is probably listening with his great, twitchy ears.

"We don't need a King," Brown Bears says, without the growl. "We've done without a King for a long time, and all Kings do is start wars."

"Just wars," I hear myself saying.

Old Crow caws. "They're *all* just wars. That's the point of war. You can't have Kings and have no wars. Didn't you learn anything from the angels?"

"Crow—"

"Look, first thing old God did was divide up the universe. Them and Us, Heaven and Hell, and shit—He's supposed to *own* it all.

"A little girl died," he added. Bastard. "I've done what I can. I've taken away the myths and the religions and the desire for anything but this, this comfort and family and friendship. It doesn't work everywhere; the human spirit is the human spirit; easily divided, easily angered. We stand in the shadow of angels."

"Oh, great, he's gonna start that again."

"I'm not going to start that again."

"You are."

"I'm not."

"Hel*loo,* do you think we could do this *after?*"

I hate that Bear. "I've armed them," I said at last, faintly. "I've armed them as well as I can. I've done what I can to make certain that the biggest weapons go to the men whose hands are most tied against their use."

"Weapons against *the* King? And that's going to work?"

"I don't *know!*" I turned to him. "I only know that when *I* see the King, *I* have to go. I am what I am; I am what I was made to be." All the old longing returns as the minutes drag on; the scent of the Winter Queen is in the air.

"But you've lived a real life. You've lived without the hoity-toity shit. You can't just go back to being a—a faceplate on somebody else's Cadillac." Old Crow cocked his head to one side. Not a pretty sight. "You were what you were made to be when you lost your little girl."

I hit him. I'm angry enough to hit him. It uses power. Power of a certain type can't be hidden for long.

"You didn't come here for nothing," he continues, feathers singed but unruffled. "It's a bad year, but it's not the only bad year."

"What do you mean? What do you mean by that?"

Brown Bear and Old Crow exchange a glance.

Red Fox comes out of hiding. I have a weakness for Red Fox. His demeanor is unpleasant, but in spirit he and I have shared much, and share much, in common.

"You always wake when it's darkest," he says. "Sleep."

"Pardon?"

"Go back to this life that you've chosen. Live it out. Send the Queen back. You don't think this is really the first time you've seen her since He left, do you? Oh, never mind. You do. I forget how stupid you can force yourself to be. You've a devious mind, I'll grant you that."

He comes up, places his paws in the center of my chest. "This is the land of the little people. And the little people are strong in their own obdurate ways. Sleep, Merlin."

I understand. I nod. "The King?"

"He returns when you will it. You were always the key. That was the agreement you made with the water sister so long ago."

"And I want—"

"Justice, I know. Over a beer we'll continue our argument of what exactly that word means, and why it shouldn't be hefted and pointed by just any powerful mage." The smell of his fur is pungent. "You were supposed to make a choice, you know."

"Did I?"

"Yes. And no. You came here, which is a good sign, but you kept His myth alive, which is a bad one. You've lived as a man for a thousand years and more. Can you not find enough in being one to be content?"

I see my little girl, dead, and old, and I hear the terrible cry in her voice that speaks of a death that's not hers, but is worse. And I want *justice,* and I know that if it were not for the wars of great men that death would never have happened, but I think that the King, when He comes, will finally end the pain.

Because I am in pain and I cannot think clearly.

Red Fox says, "You said yourself that the dead were without number when you passed the winter after the last battle. They starved. They ate their fallen. Can you not see the face of your Leofgifu in those fallen even now?"

And I do.

"Have I built her a better world?"

"Your answer. The girl got hit by the train. The women

died because of a temper tantrum. The man—the only one to respond to the heroic impulse—left his own children without a father. Give us a King, Merlin, and what will we do? How will we listen to what He says?" The paws are light but insistent. "There is not a better world. Make of that what you will.

"But let the King sleep. The time for Kings is passing, and you have made it so."

"But I didn't mean to make that choice. I sought to protect her memory, not to destroy my own."

"No," Fox says. "But the Age of Kings has passed, and you must know it. You have given power to men who cannot use it in the way that it was once used; you have grayed the world and made it smaller, but it is an infinitely more beautiful place than it was."

I think of the Winter Queen, and I despair.

"Despair, then, old fool. But think as well of the graves that aren't filled by the young and the weak. Think of the graves that aren't filled by the older and stronger who must kill and destroy each other in order to feed their young and their weak. We *do not need a King,* and a King will weaken us.

"*That* is your gift to your child. Remember it. Forget all else."

"He is too strong, this time," I say softly.

Old Crow looks at Red Fox. "He's right."

"Should we kill Him now?" Brown Bears says.

"We can't."

"Damn."

I leave them.

I have done what I can. I say this, I write this, I think this: I have done what I can. But the King will come, and He is a good King, an absolute monarch, a being who understands a swift and brutal justice. I am summoned, and I am bound by magic and oath, by blood and ritual, to his side. I have given you what you need. Choose your life, and choose it wisely; give me some sign that the world I built for *Leofgifu,* the world that is still being built, day by day, vote by vote, bureaucrat by bureaucrat, is a world that will not be destroyed by the very acts necessary to protect it.

The horns are sounding. The swords are blazing. The Winter Queen is in her shrouded castle.

Take what lessons I cannot learn from what I have learned, and help us.

Help us all.

Don't Miss These Exciting DAW Anthologies

THE CATFANTASTIC ANTHOLOGIES
Edited by Andre Norton and Martin H. Greenberg